Corin's Reach
Frost
Foxburrow
Snowhaven
Fernshade
Elderwood Forest
Have
Gladecross
Briarshade
Mosswick
Lowbranch
Ve
P
Oakridge
Seabreeze
Whalesong Bay
Anchorstone
Tidemarch
Twilight Co

ELDER MOUNTAINS

Kellgrim's Rest

Eagle's Perch

Castle Dunmoh

Breyton

Braeland

Pearlmoor

Arden's Wake

DANT
AINS

Stonebrook

Silverport

YBROOK

Stormhaven

T

THE ELDRITCH KNIGHT

THE ASHEN THRONE, BOOK 1

K.W. BUSSARD

Book Cover by: Joze Groselj 'Vitogh'

Sigil Design by: Dzmitry Zasimovich

Map by Corin Raldekaln

1st edition 2025

CONTENTS

A Fateful Night

Chapter Zero

The sky was cracked.

Storms spun in the sky like a living vortex of swirling darkness and unnatural lightning. The air crackled with raw energy. The very fabric of reality stretched thin. The valley was a hellscape made manifest on scorched earth. A cold wind tore across the ruined landscape. Ash danced in the air like fallen snow.

At the heart of this desolation stood two figures.

A man robed in indigo woven with silver threads. His staff was planted into the earth like a beacon against the dark. His face was aged, framed by long silver hair and beard. His storm-gray eyes sparked a reflection of the storm above. His name was Eamon the Wise, the last of the Eldritch Sorcerers.

If it could still be called a man, the other was wreathed in shadows darker than the abyss itself. His skeletal form was adorned in tattered black robes. Faint, arcane sigils pulsed along his bones. His face was an abomination of rotted flesh and bone. Where his eyes should be were empty sockets that swirled with an unnatural, deathly green. When he moved, the air itself recoiled from his presence.

Zharadim.

The Eternal Woe. Defiler of worlds. Architect of despair.

The name alone sent shudders through the earth. His existence was an infection that festered in the heart of creation.

The two stood silently for a time, the storm roaring around them. There was no army left to witness this battle. No banners to wave in defiance or cries to rally hope. The war had consumed an empire of men that now lay in piles of corpses across the horizon. Life rested to this moment. To these two.

Eamon raised his staff. Runes gleaned with celestial radiance. The light sliced through the shadows that threatened to consume the world.

"It ends tonight, lich," he declared.

Zharadim merely tilted his head as if amused. In a voice that was not just his own but thousands of voices woven into one, he whispered, *"Does it?"*

For just a breath, the battlefield froze. Zharadim grinned as he raised his hand. A wave of raw energy erupted, hurling toward Eamon. A force so ancient and vile that it sought to erase him from existence, to reduce him to nothing more than a forgotten whisper in time.

Eamon's staff struck the earth, and sigils of warding erupted from the ground to form a radiant barrier. The wave of darkness collided against the shield, sending out a blinding shockwave of white and black light. The force shattered the earth around him, sending molten rock and jagged shards of stone spiraling outward.

Zharadim laughed.

"Pathetic."

He raised a skeletal hand, and the very air screamed. The ground below split apart. From the infinite below, shadows rose. Their forms writhed like a tide of living nightmares. Limbs that should not exist, too many fingers, too many mouths gaping with silent howls.

The creatures lurched forward. Their forms shifted between corporeal and spectral. They did not walk, but rather bled through reality itself, closing the distance between them and Eamon in mere heartbeats.

Eamon did not hesitate.

His fingers traced runes in the air, golden glyphs burning into existence. Each symbol weaved into the next that created a tapestry of power older than the gods themselves. With a thrust of his staff, a single word spoken in the celestial tongue. A word not meant for mortal ears.

"BEGONE."

The word did not echo. It resonated, a command written into the very fabric of the world. The air ignited, and a column of searing white fire erupted that incinerated the abyssal horrors where they stood. They screeched as their forms dissolved like ink in water. Their cries reverberated across the shattered ruins.

But Zharadim had not been idle.

The moment Eamon turned his power against the horde, the lich moved in a blur of unnatural speed, his form weaved through the remnants of fire and shadow. A hand of skeletal fingers burst through the flames to claw toward Eamon's heart.

Eamon twisted, barely dodging the strike. The air behind him ruptured, the mere proximity of Zharadim's grasp decaying reality itself. His cloak disintegrated into dust where it brushed the void-tainted fingers.

He countered.

With a swift incantation, golden chains of pure energy lashed out, wrapping around Zharadim's arm, binding it mid-air. The moment the chains touched him, they burned. A divine radiance seared against the lich's decayed flesh. For the first time, Zharadim snarled in pain.

"FOOL!" The sky shook with his fury. "I AM BEYOND YOUR PITIFUL GODS!"

With a twist of his will, the chains shattered, exploding into a thousand fading embers. The backlash sent Eamon skidding backward across the broken ground, his boots digging trenches into the earth.

He barely had time to recover before Zharadim countered.

With a single twist of his fingers, the battlefield shifted again. The stars above went out. One by one, the celestial bodies that had long watched over the world flickered and died. The light of the heavens was snuffed out. Only darkness remained.

And from that darkness, the dead began to rise. The world trembled as the battlefield twisted beneath their feet. The air grew thick, sluggish, as though existence resisted what was happening. A vast, suffocating stillness settled over the ruins, broken only by the distant echoes as the dead rose.

The corpses of long-forgotten warriors dragged themselves from the earth. Their eyes devoid of light. Their bones wrapped in the spectral remains of armor. Their broken and rusted swords gleamed with a pale green fire that licked along their edges.

Eamon steadied his breath. He had seen necromantic resurrections before. But this... this was something far worse. These were not merely spirits recalled to their decayed vessels, but echoes of every soul Zharadim had ever devoured. Thousands. They stood, their skeletal faces turned toward the lich in silent reverence. Waiting.

"You cannot kill what has already been consumed, Eamon." Zharadim's voice was both a whisper and a roar, filling the battlefield from every direction. *"They belong to me."*

The dead turned, their hollow gazes locked onto Eamon as one and charged. A tidal wave of spectral warriors rushed forward with a thousand guttural war cries that shattered the silence. Their weapons screamed as they clashed against reality, the force of their charge causing the ground to fracture beneath them.

Eamon did not move. He simply closed his eyes and raised his staff. A single pulse of divine energy rippled outward. It was not an attack but a command.

A ring of blazing white runes erupted from the earth, formed a sacred circle around him. As the spectral warriors crossed the boundary, their bodies ignited in holy fire. Their souls were ripped from the lich's grip and scattered into the winds.

Zharadim raised both hands, fingers curling into a twisted incantation.

The sky cracked open more.

A deep, abyssal void tore across the heavens as if reality was being pulled apart at the seams. The battlefield bent, twisted. The ruins stretched in impossible ways. Distant mountains folded inward and warped into unnatural, spiraling landscapes that defied logic.

And from the massive wound in the sky, something moved. A shape too vast to comprehend. An immensity of shadow that seemed to pulse. Tendrils of pure blackness slithered downward as they stretched toward the battlefield. Their forms shifted and reshaped.

Even the storm recoiled at its presence. Zharadim lifted his skeletal face toward the chasm above, his voice a whisper laced with triumph.

"The veil is finally broken."

The void seethed as it answered his call with a pressure that throbbed in the marrow of bones. This was a presence that should not be. Zharadim turned back to Eamon.

"You have already lost, sorcerer."

Eamon breathed heavily, sweat beaded on his brow. His energy reserves were almost depleted. The warped reality interrupted the natural flow of magic in the land. This chaos prevented him from drawing from the land. He could feel the presence claw at the edges of his mind. This was not merely dark magic but the end of all things.

The Devourer stirred.

A cold realization settled in Eamon's chest. Zharadim was not trying to win this battle. He was trying to end the world.

"No!"

Eamon clenched his fists, summoning every last ember of power within him. The sacred runes at his feet flared brighter, casting golden light against the abyss. The weight of the heavens pressed down upon his shoulders, but he held his ground. If Zharadim wanted to unmake existence itself, there was only one way to stop him. He had to break the lich's tether to reality, even if it meant breaking himself along with it.

"Enough."

Eamon slammed his staff into the earth, and the world exploded into fire and light. The battlefield erupted with a blinding explosion of golden light, a shockwave tore outward as Eamon unleashed everything he had left. The heavens and the abyss clashed, celestial radiance crashed against Zharadim's eldritch darkness in a violent storm of pure, unrestrained power.

The world shook beneath the magnitude of their final clash. Eamon stood at the center of it with his staff buried deep into the ground. The sigils burned along its length with raw arcane force. His robes billowed out from the sheer magnitude of magic that surged from him. Divine fire coiled around his form, and light broke through the growing void overhead.

Zharadim raised his arms in defiance as shadows cascaded outward. In a deep, reverberating cascade of voices

"YOU CANNOT STOP THE INEVITABLE!"

The sky ripped open wider, and from within, the Devourer's abyssal tendrils reached downward, their edges warping in and out of existence as they sought to consume the last vestiges of light.

Eamon's fingers tightened around his staff. His heartbeat slowed. His breath steadied. And he finally understood. Zharadim had anchored himself to the abyss. His existence was no longer bound to this world alone. If Eamon struck him down as he was, the lich would simply reform, returning again and again.

This wasn't a battle of might. It was a battle of sacrifice. Eamon closed his eyes. The incantation came instinctively, an ancient spell, the first. One that had not been spoken aloud since the dawn of the world.

The sigils beneath him shifted, no longer mere barriers but chains.

Runes coiled outward, spiraling across the battlefield, carving themselves into the very bones of the earth. Celestial glyphs formed a cage, light lanced through the darkness, and sealed the cracks in reality that Zharadim had opened.

The abyss shrieked, recoiling as the runes took hold. Zharadim screamed.

His corporeal form snuffed out like a candle in a storm. He felt it. The pull. The weight. He tried to sever the tether and attempt to escape, but the sigils had already locked onto him.

Eamon lifted his gaze, eyes burned like twin stars. He spoke the final word.

"Begone."

The world imploded. The golden chains lashed outward to ensnare Zharadim's body, to bind him not just in this world but in every reality, he hoped. The lich shrieked, his screams echoed across time itself as he was ripped from existence. His essence dragged into the abyss he had sought to control.

The sky above sealed shut, and the rift collapsed in on itself with a final, deafening roar. The tendrils of the Devourer snapped, severed from the world, banished into the void once more. The ground quaked.

The last of Eamon's power poured into the spell, and as the light consumed the battlefield, he let go.

His body dissolved, not into dust, but into pure radiance. His name would not be forgotten. The chains that bound Zharadim would hold... for now.

Silence fell, and the storm vanished. All that remained was a single sigil burned into the earth, glowing faintly. It marked where the greatest battle in history had been fought... and won.

300 years later...

A cold wind howled across the ruins. The valley was nothing but dust and forgotten echoes. A dark brazier flared to life in the crumbled remains of a long-abandoned keep.

But inside the keep, the wind was afraid to move. Brittle bones littered the floor. Fractured pillars and stone thrown about from a long-ended battle. A figure cloaked in a tattered black robe knelt before a broken altar, at the heart of the ruined temple. His head bowed. Hands outstretched over a brazier. The air around them was wrong.

Heavy. Suffocating.

It was not just darkness that lingered here. It was something deeper, ancient. Something that did not belong. The figure's voice broke the silence. A whisper in a language that had not been spoken in over three hundred years. Each word scraped against reality. Such unnatural syllables twisted through the air like serrated knives.

"Latuin vex'khar... Varros el'thanal..."

The brazier flared to life, the fire within shifted from its natural orange glow to something... else. Something wrong.

A sickly green flame coiled upward. It twisted and writhed like a living thing. Its tendrils licked at the air. The ground shuddered. The keep groaned as though some unseen force pressed against its remains. The figure's voice grew louder. They did not waver or pause. The chant became a rhythmic pulse that clawed at the edges of existence.

"Your time is nigh..."

The air thickened. Something listened. A pulse of dark energy rippled outward from the brazier and crawled across the chamber like a living shadow. The very stones blackened and cracked beneath its touch. The brazier's flames surged higher as it shifted to deep violet, tendrils of black smoke curling upward like fingers stretching toward something unseen.

And they appeared through the smoke.

Figures... Twisted. Writhing. Grotesque.

Monstrous things with too many limbs, too many eyes, their forms shifting, flickering between shapes as though unable to decide what they were supposed to be.

The figure raised its skeletal hands toward the brazier. The flames cast a distorted glow beneath their hood.

"Come forth, Devourer of Light... Sovereign of the Abyss... Vael'Zharuun, Stir from your shadowed slumber and consume all."

The very air screamed. The ruins trembled, stones cracked under the immense pressure of something beyond comprehension.

From the darkness, a whisper—no, a breath. A presence that should not be. Something stirred. The brazier's fire turned black. The smoke thickened, coiling together, solidifying into something more.

The chanting stopped.

Silence fell over the ruins, a silence too deep, too absolute; the darkness absorbed the sound itself. Then, in the stillness, a voice emanated. It was not from the cloaked figure, not from the spectral horrors looming in the smoke, but from the void itself.

"It is not yet time."

The figure stiffened. The fire in the brazier crackled, sputtered, and then settled, still burning black but no longer reaching hungrily toward the sky.

The presence lingered, though unseen. It did not step into this world fully—not yet.

But it had marked the moment. It had seen. And it had chosen.

The cloaked figure slowly turned their hooded gaze toward the brazier. The dark flames reflected in the hollow depths beneath their hood.

"The herald is marked tonight."

Their voice was cold. Certain. Somewhere, far away, a child took their first breath. And in the abyss, something watched.

The birthing chamber trembled with the force of the storm outside, its walls shuddering beneath the weight of the howling winds. A deafening crack of thunder rolled through the castle, rattling the iron sconces on the stone walls. Candles flickered wildly, their flames bent and twisted by unseen hands, casting erratic shadows that slithered across the chamber like living things.

"ALDRIC!"

The cry was raw, torn from Alia's throat, her voice laced with agony and desperation. She arched off the bed, her fingers clutching the wooden bedpost so tightly her knuckles had gone white. Sweat beaded along her forehead, trailing down her pale cheeks in shimmering streaks. Her other hand flailed in the air, grasping blindly seeking something, someone, anything to hold onto.

King Aldric was already there.

"I'm here, my love," he said, rushing to her side, his voice strained but determined. His hands, usually so sure and steady, trembled as he wrapped them around hers, pulling her fingers into his grasp. "I'm right here."

Her grip crushed his fingers, her body wracked by another unbearable wave of pain.

Aldric brushed damp strands of golden blonde hair from her face, whispering softly, his voice thick with emotion.

"You're strong, Alia. You can do this. Just a little longer."

Alia's gasping breaths filled the chamber, but she barely seemed to hear him. She clenched her eyes shut, her face twisting in pain as another contraction racked her body.

"Something's wrong."

Her voice was barely a whisper, a tremor of fear woven into the pain.

Aldric's stomach clenched.

He tightened his grip, pressing his forehead to hers for a brief, fleeting moment. He didn't know what else to do. He was a warrior, a ruler, but here in this moment, he was powerless.

Aldric barely heard the storm anymore, not over the frantic activity inside the chamber.

But the castle did. A terrible wind shrieked through the stone corridors, finding its way through even the narrowest of cracks. The wooden shutters over the arched windows shuddered violently, their iron hinges straining under the force of the gale.

And the lightning came in rapid succession, not the usual silver streaks of a summer storm but something unnatural. Bolts of deep violet, crimson, and electric blue split the heavens, illuminating the chamber in horrifying, otherworldly hues.

The color of the sky was wrong. Not that Aldric saw it—but someone did.

One of the midwives had dared to glance out the window between tending to the water basins. She froze.

Aldric barely noticed her at first, not until she gasped and staggered backward, a hand clutching at her chest.

"My Lord..." she whispered, her voice trembling. "The sky..."

Aldric barely spared her a glance. His focus remained entirely on Alia, but something in her voice sent a chill down his spine.

The doctor, an older man with sharp features and weariness carved into his bones, frowned but did not turn. "Forget the damn sky!" he snapped. "Focus on the queen!"

Unbeknownst to all of them, the storm was not simply raging. It was reacting.

Its pulse... was tied to Alia's own.

Every contraction. Every wave of pain. Every step closer to the child's birth.

The sky answered.

And somewhere in the depths of the abyss, something stirred.

The chamber was chaos. Midwives bustled around the room, moving with a practiced urgency, their hands damp with sweat and stained with blood. Basins of warm water were overturned, cloths and linens piled high and stained crimson. Another midwife tried to keep her hands steady as she wiped Alia's brow, her lips moving in silent prayer. But it wasn't enough.

"No... no, no, no! There's too much blood..."

The doctor's voice cut through the frenzy like a blade. Alia's labored breaths hitched, her body arching off the mattress. Tears pooled at the corners of her eyes, and her fingers, once so tightly wrapped around Aldric's hand, were weakening. Aldric's heart clenched.

"Stay with me, my queen!" the doctor urged.

The words should have been a command. Instead, they sounded like a plea. Alia's eyes fluttered, her lips trembling. Her breathing was slowing. And for the first time, true fear struck Aldric. Aldric felt his world crack. Alia's body shuddered, her breathing coming in shorter, sharper bursts.

She was slipping. Aldric tightened his grip on her hand, willing his strength into her.

The room felt smaller.

The chamber was filled with activity, movement, sound, but all of it seemed distant to Aldric. His world had narrowed to the bed before him, to the woman fading beneath his hands, to the tremors in her breath.

A low, guttural groan rumbled from Alia's throat, her body arching weakly against the mattress. Her skin was pale, too pale, her once-rosy lips taking on a sickly hue.

And her hands were cold.

Aldric's fingers wrapped tighter around hers, desperate, as if he could anchor her to this world by will alone.

"Alia..." His voice barely carried.

She didn't answer. Aldric turned to the doctor.

"Can you save her?" His voice was rough, barely above a whisper.

"I will try, Your Highness, but we have been at this for hours now."

Alia's body shuddered, her breathing coming in shorter, sharper bursts.

She was slipping.

Aldric tightened his grip on her hand, willing his strength into her.

"Do what you must to save her." His jaw clenched. "I don't care about the cost."

For a moment, no one spoke.

Then the doctor nodded solemnly and turned back to Alia.

The storm still raged beyond the castle walls, but Aldric barely heard it now. All he could hear was her breathing; shallow, broken, and slipping away.

His chest tightened. He had seen men cut down in war, gutted in the streets, bodies run through with spears and left for the crows. He had seen the light leave their eyes, seen the vacant, glassy stare of the dead.

But not her. He would not let this be her.

His breath came heavier, his heart hammering so violently against his ribs it drowned out the sound of the midwives' whispers.

Aldric felt it, the hesitation, the weight of something left unsaid.

Then, slowly, the doctor inhaled. He lifted his hands over Alia's body, fingers trembling ever so slightly. And then the air changed. Aldric felt it before he saw it.

A shift. A pulse. Something stirred. The doctor began the incantation, stumbling through the words. His hands began to glow.

It was faint at first, a dull golden aura, flickering, unstable, as if the magic itself refused to manifest. Aldric's stomach twisted.

When was the last time he had seen magic? He always thought it to be unnatural.

And yet now he needed it. His fingers twitched at his side, as if his own body recoiled at the hypocrisy.

A gust of unseen wind rushed through the chamber, snuffing out two of the candle flames. The glow of the spell strengthened. The doctor's hands pulsed with celestial energy, runes appeared just off the palms of his hands.

Alia gasped. Her back arched violently, her mouth opening as if to scream but no sound came out. For a heartbeat, her eyes glowed too.

Not the same golden hue as the doctor's magic. Something else.

A flash of violet. A shade too close to the storm.

Then lightning struck again.

A crack of thunder so loud it shook the walls of the chamber, rattling the iron candelabras and sending shadows skittering across the stone.

The doctor stumbled backward, the glow around his hands snuffing out like a candle in the wind. Alia's body collapsed back onto the mattress, her limbs suddenly limp. Too still. Aldric's breath stopped.

And then the storm stopped.

Not gradually. Not naturally.

One second, the rain pounded against the castle. The next, it was gone.

The wind, the thunder, the howling vanished, swallowed into some unnatural silence.

The absence of sound was deafening. And in that terrible stillness sounded a cry.

A single, sharp, newborn wail pierced the hush. For a moment, no one moved. No one spoke. The midwives breathed again, shifting, hands moving quickly as they pulled the child free, wrapping him in linens stained with his mother's blood.

Aldric was frozen. A strange, paralyzing weight sat on his chest. Then, slowly, he turned toward Alia. And his world collapsed. She was still. Too still.

The tension had left her limbs, the strain gone from her face. Aldric stared, waiting for the rise of her chest. Waiting. Nothing.

"No..."

His hands moved without thought, grabbing her shoulders. Shaking her gently, then harder.

"Alia. Alia!"

No response.

"No, no, no, no, no! Alia!"

He pulled her into him, clutching her against his chest, rocking slightly, as if desperation alone could will her back to him. His throat burned. His vision blurred. A king did not weep. But a husband did. His body trembled as he pressed his forehead to hers, feeling nothing but cold.

His voice broke as he whispered, "Come back to me..."

Another cry. A wail. The child.

King Aldric's heart shattered. He fell to his knees beside the bed, clutching at Alia's lifeless hand. "My love," he whimpered, his voice cracking. Tears streamed down his face as he felt the last of her warmth fade away.

At that moment, a deep, dark resentment took root in Aldric's heart, not just towards the magic that had failed to save his beloved wife but towards the child who had survived her.

ACT I

THE DIVIDED KINGDOM

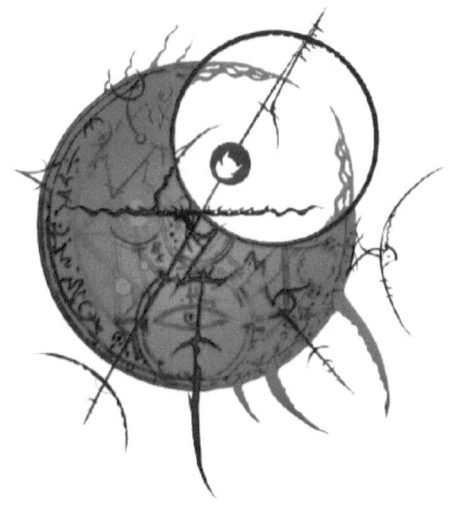

There was no before. No when. No edge to measure.
No death to fear. No shape to hold the fear in.
The void did not sleep. It did not wake. It did not wonder.
It wasn't.

And then, it was.

CHAPTER ONE

THE CHILD AND CURSE

In the wake of the storm, an eerie silence fell onto Castle Dunmoh. It was as if the shadows themselves absorbed the sound. Besides faint whispers, no one dared to speak at a normal volume to avoid disturbing the king in his grief. The storm raging on the outside had subsided, leaving only a trickle of rainfall with fog clinging to the ground. Thunder could be heard in the distance, as if someone beat a drum out of sight in some asymmetric rhythm.

Queen Alia's now empty bed lay in the middle of the chamber. Hours had passed since her body was moved. A wooden crib stood nearby, holding a baby swaddled in a soft blanket. Glowing faintly as the embers burned, the hearth flickered light across the room while wisps of flame flew up in search of air.

A faintly glowing birthmark on the baby's chest illuminated his figure inside the crib. The birthmark appeared as an intricate crest with ancient sigils. The child was asleep; his peaceful expression seemed unbothered by the weather outside as the lightning flashed briefly, illuminating the rain-streaked windows. The flickering firelight made the shadows dance across the walls like tentacles reaching for something.

King Aldric Ravenmark stood at the foot of Alia's birthing bed. His stout form cast a grim shadow over the bedding, still stained with sweat and blood. His face, usually etched with the years of age and experience, furrowed in pain and grief. Tears rushed down his face, past his hands, into his auburn beard as he attempted to cover his sorrowful weeping.

Shadows flickered with the lightning; his imagination still showed afterimages of Alia lying asleep in bed. He lowered his hands to the wood of the footboard, his grip almost digging into the wood with a strength that seemed to dent the oak. He glanced through tearful eyes at the wooden crib and the newborn child.

What is this glow? he wondered as he noticed a peculiar mark on the baby's chest. As he studied the birthmark briefly, the faint glow from it revealed a redness of anger inside him.

This child is cursed! The thought forced its way into his mind.

Waves of irrational fear and anger filled him as he continued to look upon the birthmark. It seemed reminiscent of an era long past, which struck Aldric as an ill omen. He couldn't quite put his finger on it, but it stirred a dread and hatred he could not contain.

Something about this child had caused the death of his beloved Alia. It could not be his son. Grief twisted his memories and spurred on a dark conviction regarding the boy, the tiny being who had survived his wife.

This child is a harbinger of misfortune. KILL IT!

The shadows seemed to writhe, as if talking to Aldric with urgency.

Aldric grabbed the tail of his cloak to wipe his face and hands, then tossed it back as if it offended him. "Dispose of this!" he ordered coldly to the midwife, loud enough for the door guards to hear as well. His voice was devoid of warmth or sympathy.

"I'll not have that cursed abomination in my home."

He slammed his hand on the footrail of the bed again, turned, and started walking out of the room. His boots echoed through the chamber like a grandfather clock ticking. He was unable to bear the sight of the child any longer. He slammed his hand into the door to open it, hitting one of the guards standing outside in the arm. Aldric stormed out and down the corridor without acknowledging the guard having to shift his position.

The door slammed shut upon Aldric's departure from the chamber, leaving only the child and the midwife charged with looking after him. Clara Threadmoor sat in a chair at the edge of the room. She hadn't left that chamber since the queen had gone into labor. Her heart plummeted at the king's harsh decree as the door slammed shut.

Clara was a compassionate young woman who had lost her own child years ago to illness. The memory of her lost child and the pain it had caused sparked a strength to save this child. Her mind raced with how. She knew someone who could help her, but she would have to get to her.

An hour or so later, Clara removed the newborn from the crib, still wrapped tightly in swaddling blankets. Her hands trembled with nervousness but were determined. She placed him gently into a wicker basket and gathered her things from the room. She walked toward the door and opened it.

"Where are you going?" one of the guards asked, staring at Clara and the basket.

"To dispose of the child," Clara stated, nodding toward the basket and hoping not to awaken the child. "The king's orders, to be carried out tonight. It 'never survived' the birth, same as our beloved queen. Gods rest her soul."

"Very well, carry on," stated the guard. "It's such a shame."

"The royal executioner will handle it," the other guard said. "He might still be awake at this hour."

Clara nodded toward the sentry and shuffled off down the corridor toward the servant's pathways. She wasn't going toward the executioner's chambers in the castle depths—quite the opposite entirely. She hoped the child would remain asleep through it all, as a crying baby would not aid her in escaping from the castle without raising alarm.

Each turn and doorway of the servant's corridors seemed winding and narrow. Each footstep echoed through the halls, almost in a match with the pounding of her heartbeat, reverberating from every surface. Clara pressed on; she had to get the child far away from this castle. Her heart pounded with adrenaline.

Keep moving! she thought, as if to motivate her sense of urgency.

A door to the outside! She could hear the drizzle upon the puddles outside and water running off the crevices of the castle, splashing onto the mud below. As she opened the door, dense fog hit her face as if to stop her from moving.

Perfect! Some cover.

Turning right out of the doorway, she crouched within the wall of fog and stayed as close to the wall as she could see it.

Quickly, or I'll get stuck, she argued with herself as she moved along, not wanting to linger too long in any spot for fear of sinking into the muddy path. She was following memory and sounds at this point. The fog at ground level seemed to be getting thicker. She could hear her next goal nearby: the stables.

Reaching the opening to the stable bay, the fog cleared up a little inside. She could see again. Inside the first stable she came to stood a bay mare with a streak of white along her nose. A sign that read 'Thistle' was etched into the door. She looked like a sturdy horse. Thistle neighed as Clara entered her stable, hoofing at the ground.

"Calm down, girl," Clara whispered, running her hand along the white streak. "We must hurry, and there is a long road ahead of us. Are you rested?" Clara asked Thistle as if carrying on a conversation.

She seemed to respond to her sense of urgency and whinnied softly as Clara secured a saddle and attached the basket.

"Ok, let's go, girl. Our life is in your hands."

Thistle neighed as she started to trot out of the stable.

"Who goes there?" shouted a voice from the shadowed stables.

The stable hand tried to light his lantern after being awakened by the noise. His light flickered to life, casting long, shifting beams of light. Panic surged through Clara as she held her breath but urged Thistle on.

"Yaw, girl! Let's go!" Clara urged as the crack of the reins hit the side of Thistle's neck.

The stable hand stepped closer to see who was in his stable. Clara flicked the reins, and Thistle bolted into the night, her hooves striking sparks against the cobblestones. Shouts echoed in the fog, and alarm bells began to toll. Shadows in the mist spilled out from the barracks and guard towers. Guards could be heard shouting,

"Horse thief!"

"Intruder!"

"Get 'em!"

Thistle surged forward, her powerful legs churning through the mud. Clara clung tightly to her reins, her cloak billowing behind her like a phantom in the storm. She urged the horse toward the western gate. Guards raced up the stairs to reach the battlements. The fog clung closely to the ground, obscuring all but Clara's outline. Arrows flew, with only one catching Clara's cloak.

"Move, girl!" she urged Thistle as they reached the gate.

Thunder clapped overhead as Thistle leaped over the gap in the drawbridge to the ground below, the basket jostling but remaining secure.

"Yes! Keep going, girl!" Clara urged Thistle on.

The next village along that road was Havenstead. They had to make it. She heard their pursuers in the distance behind them. She had a decent lead on them, but this was no time to slow down. The guards of Dunmoh were not known for relenting. Clara's saving grace was that the fog clung to the ground like a ghostly shroud. Visibility was obscured beyond twenty feet. Anything beyond that was left to the imagination. Mist droplets stung Clara's face as Thistle trudged through the muddy roadway with reckless abandon. She was on a mission. Her strength and endurance almost seemed unnatural.

They had to have been on the road for hours at this point. The guards pursuing her were far behind them; shouts could no longer be heard. Exhaustion weighed heavily on both Clara and Thistle.

I need to find a place to rest, Clara thought. *The sun will be up soon!*

No sooner than that thought crossed her mind, the faint outlines of Havenstead appeared through the thinning fog, and dawn was peering over the horizon.

Clara veered off a small pathway toward a barn near a cluster of cottages. The door was slightly open.

"Great, we can hide in here, hopefully," she said to herself, half talking to Thistle.

She dismounted at the door and led Thistle to a water trough inside the barn. A couple of dairy cows were in a small corral on the opposite side of the barn. As Thistle drank, Clara removed the basket and placed it on a small nestle of hay. She rushed back to the door to close it. Then she found some gaps in the planks that allowed her to peek through without being seen.

Clara could almost see the central square. Remnants of smoke still wafted up from chimneys, and the last flickers of life in a couple of street lamps burned out.

Of course, they are farmers. They're up before the sun to tend the flocks and fields.

She watched as an older villager slowly made his way down a pathway. His lamp swung with each step, and he occasionally slid in the mud.

"Oof, damn mud," the old man muttered.

"You there! Halt!" a guard suddenly shouted toward the old man.

Clara was on high alert. She looked around. *One... two guards... where's the rest of them?*

"What do you want? Botherin' me on my mornin' chores," he spat back, as if annoyed by the guard interrupting his daily pattern.

"Have you seen a woman on horseback come through here recently?" questioned the guard.

The old farmer stopped to regard the guards.

"Not seen anyone tonight but you. Just gettin' back from the fields, checkin' on the herd since the storms let up."

"If you see anyone suspicious, report it, ya hear?" the second guard spoke up. "The woman is a fugitive of the crown for stealing a horse. Anyone aiding her will be just as guilty."

The gruff old farmer nodded. "Yeah, yeah..." he mumbled. "I'll keep my eyes open. Now, let me be so I can get on with my morning chores. Cows don't care about your manhunt."

Clara breathed a sigh of relief as the guards walked away. Suddenly, the barn door creaked open.

Shit!

She slid down from the wall and attempted to hide, but was too slow. A young woman holding a pail walked inside, closed the door behind her, and froze, staring right at Clara in mid-lunge back to the hay.

"Already saw ya! Come on out, ma'am," the young lady stated.

Clara got back up from the hay, standing about fifteen feet in front of her.

"You ain't from around here... who are you?" she asked, setting down the pail near her feet, then looked over at the baby lying in a basket.

"Please don't tell anyone," Clara pleaded. "I need a place to hide myself and this baby. I'm no criminal, but I need to make it to Gladecross, and the guards won't stop until they catch me."

The young woman stared over at the baby, noticing a faint glow coming from something under the blanket. The child seemed peaceful, a newborn by the looks of it.

"This way," she whispered.

She motioned Clara toward an area in the back of the barn, enough to hide Thistle behind the hay bales. She moved a couple of planks in the floor, revealing a small crawlspace.

"You'll be safe in here for the day. Keep the babe quiet. The horse'll be fine up here, plenty to eat and drink."

Clara smiled and nodded, grateful for the generosity.

"Thank you so much," she said as she lowered herself and the basket into the cubby.

The hours seemed to drag on Clara as she fought off sleep, attempting to keep the child quiet. She would hear voices nearby occasionally, jolting her awake with anxiety. Some were just casual conversations among the villagers, mostly disdain for the sudden appearance of guards questioning about some woman.

They've been quiet for a while.

The baby got fussy. It had been a while since he'd had anything to eat.

The barn door opened.

"Can I help you?" Clara recognized the young woman's voice.

"What's in here? Anything unusual going on?" the guard asked.

"Nothin' in here but hay, milk cows, and some old tools. Got a nanny goat in the back nursin' her new kid," the woman replied.

About that time, the kid came hopping around a bale of hay.

Meehhhhh! it muttered as it hopped around in circles.

"Hmm... ok," the guard stated as he looked around from the door and walked back out.

Clara felt her muscles relax a bit. Her nerves were shot, though.

A few more hours passed as the daylight waned over the fields and dusk settled over Havenstead. The young woman returned to the barn and knocked at the planks.

"The guards are gone. It's safe to come out," she said as she helped Clara out of the hiding spot.

"If you take the west path through the wheat fields, it'll be harder to track you."

"I don't know how I could ever thankyou!" Clara exclaimed as she launched a hug onto the woman.

"Just go," the woman urged. "There will be a pathway about four hours out that'll lead back to the main road into Gladecross. And take care of that child."

Clara grabbed the basket, reattached it to Thistle's saddle, gave Thistle a long pet along her nose, and mounted up. Thistle neighed in reaction, signaling that she'd rested up and was ready.

They left the barn and followed the pathway the woman told Clara about. It was treacherously muddy, but nothing was in sight but fields of wheat blowing in the wind. This wasn't a death sprint like last night, but they trotted along, making good time.

Several hours passed, and the path veered back toward the main roadway. As dawn crept up over the horizon, she saw the woodlands and the faint silhouette of Gladecross, nestled at the edge of the plainlands and the forest. The air was still thick with the scent of soggy earth and now the whiff of oak and cedar.

She trotted through the village until she approached a modest cottage nestled on the outskirts. The cottage belonged to Mother Elaria Mooncrest, a wise and kind-hearted middle-aged woman. She had once been a court healer under the previous king but left the service behind when King Aldric was coronated. She had known of Aldric's wariness of magic even then. She wanted to preserve her knowledge and ability to practice freely, away from any scrutiny.

Clara dismounted Thistle near the side of the house by the tie-post and trough, then tethered the reins securely.

"You can rest here, girl; you did well," she said as she brushed Thistle's mane while she shook her head up and down, neighing.

"Enjoy the rest of your days."

Thistle nickered softly while stomping a hoof into the ground, nudging Clara's hand as if she understood. Clara lifted the basket off the saddle and walked around to the front door. The baby was cooing, as if content with his current situation. She placed the basket gently on the doorstep and kissed the baby on the forehead.

"Be safe, child. We'll meet again," she whispered.

She stood up and started walking back around the cottage, heading toward the forest. The trees seemed to glow in the dawning light from their recent bath. Dew stuck to the grass, creating an almost reflective sheen. Clara pulled her cloak tight around her and hurried into the treeline.

Once she felt she was a safe distance away from the cottage, she stopped in a small clearing. The trees and brush seemed to form a natural circle of undergrowth. Kneeling down on the damp ground, she pulled out a small vial of glowing liquid from her pouch. This was a potion Elaria had given her years ago for emergencies. It was only good for a single person, or she would have used it in the castle.

She uncorked the vial and poured a few drops onto the ground below. The liquid seemed to shimmer as the morning dawn rays were caught in its droplets. She corked the vial and placed it back into her pouch. With trembling hands, she rubbed them together and placed them both on the earth, now slightly glowing from the liquid.

Clara recited an incantation softly, stumbling over the words at first, but it returned to her. It had been years since she last performed this one. Eventually, the words of the spell rolled off the tip of her tongue as naturally as breathing. The air around her thickened with energy. A faint hum vibrated through her fingertips.

As if rising from the earth itself, a swirl of light enveloped her, growing brighter with each word. Clara closed her eyes as she recited the last word of the incantation. Her body was immediately enveloped with light swirls as the world blurred around her. In an instant, the forest vanished and was replaced by an alleyway off the streets of Arden's Wake.

"Well, well..." a voice said.

"A visitor perhaps?" another replied.

"Naw... not this one. She's not ready yet," the first voice stated matter-of-factly.

Clara staggered slightly, attempting to get her wits about her. She looked around for the source of the voices. The alleyway was empty, except for an odd shop displaying "Curiosities" on the sign and two imp-sized gargoyles perched above the doorway.

"Couldn't be..." she told herself while shaking her head. The spell had left her momentarily disoriented. She tried to steady herself against the nearby wall. The familiar sounds of the town grounded her in reality.

She stood up, straightened her cloak, and made her way out of the alleyway. Reaching the street, she turned back, and the alleyway was gone. It was replaced by a brick wall as if the alley had never existed.

"Weird..." she stated, then turned and continued down the street.

Faint cries of a baby cut through the remnants of Elaria's dreams, pulling her from her sleep. She sat up and looked around. The cries were coming from the door. She got up, grabbed her shawl from the chair, and wrapped it over her shoulders. She approached the door and looked through a peephole. She couldn't see anything out of the ordinary. The remnants of the rain were still filtering down from the treetops.

She unlatched the lock on her door and opened it. To her surprise, a basket was on the doorstep with a baby inside. The small child stared back at her with the wonder only a newborn could offer. She bent over and picked the child up from the basket. As she moved the swaddling around, she noticed the faintly glowing birthmark on the child's chest. She had seen this mark before... a long time ago.

"Hush, little one," she whispered as she turned around and headed back inside. "You're safe now."

CHAPTER TWO

SANCTUARY IN ELDERWOOD

In the days following Queen Alia's tragic death, King Aldric Ravenmark stood before a gathering of his most trusted advisors and enforcers deep within the royal castle. The great hall was adorned with towering banners bearing gold and crimson sigils gleaming in the dim torchlight.

"For too long, magic has been allowed to fester in our lands," Aldric's voice rang out. "It has corrupted our people. Twisted their minds. No longer."

His gauntlet-clad fist slammed onto the oak table before him, rattling the goblets and sending loose parchments fluttering to the floor. A battle-worn commander stood and bowed his head.

"What would you have us do, Your Majesty?" he asked.

Aldric leaned forward, his face contorted in rage.

"Root them all out. I want a decree sent to every corner of the kingdom. Effective immediately. Magic is outlawed. Anyone who practices it will be arrested, tried, and made an example of. Any who harbor them will share their fate."

Uneasy whispers of agreement rippled throughout the room. None dared to challenge the king's command.

By nightfall, the Royal Guard, clad in their dark uniforms emblazoned with the king's crest, marched through the streets of Arden's Wake.

At every significant square, a herald stepped forward, unrolling a heavy parchment, reading aloud.

"Hear ye, hear ye! By order of His Majesty King Aldric Ravenmark, all practices of magic are hereby forbidden! Anyone who engages in or supports magical activities shall be subject to immediate arrest! This decree is issued for the safety of our great kingdom!"

The words echoed over the city like a funeral bell. The people gathered around in small groups, listening to the heralds. In the markets, merchants paused. In the taverns, whispers of defiance barely dared to surface, all replaced by a quiet tension. A merchant shook his head as he leaned over to another shopkeeper.

"How in the name of the gods are we supposed to know who practices magic and who doesn't? Anyone could be accused."

"It doesn't matter. This isn't about finding the guilty," responded the elderly woman shopkeep. "This is about making people afraid."

Throughout Dunmoh's villages, the decree spread like wildfire. Messengers rode hard to reach every hamlet, every settlement nestled in the kingdom's hills and forests. And wherever the messengers went, the king's soldiers followed closely behind.

Friendships grew strained. Neighbors turned wary of one another. Fear was the king's greatest weapon, and with this decree, he cast a shadow over his kingdom that would be difficult to escape.

Six years since the fateful night...

Raaawwwwrrr!

The monstrous beast screamed out, flying high above. Its black scales contrasted against the snowcapped mountain peaks. Wings cut through the clouds as it dodged around peaks and dove down into ravines. Below stood a lone warrior, holding his ground with a gleaming sword, cloak chaotically flowing behind him amidst the wind.

"You are not welcome here, foul beast!" the warrior exclaimed, raising his blade toward the dragon.

Circling the area several times, the dragon landed directly before the warrior, its mouth dripping molten spital between dagger-like teeth.

"I will eat what I want, mortal!" bellowed the dragon. "And you are next."

Swiping with its front right claw, the warrior charged forward. His sword met the beast's talons in a blinding flash of sparks. Metal clashed against scale, and the force behind the warrior's blow sent the mighty dragon reeling back with a roar of frustration. The battle raged on. The ground was charred with dragon fire around the warrior. He steadied himself, raised his sword, poised for another charge, and...

Snap!

A piece of the stick fell to the ground, breaking his immersion.

Caelan sat on the grass in front of the cottage, his legs tucked underneath him. The wind rustled the leaves around him. His sword? A slightly curved stick that he was gripping firmly in his tiny hand. Stones and twigs were laid before him, depicting his grand imaginary world. He puffed out his chest as he stood up, inspecting his sword for damage.

Behind him, a chuckle sounded. Elaria stood in the doorway, watching Caelan's fierce battle unfold.

"You were quite the valiant hero!" she mused.

"Did you see me, Momma?" Caelan asked, beaming with pride. "I almost beat the dragon!" He swung the stick around and poked the air a couple of times.

"I did," she replied with amusement. "But it'll be back again later, won't it?"

"Yeah," Caelan replied disappointedly. "It ran away, but I'll get it next time!"

"Ok, well, put your sword away and go clean up. It's time for mighty warriors to eat," she said with a chuckle, patting Caelan on his head.

Setting the stick down, he dashed to the side of the cottage. The sun was beginning to set, the air carrying a crisp breeze. He rounded the corner, coming to a stop near a single stable. Thistle stood quietly near the water trough until she spotted Caelan, letting out a soft whicker and flicking her ears forward. She lifted her head, tossing her mane from side to side, stepping toward him.

"Hey, girl!" Caelan grinned, reaching up to scratch her jawline.

"I almost beat a dragon today!" he stated, puffing his chest out.

Thistle snorted in retort as if unimpressed by his grand tale. Still, she nudged him gently with her muzzle, almost knocking him off balance.

"Hey!" Caelan giggled. "Okay, okay, maybe next time I'll really beat it."

Thistle neighed and stomped at the ground. Caelan returned to the water trough, ran his hands through a couple of splashes, splashed some up on his face, and then rubbed his palms together to wash away the dirt. He patted his hands several times on his clothes, then gave an affectionate pat on Thistle's muzzle.

"See you later, girl!" he said to Thistle as he turned and darted back to the house.

The door creaked as he pushed it open. Caelan was greeted by the rich aroma of roasted vegetables in a beef stew and freshly baked bread. The hearth crackled with a few wood logs, giving a stage to dancing fire and wisps of embers escaping free into the air. He ran up to the table and sat down. Elaria set down two steaming bowls of the stew, arching an eyebrow at Caelan as he adjusted his seat.

"Did you clean your hands?" she asked, almost knowing the answer already.

Caelan held up his hands, still slightly damp with water. "Mostly."

Elaria shook her head and set the bowl of stew and a chunk of bread before him. Her expression was filled with love.

"Mighty warriors and playful children need their strength all the same; eat up."

Meals were generally a time for reflection. Elaria taught Caelan to enjoy the meal in its entirety—the fragrances and the tastes of the different herbs and spices. Each meal was precious and made with love. The body needed the nourishment it provided. Although Caelan was only six years old now, he tried to. Mainly, he would almost inhale the food provided in a frenzy only a hungry boy could muster. Elaria watched him as she took her bites in smaller spoonfuls.

Tap, tap, tap... meow! Came from the windowsill.

Caelan looked up with a mouth full of stew. Elaria turned her head toward the noise and noticed a sleek black cat perched on the windowsill. The cat turned to regard Elaria with piercing green eyes that glowed in the dim light. A thin silver cord tied a small parchment scroll around its neck. She dabbed her mouth with her napkin before getting up from the table. Elaria walked over to the window and opened it.

"Well, hello, Zoe! Do you have a message for me?" Elaria recognized the familiar.

Zoe meowed and started purring at the recognition. Elaria unfastened the silver tie and retrieved the parchment. Zoe stretched lazily, leaped into the house, trotted to the chair near the hearth, and laid down as if she owned the place. Elaria unrolled the parchment and began to read:

Dear Cousin,

I hope this message finds you well and that Zoe isn't too bothersome. I fear I have bad news for you and young Caelan. The king's decrees against magic have worsened, just as you predicted. He has gone mad, arresting anyone caught using magic. It may no longer be safe for any of us. There may still be a few safe havens left. I have located and taken refuge at the Sanctum that you told me about years ago. You were correct in their teachings, but I am doing well in my studies. Keep in touch. I hope to hear back from you soon.

With love,
Clara

Elaria exhaled slowly as she read the message, firelight flickering in her eyes. Caelan looked up from his bowl of stew, sensing her change in demeanor.

"Momma?" he asked.

Elaria glanced at him with a reassuring smile. "Finish your stew, love."
Zoe continued to catnap on the chair near the hearth fire.

A few days later, Elaria and Caelan entered the village for fresh vegetables and maybe some sweets if Caelan behaved. The town square was alive with its usual activities. Merchants called out their wares. Carts rattled over cobblestones as they moved down the street. The smell of bread and music wafted through the air. Caelan hurried his little legs to stay close to Elaria, holding her hand tightly.

Closer to the square, a man stood at the edge playing his flute. His fingers danced over his instrument, creating a heavenly melody. As he played, tiny wisps of light flicked around him, dancing in the air like fireflies. Caelan stared in awe at the performance. Such beauty.

Nearby stood another child, no older than Caelan, with his mother. His eyes went wide as he held onto his favorite rabbit doll. He was also staring at the street performer, but something else happened. The doll he was holding began to float, levitating lazily in the air. For a moment, it was almost beautiful.

"Magic! He's using magic!" someone screamed.

The music stopped abruptly, and the crowd went silent. The street performer froze. An expression of realization and horror covered his face. A group of guards shoved their way through the crowd.

"Him!" one barked, pointing at the musician, then pointing at the child. "And the boy, too!"

The street performer took a step back, hesitant, thinking of fleeing.

"I was only entertaining. There was no harm done."

A baton cracked across his ribs.

"Silence!" the guard growled, grabbing the man by his shirt. "Magic is forbidden under the king's decree. You know the punishment."

The boy screamed in fear, trying desperately to hold onto his mother as another guard attempted to grab him.

"No! I didn't mean to... I... I don't know what happened. I was just listening to the music with Momma!"

His mother desperately clawed at the guard's arms.

"He's just a child! PLEASE... have mercy!"

The crowd just stood, watching the entire event take place. Most were dumbfounded at what was happening. Some patrons cast their eyes downward, others whispered in hushed breaths, too afraid to speak up.

Caelan was frozen in place at Elaria's side.

"Momma?" he whispered, looking up at her as her grip tightened on his hand.

"Enough!" a voice cut through the crowd. It was the Magistrate of Gladecross.

Everyone stopped. His eyes looked from the street performer, still writhing on the ground, to the young boy. Then he addressed the guard.

"The king's decree applies to those who practice willingly," he stated. "This child did not. Release him."

The guard complied, and the boy stumbled back toward his mother, clinging desperately to her side now, sobbing uncontrollably.

"He, however, knew what he was doing. Take him," the magistrate ordered with a flick of his hand.

Two guards lifted the man to his feet, dragging him to the town jail. His flute lay broken in half in the dirt. Elaria let out a slow breath, tightening her posture, then started walking in the opposite direction, pulling Caelan with her.

"We must go," she whispered.

Their journey home was silent. Caelan held Elaria's hand as tightly as he could as her pace quickened. The usual sights and sounds of their home felt muted. The birds chirping, the wind rustling through the trees, and the bubbling brook cascading over rocks all seemed dampened, overshadowed by what they had witnessed. Once their cottage came into view, Elaria released a slow, steadying breath. They were home, but they couldn't stay.

At the sight of their house, Caelan let go of her hand and ran toward the door, pushing it open and stepping inside. The lingering smell of the hearth, fresh herbs drying, and the morning's meal still hung in the air. Elaria stood at the doorway, attempting to calm herself. She looked over the small cottage in a panoramic view, as if looking at it for the last time. She had always known this day would eventually come but hoped it wouldn't. She finally stepped inside, shutting the door behind her.

"Caelan, love," she said calmly. "Come sit with me at the table."

He jumped up from the rug where he was playing with toys and ran over to the table, sitting in his usual spot.

"Are we in trouble, Momma?"

Elaria's chest tightened as she heard the question.

"No, son, but things are... changing," she reassured him. "It's not safe for us here anymore."

"Is it because of the guards?" he asked.

"Yes, son. Because of the guards and the king." She nodded. "But also because of what you are."

Confused and intrigued, he asked, "Because of what I am? What am I?"

Elaria looked up at Caelan with the love that only a mother could. She reached forward, tucking a strand of hair behind his ear.

"You are special, Caelan."

She then placed her hand on his chest, over his birthmark.

"You have been marked for something special. And if the king's men ever saw this..." Her voice trailed off momentarily. Then she shook her head and looked him square in the eyes with a smile.

"I won't let that happen."

Caelan thought back on the boy in the square and the floating doll. The boy was his age. The fear in his eyes.

"They would take me away too, wouldn't they?"

Elaria closed her eyes momentarily, then placed her hand on his cheek, smiling.

"I won't let them."

"Now go look through your things. Pick out your favorite toys and get your clothes ready for packing," she stated, rustling the hair on his head in a playful manner.

"We need to leave in the morning, before sunrise."

"Where are we going, Momma?" he asked.

"Deeper into the forest, love," she whispered. "Where the king's reach cannot find us."

Then she turned to regard Zoe, who was still at the cottage.

"Zoe, come here, please."

The familiar's ears perked up at her name. Stretching out and yawning, she jumped down from the chair and sauntered over to Elaria.

"I need you to carry a message back to your master. Can you do that for me?" she asked, petting Zoe on the head as the cat blinked back at her.

Dearest Clara,

Events have unfolded here. There was a musician and a little boy, no older than Caelan, while we were shopping in town. Caelan doesn't fully understand what transpired, but he is scared just the same. We must leave Gladecross. We venture deeper into the Elderwood to seek sanctuary and protection from the forest. I feel this is the best way to keep him safe. We both know the stories. The king's guard will not find us there. Zoe has been a wonderful guest these past couple of days. When you get this, keep your guard up, and do not draw attention to yourself. I will attempt to contact you once we settle.

With love,
Elaria

She secured the letter around Zoe's neck with the silver cord and gave her some head scratches.

"Travel safe and swift," she said to Zoe as the cat hopped up to the windowsill, disappearing into thin air as she jumped off the ledge.

Later in the evening, Elaria prepared for the journey. She moved swiftly but remained quiet because Caelan had already gone to sleep for the night. She gathered only the essentials: clothes, travel rations, water skins, herbs, and potions. Her tomes of magic were carefully wrapped and tucked into her unique satchel. She packed some warm blankets and bedrolls, knowing the trip would take several days and would be colder outside.

Elaria began bringing the supplies outside to her small cart. Thistle, standing nearby, shifted her weight as Elaria approached, lifting her head with her ears twitching.

"Tomorrow, girl," Elaria whispered as she ran her hand through Thistle's mane.

She shuffled, bobbing her head slightly in acknowledgment. She continued her preparations and then slept for a few hours.

Their journey began early. The following day was still. Elaria stood outside the cottage, watching the first break of dawn light over the treetops. A low mist curled along the ground, wrapping its fingers around the trees. The world was hushed, as if it held its breath.

It was time.

Elaria went inside to Caelan's bedside, sitting at the edge of his bed. She gently brushed at his dark auburn hair.

"Caelan, my love," she whispered. "It's time to wake up."

"Uh..." he protested, beginning to squirm in his sheets. "A few more minutes..."

"We need to get going soon," she said, moving to grab his blanket and folding it up for last-minute packing.

"Are we leaving now?" he asked, still half-asleep.

"Yes, the sun will peak soon. And we need to go before the roads get busy."

"Okay..." he replied, hopping up to put his clothes on and helping his mother.

As they stepped outside, the morning chill still clung to the air. Dew covered the grass like a fine mist. Thistle stood patiently in the front with their cart attached, waiting. She neighed and stomped at the ground with her front right hoof when she saw them emerge from the door.

"She knows we're leaving, doesn't she?" Caelan asked.

Elaria nodded. "She does..." running her hands through Thistle's mane, then leaning over to whisper a few quiet words in the old tongue.

"Afare li," *thank you.*

Caelan held onto his bag, packed with his favorite toys. He ran down to the cart and turned around to look back at the cottage.

"Are we going to come back here?" he asked.

Elaria turned to regard the cottage she had built, the memories held within the walls.

"No, love," she whispered. "We won't be returning."

She hopped into the cart and then reached down to help Caelan. She took up Thistle's reins, glanced back at the cottage one last time, snapped the leads, and clicked her mouth a few times.

Thistle took her first steps toward their future.

Pathways along the forest appeared to be expected. The dirt path wound gently through the outermost edges and began veering inward. The sunlight filtered in through the dense canopy. Birds fluttered from the branches, singing a light and melodic song. As they traveled deeper into the forest, the world began shifting. The air grew heavy. It wasn't oppressive, but rather, it was denser, charged even, like a storm waiting to break. The further they ventured, the stronger the sensation felt. It was almost as if eyes watched from unseen perches.

Then, the trees began to change. The further they went, the older and more wild the forest became. Trunks looked thicker, their roots twisting and furling about the ground. Their leaves darkened. The pathway they were on began to narrow into nothingness. It stopped. The path had disappeared altogether. Elaria stopped the cart, looking around at the current surroundings. She took a slow breath and closed her eyes, thinking, *The Elderwood did not welcome those who did not respect it.*

She hopped down from the cart, approaching the nearest tree. She placed her hand on the trunk, whispering an ancient phrase,

"Da ote kuvi do nobi." *We request peace in travel.*

The forest groaned in response, almost like a sigh of relief. A sudden gust of wind rushed past them through the brush, and the pathway suddenly revealed itself again, where moments before, there was nothing.

"Momma, did you see that?" Caelan exclaimed in awe.

Elaria smiled. "The forest is watching us. But it knows we mean no harm."

She hopped back into the cart, and they continued down their path, further into the unknown. The Elderwood welcomed them inside.

Several hours later, Thistle steadily pulled their cart down the trail as it meandered through the woods. The mossy ground was soft on her hooves. Elaria decided to walk next to the cart to help ease the load on Thistle a tiny bit. Caelan sat nestled inside the cart, playing with some of his toys and looking around in wonder.

"Momma," he finally said, breaking the silence. "Do you think the forest knows we're here?"

"Yes," she replied. "It's been watching since we arrived."

Continuing for several more hours, the forest began to warm up to them, in a manner of speaking. The sides of the pathway they were traveling bloomed tiny white flowers to help show the way in the setting light. Branches started moving out of the way before Thistle brushed into them. The magic in the air was getting thicker and more vibrant.

As the sun set, the forest brought them to a small clearing with a creek nearby. It was the perfect campsite for the night. Elaria led Thistle to the side, disconnecting the cart and leads from her for the night.

"Good job, girl, thank you," she whispered to Thistle, brushing her mane slightly. "Rest up."

"Are we sleeping here tonight?" Caelan asked as he hopped down from the cart and started running around the perimeter of the small clearing.

"Yes, dear," Elaria responded. "Can you please gather some large sticks and bring them right here?" she asked as she started to place some nearby rocks into a circle.

Caelan happily ran around, picking up sticks of various sizes and bringing them back to the circle. Elaria started the campfire when there was enough.

"Okay, some larger pieces now. Big ones, so they burn longer," she asked him.

Caelan was running around, swinging his 'sword' and making noises. He was almost lost in his own imaginary world again, but he heard her and started bringing back larger pieces of fallen wood like it was a game. Elaria began making a small meal from the rations they had. It wasn't much, just some dried meat, bread, and cheese. She brought a pail of water from the nearby creek to drink. Thistle was already grazing on some of the taller grass.

"Caelan, come get some dinner," Elaria stated.

Caelan came over and sat beside her on the ground, his legs crossed near the fire.

"Momma," he inquired while biting into a chunk of bread. "How do you know where we are going?"

Elaria glanced up from her plate, the flickers of flame catching her green eyes.

"I don't," she admitted. "Not exactly."

Caelan asked, confused, "Then how do we know we won't get lost?"

She smiled, reaching for a small stick to draw on the dirt.

"The Elderwood isn't like other forests," she explained. "It doesn't follow maps or have roads. It only opens paths to those who respect it."

Caelan observed the intricate, intertwining circle that Elaria drew on the ground.

"So... it chooses who can walk through it?"

"In a way, yes." Elaria nodded. "And if the forest decides you don't belong, you'll find yourself walking in circles until you turn back."

"So, will the guards find us here?" he asked, remembering the events from yesterday.

"No, son. They don't come here," she said. "The king's guard stays clear of the Elderwood."

A gentle breeze started to blow. Somewhere off in the distance, the echoing hoot of an owl could be heard.

"Are we going to be safe?" Caelan asked.

"Yes, dear," she whispered, watching him finish his meal. She leaned over and kissed him on his forehead.

"We will be safe here."

The night was calming. Elaria set out their bedrolls, and they curled up under their own blankets. The campfire crackled while embers danced in the air. Sleep found them both quickly.

As the first hints of morning light filtered through the dense canopy, a fine mist clung to the air, weaving about in an almost visible dance. Its crispness kissed Elaria's cheek, stirring her slightly. She blinked a few times, then sat up to stretch. The campfire was clinging onto the last of its embers within a pile of ash. She turned to look at Caelan. His delicate figure was still curled underneath his blanket in what seemed to be the most restful sleep she'd ever seen him have. She sat there watching him sleep for a few minutes before reaching over.

"Caelan, love, it's time to wake up," she whispered as she stroked his hair.

"Mmm... five more minutes," he groaned, pulling the blankets tighter around himself.

"We have a long journey, little one. Come on now," she retorted, trying not to laugh.

"Fine..." he moaned as he opened his eyes, rubbing his face.

"Make sure to go wash your face; the cool water will do you some good," Elaria said, amused, watching Caelan stumble out of his blanket.

He slowly stumbled over to the water while she packed everything into the cart. She whistled over to Thistle, lying in a nearby patch of grass. Thistle neighed in defiance but stood up and sauntered over to the cart. Elaria bribed her with an apple from her satchel and began strapping the cart back onto Thistle's harness.

"Just a little further, girl," she whispered. "We're almost home."

Caelan made his way to the cart, jumping up into the back, dangling his legs off the edge.

"How do you know?" he asked, looking out into the forest.

Elaria smiled. "I can feel it."

She climbed into the cart, took hold of the reins, and with a click of her tongue, Thistle gently started off. Several more hours down the twisting paths, they continued to journey further into the heart of the Elderwood. The trees seemed even wilder than before, older, like they had seen hundreds of years. Some trunks were wider than most cottages Caelan remembered seeing back in Gladecross. He was in constant awe, though. Squirrels launched from branch to branch. Distant shadowy outlines of birds flew high above.

Occasionally, he would see figures darting in the shadows, almost following them, eyes always watching. The forest was alive today, even more so than before.

"Momma!" Caelan exclaimed excitedly, pointing at some silvery insects flying off to the side. They left a streak of silvery blue trailing their aerial dance.

Thistle crested over a small hill, heading towards a pair of trees leaning into the pathway, almost blocking it. Then they groaned as they lifted and parted, opening the way for them. Thistle huffed at the trees and stomped at the ground until the way was open enough for her to pass through.

Before them stretched a secluded glade nestled deep within the Elderwood's embrace. Caelan glanced around with wonder. Elaria's heart skipped a beat as she took in the sight. The air was rich here, full of earthy tones and alive with magic. A gentle stream wound around the clearing, falling over some stones before continuing down and back into the forest. The trees stood almost in a perfect circle, their branches interwoven together to form a protective canopy. It was too perfect for mere coincidence.

Caelan turned to his mother. "Momma, did the forest make this for us?"

Elaria, still in awe at the sheer beauty of it all, took a deep breath in. She felt the glade's energy rush through her and back out as she exhaled.

"Yes, love," she whispered back. "It did."

She stepped into the canopy covering, brushing some of the trees with her hands, feeling the life tingle her fingertips. Closing her eyes briefly in silent gratitude, she breathed out softly.

"We are home."

CHAPTER THREE

HAVEN OF MAGIC AND MYSTERY

Eleven years since the fateful night...

The ground blurred beneath Caelan's feet, each bootfall a muffled beat against the damp forest floor. Morning light filtered in slanted rays through the towering canopy of the Elderwood, casting flickers of gold across the moss and underbrush. His breath came in sharp pulls, steady but quick, his lungs drinking in the cool, pine-scented air. Wind tugged at his tunic as he leapt over a fallen log, then launched himself up onto a moss-covered boulder, grinning as he landed in a crouch.

Behind him, the forest stirred.

A flicker of movement to his left—a sleek streak of white, black, and grey darting through the ferns.

The fox was back.

Caelan's grin widened. "So we're playing this game again," he thought, eyes gleaming with recognition.

For as long as he could remember, the fox had haunted the edges of their glade. Not like a ghost—more like a quiet watcher, a shadow that refused to stray too close, but never quite disappeared either. It had grown up alongside him in a way. Never tame. Never a pet. But always there.

Some days it would sit at the edge of the clearing, unmoving. Other days, like this one, it would appear behind him during his runs, darting through brush, weaving through trees, always just out of reach but never far behind.

Caelan pushed himself harder, arms pumping, his legs working to widen the gap—but the fox kept pace easily, gliding through the forest like water slipping between rocks.

"Bet you can't catch me!" Caelan called over his shoulder with a laugh, though he knew the fox wouldn't answer. It never had. But it didn't need to. The chase was the language they shared.

He ducked beneath a low-hanging branch, then pivoted sharply as the terrain sloped downward. His boots slid slightly in the loose earth, catching purchase just in time to spring forward again. The thrill of it all surged through him—freedom, movement, the unspoken bond with something wilder than himself.

Then, the forest changed.

A whisper of space opened before him—a narrowing in the trees, a flicker of something ancient in the air. He slowed instinctively. Just ahead, the brush parted, revealing a circular clearing ringed by massive stones, half-buried in earth and tangled in ivy.

Caelan skidded to a halt, breath catching.

The fox stopped too. It stood at the edge of the circle, ears high, body still as stone.

Something was different here. The air was heavier, vibrating with a pulse he could feel in his chest. A slow, deep hum rolled outward from the stones, like distant thunder echoing across an invisible sky.

Caelan's exhilaration faded into quiet awe.

He took one step forward, then another, drawn toward the nearest stone. Its surface was rough beneath his fingertips, etched with weathered grooves that hummed faintly beneath his touch.

"Mother!" he shouted over his shoulder, his voice cutting through the hush. "You have to see this!"

Leaves rustled as Elaria emerged from the trees, her pace slowing the moment her eyes fell upon the circle. She stopped short just inside the clearing, her gaze locked on the ancient stones.

"By the gods, Caelan..." she whispered, her voice barely more than breath.

Her expression shifted—no longer the calm, measured look of a mother on a morning stroll. Awe flooded her features, the kind of reverence Caelan had only seen once before, when she had spoken of the temple ruins hidden deep within the eastern marshes. But this... this felt different.

She stepped forward slowly, her fingers brushing over the moss-covered surface of the nearest standing stone. Her hand lingered there, eyes scanning the faint carvings etched into the face. Grooves like veins ran through the stone's surface, pulsing faintly with magic that didn't hum—it breathed.

Caelan watched her closely, trying to understand. "How old do you think they are?" he asked.

Elaria exhaled slowly, her palm still resting against the stone. "Older than anything I've ever seen," she murmured. "These stones are alive, Caelan. I believe they've been here since before the trees took root."

Caelan turned slowly, taking in the entire circle now. Each stone was different—some taller, others tilted or half-swallowed by earth. One was split down the center, as if struck by lightning centuries ago, yet the two halves still stood, leaning into one another like quiet sentinels.

A squirrel chattered somewhere high in the trees. A breeze stirred the tall grass that had sprung up inside the ring. The air inside the circle felt still, yet alive—watching. Waiting.

Elaria knelt, motioning for Caelan to join her beside a wide, flat stone near the center. "Sit," she said gently. "And close your eyes."

He obeyed, dropping to the soft grass, folding his legs beneath him. She guided his hand to the surface of the stone.

"Feel the current," she instructed. "Let it pass through you. Magic is not something you command. It's something you join."

Caelan inhaled deeply, the scent of moss and dew soaking into his senses. He closed his eyes.

For a long moment, he felt nothing.

Then, like the slow warmth of a sunrise, it came. A subtle thrum at first, then a low resonance in his chest. Not a sound, but a feeling—like his heartbeat syncing with something far older, deeper. He couldn't explain it, but it wrapped around him like the forest's embrace.

"It's warm... and different," he said quietly.

Elaria smiled beside him, her own eyes closed, her hand on a neighboring stone. "Yes. The circle is listening."

They stayed like that for a long while—mother and son, seated among the ruins of a forgotten age, wrapped in the quiet rhythm of something timeless. No lesson, no pressure. Just presence.

Finally, Elaria opened her eyes.

"We'll come back," she said. "There's much more to learn. But for now, it's time to go home."

As they rose, Caelan glanced once more at the fox. It still stood at the edge of the clearing, watching.

Waiting.

And then, without a sound, it turned and disappeared back into the forest.

The scent of rosemary and hearth smoke hung in the air as the first golden rays of morning spilled across the glade. Dew clung to every blade of grass outside, glistening like tiny crystals. Birds called from the branches overhead, announcing the sun's arrival with melodies that drifted down to the cottage nestled in the trees.

Inside, warmth radiated from the heart of the home. Elaria moved about the kitchen, her sleeves rolled past her elbows as she stirred a pan over the fire. The hiss of eggs cooking mingled with the occasional clink of utensils. She hummed a quiet tune to herself, one she hadn't sung aloud in years—half lullaby, half spell.

Sunlight reached through the windows, catching on jars of dried herbs suspended from wooden beams. Lavender, hyssop, mugwort—each neatly bundled and tied with colored thread. Her drying shack stood just beyond the back door, its frame barely visible through the condensation on the glass. A pot of tea steeped gently on the windowsill, the scent of chamomile wafting through the air.

Years ago, this clearing had been wild and overgrown, untouched by anything but nature. But Elaria had seen potential in its solitude. With the help of forgotten tomes and whispered incantations, she had bent the land to her will—gently, respectfully—never forcing it, only guiding it.

She had summoned spectral axes to gather fallen timber, called stones to stack and fuse, carved out a home from the bones of the forest itself. Now it was a sanctuary. A small greenhouse stood on one side for delicate herbs, a shed on the other to dry roots and store mixtures. The cottage had two rooms—one for her, one for Caelan—and the main living space where most of their time was spent: hearth, kitchen, and the heavy wooden table where so many lessons began.

A creak sounded from one of the back rooms. Elaria glanced up with a small smile. Right on cue.

Caelan stumbled out of his room, rubbing the sleep from his eyes with the back of one hand. His hair stuck up unevenly, a mess of dark auburn waves. He yawned, stretching his arms wide, then blinked at the light.

"Good morning, love. Up with the birds today?" Elaria asked with a chuckle.

"I could smell breakfast," he mumbled through another yawn.

"Ah, so your stomach gets credit, not the sunrise."

He plopped into his chair at the table as she turned with a plate—eggs cooked with herbs, thick-cut bread, and a smear of black-berry jam.

"Eat up," she said, setting it before him. "Growing boys need their food."

Caelan's eyes lit up as he dug in.

"After breakfast, we're going for a walk," she added, moving to pour two cups of tea. "I need to gather a few herbs from the northern stretch."

He perked up. "Are we going back to the stone circle?"

Elaria shook her head gently. "Not yet. That place is... special. You must learn to listen to smaller things first—the roots, the plants, the creatures. Magic starts there."

Caelan nodded, chewing quickly now, clearly excited. He wolfed down the rest of his food, wiped his mouth on his sleeve, and dashed off to get ready.

Elaria laughed softly and shook her head. "I'll meet you outside," she called after him.

She finished her tea, then made her way to the drying shack. The door creaked open to reveal rows of hanging herbs, a soft earthy fragrance wrapping around her like a blanket. Glass jars lined the shelves, each one labeled with hand-drawn symbols. She retrieved her satchel from the table and added a few fresh tools—a set of shears, spare parchment, wax paper for wrapping, and several small vials for collecting.

When she stepped outside again, Caelan was already running wide circles around the yard, arms outstretched like wings. He spun when he saw her.

"Ready!" he beamed.

Elaria adjusted the strap of her satchel and started toward the northern trail. "Alright, son. Let's go."

Caelan darted to her side, matching her pace for all of three seconds before running ahead again.

Elaria let him go. She always did.

The trail curled like a lazy stream through the northern stretch of the Elderwood, narrowing between thickets and winding past crooked trees whose roots jutted from the soil like gnarled fingers. Ferns brushed at Caelan's knees as he darted ahead, leaping over patches of uneven ground, stopping every few feet to poke at something with a stick.

Elaria followed at a steady pace, her steps quiet and deliberate, eyes scanning the path for signs of useful growth. She barely looked where she walked—her familiarity with the terrain allowed her to move fluidly, letting her senses lead her gaze.

"You need to slow down, son," she called ahead with amused patience. "We're not out here for your acrobatics."

"But we've been walking forever!" Caelan called back dramatically, twirling once before ducking under a branch.

"It's been thirty minutes," she replied with a smirk.

"Feels like hours."

She chuckled softly, then stopped where the trail broke slightly and pointed. "There. At the base of that maple."

Caelan skidded to a halt and squinted in the direction she indicated. "It's just a plant."

"Not just any plant," Elaria said, already kneeling beside it. "This is wild sage."

He trotted over and knelt beside her, eyeing the velvety green leaves.

"Go on," she encouraged. "Rub one between your fingers. Then hold it to your nose."

He hesitated for a moment, then obeyed. The leaf crumbled slightly, releasing a warm, earthy aroma that hit him with instant familiarity.

"It smells like the tea you make when I'm sick," he said.

"Because it is. Wild sage calms the mind and soothes the body. It can be used in potions, teas, even rituals. But you need to know where and how to harvest it."

She carefully plucked a few leaves from separate stems, never over-harvesting any single plant, and tucked them into her satchel.

"What do you notice about where it's growing?" she asked.

Caelan narrowed his eyes, thinking hard.

"It's in the shade," he said slowly, "and the dirt's soft... not rocky like the glade."

"Good," Elaria said with a nod. "Sage likes shade and rich soil. Plants are like people. They thrive in places that suit them. And if you take too much from one place, it may not recover."

Caelan nodded, though his attention was already drawn to another patch of green further along the trail. He darted over to it, poking his stick into a rabbit burrow nearby, before crouching down to inspect the leaves.

"I think I found another one!" he called triumphantly.

Elaria raised an eyebrow. "Don't guess. Smell."

He did, and a broad grin spread across his face. "Sage again!"

"Well done."

They moved onward. A clearing opened before them a few minutes later, filled with sunlight and speckled with wildflowers. Caelan ran ahead, stopping beside a tall cluster of purple, bell-shaped blooms.

"These are pretty," he said, reaching out.

Elaria's hand caught his wrist gently. "Careful. That's foxglove."

"Why? It's just a flower."

"In small doses, it strengthens the heart. In large ones, it stops it entirely."

Caelan blinked. "It's poison?"

"It's balance," Elaria said. "Magic is the same way. Every herb, every spell—it all comes with cost and consequence."

She plucked a few of the lower blooms and tucked them carefully away.

Nearby, Caelan pointed again. "Those look like tiny daisies."

"Feverfew," Elaria said. "Good for easing headaches and fevers. But like the foxglove, too much can do harm. You're beginning to see the pattern, aren't you?"

He nodded, his tone quieter now.

They walked deeper into the clearing, and Elaria paused beside a patch of low white flowers with delicate, feathery leaves.

"This one is special," she said, crouching. "Yarrow. Useful for stopping bleeding. Strengthens the body. It's one of the first herbs I learned about as a girl."

Caelan crouched beside her, running his fingers lightly along the fronds.

"It feels soft... but the stem is strong."

Elaria smiled. "That's why it's used in protection magic. It survives. Fire, cold, bad soil—it keeps growing."

He considered that quietly, then plucked a single sprig. "I want to keep this one," he said, slipping it into his pouch.

Elaria nodded her approval.

As they made their way back toward the glade, Caelan walked with less spring and more thought in his step. His eyes scanned the underbrush with new awareness. He didn't run ahead this time. He walked beside his mother, matching her pace.

"You're beginning to see it differently, aren't you?" Elaria asked.

"Yeah..." he said softly. "I think so."

The sun had shifted well past its peak by the time they returned to the glade. A gentle breeze rolled through the trees, tugging at the leaves and carrying with it the scent of pine and distant wildflowers. Thistle raised her head from the trough in lazy acknowledgment as Caelan and Elaria approached the cottage.

Inside, the air was cooler. The hearth had burned low, leaving only faint embers in the ash bed. Elaria pushed the door open, and Caelan bounded in ahead of her, unfastening his satchel and slinging it onto the wooden table. Elaria followed, setting hers down beside it.

"Now comes the important part," she said, voice calm but firm.

Caelan straightened, sensing the shift in tone.

Elaria began to unpack her herbs with a practiced rhythm, laying each one gently on the table. Feverfew. Wild sage. Yarrow. She separated them into neat piles. Caelan mirrored her movements, though his hands were less precise. She didn't correct him—yet.

"We'll start simple," she said, selecting the feverfew sprigs and laying them closer. "You'll make your first tincture."

Caelan's eyes lit up with curiosity.

"Potion-making," Elaria continued, "is not about throwing herbs into a pot and hoping for the best. Every ingredient has a purpose. But preparation... that's what determines power."

She unsheathed a small silver knife from a drawer and began slicing the stems into precise lengths. Each cut was smooth and deliberate. "Watch carefully," she said.

Caelan leaned in, his brow furrowed as he studied her hands.

"See how I separate the flowers from the leaves?" she asked, demonstrating. "The flowers hold the healing oils, but the leaves carry the bitter agents that bind them. We'll use both, but in different ways."

He picked up the next sprig and tried to imitate her. His cuts were jagged, uneven. One flower bent instead of slicing cleanly.

Elaria gently took his hand. "You're not slicing meat, love. Let the blade do the work. Precision, not pressure."

Caelan tried again—slower this time. Better.

"Good," she said with a nod. "Now, into the vial."

She brought forth a glass bottle already half-filled with alcohol. "Tinctures draw the essence from the herb into the liquid. It'll take time—weeks, sometimes. But it lasts much longer than a tea."

Caelan dropped the prepared feverfew into the jar, then corked it tightly. He held it up to the light, watching the flowers swirl inside.

"What if someone needs it now?" he asked.

Elaria smiled. "Then we brew tea or make a salve. Not every remedy can wait."

She moved on to the wild sage, placing a few leaves in the stone mortar. "This one's for tea," she said, handing him the pestle. "Press and roll. Don't crush."

He nodded and began grinding, slower than before. The scent released immediately—strong, herbal, clean.

Elaria added hot water from the kettle, watching as the liquid darkened, curling into green-brown ribbons. "Let it steep," she said. "Magic, like tea, takes time."

Caelan leaned in and sniffed. "It smells like the forest after rain."

"That means you did it right," she said, then handed him a small cup.

He sipped. His face twisted. "It's strong..."

Elaria laughed, handing him a small jar of honey. "A bit of sweetness helps."

He stirred in a spoonful and sipped again. This time, he nodded in approval.

Finally, Elaria reached for the yarrow. "This one's for a poultice."

She crushed the dried flowers between her fingers, then added a dab of thick bark paste and a splash of water. Mixing it slowly, the concoction formed into a firm, herbal paste.

Caelan poked it curiously. "It's cold."

"Try a little on your arm," she said.

He smeared some along his forearm. The cooling sensation hit first—then came the warmth. A subtle tingling spread under his skin.

"It feels weird," he said, "but kind of... alive."

"Yarrow always knows where to go," Elaria said. "It finds the hurt and begins the work."

They worked for the next hour, preparing and preserving the rest of the harvest. Soon the table was scattered with small vials, tightly-wrapped pouches, and jars of dried leaf blends. Caelan stared at them with a strange pride.

"I thought magic was all spells and sparks," he admitted, "not... chopping herbs and boiling water."

Elaria placed a hand on his shoulder.

"Magic is many things, son. Power is only one part of it. Real magic is knowing when to act—and when to let the world do what it does best."

She gave his shoulder a gentle squeeze.

"Now go wash up. You've earned your tea and your dinner."

Caelan grinned and bounded for the door. "Thistle!" he shouted as he ran outside. "Guess what I made today!"

Elaria just smiled and returned to her work, her hands moving with practiced ease.

But tonight, she thought, the real lessons begin.

The sun had dipped low, casting long shadows across the glade. The hearth fire crackled again to life, newly stoked. Its flickering light danced across the walls, casting soft, amber hues onto the woodgrain and shelves. Outside, the forest began its nightly chorus—owls hooting from unseen perches, crickets humming beneath the leaves, and distant rustlings in the underbrush. Within the cottage, a gentle stillness settled.

Elaria sat at the wooden table, rolling a dried sprig of yarrow between her fingers. The petals had turned brittle and white in the drying process, yet they still gave off their subtle, herbal scent. Caelan sat across from her, elbows on the table, chin resting on his fists. He watched her hands, his eyes focused, calm. The energy from earlier had mellowed. He wasn't fidgeting or rambling. He was ready.

"Tonight," Elaria said softly, "we begin your true lessons."

Caelan blinked. "I thought I already was."

She smiled faintly. "The herbs, the potions, learning the land—those are the foundation. But magic... real magic... is more than recipes and rituals. It's intent. It's balance. It's knowing when to act, when to hold back, and how to feel the pulse of the world."

She gestured to the yarrow. "You remember what I told you about this?"

Caelan sat up straighter. "Yarrow is for healing. It stops bleeding, helps you recover... and it protects."

"Exactly. It's used in wards and charms, too—against danger you can't always see."

She reached across the table and pulled a shallow dish toward her. Inside were bits of chalk and powdery residue from past lessons. She selected a piece and, with a few steady motions, began drawing a looping, curved symbol on the tabletop between them. It resembled a closed eye—a circle bisected by a crescent-like arch.

"This," she said, "is a protection rune. Old. Simple. But strong."

Caelan leaned in. "So magic is just symbols?"

"No," Elaria replied, "Symbols are just anchors—tools. This is just a shape until you give it purpose."

She took the sprig of yarrow and placed it in his hand. "Close your eyes."

He hesitated, then did so.

"Feel the herb," she said gently. "Don't just touch it—feel it. The texture. The warmth in the leaves. Let your breath slow. Let your thoughts settle."

Caelan inhaled slowly. The scent of the herb mingled with the smoke from the hearth, earthy and familiar. He imagined their walks in the forest, the feeling of safety in his mother's presence, the unspoken trust he felt under the canopy of the Elderwood. He remembered the warmth that had pulsed through his chest earlier at the stone circle—alive, ancient, comforting.

"I want you to think about what protection means to you," Elaria continued. "Think about moments where you felt safe. Think about why you want to protect others. Let that feeling rise."

A warmth stirred within Caelan's chest—slow, like embers catching fire. It pulsed gently, then spread through his arms, into his fingers.

"Now," Elaria whispered, "place your hand over the rune. Let the yarrow touch the chalk. And exhale. Give it purpose."

Caelan lowered his hand.

The moment the yarrow met the rune, a flicker of silver light shimmered across the lines. It was faint, but unmistakable—like starlight catching on still water. The glow traveled the symbol's path for a moment, then faded into nothingness.

Caelan's eyes flew open.

"I... I did that?"

Elaria nodded. "You did. That was your will. Your intent. You gave the magic something to hold on to."

Caelan stared down at the chalk lines, then at the sprig still resting in his palm. "It felt alive."

"It is," Elaria said. "Magic is everywhere. In everything. But it doesn't move unless called."

She sat back, satisfied, and folded her hands in her lap. "That's why we start with protection. It is the oldest, most sacred form of magic—not because it's the strongest... but because it teaches you why we use magic at all."

Caelan looked down at his hands, flexing them slowly. He didn't feel powerful—but he felt different. Like the world had opened just a little wider.

"And what's the lesson?" he asked.

Elaria reached over and brushed a stray lock of hair from his face, placing a soft kiss on his forehead.

"That true strength," she whispered, "is in defending what matters."

The fire burned low in the hearth, casting long shadows that stretched and danced across the cottage walls. The warmth of the yarrow poultice still lingered faintly on Caelan's skin, and the chalk rune from earlier had faded to a ghost of itself on the tabletop—but the glow it had given off lived fresh in his memory.

Elaria sat across from him, tea in hand, her mending set aside and forgotten. She had watched him closely all evening, saying little as he sorted through the feeling of what he'd done—his first spell. Not something he copied, but something he created, even if only for a heartbeat.

Caelan finally broke the silence. "Is that what magic always feels like?" he asked. "That... warmth?"

Elaria gave a small nod. "When it's used with care. When it comes from the right place."

He sat back in his chair, still absorbing the moment. "Have you ever used it... for more? Not just potions and plants. I mean for something bigger. To protect someone, really protect them?"

A smile tugged at her lips—warm, but a little sad.

"Yes," she said. "Though the best protections are often the quietest ones. The ones no one sees."

Caelan glanced down at his hand again, curling his fingers into his palm. "Do you think I'll ever be strong enough to protect people like that?"

Elaria set her cup down gently. "Strength isn't just power, Caelan. And magic isn't about how much you can do—it's about why you do it."

She leaned forward slightly, her tone shifting.

"There was a mage, long ago. One I think of often. His name was Eamon the Wise."

Caelan's brow furrowed. "I think I've heard that name before."

"You have," she said. "All mages do, eventually."

She turned her gaze toward the fire, and her voice grew softer, more rhythmic, like a story passed down from candlelit rooms and whispered over pages.

"Eamon lived over three hundred years ago, during the twilight of the old age. A time when the kingdoms still held court with magic openly—but trust in it was beginning to fray. He was powerful, yes, but not in the way most imagine. His spells weren't flashy, and he didn't crave attention. He was a builder. A healer. A protector."

She paused, watching the fire.

"They say his wards could hold back entire armies. That his runes glowed with starlight when carved by hand. That he could feel the flow of the world's pain and bend it away, like stone diverts water. But more than any of that... he chose not to use his strength unless there was no other path."

Caelan leaned in, listening intently now.

"There came a time," Elaria continued, "when something rose out of the forgotten places—something no mortal army could face. A creature of ancient hunger. Not just dark... but devouring. It was said to be the end of all things. Cities fell. Even kings fled. But Eamon stood his ground. Alone."

She didn't raise her voice. If anything, it grew quieter—as though the very telling required reverence.

"No army at his side. No fanfare. Just him, and the light he carried."

She looked at Caelan again. "He didn't win with fire or force. He won because he refused to let the world break. Because when everything else gave in to fear, he stood."

Caelan was silent for a long time. "What happened to him?"

"No one knows for sure," Elaria said. "Some say he perished. Others believe he ascended—became part of the magic itself. A guardian watching over those who still honor the balance."

He swallowed hard, eyes still fixed on the fire. "Why haven't you ever told me that story before?"

"Because you weren't ready to hear it," she said simply. "Magic isn't about knowing all the stories. It's about knowing which ones to carry."

He looked down at his hands again. "I want to carry that one."

She reached across the table and squeezed his fingers.

"Then learn what he knew: That the greatest strength... is in defending what matters most. Even when no one sees it. Even when you stand alone."

The fire crackled softly in response.

Chapter Four

A Kingdom Under Shadow

Fourteen years since the fateful night...

Soaring high above the kingdom of Dunmoh, a lone hawk sliced through the morning sky. His vantage of the vast expanse of blue stretched infinitely in every direction—smooth sailing, except for the occasional turbulence, forcing a left or right sway, making a game of flying up and through clusters of clouds, calling out to the world.

Kree-eee-ar

Far below, Dunmoh stirred at dawn's first light. The night's shadow was visibly retreating from the dawn's approach. The hawk looked around, surveying its domain. The Verdant Plains stretched out below, veined with rivers. Farmers starting their days appeared no bigger than ants at this height. To the north, the jagged peaks of the Elder Mountains loomed with their snow-capped summits. To the south, the golden line of the Twilight Coast shimmered.

The hawk looked downward, folded its wings, and dove. Wind howled around it as it plummeted. No more than a blurred streak of brown if one could have witnessed such a sight. The landscape rushed in closer, details beginning to define themselves clearly. Fields turned to forests, forests to roads, roads to the towering stone walls of Castle Dunmoh. The mighty fortress stood as a proud, unwavering sentinel above the capital. The towers stabbed the sky in defiance of the heavens.

Kree-eee-ar

The hawk veered sharply, bringing itself more horizontal in flight, skimming just above the rooftops of buildings. Rushing to the senses were scents of stone and iron. Passing over the sparring yard, the stables, circling around the battlements, passing over the grand hall and the garden walkways. Finally, tilting slightly upward, the hawk lifted in elevation, aiming toward the highest tower at the castle's center. A lone figure stared out of the window as the hawk rushed up above and perched on the ledge directly above the giant window, open to the morning air. King Aldric barely flinched as the hawk passed. His gaze remained fixed upon the horizon.

Standing vigilant around the room were the Gray Cloaks, the elite personal guards to King Aldric. Their ashen mantles draped them in half-shadow, standing more like statues than men. They did not fidget, only waiting, watchful, unwavering. The hearth crackled nearby, then a rustling of parchment, followed by a quill scratching.

"Your Majesty." Sir Reginald broke the silence.

He had spent years navigating Aldric's moods. Sir Reginald was Aldric's closest advisor, often dealing with the administration of affairs. His signature carried the king's authority. Sitting at a desk near the middle of the room, Reginald lifted a report, pretending to read from it.

"There have been increased reports of magical activity in the northern villages," he continued. "One, in particular, stands out, sire; talk of a healer in Snowhaven. They practice openly, defying your decrees."

Aldric visibly tensed at the mention. Magic. He shifted his gaze toward Snowhaven slowly. Jagged shadows cast across the hard lines of his face. His disdain radiated from him like a miasmic aura.

"Increase the patrols," he commanded. "Bring this healer to the dungeon. I will not allow such open violation to spread hope."

The finality of his words left no room for question. Sir Reginald inclined his head in acknowledgment. He dipped his quill in the vial of ink sitting on the desk. A few drops left the tip as he brought it to the parchment, scribbling King Aldric's command. He returned the quill to its holder and picked up the heated wax. He poured a small puddle next to the signature, then stamped it with the royal seal. He blew on it briefly to cool the wax, stood up, and made his exit from the room.

As Reginald finalized the command, Aldric reached for something he kept in his pocket. His fingers lingered on a small locket. The locket was worn and slightly dulled after many years. Still, its significance could not be mistaken by anyone close to Aldric. He lifted it out of his pocket with quiet reverence, tracing the patterns with his calloused thumb before pressing the button to open it. Inside was a miniature portrait of Queen Alia. With her long golden hair and soft blue eyes, she was an angel in his eyes. Her soft features had never known hardships or sorrow. She was the light of his life, but now, without such light, only darkness remained.

"Alia," he whispered. His voice slightly cracked at the mention of her name.

"I do this for you. To cleanse the land of the chaos that took you from me."

The morning pressed on, and Aldric did not move from his windowed view. The walls surrounding this very chamber hosted several tapestries bearing the proud history of Dunmoh. Intricate weavings that told of past kings who built legacies, warriors who secured the realm, and scholars who led the kingdom into enlightenment. Yet for all their grandeur and glory, none told the tale of a king haunted by the past, consumed in hatred and sorrow.

His hand tightened around the locket. His thoughts wandered back to the night Alia died years ago. The chamber had filled with the scent of lavender and blood. The healer had promised to save her. He had stood by, watching their hands glowing, chanting, meaning to bring life back to her failing body, but it never came. Except for the child. That cursed child. Seeing the glowing sigil upon its chest had been a slap in his face. It was a mockery of the gods that his beloved had lost her life so that the abomination lived.

"Your Majesty." Sir Reginald interrupted Aldric's brooding, but he did not turn around.

"The patrols are ready to be dispatched at your command."

Reginald stepped forward slightly as he addressed his king. His grip held onto some more parchments with reports, but he did not mention them.

"Do it," Aldric stated. "And no leniency or quarter for those who defy my decree."

Sir Reginald inclined his head to acknowledge his king's order, took a step back, turned, and exited the chamber again. Below in the staging yard, soldiers were preparing to roll out, and servants were rushing about the castle, engaged in their daily duties.

Only Aldric moved slightly to another window in his chamber to get a better view of the north. Silence clung to the chamber long after Sir Reginald departed. Aldric remained at the window, looking northward at the towering silhouette of the mountains. The Gray Cloaks stood still, like statues behind him. Watching... Waiting... Always silent shadows of duty. Aldric exhaled slowly.

"You are dismissed," he ordered without looking back.

For a moment, there was no movement. Then, in perfect unison, the guards bowed their heads and departed. The weight of their boots slowly faded down the corridor after the chamber door shut behind them with a hollow thud. Now, he was finally alone.

Aldric turned from the window, walking across the vast room. The fire in the hearth was burning low. He reached down and tossed a couple of logs onto the embers. Sparks flew up in protest as they landed. The sun was setting outside, and the light from the hearth flickered against the walls. Not too far from the hearth sat a polished oak table. Resting upon it was an ornate decanter paired with a set of crystal goblets. A deep crimson liquid rested inside the glass. The vintage had been untouched since his coronation. His rough hands picked up the decanter and opened it, bringing it to his nose to inhale the aroma of distilled fruits and honey.

Aldric poured his first glass with a steady hand, then set the bottle back down. He lifted the goblet to his lips and took a sip. The flavor was accompanied by memories of his coronation feast, Alia and himself enjoying the vast banquet in cheerful glee. Oh, the memories. The warmth softly burned down his throat and spread through his body, but it did not warm him. Soon, the second glass, then the third. The mead dulled the edges of his thoughts but did not soothe them.

His gaze shifted back to the window and toward the northern mountains. The north. His thoughts wandered back to the days before the fateful night that he lost Alia.

The air bit at his skin when he stood at the heights of the Frostspire Temple. He had never felt more alive. Alia stood at his side. Her laughter carried through the wind as her hair danced underneath her hood.

"You're shivering," he told her as he reached to pull her cloak tighter around her shoulders.

"And you are not?" she teased, a crisp cloud escaping her mouth.

She pressed closer into him as they stood before the temple gates.

"We should go inside, my dear," he murmured.

"Not yet," she said, lifting her gaze to the ice-carved pillars in wonder. "Look at it, Aldric. Isn't it beautiful?"

"It is, my love."

The temple was carved into the very bones of the mountain. Inside, the monks spoke of balance, unseen forces, and destinies written long ago. Aldric had paid no attention to it then. He only watched Alia, bathed in candlelight, as her fingers brushed over the sacred texts with curiosity. She had always sought knowledge and history. He had only wanted her.

The mountains had given them more than just the temple. They had traveled to Kellgrim's Rest, a highland shrine of a legendary mountaineer. Alia had wanted to visit to provide offerings and whisper a prayer to the gods. He took another sip of his mead, remembering their trip to Eagle's Perch.

"Aldric, we must go." She jumped excitedly.

"For what?" he asked.

"For flowers!"

"You would climb half a day for a handful of petals?" he mused.

She laughed, grabbed his hand, and ran toward the path. They climbed together until they reached the narrow ledge overlooking the world below. The wind howled at their backs. Cloaks flapped about violently. They did not care. The fields below stretched far beyond their sight. A few more feet above them plateaued a cliff flat, where wild blossoms sprouted up in defiance of the cold. Alia knelt and reached out her hand to cup the delicate petals.

"They only grow here," she smiled, looking up at Aldric, then back to the flowers. "Nowhere else in the world."

Aldric hadn't understood it fully then. He only watched the way she looked at them. The way she looked at everything... with wonder and light.

He blinked. The mountains were gone. Only the window remained, with the hearth crackling behind him, shadows dancing and reaching about the room. Alia's laughter would no longer be heard, only silence. His grip tightened around the goblet.

"You would climb half a day for a handful of petals?"

The realization slapped him in the face. He never understood back then. Some things will only bloom once. When they are gone, they never return.

Aldric's hand trembled as he started to lift his goblet again. He could barely taste the mead anymore. The warmth in his chest was now replaced by something colder. Something that seemed to curl within him, refusing to leave. He drunkenly gazed back toward the hearth. The embers blinked briefly, then the flames stretched unnaturally for a moment before settling down again. He was tired. Gods, was he tired.

He stumbled over and slumped into the great chair beside the hearth. The weight of it all pulled him down. His eyes blinked for a few moments, then shut. His grip on the goblet loosened, allowing it to fall toward the floor, shattering. Then, blackness.

He was back in Eagle's Perch. The dream seemed so vivid, so surreal.

"Aldric, we must go." Her voice echoed, full of excitement—just as he remembered.

"For what?" he responded.

"For flowers!" she stated with a laugh.

She grabbed at his hand, pulling him up the rocky incline. He reluctantly followed. He had always followed her. Then, they were at the ledge. The blossoms swayed in the wind, a small field of frost-kissed blue and white. Alia knelt to cup the flowers.

"They only grow here," she whispered. "Nowhere else in the world."

Aldric drank in every detail. She was alive. He had her again. Then, the wind stopped. The once vivid sky bled into darkness. The mountains stretched out, their peaks twisting into jagged, unnatural shapes. The valley below swallowed itself, replaced by an endless abyss. The warmth left his hands. He looked back. The Alia he remembered was gone. The flowers where she had knelt withered before his eyes, turning black, rotting in her hands. The rot spread quickly, devouring everything, even the earth itself.

"Alia?" he gasped.

Her skin faded to gray, the pallor of death settling into her features. The veins on her body blackened, spreading like cracks on porcelain. They bulged underneath her flesh. She stood up slowly and turned toward him, unnaturally lifted by unseen things. Her eye sockets were hollowed voids. Her lips parted, but no words came out. Only silence... She reached out for him. Her fingers were now withered, skeletal, skin stretched too tightly over bone. The black veins pulsed, swelling like something was alive beneath her skin.

Her smile was the last thing to go. Her lips curled and deformed as rot took hold, eating away until nothing but a toothy skeletal grin remained. Then, her body began to crumble. First, her fingers dissolved, curling into dust. Each particle caught the air, spiraling into the abyss, swallowed by the void.

"NO! No, no... not again!" his voice echoed as he tried to move.

The mountains were now completely gone, only blackness remained. The shadow remained. Then, it spoke. A voice low and guttural, a scent of a thousand graves filled the air.

"She is gone, Aldric."

The air shuddered. The darkness coiled.

"She is gone... but they remain."

The whisper seeped into his bones, a breath against his ear, a presence he could not see.

"Magic took her from you. Magic defied the order of life and death. Magic was chaos."

Aldric clenched his fists, his breath coming in ragged gasps.

"You know this to be true."

The abyss swirled, shapes shifted within the darkness, distorted figures cloaked in shadow, their hands glowing in unnatural greens and purples. He knew them... The Healers.

"THEY LET HER DIE!"

A flicker of green flame ignited in the dark.

"You were right to cleanse them from this world."

Suddenly, an ungodly scream pierced his ears, resonating on frequencies no mortal could fully comprehend. Aldric turned away, attempting to run, but there was no escape. The shadow stretched and contorted, swirling like a black mist. The mere presence of it was suffocating. Aldric tried to move... breathe... wake up... nothing worked.

The darkness reached for him.

He gasped awake, launching from his slumber. His chest heaved with forceful breathing. His head felt as if it would pound right out of his skull. The fire had all but died, but the embers smoldered a faint shade of green. Aldric's hands trembled on the armrests, attempting to steady himself.

It was just a dream. Wasn't it? Aldric thought.

He reached for the goblet, but it lay shattered on the floor. The wine splattered in a crimson pool-like blood splatter. The air felt colder. The silence deepened.

"We are not done yet."

CHAPTER FIVE

IN THE WAKE OF THE DECREE

Snowhaven lay hushed beneath a sky bruising toward indigo, the light fading as though the mountains themselves pressed it out. Frost had settled into every seam of stone and timber, turning each rooftop into a brittle crown. Along the lane, villagers moved with quiet haste. Shutters slammed closed. Curtains drew tight. Doors barred with a firmness that spoke less of routine and more of unease.

Lysandra carried her bundle of kindling close, the weight not heavy but awkward, pressing against her ribs with each careful step. Her breath curled white into the air, visible proof of how cold the mountain had turned. Yet it was not the chill that slowed her. It was the hush that followed her wherever she walked. The hush of doors shutting before she arrived, of voices silenced mid-word, of spaces that had once welcomed her now drawing away as though she carried a sickness.

The tavern ahead had been lively when she left that morning. Now, as she rounded the corner, the heavy oak door swung to with a final, muffled thud, smothering laughter and lamplight alike. Across the lane, the cobbler's window was already dark, the candle snuffed hours before its usual time. Even the dog that barked once from an alley broke off mid-sound, silenced not by command but by some instinct older than obedience.

It had not always been this way. Just weeks ago, she and her mother had made the same walk side by side, arms laden with herbs and bark, exchanging remedies for smiles. People would pause to greet them, sometimes to ask for a poultice or a tincture. The road had felt part of home then. Now, the only things that marked her were glances too quickly turned aside, the weight of silence, the knowledge that she was no longer simply Lysandra. She was the healer's daughter, the strange girl from the smoke-scented cottage at the edge of the village.

At the crest of the path her gaze lifted. Their home sat half-buried in snow where the ridge curled against the mountain. The chimney jutted black against the indigo sky, and perched atop it was the raven. It had been there that morning when she left. It was there still, feathers glossy in the last light. Watching. Waiting. It cawed once as it turned it's head and titled to look at Lysandra.

"I see you," she whispered into the wind as she looked up at the raven.

The gate stood stiff with frost when she reached it, the latch rimed white and brittle beneath her fingers. She paused there, wood pressed tight against her chest, and let her gaze sweep the garden. Where summer had spilled green across the beds, only withered stalks remained, bowed beneath snow that glittered faintly in the dim. The air held no fragrance now, only the sharp scent of cold earth sealed under ice.

Beyond the slats, the cottage windows glowed with muted firelight, curtains drawn but not so tightly that they could keep it hidden. The warmth beckoned, a promise of refuge against the village's closing doors. For a moment Lysandra allowed herself to stand still and breathe. The weight of the silence pressed at her back, yet here at least, at this threshold, something softer waited.

She lifted the latch, pushed the gate inward, and stepped into the yard. The snow crunched under her boots, brittle and sharp, and the garden's dead stems brushed against her cloak as if in parting. At the door she shifted the wood to one arm, freed her other hand, and pulled. The hinges groaned faintly, and the warmth within spilled out like a living thing.

The air met her with scents she knew as well as her own skin: smoke from the hearth, rosemary drying above it, and the faint sweetness of thyme steeped too long in honey. Shadows flickered along the beams overhead, dancing with the sway of herb bundles strung on their hooks. Rows of jars lined the shelves, their glass catching firelight in muted tones of green and amber.

Lysandra nudged the door closed with her heel, letting the thud cut her off from the silence outside. The sound seemed final, sealing the night out and holding the warmth in. Her arms loosened for the first time since leaving the woods, and the weight of the kindling shifted to rest at her side. Her deep red hair was slightly dusted with snow.

At the table, her mother sat waiting. Ksara's sleeves were rolled, her hands steady over a strip of linen folded neatly. She glanced up, eyes warm, and smiled as though nothing in the world had shifted.

"Welcome back, love," she said, her voice soft as the fire behind her.

Lysandra laid the firewood beside the hearth and rubbed her hands together until the sting of cold began to fade. Her fingertips were red, the skin raw from the bite of mountain air, but the warmth in the cottage was already softening them. She crossed to the table without needing to be asked. Ksara slid a small bowl toward her—dried golden-root shaved thin—and set the mortar between them.

Without a word, Lysandra took up the pestle. The motion was familiar, yet her hands betrayed her, moving too quickly at first. The pestle scraped against stone in sharp circles, scattering more than it ground.

"Steady," Ksara said, not unkindly. Her voice carried no scold, only correction. "Let the stone do the work. The root will give if you're patient."

Lysandra slowed, adjusting her rhythm until the scrape softened to a whisper. Golden flecks powdered beneath the weight of the pestle, curling into dust at the rim. She focused on the sound, on the pressure through her arm, and tried not to think of the closed shutters outside.

Her mother's hands moved effortlessly folding linen, binding herbs, and tying knots that would not loosen. She did not glance down often; her fingers knew their place without sight. Watching her always felt like watching certainty itself, as though Ksara's calm could tether the very air around her.

The fire popped in the hearth. Shadows leaned across the ceiling beams. For a time, only their shared work filled the room—the scrape of pestle, the crackle of fire, the soft slide of linen folded neat.

Finally Lysandra spoke, her voice lower than before. "They shut the door on me today. At the tavern."

The pestle slowed in her hand, though she did not stop.

Ksara looked up, the strip of linen paused mid-fold. She did not answer right away. When she did, it was with the quiet weight of someone who had already thought the words many times. "They're afraid. Fear makes people turn away from what they don't understand. And lately, they choose fear over truth."

Lysandra pressed harder against the mortar, grinding the root to dust. "But they used to come to us for everything."

"They will again," Ksara replied. Her voice was calm, but the linen in her hands had been folded twice more than necessary. "Not all at once. Not always kindly. The world shifts before we notice it, and here at the edge of things, we feel it first."

The words lingered in the air, heavier than the scent of herbs. Lysandra blinked down at the powder she'd made. It looked almost too fine, as if it might blow away with a single breath.

The goldenroot dust gathered fine and pale in the mortar, clinging to the stone in yellow streaks. Lysandra slowed her grinding until the sound of it all but disappeared. She sat back a little, hands loose on the pestle. Her eyes stayed on the powder, though her voice carried across the table.

"Someone asked about your tincture last week," she said. "A man with a patchy beard. He said his sister took a few drops and felt... too calm. He asked if you'd put something else in it."

Ksara's hands stilled. She had been folding another length of cloth, and now it lay idle in her lap, the crease half made. Her eyes narrowed. "And what did you tell him?"

"That you gave her exactly what she asked for," Lysandra answered quickly. She glanced up, met her mother's gaze, then looked away again. "He didn't believe me. I could see it in his face."

Her mother drew a long breath through her nose, the way she did when she was testing a draught for balance. "He was from the millhouse?"

Lysandra nodded.

The cloth in Ksara's hands was folded once more, sharper this time, until it looked almost like a blade. She set it down carefully. "I warned her about valerian. Too much and the mind drifts, floats away from its tether. Some call that peace. Others mistake it for danger."

Lysandra's jaw tightened. "Are we in danger?"

The question came out quicker than she meant, and sharper. The fire cracked behind her, sending sparks chasing upward. For a moment the room seemed smaller, shadows reaching in too close.

Ksara's gaze did not waver, though something behind her eyes shifted, as though she weighed the truth against her daughter's need for calm. "Not yet," she said at last.

The words hung heavy. Not yet. They were a door left ajar, not an assurance.

Lysandra hugged her arms across her chest. She wanted to believe the quiet of the room, the warmth of the fire, but she could feel the memory of the tavern door shutting still pressed against her. As if the whole village had already chosen which side of that door she belonged on.

The mortar sat quiet between them, its rim dusted in gold. For a while neither moved. The hearth crackled, throwing light that made the herb bundles sway as though they breathed. Outside, the wind slid along the shutters and pushed a faint draft through the seams of the door.

Lysandra shifted in her chair. Her voice came softer this time, as though speaking too loud might make the thought real. "Do you think something's going to happen?"

Her mother didn't answer at once. She turned her head toward the window instead, though the shutters were drawn tight. Her fingers brushed the frame, a gesture so light it seemed more like listening than touching.

"Balance always tips before it breaks," Ksara said at last. "We cannot stop the tipping. But we can choose how we stand when it comes."

Lysandra let the words settle, unsure if she found comfort or dread in them. The fire popped behind her, sending sparks tumbling into the chimney. She whispered back almost without meaning to: "Balance in everything."

Ksara's gaze returned to her, steady and calm. "Not only in herbs, child. In all things. Even the ones we cannot see."

The silence that followed was not empty. It pressed against the walls and floor like water in a vessel, filling every corner until it seemed the whole cottage breathed with them. Lysandra looked down at her hands, powdered faintly with goldenroot, and tried to still the faint tremor that had begun in her fingers.

Above, something stirred the chimney. A hollow caw drifted down—low, unhurried, almost like an answer. Lysandra's head lifted, but her mother did not move. The raven had not left its perch. It only waited.

The draft slipped through the door again, sharper now, and the candle nearest the hearth guttered. Ksara set her hands flat against the table, eyes still distant, and said in a voice near to a whisper: "The wind's shifted."

The hearth's crackle faded beneath a new sound. A single strike rattled the cottage walls, loud enough to make the jars quiver in their shelves. Lysandra flinched, hands flying to the table's edge. For an instant she thought it thunder, but no storm rolled above the mountains.

Another blow followed, harder, the wood of the door groaning under its weight. Dust drifted down from the beams.

A voice cut through the cottage, muffled by timber but sharp with command.

"By order of King Aldric, open this door!"

Lysandra froze. Her chest seized with the kind of fear that seemed to hold the very air still in her lungs. She looked to her mother, waiting for alarm, for panic perhaps, but Ksara's face had already hardened to something else.

She stood quickly, chair scraping the floor, and crossed the room in three steps. "Lysandra," she said, and there was no fear in her tone. Only decision. "Behind the shelf. Now."

The girl didn't move. Her body felt locked in place, heart hammering, mind still catching up to the sound that had shattered their evening.

Ksara dropped to one knee beside the far wall and pulled a low shelf away with practiced force. Behind it gaped a hollow lined with wool and birch bark. They had spoken of it before, rehearsed it as a kind of drill, but never once used it. Until now.

"Go," Ksara urged, her voice lower but no less firm. "Stay silent. Survive."

"I—"

"Now!"

The word cracked like a whip. It cut through her hesitation, and Lysandra's body moved at last. She dropped to her knees, crawled into the hollow, and pressed herself small against the earthen wall. The shelf slid back into place, sealing her into darkness.

Through a narrow gap between the boards, she saw only the sliver of golden firelight left to her and the outline of her mother turning back toward the door as the third strike shook it loose from its hinges.

The latch splintered. The door crashed inward in a spray of wood shards, wind roaring in to snuff half the candles at once. The warmth of the cottage broke apart, scattered into cold and smoke. The door slammed against the wall, a crash that made the floor tremble beneath her knees. Boots stamped inside, the rhythm of iron nails on wood echoing far louder than it should have in such a small house.

"Ksara of Snowhaven!" a man's voice barked. "You are hereby under arrest for the practice of illegal magic."

Darkness swallowed her as the shelf slid into place. The air inside was close, stale with dust and the faint tang of wool packed against the walls. Lysandra pressed her forehead to the wood, fighting to slow the rhythm of her breath. Each exhale sounded too loud, as though it might give her away.

The same voice barked again, closer now. "You are charged with unlawful craft. Confessions have been heard, witnesses named. You will answer to the crown."

Through the slat of light, Lysandra saw only the edge of a boot, thick leather bound with iron buckles. Her mother's voice answered, calm and even.

"I am a healer."

"You brew tinctures that cloud the mind. You craft potions without sanction. These are crimes against decree."

"I treat burns and fevers. I do no harm."

"The crown will decide that."

The scrape of leather straps followed, harsh and final. Lysandra clutched her arms to her chest, biting her sleeve to smother the sound of her own breathing. She wanted to cry out, to tear the shelf back and reach for her mother, but her body wouldn't move. Every muscle locked tight, every sound outside magnified until it drowned her thoughts.

The table overturned with a crash. Glass shattered. The air filled with the sharp tang of herbs and tinctures spilled to the floor. She heard her mother's breath catch.

Then came the heavy stomp of boots turning toward the door, dragging her mother with them. The hinges groaned once more. Cold wind rushed back in. And the door slammed shut.

The cottage was left to silence. Except for the boots that had not left.

The silence stretched only a heartbeat before boots scraped against the floor again. Heavy, deliberate. One pair moved toward the hearth, glass crunching underfoot. Another kicked at a chair, sending it toppling with a crack of splintered wood.

"You smell that?" a younger voice muttered. "Mint. Maybe sage."

A laugh followed, coarse and too loud for the small cottage. "Witch's brew. Bottle the stench and grave robbers would pay for it."

Through the narrow slit, Lysandra caught flashes: iron buckles, muddied soles grinding petals into the floorboards, the shadow of a hand pulling down the drying rack until bundles of lavender and yarrow fell in a scatter. She pressed her forehead harder against the shelf, willing herself not to make a sound.

Another voice cut through that was a bit older, gruffer, and one she knew.

"Leave it. We're here for evidence. If it looks magical, it burns."

Her chest seized. The voice belonged to Captain Rendar. She remembered him from a harvest festival years ago, dancing with a pie in each hand, mustache dripping with cider. Now his tone was iron, each word snapping into command.

"She didn't fight," one of the younger guards said.

"Why would she?" Rendar answered. His boots stopped near the shelf, so close Lysandra could see a scuff worn smooth at the toe. "She knew what was coming. And she didn't want her daughter caught up in it."

The blood drained from Lysandra's face. Her nails dug into her arms until they ached.

"They say she has one," the younger voice pressed. "A girl. About ye high. No more than thirteen years old. Haven't seen her around much lately."

A pause. The boots shifted, leather creaking.

"She's smart," Rendar said at last. "Probably sent the brat to a neighbor."

Relief and terror tangled in her chest, so sharp it almost hurt.

"Should we check the outbuildings?" another asked.

"No," Rendar snapped. "The crown will pull it all down soon enough. Let the snow have what's left."

Glass shattered—a jar thrown or dropped. More laughter rose, then ebbed. Each sound dug deeper into her ears: herbs crushed, shelves overturned, her mother's cloak tossed to the ashes. She wanted to scream, to fling the shelf aside, to drive them out. Instead she held still, her body shaking, heart pounding like a hammer inside a locked box.

The cottage that had been a sanctuary was becoming ruin under their boots, and all she could do was listen.

The storm of boots and laughter dragged on longer than Lysandra thought possible. Every crash seemed meant to draw blood from memory, to tear her mother's presence out of the very walls. A chair scraped, something heavy toppled, then another burst of laughter that cut too sharp in the confined space.

At last, Captain Rendar's voice cut through the din. "Enough. We've what we need. Out."

The shift in the room was instant. Boots shuffled, wood creaked, glass crunched under hurried steps. One last bundle of herbs was ground under heel, a petty parting gesture. Then the door opened, groaned, and slammed shut. Cold air flooded in and swept out again.

Silence.

Lysandra stayed where she was, pressed into the hollow. Her muscles ached from holding still, but she dared not move. Not yet.

A floorboard popped somewhere in the cottage. Her heart surged to her throat. Was someone left behind? She held her breath until her chest burned. Nothing followed—only the faint moan of the wind pushing through the chimney stones.

Still she waited. Seconds became minutes, stretching until time itself lost shape. Every beat of her heart felt like it might give her away.

Only when her legs began to cramp so badly she thought she might faint did she shift her hand and ease it against the wall. With a trembling push, she nudged the shelf forward an inch, then another, until a sliver of the room appeared.

The fire had guttered low, embers dim beneath their own ash. Shadows sprawled where furniture had been overturned. The air smelled of crushed herbs, spilled oil, and something bitter that didn't belong.

There was no longer any boots or voices. The cottage was empty.

Lysandra pressed harder against the shelf until it scraped outward just enough for her to squeeze through. Golden light spilled across her face, faint and uneven from the embers still breathing in the hearth. She crawled forward, her arms trembling beneath her, and pulled herself into the open.

Her legs gave out the instant she cleared the space. She collapsed onto the floorboards, the cold biting at her. For a moment she lay there, cheek pressed to the wood, lungs heaving like she had run a mile though she had not moved more than a hand's span.

When she lifted her head, the cottage no longer looked like home.

The table had been overturned, one leg snapped clean, the other wedged crooked against the wall. Glass from shattered jars glittered dully in the firelight, their spilled powders dusting the floor like strange pollen. A drying line had been torn down, its string dangling limp, bundles of sage and thyme crushed into the dirt.

Near the hearth lay her mother's cloak, the green one with the sun-faded trim. Ash clung to it, boot prints stamped dark across the fabric. Lysandra stared at it for a long time, unable to move closer.

Her hands shook as she reached for a shard of ceramic from their kettle. The smooth glaze was cracked and jagged now, sharp enough to cut. She set it down, only to pick up another piece: the dented tin cup she had used as a child, small enough to fit in her palm. The dent was still there, from the time she dropped it against the hearthstone. Her breath caught, and for a moment she could almost hear Ksara's laugh from that day.

The sound wasn't here now. Only the groan of settling beams and the soft hiss of the embers.

Lysandra folded over herself, her arms wrapped around the cup like it was something living. She waited for the tears to come, but none did. Her throat was raw, her chest aching, yet her eyes burned dry. A part of her was still back in the crawlspace, waiting for her mother to open the shelf and say it was over.

But the shelf was empty. And the only voice in the room belonged to the wind.

The cottage pressed in around her as ruin wearing familiarity. Every overturned chair, every broken jar. The smell of rosemary and sage lingered, but soured beneath the bitter tang of spilled tinctures and ash.

Lysandra dragged herself upright, her knees stiff from crouching so long in the crawlspace. She braced against the edge of the overturned table, her arms trembling as she forced herself to stand. Her vision swam, the wreckage tilting as though it would swallow her. She closed her eyes, steadied her breath, and opened them again.

That was when she saw it.

Half-hidden beneath the fallen shelf lay the corner of a leather strap. She bent, fingers fumbling as she pulled it free. A satchel. Her mother's travel pack she always kept ready "just in case." Lysandra sank to the floor with it in her lap, hands shaking as she loosened the flap.

Inside were bundles of herbs wrapped in linen, a waterskin still half full, and a small pouch of coins knotted in cloth. Not much. But it felt like more than the broken house around her. As if Ksara had left her a path forward.

Her fingers lingered on the satchel's strap, unwilling to let go. Then, as she shifted, a floorboard creaked under her boot, one of the loose planks by the hearth.

She knelt quickly, prying it up with careful hands. Beneath, wrapped in linen and twine, lay her mother's knife.

She unwrapped it slowly, reverently. The handle was smooth birchwood, worn by years of use. The blade caught the emberlight, clean and sharp. It had cut herbs, carved roots, pared cloth. It was no weapon. And yet, in her hand now, it felt like one.

She remembered the first time her mother had guided her grip, showing her how to hold it steady.

Lysandra laid the flat of the blade against her palm. She wasn't angry. Not yet. But something deeper was already rooting itself inside her, something that would not bend as easily as the herbs they once gathered.

She rewrapped the knife and slid it into the satchel, securing the strap tight. Then she looked around the cottage one more time... At what she knew she would have to leave.

The satchel sat open in her lap, its leather worn smooth in places where Ksara's hand must have rested countless times. Lysandra breathed once, steadying herself, then began to fill it with care.

Bundles of herbs first: yarrow, goldenroot, feverfew. Their scents were faint but distinct, each one a fragment of her mother's voice naming their uses. She tucked them tightly into the bottom, wrapped to keep dry.

Food followed: the heel of bread, two thin strips of dried meat, and a pouch of bitter nuts. Hardly enough to last, but more than nothing. She wrapped them again, binding the cloth carefully before setting it beside the herbs.

The pouch of coins came next. She turned it over in her hand, the metal clinking softly inside — three silvers, seven coppers. Not much to others, but here, in this moment, it was wealth. She slipped it into the side pocket of the satchel and tied the flap tight.

Her fingers brushed the wrapped knife. She placed it near the top, where she could reach it quickly if she must. It rested there heavier than its weight should allow.

Finally, she looked toward the hearth shelf. A small carved bear sat at the corner, no larger than her palm, its edges worn smooth from years of handling. Ksara had given it to her when she was little. It was something to hold when storms rattled the shutters. A totem of courage, her mother had called it.

Lysandra reached for it, her hand closing around the familiar shape. For a moment she held it to her chest, eyes shut, willing the courage to seep into her bones. Then, slowly, she placed it in the bag as well.

She was no longer a child hiding from thunder, but it was a memory that didn't take much space in her satchel. One she might need to call on later.

The satchel's flap was cinched shut. Her mother's cloak was still littered with soot and ash as she lifted it up and drew around her shoulders. Its smell clung to her, smoke and yarrow woven into every fiber.

Her gaze swept the room one last time, looking for something that would burn well. The satchel weighed firm against her side as she crossed to the storage bin beneath the counter. Her fingers worked without pause, drawing out dried elderbloom and foxwood bark, the herbs brittle but still fragrant. She scattered them across the rug near the hearth, petals bright even in the dim emberlight. Their perfume rose sharp and sweet, clinging in the air like memory.

Next she searched the windowsill, where a beeswax taper had been left half-melted by the sun. She took it in both hands and carried it to the hearth. Kneeling, she coaxed its wick against the embers until a thin flame sprang to life.

For a moment she held it there, cupped between her palms. The light flickered across her face, painting her cheeks in amber. It was more than a candle... It was prayer, farewell, and vow all bound into one.

She crouched low and pressed the candle's base into the spread herbs. The flame caught slowly at first, curling around petals and stems. Then it spread, foxwood bark snapping as it yielded. Smoke rose in delicate tendrils, gray against the beams above, winding upward like ink in water.

The fire lightly danced as it whispered smoke. Lysandra stepped back, watching it take hold. Shadows flared against the walls as the blaze grew, swallowing the overturned table, licking at the herbs crushed into the floorboards. The cottage filled with the smell of rosemary, yarrow, and ash.

This place had been full of stories, of her mother's laughter, of quiet evenings with tea and tales by the fire. Now it would be reduced to ember and soot. And somehow, that felt right. Better ash than to let the King's men turn it into evidence of some imagined crime.

She tightened the cloak around her shoulders, turned to the door, and lifted the latch. Cold air struck her cheeks as she stepped outside. Behind her, golden firelight spilled through the shutters, shifting to orange, then deepening toward red.

She did not look back.

The night closed in around her as soon as she left the cottage behind. Wind hissed through the pines, shaking snow loose in thin veils that dusted the path ahead. She ran anyway, boots slipping against patches of hidden ice, the satchel banging against her hip. The kindling weight of the cloak dragged at her shoulders, but she clutched it tighter, refusing to let it go.

Snowhaven fell away behind her. The village rooftops vanished first, then even the glow of the flames dwindled until it was no more than a smear of orange against the horizon. For an instant it might have been a sunrise — but one that belonged to no dawn she wanted.

The forest took her in. Trunks rose high and skeletal, their branches stretching like black arms against the sky. The ground was uneven, roots twisting up through frost and stone. Branches clawed at her sleeves, slapped her cheeks, caught in her hair. Her lungs burned with every breath, sharp knives of cold tearing down her throat. Still she ran.

A root caught her boot. She stumbled, flung out a hand, and caught herself against a drift of snow. The impact jarred her shoulder, and pain radiated down her arm. She staggered upright again, ignoring it, and pushed forward.

Her body ached already, knees bruised from the crawlspace, palms sliced with tiny cuts from shattered glass. Each step throbbed through her legs. A stitch grew hot beneath her ribs, but she pressed her hand to it and forced herself on.

The forest offered no road, no mercy. It only swallowed her in shadow and silence.

Her legs carried her until they no longer could. One misstep on a buried root sent her tumbling hard to the ground. Snow bit into her palms and scraped her cheek as she slid against frozen earth. The satchel spilled half-open beside her, spilling cloth bundles into the frost. For a moment she only lay there, gasping, mouth full of cold air that burned more than it soothed.

She rolled onto her back and stared upward. The branches overhead webbed across the sky, their black silhouettes cutting the stars into jagged pieces. Each breath rattled her chest, uneven, edged with pain. Her ribs ached from the fall, her throat raw from the running.

And then the sound came from within. A sob clawed its way up her throat, sharp and sudden. She pressed both hands to her face, trying to hold it in, but it broke past her fingers anyway. A second followed, then another, until her chest heaved with them.

The forest gave her no answer, only silence. Her cries sounded too loud in the emptiness, as though the trees themselves were listening. She hated the sound, hated the weakness of it, but there was no stopping it now.

Tears streaked down into her hairline, stinging her cold skin. She curled on her side, knees drawn up, body trembling with the force of what she had held back for too long. Not since the knock at the door, not when her mother had been dragged away, not even when the guards had torn apart their home had she allowed it. But here, with no one to see and no strength left to hold the dam, it spilled out of her all at once.

She sobbed until her voice was little more than a rasp, until her chest ached from the convulsions, until the tears ran dry and left only a hollow ache behind. The snow beneath her had grown damp from her heat, but she barely noticed.

She was not dead. Not yet. But in that moment she felt broken, scattered across the frost like the shards of her mother's jars.

When the sobs finally quieted, Lysandra lay still for a long while, her body curled tight as though the earth itself might hide her. The ache in her muscles gnawed at her, but another truth gnawed deeper: she could not remain here. Snowhaven was behind her, but soldiers still prowled the world, and grief would not protect her if they found her on the open ground.

She forced her arms beneath her, pushed herself upright, and gathered the satchel close. Her legs trembled as she rose, but she set her weight forward, one step and then another, until she found herself moving again.

The forest offered little in the way of safety. Pines crowded close, their shadows thick between the trunks. Every ridge looked too open, every clearing too exposed. Her eyes darted from shape to shape, searching for cover, until they caught on a bramble thicket that hunched at the base of a hollow pine.

It was a cruel-looking tangle of dense, thorned branches. Which made it perfect. No one would willingly crawl inside.

She dropped to her knees and shoved her way in, thorns scraping her sleeves, catching at her cloak. One dragged a line across her cheek, sharp enough to sting, but she pressed forward. The branches gave way to a cramped hollow within, no larger than a fox den, dark and musty with damp leaves.

Lysandra collapsed into the space and curled tight, the satchel pressed against her ribs as if it were part of her. She drew her cloak around herself, though it snagged on the thorns. Her knees tucked against her chest, her chin pressed low. It was not comfort. It was survival.

The wind hissed through the pines outside, but here the brambles muffled it, dulled the sharp edge of the cold. Her breath came fast at first, harsh in her ears, until she forced it slower. In through her nose, out through her mouth. Steady. Again. Again.

When fear rises like a fever, breathe as though you are cooling the blood. Her mother had said that. She clung to it now like a rope in floodwater.

Her hand drifted to the satchel. She didn't open it — only rested her palm against the wrapped knife inside, feeling the faint shape of the blade through linen. Its weight anchored her, reminded her she was still here.

The bramble hollow was damp and bitter-smelling, but it held her. And for tonight, that was enough.

The hollow pressed close on every side, the brambles above arching like twisted fingers laced in prayer. Darkness pooled thick, broken only by the faintest leak of moonlight through the thorn canopy. The cold clung stubbornly, but it was fear that held her rigid.

Lysandra pulled the satchel closer and opened it with fumbling hands. Inside, she found the wrapped bundle of linen and eased it out. She unfolded it one layer at a time until the birchwood handle gleamed faintly in the dim.

The knife was plain, yet beautiful in its simplicity. Ksara's hands had polished the grip smooth, each curve worn. Lysandra ran her thumb along the flat of the blade, not enough to cut, just enough to feel the steel. Its chill grounded her, sharper and more real than the nightmare blur of the last hours.

She remembered the lessons that had come with it. How her mother had guided her grip, steadying her trembling hands. *Never cut angry,* Ksara had said, her voice gentle but firm. *Knives carry your intent.*

Lysandra held the blade across her lap and let those words root inside her. She wasn't angry. Not yet. But intent had already begun to take shape — something quieter, heavier, growing at the core of her grief.

She rewrapped the knife carefully and pressed it against her chest. The linen smelled faintly of hearth ash and rosemary. She closed her eyes and drew in a slow breath, holding it, then letting it out in measured rhythm. Each cycle was steadier than the last.

Her lips moved without thought, shaping a whisper from childhood, half-prayer, half-song: *From root to bloom, from ash to flame, keep me safe and keep me sane...*

The words barely touched the air, but saying them made her feel less hollow.

Outside, the forest shifted. Branches creaked, something small scurried through the underbrush, and the wind groaned low through bare pines. Each sound pulled her taut again, but the knife at her chest reminded her she was not empty-handed.

She pressed her forehead against her arms holding the satchel and clung to that thought until the tremor in her hands began to ease. She had to keep herself from freezing.

The hours stretched thin, marked only by the shift of cold through her bones. At first it was the ache in her legs that gnawed at her, then the hollow in her stomach. The fear had hidden it for a while, but now the emptiness growled, low and insistent.

She unfastened the satchel and dug through its bundles with trembling hands until she found a strip of dried meat wrapped in waxed paper. She tore at it with her teeth, careful not to make a sound louder than her own breath. Each chew was slow, her jaw stiff, throat dry. She made herself count the motions before swallowing, stretching every mouthful. This wasn't dinner. It was survival.

When the meat was gone, she tucked the empty wrapper deep into the satchel, unwilling to leave even that trace for the wind to scatter. She pressed the bag tight against her ribs again, her hand resting on the place where the knife lay bundled.

The forest answered her stillness with sounds she could not ignore. A branch snapped somewhere beyond the brambles. Her breath halted in her throat. Was it a deer? A fox? Or boots crunching where snow had drifted?

Silence followed. Then the faint drag of something... a brush against bark, a shift of weight. It might have been the forest settling into itself, but to Lysandra it was too deliberate.

Her heart hammered until the thorns seemed to rattle with it. She pressed her back harder against the frozen ground, curling into herself, wishing she could vanish into the roots. Every nerve strained to catch the next sound.

Another creak. The groan of a tree swaying. Then quiet again.

The noises blurred together after that. Wind whining through bare branches, leaves rasping like whispers. Even the cry of an owl that seamed too close to a scream. Each one landed heavy, carrying intent whether it had any or not.

She clenched her teeth until her jaw ached. Fear pressed tighter than hunger ever could, and still she listened. Because if she stopped, if she let her ears rest, she might not hear them coming.

The longer she sat in the hollow, the heavier her body grew. Shivers wracked her arms until they turned numb, her eyelids burning from strain. She fought them at first, blinking hard, forcing her gaze to stay open to the dark lattice of brambles overhead. But her body was not made to hold fear forever.

Sleep came in fragments.

She startled awake at the snap of a twig, heart hammering, fingers halfway to the knife. Nothing waited outside but the sway of branches. Her eyes closed again before she meant them to.

This time she dreamed her mother by the hearth. Ksara's hands folded linen, her sleeves rolled as always, her face softened by firelight. "Balance, Lysandra," she murmured. "In all things."

The words echoed in Lysandra's chest, comforting for a heartbeat until the dream broke. Ksara was no longer at the table. She was being dragged through the cottage doorway, arms bound. The slam of the door jolted Lysandra awake again, breath ragged in the cold hollow.

She pressed her forehead against her arms, trying to steady herself, but her thoughts frayed as exhaustion pulled her down once more. Images tumbled together in her mind of her child's tin cup dented at the rim, the herbs crushed beneath boots, the fire climbing the beams of their cottage, and her mother's cloak sprawled in the ash.

Her lips shaped a name without meaning to. "Mama..."

The sound was little more than a broken breath.

She curled tighter around the satchel, the bundled knife pressed against her chest, and drifted again into the darkness of sleep... shallow, uneasy, and restless. There was no peace, but she was still breathing.

She woke with her jaw clenched tight, breath fogging in uneven bursts. The hollow around her had grown pale with the first touch of light, bramble thorns rimed in frost that glimmered faintly as the sun broke the horizon.

Lysandra pushed herself upright, wincing at the stiffness that locked her joints. Her back ached from sleeping curled against roots, her legs cramped from too long spent bound in fear. She flexed her fingers, but the cold had numbed them to clumsy stubs.

The forest lay hushed. No voices. No boots. Only the faint groan of trees shifting in the wind and the distant chatter of a bird waking high in the pines. Snowhaven was gone now, hidden beyond ridges and memory.

She pulled the satchel into her lap, needing to see, to know. She opened it carefully, her hands clumsy with cold. Inside, everything was still where she had packed it. She only needed to look, to be reminded she hadn't lost everything.

Her breath came steadier for it. Proof of her existence sat in her lap.

She emptied the satchel piece by piece, laying the contents in neat rows across her knees. Yarrow, goldenroot, feverfew. The heel of bread, the strips of meat, the pouch of nuts. Three silvers. Seven coppers. The knife, wrapped in linen that still smelled faintly of ash and rosemary.

For a moment she let herself linger, fingertips brushing each as though it were holy. They weren't just supplies. They were memory, and they were the thread between who she had been and who she must become.

Then she began to pack again but not as before. Now each placement was chosen with care. Herbs sealed tight at the bottom. Food next, wrapped snug. The coins tucked into a hidden pouch. And the knife near the top, where her hand could reach it first.

When the bag was full, she drew the flap tight and cinched the strap. This time it didn't feel like her mother's satchel anymore. It felt like hers.

She whispered aloud, voice hoarse but firm: "I have what I need." as a declaration.

She rose from the hollow, dragging the cloak tight around her shoulders. The forest stretched in every direction, endless trunks fading into gray. She turned slowly, letting the faint beams of morning touch her face. The ridge lay behind her. South was ahead.

Gladecross. Ksara had spoken the name only a handful of times, but it had lodged in Lysandra's memory. A place where knowledge moved more freely, where the King's decree carried less weight. If safety existed anywhere, it was farther from Dunmoh's immediate reach, or so she believed. It was the next village south along the roads. She had to head south to stay warm. If she remained near the mountains, she would likely freeze to death within the coming days.

She looked once more at the bramble hollow, the place that had held her in her breaking. Then she turned away. The sun had risen. And so had she.

At the edge of the clearing, she stopped. Pines towered ahead, their trunks silvered by frost, their shadows deep and endless. The path forward was not marked, no trail offered. But she didn't need one.

She placed her palm against the nearest tree. The bark was rough, grooves biting into her skin. She closed her eyes and let the contact steady her, grounding her in the present. She was here, alive, and unbroken enough to stand. She breathed in once, sharp and cold, and released it slow.

Her first step was cautious, boots crunching against brittle grass. The second held more weight, more certainty. By the third, her stride had found rhythm. She kept close to the trees, following the natural lines of deer trails, letting the undergrowth conceal her as best it could.

Her eyes scanned each shadow, every ridge and hollow, but she no longer moved like prey. Fear still pulsed inside her, but it was tempered now.

The forest's voice shifted with her. The chatter of a squirrel in the canopy, the sudden flight of birds between branches, the sigh of wind through needles. They were all sounds she had bristled against in the night. Now she listened differently. They had their own language, their own pattern.

Behind her, the last smoke of the fire would be rising faint into the sky, dissolving as the morning advanced. She didn't turn to look. That life was ash now, and she had given it to the flames with her own hand.

The satchel brushed her hip with each step. The knife rested within reach. The cloak, though stained, still smelled faintly of pine and yarrow. These were all that remained and all she required.

She slipped deeper into the trees, her figure soon swallowed by shadow and frost. Her steps were light, her hands steady at her sides.

The kingdom's lie would not endure forever. And it would begin to unravel with a girl who had nothing left to burn.

CHAPTER SIX

FOX IN THE BURROW

Fifteen years since the fateful night...

The sky was still dark when Caelan stirred, the first edge of dawn only beginning to stretch across the treetops. Mist clung to the forest floor, curling around roots and mossy stone beyond the cottage window. The sharp, earthy scent of pine filled the air, clean and cool.

He sat up slowly, rubbing the sleep from his eyes. Today was different. Today, he would go alone.

His boots waited by the door, and beside them his satchel leaned against the table leg. He had checked it again and again the night before—dried fruit, coin pouch, parchment list, flask, a bundle of cord. None of it heavy, yet this morning it felt as though every piece carried more than its weight.

Elaria moved softly about the kitchen, already wrapped in her moss-green cloak. She moved with the quiet ease of someone at home in the forest, her presence as steady as the trees themselves. A kettle hissed over the fire, and bread with berries waited on the table.

"You're up early," she said without turning.

"So are you," Caelan answered, tugging on his boots.

When she turned, her smile was gentle but did not quite hide the worry beneath it. She held out a small bundle wrapped in cloth. "I made you something for the road. Oatcakes and honeyroot. You'll need the strength."

He accepted it and slipped it into his satchel. "Thank you."

She stepped close, her hand lingering on the strap across his shoulder, her voice softer now. "Do you remember everything?"

"Grains, salt, parchment, glass vials, fabric, and a new mortar if I can find one, and—"

"—no magic," she finished for him, as she always did. "Blend in. Watch, don't speak. Let them think you harmless."

"I know," he said, though a flicker of impatience slipped into his voice.

Her hand stilled on the buckle of his satchel. "You've never gone this far alone."

"I'm not a child anymore."

Her fingers tightened, then slowly released. "No. You're not."

She pressed a pouch of coin into his palm. "Use it sparingly. Barter when you can."

He nodded, the solemn weight of her trust heavy in his chest.

Together they stepped outside. Dawn spread gold and lavender through the trees, and birds called faintly in the distance. At the edge of the path, he looked back.

"You'll be alright," Elaria said, folding her arms loosely though her eyes never left him. "Trust your instincts."

He hesitated. "Do you trust me?"

For a long moment she said nothing. Then she touched his shoulder and met his eyes. "I trust the heart I've raised. Now go, before the day escapes you."

The cottage faded behind him as he set out. A thrill, sharp and uncertain, tugged at his chest. For the first time, the world ahead belonged only to him.

The trail was damp beneath his boots, soft with morning dew. Every step left an imprint, swallowed almost at once by the underbrush. The satchel bounced at his side, not a burden, but a constant reminder that this was his journey.

Birdsong flitted high in the canopy, fading as he pressed farther into the forest. In the past, Elaria's steady stride and quiet hum had carried him through such walks. Now the only voice was the whisper of the wind in the trees, rustling their leaves with secrets.

He followed the familiar trail, its mossy stones and gnarled roots as known to him as the lines on his palm. He had made this journey countless times before, but today he was by himself.

As the hours went by, faint memories of Gladecross came back to him with the rush of strangers, the glare of soldiers, and the helpless fear as a child. He remembered hiding behind Elaria's cloak.

Not today. Today belonged to him.

The canopy broke, sunlight spilling golden across wild grass and flowers. The Elderwood gave way to open sky. A river shimmered in the distance, winding past low hills and misted treeline. Nestled at the base of one of those hills waited Foxburrow.

From here it looked simple and harmless. Thatched roofs. Thin smoke curling from chimneys. Villagers bent to carts and baskets. Ordinary.

Caelan lingered at the treeline, breathing in the last of the forest air. Then he stepped into the light, following the pathway ahead. The pack shifted against his shoulders. He ignored it and kept walking. He crested a rise and paused. Foxburrow sprawled below, tucked between the river's bend and the edge of the mountains. Its cottages stood quiet, gardens spilling with herbs and flowers, smoke drifting from squat chimneys. Yet it was not the village itself that held him in awe, it was the land around it.

Hills rose behind, dotted with rocky outcrops and shallow caves like the dens of wild creatures. Trails wound through the grass, narrow and uncertain. Foxglove and thistle clustered thick around the stones, and flashes of white and russet fur darted between them. Foxes. Dozens of them. Some sunning themselves. Some watching. Some slipping into shadow. They were everywhere, chasing after each other in play.

Caelan exhaled, tightening his pack.

The Elderwood was behind him.

And Foxburrow waited.

The dirt path wound gently between the fields, carrying Caelan closer to the heart of Foxburrow. His boots pressed through tufts of tall grass that leaned into the morning light, brushing against his legs with a soft hiss. A pair of foxes lingered on a nearby rise, their sleek bodies still against the slope. One tilted its head as if measuring him, ears pricked and sharp, while the other stretched lazily, rolling onto its side in a ripple of russet fur before settling back into the grass. Their indifference was strange comfort. He had expected them to scatter, yet they remained, content to watch him pass as though he belonged here as much as they did.

The path narrowed as it drew him closer, and Caelan kept his stride steady, breathing in the clean air of the fields and trying to calm the tightening in his chest.

Foxburrow revealed itself without spectacle, as though it had always been there, content in its rhythm. The morning sun had lifted the last shreds of mist, leaving the air clear and bright. Gardens stretched in tidy rows beside the cottages, their soil dark and rich, already touched by the careful hands of those who worked them. Stacked stone fences marked the edges of fields, moss creeping into the cracks, giving the impression that they had stood for generations.

The cottages themselves sat low and humble, roofs thatched and windows latticed with dark wood. From several chimneys rose thin columns of smoke, carrying the scent of pinewood and cooking fat. Somewhere deeper in the village, a bell rang with a muted clang, only a reminder of the hour, the sound blending into the slow current of daily life.

Caelan slowed his steps as he left the fields behind and set his boots upon the worn earth of the village edge. He took it all in quietly, allowing the weight of the moment to settle against his chest. This was no bustling city, no grand fortress. Yet to him it felt immense, a place alive with its own pulse.

Children darted barefoot through the grass, chasing one another in bursts of laughter that rang brighter than the bell. Their joy carried freely, spilling across the lanes as if the world beyond the village did not exist. A woman stood nearby, stretching a line of twine between two trees. She lifted damp sheets from a basket and draped them one by one, the fabric snapping lightly in the breeze until it swelled like sails on a quiet sea.

At the edge of a courtyard, an old man moved beneath the weight of a basket filled with kindling. His back curved under the burden, yet his grip was firm. As he paused to catch his breath, a curious fox padded close, nose twitching toward the wood. The man waved it away with a half-hearted swat, his expression one of weary familiarity, as though such encounters were part of the day's routine.

All around, the village moved with the rhythm of ordinary life. The hum of chores, the scatter of laughter, the murmur of voices woven together into something that felt at once comforting and impenetrable.

Caelan drifted farther into the village, his steps steady but cautious. A few glances passed between him and the townsfolk. A nod from a man tightening the harness of a mule. A quick flick of the eyes from a woman gathering herbs at her doorway. To them, he was only another traveler with a pack, another pair of boots on the road.

The ease of it unsettled him. He had expected whispers, perhaps even stares. He had imagined the weight of strangers' eyes tracking his every move, questions about his name or the purpose of his journey. Instead, there was nothing. The villagers carried on, their attention fixed on their own lives, and the absence of interest pressed against him more heavily than any scrutiny would have.

He reminded himself of Elaria's words. *Blend in, keep quiet, let them overlook you.* This was good. This was what he needed. Still, the quiet felt strange. He adjusted the strap of his satchel, drawing a slow breath.

The village square opened before him, shaped by the slow rhythm of trade. A stone well stood at its center, the worn lip darkened by years of use, while around it merchants had arranged their stalls in uneven rows. The scents reached him first of fresh bread mingled with boiled roots, sharp herbs drying in bundles, and the faint tang of lamp oil. Voices rose here and there.

Caelan moved carefully among them, head lowered beneath his hood, his hand never far from the pouch at his side. He stopped at a narrow stall where parchment and ink lay stacked in neat bundles. The merchant accepted his coins without a word, sliding the supplies into a small wrap of cloth. From there Caelan moved on to a sack of grain, then a measure of salt, each exchange swift and quiet.

The errands themselves were simple. He felt the weight of Elaria's trust in every coin he spent, the satchel at his hip slowly filling with the proof of his task.

At the edge of the square, a stall displayed bolts of fabric stacked in careful layers. Flax and wool lay side by side, dyed in soft shades of green, brown, and faded blue, the colors drawn from roots and bark rather than foreign dyes. Caelan reached out, letting his fingers trace the weave of a rougher cloth. It was coarse but sturdy, the kind of fabric that would last through seasons of wear if Elaria set her hands to it. He lingered only a moment, imagining how she might shape it into something useful, before stepping back.

A shimmer of light caught his eye farther along. Across the row, another stall held a neat line of glass vials arranged like soldiers on parade. Sunlight slid across their curved sides, scattering into pale glints that tugged at his attention. They stood out against the muted tones of the square, too precise, too polished to ignore. He adjusted the strap of his satchel and began to make his way toward them, his pace measured, his eyes careful not to betray eagerness.

Caelan had nearly reached the stall with the vials when a voice cut across the square. It was sharp, carried with authority, and it did not belong to any villager.

"Step aside, merchant."

The words seemed to strike the air itself. The chatter of the square faltered. A merchant's call trailed off mid-sentence. The clatter of children's laughter stilled into uneasy quiet. Even the fox kit that had been prowling near a vegetable cart darted back into the grass, vanishing like smoke.

Caelan turned with the others. At the far edge of the square stood a small group of armed men. They wore black-and-iron cloaks trimmed in silver, their armor polished until the raven crest of Aldric Raven-mark glinted against the sunlight. They did not need to shout or march in formation—the weight of their presence was enough.

There were four in all. One stepped forward, broad-shouldered, a long scar carved from temple to cheek. His helm rested beneath his arm, his eyes cold and unblinking. The others flanked him in loose formation, their hands resting easily on hilts, their stares sweeping the square with practiced detachment.

The stillness of the village deepened, heavy as stone. What life had stirred moments before now seemed to fold in on itself, retreating into silence.

The guards crossed the square with unhurried steps, their boots grinding against the cobblestones in a rhythm that seemed louder than it should have been. They stopped before a modest stall near the well, where an older man had arranged seashells, bits of driftwood, and small pendants carved from resin and wood. The trinkets glimmered faintly in the sunlight, unassuming but carefully displayed.

The merchant's hands lifted slowly, palms outward, his face drawn but steady. "I swear, gentlemen," he said, his voice thin in the quiet, "they're only trinkets from the coast. Nothing more."

The scarred captain studied him without shifting his stance. "We have reports that enchanted objects have been sold in this region. Your stall matches the description." His words fell like a verdict rather than an accusation.

"They're charms, carved by hand," the merchant replied, though a tremor had entered his voice. "Wood and resin. If there were magic in them, I would not know it."

The captain did not blink. "And yet they find their way into the hands of those who disappear. You expect me to believe that is chance?"

Around the square, villagers edged away. Some turned their backs as if distance would erase the scene. Others slipped quietly into door-ways, their movements too practiced to be coincidence. Only a few remained, frozen like Caelan, drawn to the gravity of the moment and unable to look aside.

The merchant tried to steady himself, though his hands trembled against the stall. "Please," he said, his voice carrying a raw edge now. "I've traded in this square for over twenty years. These are keepsakes from Anchorstone, nothing more. I swear it."

One of the younger guards shifted at the captain's side. His palm slid along the grip of his sword, before raising it from it's sheath into the air, impatience written across his face. "We should search the crates," he muttered. "Tear it down, strip it bare. No point in listening to lies."

The captain's expression did not change. His gaze fixed on the old man.

The merchant's plea sharpened, urgency breaking through fear. "I swear on my life, there is no magic here. I am loyal to the crown."

But loyalty was nothing to them. The younger guard moved before the words had settled, his blade flashing down. It was the impatient cut of someone who had forgotten that life sat at the other end of steel.

The arc came down hard and fast. The blade tip cut across the merchant's shoulder, dragging a shallow line across his chest. His cry broke into the silence as he collapsed to his knees, clutching at the spreading stain that darkened his tunic. Blood welled quick and heavy, dripping down his arm before pattering against the cobblestones.

The crowd recoiled in a ripple of movement, yet no voice rose. No hand moved to stop it. The square held its breath, smothered beneath the weight of fear.

Caelan felt the moment break inside him as surely as the blade had broken the merchant's flesh. Heat rushed through his chest, through his birthmark, sharp and sudden, the pressure of magic rising like water against a dam. His fists clenched at his sides before he realized it, nails biting into his palms. He could taste iron in the air—blood, stone, and the raw heat of anger blooming behind his eyes.

The urge came not from thought but from something older, deeper. Before he could stop it, before he even understood it, the word ripped from his throat.

"Stop!"

The sound crashed through the square with unnatural force, sharper than steel, louder than any single voice had a right to be. It seemed to strike the air itself, echoing against walls and rooftops, hanging there as though the village had been waiting for someone to speak.

For one fractured heartbeat, everything froze. The guards stilled. Merchants held their breath. Even the children who had been watching from behind the safety of a stall stood wide-eyed, clutching each other's hands. The world paused, caught in the echo of that single command.

All eyes turned toward him.

The captain turned with deliberate slowness, his scarred face angling toward the sound. His eyes found Caelan through the crowd as if there had never been any doubt who had spoken. The gaze was steady, sharp, and unyielding, the kind of look that could pin a man in place without a single step taken.

Caelan's breath caught in his throat. He had not meant to reveal himself, not like this, not with everyone watching. Yet the moment was past saving; the word was already loose, impossible to gather back. His heart pounded so hard it felt as if it might shake him apart.

The captain studied him for a long, unbearable silence. Then his voice carried across the square, each word falling heavy. "Mind your business, boy. Unless you wish to share his fate."

The crowd shifted uneasily, some turning their eyes away from Caelan as though distance might absolve them. But the captain's focus did not waver. It was as if the whole square had narrowed to the space between the two of them.

Caelan stood rooted, the weight of that gaze pressing against his chest.

The magic had already risen to the surface, alive beneath his skin, sparking at the edges of his senses like fire pressing against stone. It begged for release, demanded it, the way storm clouds strain to break into thunder. Every part of him wanted to act. The birthmark on his chest burned with it, his hands shook with it, and his eyes lingered on the blood spreading across the old man's tunic until it seared itself into memory.

He could end it. He could hurl the guards back with a single breath, strike them down with power none of these villagers could imagine. The thought blazed inside him with chaos.

But so too did Elaria's voice.

Blend in. Watch, don't speak. Let them think you harmless.

The words clashed with the roar of magic until he felt torn in two. His body trembled with the strain of holding both truths—the fury of what he had witnessed, and the knowledge of what it would cost to intervene. He had heard the stories of dungeons that swallowed men whole for lesser acts. He had seen soldiers drag innocents away in chains while others stood by in silence.

He forced himself to draw a breath, slow and deliberate, as if he could cage the storm within. His fists unclenched one finger at a time. The power bled back into his chest, settling there like coals hidden beneath ash. His jaw ached with the effort, but he lowered his gaze in restraint.

The captain studied Caelan a moment longer, his expression unreadable. Then, with a flick of his hand, he dismissed him as if he were nothing more than a nuisance, and turned his attention back to the merchant laying on the ground.

"Clean this mess up."

Two of the guards moved at once, seizing the merchant beneath his arms. The old man groaned as they dragged him to his feet, his tunic already soaked with blood. His trinkets lay scattered across the stones, shells and pendants tumbling in the dust, forgotten. The guards hauled him away like a sack of grain, his feet scraping against the cobbles with every step.

No one moved to help. No one spoke. The villagers kept their distance, heads turned, eyes lowered. A mother clutched her child tighter, whispering hurriedly before pulling him out of sight. One of the merchants bent over his stall again, rearranging his wares with a hand that shook only slightly.

Then, slowly, the square returned to life as if nothing had happened. A hammer rang from the blacksmith's forge. A woman resumed calling out the price of her bread. A dog barked at the edge of the lane. The silence dissolved, but what had filled it lingered in Caelan's chest, heavy and unshaken.

He stood rooted where he was, breath shallow, every muscle tight with the effort of restraint. No one looked at him now. No one whispered or pointed in his direction. It was as though the moment had been swallowed whole, leaving only the weight of it pressed against his heart.

Caelan forced his feet to move, though he could scarcely remember the motion. The market had already settled back into its rhythm, merchants calling out, villagers passing between stalls as though blood had not just darkened the stones. The square carried on, burying the moment beneath routine.

The pool of blood was gone, trampled into the dirt by the shuffle of boots. The scattered trinkets had vanished as if they had never been there. The old man was nowhere to be seen, carried off like refuse. And still the village pretended nothing had happened.

Caelan kept his head low, his body moving through the motions, but his thoughts circled the moment like a snare. Every step felt heavier, every breath caught on the truth of what he had witnessed.

At the far end of the square, a narrow shop bore a pane of glass polished smooth as a mirror. Caelan caught his reflection there and stopped. For an instant he almost expected to see the boy from the glade—the one who trailed behind Elaria's stride, who listened to her lessons with wide eyes and believed the world would bend to the strength of her guidance.

But the face in the glass was not that boy. His eyes were flat, their light dulled, shadows pressing deep at their edges. His jaw was set too tight, his mouth a hard line. He looked like someone hollowed out, as though he had swallowed something bitter that refused to leave.

He pressed his lips together, fighting the words rising in his mind. Why hadn't he moved? Why hadn't he acted? The questions looped endlessly, a chain he could not break. The guards had swords, the villagers had silence, and Elaria's warnings had bound his hands before he ever thought to raise them.

Still, none of it felt like enough. The reflection stared back at him with an accusation he could not answer.

He turned from the glass and forced himself back into motion. The list still waited, though it now felt absurd in its simplicity. He stopped at a stall with bolts of fabric, choosing a length at random and paying without a word. The merchant gave a tired smile, polite but distant, and handed the cloth over without meeting his eyes.

At the next stall, rows of glass vials gleamed in the sunlight. He selected several, sliding them carefully into his satchel. The exchange was quick, quiet, and unnoticed by those around him. Coins changed hands, and that was all.

By the time he reached the edge of the square his pack was full, every item Elaria had asked for tucked neatly inside. Yet the weight pressing on his shoulders had nothing to do with grain or salt or glass. It was the silence he carried—the silence of the villagers, the silence he himself had chosen when the moment had demanded more.

The sun had climbed higher, stretching shadows long across the cobblestones. Caelan tightened the straps of his pack and set his feet on the road that would carry him home. He did not look back at the square, did not seek the faces of those who had watched and then turned away. The market had already swallowed what had happened, but he could not.

Every step away felt heavier, as though the village itself clung to him. His jaw clenched against the questions still burning in his mind. He hated the guards for their cruelty. He hated the villagers for their silence. And more than either, he hated himself for standing among them and doing the same.

The path ahead waited, bright with afternoon light. Caelan walked into it with his satchel full and his heart hollow.

The forest felt different on the return. The same path that had carried him out that morning now seemed longer, narrower, as though the trees had shifted in his absence. The wind pressed against him in restless gusts, whispering through the grass and shaking loose the higher branches. Shadows stretched across the trail, sharp and dappled, thrown long by the sun as it dipped toward the horizon. Every step sounded louder than it had before, each crack of a twig echoing in the stillness.

Caelan kept his eyes on the ground, his boots scuffing against the dirt. The pack on his shoulders weighed more heavily with every stride, because of what clung to them... the silence, the memory of the square, the guilt of standing still when he should have done more. What he carried was no longer food and parchment and vials. It was the weight of what he had not done.

The forest, which so often soothed him, gave no comfort. The birds still called, foxes still wove through the underbrush, clouds still shifted overhead, yet none of it reached him. His thoughts gripped too tightly to what had happened behind him. Or worse... what had not.

The scene refused to leave him. It looped through his thoughts in fragments... the merchant's raised hands, the hollow steadiness of his voice, the sudden flash of steel. He saw the old man collapse again and again, his body folding as blood spread across his tunic. He heard the gasp ripple through the crowd, the scrape of boots shifting back, the silence that followed.

He had shouted. He had felt the fire rise inside him, fierce and ready. For a heartbeat he had believed he might act, that he might turn the tide. But the moment had passed, and he had not moved.

Elaria's lessons wove through the memory like a second voice, quiet but insistent. *Stay hidden. Let them underestimate you.* The words pressed against him like a hand forcing him down.

He clenched his teeth until his jaw ached. That was what the villagers had done. They had let the guards cut a man down, let fear choke their voices, let silence become their defense. And in the end, he had stood among them, no different.

His fists tightened at his sides as he walked. Nails bit through the fabric of his gloves, and each breath grew sharper, heavier, until the forest itself seemed to lean in around him, listening.

Every tree he passed felt like a witness. Their trunks stood silent, tall and unbending, while foxes slipped across the path with quick flashes of russet fur, their eyes glinting as if they saw more than they revealed. The weight of it all pressed tighter against him, a silence that would not ease.

It wasn't fair. It wasn't right. He should have done more... should have shouted louder, should have stepped forward, should have let the power inside him break free. He could have made them stop. He could have made them see.

But then the other voice rose in him, quiet and merciless. What would you have done, Caelan? Burn them where they stood? Draw steel against four guards with a hunting knife? Die bleeding in the square while the world turned its back?

The questions gnawed at him with every step, and he had no answer that did not leave a bitter taste in his mouth. His anger clawed at his chest, but beneath it lay something colder: fear. He hated it more than anything. The feel of it creeping along his spine, chaining his hands, and drowning his voice. He hated the guards for their cruelty. He hated the villagers for their silence. And most of all, he hated himself for standing among them, no different from the rest.

The path seemed to stretch endlessly before him, winding through a forest that no longer felt like home. Its stillness offered no refuge. The Elderwood had always been his shield, but tonight it only watched, indifferent.

By the time Caelan stepped out of the trees, the sun had sunk low, its light spilling gold across the clearing. The glade stretched before him, swaying grass, and birds singing as though nothing in the world had shifted. From a distance, it looked untouched, the same sanctuary it had always been.

Yet to Caelan, it felt altered. The glow through the branches struck him less as warmth than as bars of light fencing him in. The hush of the place, once comforting, now pressed against him like a silence too heavy to carry.

Thistle raised her head from the trough as he passed, ears flicking, breath huffing in recognition. For a moment, he almost reached to stroke her neck, to let the familiar steadiness of her presence ground him. But the weight inside him dragged his hand back, and his gaze dropped to the earth instead. He walked past without a word.

The cottage door stood ajar, and the sound of home drifted out to meet him... the faint clink of pottery, the rhythm of a knife against a board, and the fragrance of herbs simmering over the hearth. Everything was as it should be, every detail wrapped in familiarity. But as he crossed the threshold, Caelan knew nothing was the same.

The air inside the cottage was warm, scented with lentils and thyme. A low fire glowed in the hearth, its light stretching across shelves of jars and bundles of herbs strung to dry. Elaria stood at the table, knife in hand, rhythmically cutting roots into neat slices.

She looked up as Caelan stepped through the door. Her hands stilled, her eyes narrowing slightly as she took in the slump of his shoulders, the stiffness in his stride, the silence that clung to him as tangibly as the satchel at his side.

"You're late," she said softly, setting the knife aside. "Did you find everything?"

Caelan gave no answer. He unfastened his pack with sharp motions and dropped it onto the table, the contents thudding inside. Without meeting her gaze, he began unpacking the grains, salt, parchment, fabric, and the vials, placing each item down. His hands moved too quickly, as though he could bury the day's weight beneath the task.

Elaria did not interrupt. She only watched, her expression calm but searching, until he reached the last of the supplies and froze, his fingers pressed hard against the table's edge, his back turned toward her.

Her voice, when it came, was quiet. "What happened, son?"

Caelan didn't answer at first. His shoulders tightened, his fingers curling into fists against the table. When his voice came, it was low and uneven.

"There was a merchant."

He kept his back to her, eyes fixed on the grains he had set down as though staring hard enough might erase them. "He was selling trinkets. Seashells, carvings. nothing dangerous. But the guards..." His throat caught, and he forced the words out. "They said it was magic. Accused him. Said there were reports against him."

His hand lifted, slicing through the air in a sharp motion. "They didn't even hesitate. Just—" He stopped, his jaw trembling before he set it hard again. "Cut him down."

Elaria stepped forward a pace, though she held her silence.

Caelan's words tumbled faster, his voice growing sharp. "No one moved. They stood there, watching. Turning away. And I... I just stood with them. I shouted for them to stop, but that was it. I didn't do anything. I let them..." His voice cracked, breaking beneath the weight of it.

At last he turned toward her, eyes glistening, anger rising fierce beneath the grief. "I could have stopped them. I felt it. The magic was there, ready, waiting. I could have done something!"

Elaria's gaze remained steady, her voice even. "But you didn't."

"Because you told me not to!" The words tore out of him before he could stop them. His breath caught in regret, but he didn't take them back.

"I did what you taught me to do," he pressed, his voice raw. "I buried it. I hid. I let them walk away like nothing had happened. And now he's gone. And I—" His chest heaved. "I hate it. I hate all of it."

Elaria did not flinch at the sharpness in his tone, she only starred at him. Her heart was broken that he had to endure this, but knew that he made the right decision.

"You wanted to act."

"Of course I did!" His voice broke, thick with anger and grief. "I had to."

"But you didn't."

Her certainty struck harder than any shout could have. Caelan spun from the table, pacing the narrow space, his fists clenched at his sides.

"Because I was afraid," he said, louder now, his voice straining. "Because you taught me to wait, to hide. To protect only when it's safe. But when is it ever safe, Mother? When will it ever be safe to do the right thing?"

Elaria's expression did not harden, nor did it soften. She held herself straight, her voice calm and firm. "I taught you to survive. Because the world beyond these trees does not care how noble your cause is. If you fall, you cannot help anyone."

Caelan's fists trembled, his whole frame taut with the fury he could no longer contain. "So what then? I'm meant to stand by and watch? To let them bleed and suffer while I keep my head down, waiting for some perfect moment that never comes?" His voice rose, filling the small cottage, rough and jagged with grief.

Elaria didn't retreat. Her composure was unshaken, steady.

"No," she said quietly. "I'm saying that one moment does not define you. Nor will it define the man you'll become."

Caelan turned away, dragging a sleeve across his eyes. The tears fought their way past anger, sharp and unwanted.

"I felt it," he muttered, softer now but no less fierce. "The magic. It was ready. I was ready."

Elaria stepped closer, her voice lowering though it carried the same weight. "And yet you held it back. That choice... the one that feels like failure now... was your first lesson in power. Not in using it, but in choosing not to."

Caelan shook his head hard, jaw tight. "It doesn't feel like wisdom. It feels like cowardice."

"It wasn't." Her hand rested lightly on his arm, grounding him. "You're angry because you care. That anger is not weakness, Caelan. It's the beginning of strength. But strength without purpose, without patience, without control..." She let the thought trail, her eyes never leaving his. "That becomes something else."

His gaze met hers, rimmed red, fierce and searching. "Then when? When do I stop waiting?"

Elaria studied him in silence, her presence as unyielding as stone. At last, she answered. "When you stop asking when."

The words landed, soft yet immovable.

The room settled into silence. The only sounds were the faint crackle of the hearth and the steady rhythm of Caelan's breathing as it slowly evened. He stood at the table with his hands pressed to the wood, staring at the supplies he had brought home. Grain. Salt. Fabric. Vials. Harmless things, ordinary things... yet they now felt like a cruel reminder of how small his actions had been compared to what had unfolded in the square.

He wasn't the boy who had left that morning. He wasn't the child who trailed after Elaria's step, who trusted the forest to be his shield. Something inside him had shifted, and he knew it would not shift back.

He turned slightly, catching the weight of Elaria's gaze. She had not moved from her place, her expression steady, waiting. He wanted to speak, to ask again, to argue, but the words would not come. His throat felt tight, his chest hollow.

So he said nothing.

Instead, he lowered himself into the chair by the table, staring at the supplies as though they belonged to someone else. The firelight flickered against the walls, painting the cottage in soft gold. Outside, the last of the daylight slipped through the trees, breaking across the glade in thin bars of fading light.

Caelan sat in the quiet, his heart heavier than the pack he had carried home. He was no longer a child, yet he was not ready to be the man the world demanded. Somewhere between the two, something had begun to awaken, and it would not be stilled.

CHAPTER SEVEN

UNDER THE RANGER'S TUTELAGE

A few weeks had passed since the incident in the village, but its weight still clung to Caelan. Elaria saw it in the way his fingers drummed against the table absentmindedly, in the way he stared out at the trees for longer than usual, lost in thoughts he wouldn't share. He carried himself differently now with his shoulders squared, steps more deliberate, and burdened by guilt and anger.

She had always known this day would come. The years she spent teaching him had been filled with lessons about balance, restraint, and wisdom. But there were things she could not teach him. Lessons that required a different hand.

One evening, she watched him from the cottage doorway as he moved through the clearing, practicing strikes with a wooden staff. A make-shift weapon that he had made from one of their broom handles. His movements were unfocused, driven by frustration more than any semblance of technique. He needed something more.

With a slow breath, she turned back inside, brushing her fingers over a parchment already sealed and bound with twine. The ink had dried hours ago, but the decision had settled in her heart long before she wrote the words. She looked over to Zoe, still casually lying on the chair after bringing the most recent letter from Clara.

"Zoe, dear... I have a letter for you to carry, but not to Clara," she said.

Zoe stirred, reaching out with her paws, stretching, and giving a huge yawn. She looked like she had been dreaming of being a panther on some distant adventure. Elaria just smiled and walked over to her.

"Please take this... You'll find him along the north-western paths of the mountains," she ordered Zoe, who gave an intriguing frill and waited for head scratches.

Elaria was reaching out to an old friend who could teach Caelan. She hadn't seen or talked to him in years, but if anyone could guide Caelan, it was him. The last time they had spoken, he had sworn he would never take another student. But Caelan wasn't just any student. And she had called in a favor he could not ignore. The letter outlined the details of a meeting. It would change everything. She only hoped that Caelan would be ready. Zoe meowed in acknowledgment, then jumped out the open doorway, disappearing into a sparkle of fairy lights that danced for a split second before vanishing completely.

The Elderwood stirred with life, birds flittering through the branches, chirping their melody that paired with the distant rustling of other creatures running around out of sight. Caelan followed close behind Elaria, his breath steady, though his mind raced with unspoken questions. He had noticed her unusual silence. She was seemingly lost in thought. She always hummed while they walked, but today's tune differed slightly. Not absentminded or lighthearted, but deliberate. Almost... solemn.

They had been walking for hours, weaving through narrow, winding trails he hadn't seen before. Then, the world opened before them. They stepped into a clearing where the sun broke through the tree canopy. Golden rays cascading in brilliant, shifting columns. The space felt untouched by time. Caelan took it all in. Why had she brought him here?

The silence in the clearing was momentary.

kree-eee-ar

The sharp cry split the air, cutting through the stillness like a blade. Caelan's gaze snapped upward just in time to see a hawk circling overhead. Its broad wings outstretched as it rode the air currents without effort. The bird tilted, banking into a slow descent, its golden-brown feathers catching the dappled light filtering through the canopy. Caelan followed its path, his eyes narrowing as it dove lower and lower. Then he saw him.

A lone figure stood at the center of the clearing, unmoving. As if the forest had conjured him from the shadows and earth. The hawk gave one final, powerful beat of its wings before landing gracefully upon the outstretched arm of the man below.

He stood tall and lean. His hair was a tousled mane of dark brown streaked with gray that fell just past his shoulders. A trimmed beard framed his weathered face, peppered with age and wisdom. There was a sharpness to the gaze in his green eyes.

His attire was built for the wilds. A dark green tunic, worn but well-kept. Leather bracers strapped to his forearms. Sturdy boots, laced up to his knees, bore the scuffs of years traveling paths. Draped over his shoulder, a mottled cloak of browns and greens shifted slightly with the breeze, a pattern made to disappear into the trees at a moment's notice.

A finely crafted sword rested in its sheath at his side, the leather-wrapped hilt well-worn from use, along with a bow and quiver, lay slung across his back. The hawk upon his arm ruffled its feathers before settling as if content.

Caelan glanced at Elaria. She met his gaze briefly, then returned to the man before them.

"Torin!" she greeted him, her voice calm but carrying a familiarity.

"You took your time walking through the woods, as always." He smirked as he turned to regard her.

Elaria stepped forward into the clearing. Caelan followed closely behind. His pulse quickened with anticipation. She stopped a few paces from the man.

"Caelan, this is Torin. An old friend from years past. He's lived as a ranger for many years. His skills are unmatched." She stated. "Torin has agreed to teach you."

Torin dipped his head slightly in acknowledgment. His sharp green eyes assessed Caelan.

"It is an honor to meet you, Caelan," he said at last, his voice carrying. "Your mother speaks highly of your potential."

Caelan swallowed nervously, with a bit of excitement building up in his chest. He straightened his posture before bowing respectfully.

"The honor is mine, Master Torin. I am ready to learn."

A flicker of amusement crossed Torin's face, the barest ghost of a smile tugging at his lips.

"We shall see," he said. "The path of the sword is not easy."

Something caught his attention briefly, and his eyes darted to the surrounding trees, pausing his sentence to determine what it was before returning to Caelan.

"But with dedication and an open mind, you will find the strength you never knew you had."

Elaria placed a reassuring hand on Caelan's shoulder.

"Listen well to Torin. His lessons will serve you in ways beyond the blade," she said.

Then, without another word, she turned and began walking back toward the forest path. Caelan watched her go, a flicker of hesitation rising within him before he exhaled, grounding himself. The clearing felt different now; its natural beauty was no longer just serene but charged with a feeling of anticipation.

He turned back to Torin, waiting for his first lesson to begin.

Just as the Elderwood began to stir each morning, Caelan would rise before the sun fully crested the horizon. The first light spilled through the trees, painting the clearing with a muted gold. The place had become his proving ground.

The clearing was surrounded by ancient trees, appearing to have moved out of the way for the training grounds. The ground was soft beneath his boots, a bed of moss and grass that easily cushioned his falls. The hush of the early hours was broken only by the distant calls of birds and the whisper of leaves shifting in the breeze.

Nestled at the wood line, a small camp lay undisturbed, save for the faint embers within the fire pit. A few tents, simple logs for seating, and a makeshift weapons rack stood.

Torin was always there first, though. When Caelan arrived each morning, his mentor had already prepared the day's training tools. He would wait near the sparring ring, his arms folded as he observed Caelan's approach. The sparring area was lined with stones and twigs to mark the boundaries. Their weapons for the day were laid out neatly: a pair of wooden swords.

They had not yet moved to steel. Torin had made it clear from the first lesson.

"The sword is more than metal and its keen edge," he said on the first morning, running his calloused hand down the blade of one of the training weapons. "Without control, it's just another tool for butchery."

He pointed the wooden blade to the ground as he finished the sentence.

"We will train with wood first. It's not to spare you but to teach you the weight of that control and discipline before we move on to something more... lethal," he continued.

The blades were dull wooden swords, but they would leave bruises, a painful lesson that Caelan had already learned firsthand.

Each morning before they sparred, Torin would lead Caelan through a relentless series of warm-up exercises. The routine never changed. They would run laps around the clearing, followed by stretching and calisthenics that burned his muscles before touching a sword. Push-ups, sit-ups, holding planks until his arms trembled. Caelan gritted his teeth, sweat forming along his brow as he pushed himself through another set. His body ached, his lungs burned, but he refused to quit. Torin's voice cut through the early morning air as they stretched.

"Every movement in fighting is an extension of your natural motion," he explained as he reached for his toes. "You must condition your body to enhance that motion, not fight against it."

Torin's methods were unyielding but never cruel. He did not tolerate weakness but never demanded anything beyond Caelan's potential.

"A tired body leads to a tired mind," he remarked as Caelan collapsed from a plank into the dirt, panting. "And a tired mind makes mistakes."

Torin crouched down beside Caelan, tapping a knuckle lightly against his temple. "Out there, one mistake can mean death."

Caelan exhaled sharply, then forced himself back onto his elbows, refusing to show defeat.

Only then did they finally turn to the sword. Torin handed Caelan his wooden blade and watched as he wrapped his fingers around the hilt.

"Grip it firm, but don't strangle it," he said, adjusting Caelan's hand slightly. "If your grip is too tight, you lose fluidity. If you hold it too loosely, you will lose control."

He stepped back, raising his own wooden sword.

"Your sword is your partner, an extension of your arm." Torin moved effortlessly, the blade gliding through the air as if it weighed nothing. "Learn its rhythm, and let it complement your own."

Caelan mimicked the movement, trying to copy the grace of his mentor. He felt the weight shift in his hands, the unfamiliar strain of muscles adjusting to the motion. Torin didn't let him rush.

Every morning, before they sparred, he would correct every grip, every stance, every motion until the sword felt like less of a burden and more of a part of him.

Torin believed in a holistic training approach, which Caelan began to understand with every grueling session. Every exercise was deliberate, building strength, agility, focus, endurance, and discipline.

The days turned into weeks.

The first few sessions had been grueling, but Caelan soon realized that the exhaustion never truly faded. His body simply learned to endure it. His muscles burned after every session, his arms trembling from endless repetitions, his legs unsteady from punishing footwork drills. Each morning, he woke with stiffness in his limbs, each movement a dull reminder of how far he had left to go.

And yet, Torin never allowed him to stop.

Caelan quickly learned that his mentor was relentless but not ruthless. Torin watched his progress with the sharp eye of a man who understood limits. He knew when to push, when to pull back, when to demand more, and when to allow recovery. If Caelan faltered too much, Torin would step back, reevaluate, and adjust the training regimen, ensuring growth without breaking him completely.

But there are days when it felt impossible.

One morning, under the heat of an unrelenting sun, Caelan's breath came in ragged gasps, his legs trembling beneath him. Sweat dripped from his brow, stinging his eyes, but he had no strength left to wipe it away. His wooden sword felt heavier than ever. Finally, his knees buckled, and he collapsed onto the mossy ground, panting.

"I ca... I can't do it," he gasped, his chest rising and falling rapidly. The weight of his fatigue crushed down on his body.

Torin approached, stepping into his line of sight. He didn't offer a hand. He didn't offer sympathy. His voice was firm but steady.

"You can, and you will," Torin stated simply.

Caelan clenched his fists in the dirt, his frustration simmering beneath exhaustion. Torin crouched slightly.

"Your body is stronger than you think. It's your mind that needs convincing," he continued.

For a long moment, Caelan stared at the ground, every fiber of his being telling him to stay down. But then, slowly, he forced his arms beneath him, pushing against the shaking protest of his muscles. Torin gave a slow nod.

"Drink some water," he said as he tossed Caelan a flask, "then get back up."

Caelan caught it clumsily, his fingers still unsteady, but he didn't hesitate. He drank, cool relief spreading through his parched throat. And he rose back up.

Caelan pushed through the pain. He had to. He learned to embrace the discomfort. To welcome the burn in his muscles and the ache in his bones. Every single bruise and sore limb was his proof of progress, not punishment. The pain was no longer an enemy. It was weakness leaving his body.

And yet, strength alone was not enough.

Torin was like the wind. His movement was swift and fluid, each motion an extension of the last. His footwork never faltered, his strikes never wasted movement. The way he handled the blade was effortless. Caelan, on the other hand, looked like a lumbering ox trying to dance.

His early attempts to mimic Torin's movements were a clumsy dance with two left feet. His swings were either too hesitant and lacking conviction or too forceful, wild, and unrefined. Every strike felt too late or too soon, and his footwork lagged behind his intent, making his movement jerky and uncoordinated.

Frustration became a constant companion.

The wooden sword felt like a stranger in his hands. It was too light, yet unwieldy, and an unbalanced extension of himself. He had imagined that wielding a blade would come naturally to him and that instinct would guide his movements. Instead, at this time, his instinct led him to mistakes. And mistakes meant bruises.

Torin watched in silence. His sharp gaze taking in every misstep, every flinch, and every wasted motion. He didn't interfere and didn't correct immediately. He was waiting to see if Caelan would adjust on his own. Torin's voice cut through the clearing like a blade when the boy hesitated on his next strike.

"Again," Torin stated.

A miscalculated step sent him stumbling forward. In an instant, Torin's blade struck his ribs with a solid crack. Pain exploded across his ribs, a deep, throbbing ache spreading through his side. His vision blurred for half a second, his breath coming in sharp gasps. He barely had time to register the sting before the next strike, a flick of Torin's sword against his wrist, jarring the wooden hilt from his fingers. It clattered against the mossy ground.

"Pick it up, ready your stance," Torin ordered, "again."

Caelan's grip tightened around the wooden sword, his arms aching, his breaths coming sharp and uneven. He had been at this for weeks. Long, grueling weeks of bruises, missteps, and failure. And today was worse than ever. Another miscalculated strike. Another sloppy movement. The sword felt like a dead weight in his hands, resisting him at every turn. Caelan hurled the blade to the ground with a frustrated growl, chest heaving.

"I'll never get this right!" he exclaimed, his voice cracked.

Torin stood still, watching him with the same patient intensity as always. He said nothing at first, letting the silence settle like a stone. Then, without a word, he bent down, picked up the fallen sword, and held it out.

"Perfection takes time, Caelan," he said steadily. "Every mistake is a lesson. You have to learn from them. Adjust and improve. That is the only way forward."

Caelan hesitated before reaching out to take the weapon back. His fingers curled around the hilt. Torin had said that phrase several times before, but today, it hit him differently. Slowly, something shifted.

The days passed, and though his frustrations did not vanish, something within him began to change. His grip on the sword became more natural, his stance more solid, his strikes less hesitant. The weight of the weapon no longer felt foreign in his hands. It was becoming a part of him. The clumsy swings, the wasted movements. Oh, they were still there, but much fewer now. And Torin saw it, too.

Each evening, when training ended, they would sit by the fire. The flames danced into the cool night air, with the occasional crackle accompanied by the distant hoot of an owl.

Caelan rubbed his sore wrists. The ache was deep but familiar now. Torin watched him for a moment before speaking.

"You're getting stronger, Caelan," he said simply while poking a stick into the fire, "keep it up."

Caelan looked into the flames. A slow breath escaped his lips, and for the first time, he believed it.

Caelan's confidence grew with each passing week. He looked forward to the challenges. No longer seeing them as obstacles meant to break him, but a measure of his growth.

He still stumbled, still miscalculated, but it was less often now. His movements were more measured, his instincts sharper. His muscles no longer screamed in protest but instead endured it. The swords, stances, and endless drills now became second nature.

Weeks turned into months.

Each morning, the rhythm of training had become ingrained in him. The footwork, the strikes, the sweat, the exhaustion, and the quiet satisfaction when it all came together. But the path of a swordsman was never linear. For every success, there was a failure. Some days, he moved with precision and control. On other days, he tripped over his own footing, giving in to frustration. Two steps back for every step forward.

And Torin took note of it all.

When he saw Caelan's improvements: footing steady, his reflexes sharpen, his strikes gain confidence. Torin would raise the stakes. The drills became faster. The sparring, harsher. Torin pushed him towards more advanced techniques. He began to show Caelan unpredictable maneuvers, feints, and counters that tested his reaction time.

On one crisp morning, a light mist clung to the forest floor as it curled around the bases of nearby trees. Caelan's frustration burned hotter than ever. His sword slipped from his sweaty grip again, falling to the ground.

"Why is this so difficult?" He burst out, throwing his hands up in exasperation. "I can't control my blade like you do!"

Torin picked up the fallen sword and handed it back to him, like he had done many times before.

"Caelan, you need to control your emotions." His voice was firm. "Your frustration is clouding your focus. The blade follows your arm, and your arm follows your mind. If you aren't right up here..."

Torin tapped a finger against Caelan's forehead.

"It won't matter what else we do." Torin continued.

He took a step back and gestured to Caelan to retake his stance.

"Let us try a different approach," he said, eyes steady. "Forget about trying to perfect each move. Let your emotions flow, but don't force them. And don't let them control you either."

Caelan took his stance. This time he hesitated less. Torin had slowed the pace. His movements were no longer sharp and punishing. They were fluid and deliberate. Caelan followed. At first, it felt strange and unnatural. But as he moved, something shifted. He stopped forcing the blade into position and stopped trying to fight against it. He let it move with him rather than trying to drag it into place.

The tension in his body eased. His breathing evened. His swings no longer felt like isolated actions but part of something more connected. Torin's eyes tracked his movement, and he gave a slow nod after a moment.

"Good," his voice held the rare approval, "now you're starting to understand."

Caelan slowed to a stop, his chest rising and falling, but no longer with frustration.

"Sometimes, letting go just a little can give you better control," Torin added.

Caelan felt the truth of those words for the first time, not just heard them.

As the sun climbed higher, filtering through the leaves and casting shifting patterns of gold and shadows across the clearing, Caelan felt something shift within him. Subtle at first. A flickering of understanding just beyond his grasp, but with each movement, it grew stronger.

The blade no longer felt like a separate weight in his hand. It wasn't something to wrestle into obedience. Instead, it moved with him. It was no longer an object to control but an extension of his intent. He flowed through the sequences. The rhythm of his strikes and footwork were no longer mechanical but instinctual. For the first time, it felt right.

Caelan's heart pounded with confidence. He executed a particularly complex maneuver he had fumbled through countless times before. This time though, was smooth. The sword sang through the air. As he landed the final step, his balance was firm. He exhaled in quiet amazement. A small smile broke through.

"This is it, isn't it?" he asked, turning to Torin.

Torin watched him for a moment, then returned the smile. Small, but genuine.

"Exactly," he replied, "you need to trust yourself as much as you trust your blade."

He tapped two fingers lightly against his own chest.

"Trust is key. Without it, the sword is just a piece of steel in your hands. With it, it's an extension of you."

Caelan turned his gaze back to his weapon. He felt for the first time that it was no longer separate from him.

Once Caelan made his breakthrough with the sword, Torin turned his focus to something even harder to master. Himself.

"The sword is only as steady as the hand that wields it," Torin said, "and the hand is only as steady as the mind behind it."

He had said this many times. Only recently did Caelan finally start to understand. Strength alone could not win battles. Torin taught Caelan to maintain focus under pressure, to read an opponent's movements before they struck, to react not out of fear or aggression, but from a calm and reasoned judgement.

"Clear your mind, Caelan," Torin instructed, "a cluttered mind is slow. And in battle, hesitation is fatal."

These lessons were conducted as the afternoon sun began to set.

Caelan resisted at first. His thoughts fought against the silence. His mind was plagued with flashbacks of his past failures. Haunted by the weight of his frustrations and the constant urge to move.

"Do not fight the thoughts," he said, "let them come. Acknowledge them and let them pass. Like ripples on water. Do not try to hold them. Just let them fade into the distance."

Caelan felt this was infuriating at first.

How could he do nothing? How could inaction be part of training?

But as the days passed by with each session, he finally began to understand. Letting his frustrations flow through him instead of chaining him down.

The following day, Torin drove him harder than ever. The drills were relentless. Footwork, counters, and feints. One after another, with no pause to catch his breath. The weight of his sword felt heavier than before, his muscles burned, his lungs strained. And Torin did not let up.

Every hesitation was punished. Every misstep is exploited. Caelan swung too slow. Torin's blade met his with a sharp crack, forcing his arm back. He adjusted, lunging forward... too reckless. Torin sidestepped and struck him hard across the ribs. His body ached, his vision blurred, and his mind screamed to stop.

"I'm not good enough." Caelan thought it was only internal, unbidden, it slipped past his lips in a breathless whisper. But Torin heard it.

The session halted. Torin stood still, his eyes were locked onto Caelan.

"What did you say?" his voice was quiet, but there was no mistaking the weight behind it.

Caelan swallowed. His body trembled with exhaustion.

"I'm not good enough," he repeated himself louder this time.

The words came out raw. Fueled with frustration and anger at himself... at everything. The moment lingered. Then, Torin stepped closer and placed a firm hand on Caelan's shoulder. Not to correct or guide but to ground him back to the training session. He was lost in his mind again.

"You are good enough, Caelan. But you have to believe it," his voice held no pity, no coddling, only the truth.

"No one can do that for you. Not me, Not Elaria, not anyone. You must find that belief within yourself," he continued.

Caelan's breath came slower now. Torin didn't move, didn't look away. And Caelan realized that this was the actual test. Belief in himself.

That evening, they sat by the firepit to rest and enjoy freshly caught fish cooked on skewers. The fire burned low and steady, casting flickering shadows across the clearing. All of their nights lately ended much like this. Caelan and Torin would take turns washing themselves in the nearby creek. Torin's hawk usually dropped several fish that it caught, hunting for its master. They would spend the rest of the night telling stories.

Caelan sat cross-legged near the flames. His body still ached from the day's training. Torin sat across from him and stared into the fire momentarily before speaking.

"When I was younger, there were times I didn't believe in myself either," he admitted.

The flames reflected in his sharp green eyes, making them seem older. They were wise and filled with memories that had long since healed into scars.

"It took me years to learn," Torin continued, "and many failures."

He poked the fire with a stick, stoking the embers, causing them to flare for a moment before settling again.

"More times than I care to count, I fell flat on my face. But I rose back up every time."

Caelan remained silent, but the words settled deep inside him. He had spent so much time fighting himself and energy wasted on doubt. But Torin didn't just tell him a story tonight; he was bearing the truth for him.

Failure wasn't what defined a warrior. Getting back up was. This was the lesson he needed most.

Caelan pushed himself harder, not just physically but mentally. Before the first stroke of a blade or the first step into a drill, he sat in stillness each morning. His eyes closed. He focused on his breathing. Counted each inhale, each exhale. His frustration never disappeared entirely, but he learned to control it.

Too often he found himself angry at simple mistakes. A misstep here. An unbalanced strike there. Fumbling his grip. But instead of lashing out or tightening his hold on the sword until his knuckles turned white, he forced himself to pause. To center himself. To let the moment pass before making adjustments and trying again.

The difference was undeniable. When his mind calmed, his body followed. But there were still days when doubt crept in, and he fumbled backwards. The connection between his mind and body had always been there. He had just never understood it before.

One evening, as they sat by the fire, Torin looked up as they ate. He stared at Caelan, taking a sip of water from his flask.

"You're getting stronger, Caelan," he stated with approval, "keep it up."

Caelan didn't respond right away. He looked down at his hands as he gently flexed his fingers as if measuring it for himself.

"Thank you," Caelan replied.

He no longer questioned whether he had the strength to continue. Now, he knew he did.

Caelan's confidence grew with each passing week. What he once felt impossible was now second nature. He welcomed the challenges. Torin never made training easy. Each session pushed him further than the last.

Instead of dreading the failures, Caelan learned to see them for what they were... mere stepping stones. It was always the tiny victories that meant the most.

A strike landed cleanly where he had once hesitated. A parry executed with perfect timing instead of second-guessing. The first time he sensed an attack coming before it arrived, his body reacted before his mind caught up. Those moments were his true milestones.

Months turned into years.

The changing seasons marked the passage of time in the Elderwood. Lush green summers gave way to the golden browns and yellows of autumn, then the sharp bite of winter's frost before the cycle began anew.

Caelan grew. The once awkward, unsure boy who had first held a wooden sword in his trembling hands was gone. In his place stood something more. Not yet a master. Not yet the warrior he aspired to be. But closer than before.

CHAPTER EIGHT

THE GHOST GIRL

Three years since Snowhaven...

The breeze carried a chill through the trees, sliding beneath Lysandra's threadbare cloak as she crouched at the edge of a narrow stream. The water wound across the forest floor like a ribbon of tarnished silver, its surface rippling faintly as pebbles shifted in the current. Dawn had not yet broken, but the light was coming—soft and grey, the kind that dulled every shape and drained the world of warmth.

Her fingers ached as she tightened the strap of her satchel and checked the knife at her hip. The hilt had worn smooth where her hand gripped it, its weight as familiar now as breath. Each motion came without thought, the repetition of habit long practiced, built into her bones by necessity rather than training.

She leaned forward, watching the water swirl in slow eddies around the stones. Her gaze held, but her mind slipped elsewhere.

She stared into the current, but the shapes of water and stone never settled into meaning. What she saw instead lived behind her eyes: the hollow stretch of time that marked the last three years. That was how long it had been since fire had devoured her home, since soldiers had dragged her mother away, since the world had closed its hand and crushed the girl she had been.

The weight of it lingered in her chest, heavier than hunger, sharper than the cold. She had not allowed herself to count the days after the first few seasons passed. Days were for children who believed tomorrow would be hopeful. For her, there had only been survival.

Her hands tightened briefly in her lap. She did not cry then, and she would not cry now. That girl—the one who could—was gone.

Lysandra reached for a flat stone beside her knee and flicked it across the water. It danced once, twice, three times before it sank, leaving only widening rings to fade downstream. She followed its path until nothing remained, then let her hand fall still again.

That was what they said about her now in taverns and along roadsides. The ghost girl. The one who listened but did not speak, who watched from the edges without stepping forward. They thought her less than she was, or perhaps more. A figure blurred by rumor, easier to whisper about than to know.

She welcomed it. Let them believe she was something other than a girl holding herself together with silence and stubbornness. The distance their stories gave her was safer than the reach of kindness or pity.

The scar on her left hand itched, a thin pale line that ran from the base of her thumb across the palm. She flexed her fingers, remembering the sting of the blade when it slipped months ago during a barter turned sour. The wound had bled freely, but she hadn't cried. Not because the pain was small, but because crying had long since become a luxury she couldn't afford.

Tears were for those who still believed someone might hear them. Warmth, safety, and softness... those belonged to another life. Survival demanded harder things. She had learned to swallow pain and carry it forward, just as she carried the scar.

Her lips were dry and cracked. She wet them absently with her tongue, then pulled her hood lower against the cold that threaded through the trees.

A wolf's call drifted through the valley, long and low, carrying over the trees until it broke into silence. The sound seemed to empty the air itself, leaving a stillness so complete it pressed against her ears. Lysandra drew her cloak tighter, listening to the quiet that followed, the kind of quiet that swallowed everything whole.

She closed her eyes and let the stillness settle over her. To survive was to match it, to learn how to move without sound, to listen without being seen. The world had not grown quieter over the years, she had simply stopped reaching for its voice. Silence was her shield now.

Stay silent. Survive. The words echoed like an old commandment etched into her bones.

With the silence came memory, sudden and unbidden. She smelled crushed lavender, saw the pattern of wooden floorboards in her childhood home, and felt her mother's hand press firmly against the back of her neck, guiding her toward the narrow nook where the shadows would hide her.

The image rose sharp and clear, but Lysandra forced it back. That moment belonged to another girl, one who had still believed she could be kept safe, one who had not yet learned that safety was a word meant for other people.

Her eyes opened to the cold light of the forest. She adjusted the strap of her satchel, testing its weight, grounding herself in the present. Dreams had no place here.

Three years prior...the morning after...

She stood slowly, joints stiff from the ground's bite, and studied the tangle of underbrush ahead. Somewhere beyond the dark ferns and bramble lay the road, a pale ribbon that promised speed and exposure in equal measure. She kept to the trees. Their shadows were not friendly, yet they were honest. They hid what they hid and asked for nothing in return.

Her stomach complained often, but she tried to ignore it and kept moving.

The first night after Snowhaven had taught her what the cold could take. It crept through cloth and skin and settled in the hollows of bone, and once it settled, it did not hurry to leave. Branches clawed at her shins as she pushed deeper. Breath rasped in short clouds, loud to her own ears. She did not know where the path would lead. She only knew she could not stop. The satchel thumped against her hip in a clumsy rhythm. She had packed it in haste, because there had been no time for care: a flask, a few bundles of herbs, a threadbare cloak, and the knife.

Her mother's knife.

It rode the satchel's side pocket in its sheath, always within reach. She had never carried it for protection before. Her mother kept it bright and clean and used it for small, exacting tasks. A sprig cut here. A charm shaved thin there. Now it belonged to Lysandra, and that changed what it meant. If she failed to defend herself, no one would step between her and harm. The truth sat plain in her chest and did not argue.

When the shaking in her knees grew worse than the ache in her calves, she slid down by a long-dead log and folded herself tight. The cloak had no more warmth to give. Damp earth breathed against her cheeks. The dark closed in with the patience of a hand that knew it would win.

She did not sob. Tears came quiet and hot through the grit on her skin. She tasted salt and loam and said the words that had formed without her permission. "Stay silent," she whispered. "Survive." The phrase held. She repeated it until the cold thinned her voice and the tremor in her limbs wore itself out. Sleep did not welcome her; it took her anyway.

The ground had no mercy. It drank warmth faster than the wind ever could. Lysandra woke curled beneath the roots of a crooked tree that jutted from the slope like bones pressing through skin. The shallow alcove gave little shelter. It was just enough to blunt the worst of the night air, but never enough to keep the damp from seeping into her clothes. Her cloak clung heavy with moisture, and each movement sent a shiver from her shoulders to her fingertips.

She rubbed her palms together until the friction stung, but her fingers stayed stiff and red. They no longer bent with ease, scraped raw from branches she had clutched during her flight. Bruises lined her shins from hidden roots she had tripped over in the dark. Every part of her body bore proof that the forest did not care if she lived through the night.

The forest had changed once the sun fell. By day it had been a maze of branches and undergrowth. By night it became something larger with trees closing ranks above her, leaning inward as though to listen. Bark creaked in the wind, leaves fluttered with unseen wings, and every sound begged to be an enemy. She told herself it was only the woods. She did not believe it. Shapes swam in the corners of her sight. Men behind trunks. Wolves in the brush. Shadows that bent the wrong way.

She stayed still. Stillness was the only weapon she could trust.

When a squirrel scurried across the leaves nearby, the sound shattered her calm. Her heart lurched into her throat. She had grabbed the knife and held it tighter. The sheath had trembled in her hands, yet the weight of it steadied her. At least she was holding more than fear.

Her stomach cramped, sharp enough to double her over. She pressed a fist to her abdomen, fighting back the pain. She had packed nothing proper to eat. Feverfew and herbs had their uses, but they did not fill her belly. The dried meat was gone now. The single piece of bread she carried had hardened to stone. She gnawed at its edge anyway, chewing until her jaw ached and forcing it down like punishment. Hunger was not a foe that listened to reason.

For a moment she shut her eyes and tried to picture home. Wooden floors warmed by the hearth. The soft clatter of bottles as her mother sorted them. The smell of lavender from the bedroll. She held the memory close, but the damp earth pressed harder. The forest's breath smelled of mildew and moss. When she opened her eyes, the illusion broke. Her mother was gone, and the home in Snowhaven was ash.

She reached into her satchel and drew the knife. Moonlight slipped through the branches above, catching the steel in broken flashes. The blade was simple, its handle worn smooth where her mother's fingers had worked over years of use. Lysandra turned it slowly, thumb tracing the grooves in the hilt. It did not feel heavy, though she expected it to. She clung to it all the same, as if its edge might cut away the loneliness crowding her chest.

Her eyes grew heavy. She curled tighter beneath the root arch, the knife pressed flat to her sternum, and let exhaustion win the fight her body could no longer carry.

The night bled into morning with no gentleness. Damp mist crept between the trees, carrying the sharp scent of pine and wet soil. Lysandra stirred, every joint stiff, her body curled as though the cold had shaped her into its own likeness. For a moment she did not remember where she was. She reached instinctively for the hearth that should have been at her back, for the warmth that should have wrapped her. Her fingers closed instead around damp roots and the hard hilt of the knife.

She drew her knees to her chest, arms wrapped tight, and let the knife rest across her lap. The steel was dull in the pale light, but it caught her eye with every breath. It was proof. Proof that she was still here. Proof that she could hold on.

She whispered the words again, the ones she had claimed in the dark. "Stay silent. Survive." The phrase steadied her like roots gripping soil. It gave shape to the air in her lungs, to the trembling in her fingers. She repeated it until her voice rasped into nothing.

When at last she rose, the girl who had fled Snowhaven did not rise with her. She left that child among the roots, folded into the damp earth. What stepped forward was thinner, hungrier, but sharpened by loss. Each step carried her farther from who she had been and closer to something she did not yet recognize.

The forest opened a narrow path ahead, uncertain and wild. She gripped the satchel, adjusted the knife at her side, and walked into it.

By the third day, hunger had settled into her body like a sickness. It dried her mouth, hollowed her belly, and left a bitterness clinging to the back of her throat. Every step felt slower. Every thought came with the dull weight of ache. Still, she forced herself down toward a stream she had heard before dawn, the faint trickle carrying through the trees like a promise.

She crouched at its bank, knees sinking into mud. The water moved sluggishly, catching light in broken ripples. Silver flashes darted beneath the surface... Fish! She had broken a branch and shaved it to a crude point with her mother's knife, holding it low now as though it were a spear fit for a hunter.

Her eyes tracked the movement. She stilled her breath, teeth biting the inside of her cheek until blood rose, sharp and metallic. Pain kept her awake. Focused.

A ripple disturbed the surface. She struck hard, driving the sharpened stick downward. The crack of wood against stone snapped through the clearing, loud enough to startle birds into flight. The fish scattered in a blur of silver shadows.

Her hands shook as she lifted the broken stick. Splinters bit her palm. She let it fall into the water and hissed through her teeth. It was the first sound she had made aloud in two days.

Her stomach answered with a knot of pain, curling her forward. She staggered back from the stream and pressed both arms to her middle, fighting the urge to cry out. There was no one to hear. No one who would care if they did.

She sat heavily on the bank, wiping sweat from her brow with a sleeve already stiff from mud and rain. Above, a squirrel scolded from the safety of a high branch. The chatter rang shrill in her ears. Without thinking, she scooped a stone and hurled it. It clattered harmlessly against bark and thudded into the underbrush. The animal was gone before the stone even landed.

Her breath shuddered. The scream that built in her chest never left her throat. She swallowed it down with the same discipline she had given her tears. Outbursts wasted strength she didn't have.

Pushing back to her feet, she followed the stream a little farther until the bank widened into a patch of reeds. Her eyes caught on the familiar shape of cattails. Her mother had spoken of them once. The roots were edible if stripped and cleaned. She dug one free, rinsed it in the current, and hesitated. The smell was foul, earthy and sour. Hunger left her no choice. She peeled away the mud-stained layers and bit into the pale stalk within.

The taste was bitter, fibrous. She forced herself to chew until her jaw ached, then swallowed. The cattail did not ease the hunger, but it kept her standing. That was enough.

She pulled more from the bank, laying them in her satchel. Not plenty. Never plenty. Just enough to carry her through the day.

By the time she dragged herself back to the shelter of a fallen tree, the light had begun to fade. She laid the cattail roots on a flat rock to dry, their pale stalks dull against the grey bark. Her stomach grumbled at the sight, but she forced herself to leave them. Hunger gnawed, but desperation had to wait.

She broke another branch and began to carve it down, her knife biting awkwardly into the bark. The steel slipped, too quick for her tired grip. A sting flared across her palm. She dropped the wood, clutching her hand tight as blood welled along the shallow cut.

For a moment she only stared, her chest rising fast. The wound was small, but the sight of red spilling from her own hand seemed larger than it should have been. Her eyes burned. Not from pain—though it stung sharply—but from how foolish it felt, how helpless.

She pressed her sleeve to the cut until the fabric darkened. Then, with clumsy fingers, she tore a strip free and bound it as best she could. The knot came loose twice before it held. Each time her frustration climbed higher, her throat tightening, until at last she forced it steady.

When the trembling eased, she turned to the circle of stones she had built earlier. A fire meant warmth. A fire meant safety. She gathered what little she had seen her mother use: scraps of birch bark, bits of moss, twigs small enough to snap between her fingers and flint. She struck her knife against the flint, spark after spark, smoke rising only to gutter and die.

Her first attempt failed. So did the second. And the third. Her eyes blurred with fatigue, but she kept striking. Her hands stank of blood and sap, and still she pressed on.

On the fourth try, a single ember kissed the bark. The moss caught, faint at first, then growing into a thin flame. She shielded it with her body, feeding it slivers of twig until the light grew strong enough to stand on its own.

Lysandra sat back, watching the fire climb in flickers. The glow painted the bark around her in shades of gold and shadow. The cold did not vanish, but it bent beneath the warmth.

She sat for hours without moving, her face lit by the flames. The forest pressed in as it always had, vast and indifferent, but the shadows no longer swallowed her whole. For the first time since running, she felt the smallest thread of control.

The cut still throbbed. Her stomach still ached. Yet the fire burned. And for that night, it was enough.

Morning came grey and damp. Mist pooled in the hollows of the forest, and the fire she had nursed through the night smoldered in faint embers. Lysandra crouched beside it, her satchel open, her mother's knife resting across her palms. She unwrapped it from the cloth she kept dry against her chest, smoothing the folds with deliberate care.

Each morning she touched its edge, tracing the line with her thumb. She did not press hard enough to bleed. She only needed to feel its presence, to remind herself that something of her mother still remained. That ritual gave rhythm to days that had none.

The first time she used it in truth was to clean a fish she had trapped in a shallow pool with a ring of stones. The fish was small and her inexperience made a mess of the work. She cut too deep, tore the skin in jagged strips, wasted more than she saved. The smell turned her stomach, and when she burned it over a weak fire, the meat tasted of ash and bitterness. She forced every bite down, gagging against the taste, because she could not afford waste.

That night she sat before the flames, knife balanced across her knees. It did not feel like a weapon. It felt like a tether. Each time her hand closed around the hilt, she remembered who had carried it before her, and she refused to let go.

In the days that followed, she carved branches with slower, steadier strokes. She mimicked the way her mother's wrist once turned, shaving thin curls of bark without wasting the wood beneath. Her grip improved. Her hands steadied. Each cut was cleaner than the last.

When she began moving again, she marked her path with the blade. Small notches in bark. Scratches at the base of stones. Shapes that meant nothing to anyone but her—triangles for safe camp, half-circles for danger, a simple slash for places she had traded or scavenged. None of it was meant as protection. It was a rhythm, a way of proving she had passed through and endured. A story written in secret, one only she could read.

One evening, she found a grove dry enough to linger. She laid the knife in her lap and took time to polish it properly. A torn scrap of linen wiped the steel until it caught the firelight. The worn handle warmed beneath her touch.

The first sign of the camp was the faint smell of smoke, lingering in the damp air like a memory. Lysandra slowed her steps and pressed herself into the cover of the trees, watching the clearing ahead. A ring of stones marked the remains of a fire, the coals faintly warm even though the flames had long since died. A tarp sagged between two branches where rain had stretched the rope thin, and beneath it rested a pack, left careless in the open.

The place looked abandoned, but not long enough to be safe. Whoever had kindled that fire might still be close, just beyond sight, and she knew better than to mistake silence for safety. Hunger, however, had its own persuasion. Days of gnawing emptiness pulled at her ribs, and her cloak was still heavy with the damp that no fire of hers could drive away. That pack might hold food, or cloth, or even the tools of fire-starting her mother had once taken for granted.

She crouched at the tree line and watched. A bird called once and went still. The leaves shifted with the wind, but no voice carried across the clearing, no boot struck the ground. She waited until her legs grew sore from holding still, then gathered her resolve and stepped forward.

Her movements were cautious, each foot placed with care, but every sound seemed too loud. The brush of grass against her ankles. The creak of leather straps as her satchel shifted. Even the rasp of her breath felt as though it might give her away. She reached the pack and laid her fingers on the flap, the rough fabric prickling beneath her touch.

The crack of a branch split the quiet.

She turned sharply, heart hammering.

At the edge of the clearing stood a man. His cloak was patched and frayed, his beard wiry, and though a smile touched his mouth, his eyes were sharp. He did not rush toward her. He simply stepped forward, deliberate and easy, as though he had already decided the outcome.

"Well now," he said, his voice thick with bile and ill intent. "You've got nerve, creeping into a camp that isn't yours."

Lysandra did not answer. Her hand slid closer to the knife at her side, the hilt already familiar beneath her palm.

He lifted one hand in mock reassurance, his grin widening. "No need for that, girl. Cold nights are easier with company. I've got a firepit, you've got a spark in your eyes. Why not share a little warmth?"

Another step brought him closer. The distance between them felt thinner than it was.

His gaze flicked toward her satchel. "Or is it the pack you're after? Looking to steal what isn't yours? I could show you how to earn it properly. How to use that knife for more than trembling."

His words were almost gentle, but his eyes betrayed the promise behind them. Then, without warning, he lunged.

The lunge came faster than she thought. His hand reached for her cloak, fingers outstretched to seize and pull. Instinct, sharper than hunger or fear, tore through her. Lysandra's arm moved before her mind caught up, the knife drawn and driven forward with the full force of her trembling body.

The blade struck low, sliding beneath his ribs. A startled gasp burst from him, wet and ragged, as though the air itself betrayed him. He staggered back, eyes wide, one hand clutching the wound while the other reached toward her in disbelief.

"You little—" The words broke into a cough, dark spittle flecking his lips. He turned clumsily, stumbling into the trees. Branches tore at his cloak as he vanished into the undergrowth, his retreat marked only by the heavy sound of breath and the smear of blood left behind.

Lysandra stood rooted to the clearing, the knife still in her grip, crimson sliding down the hilt and pooling at her wrist. Her chest heaved with shallow, desperate gasps. The clearing seemed to tilt, her vision narrowing to the blood on her hand and the weight of the blade she no longer recognized.

Her knees buckled, and she collapsed beside the firepit. The knife slipped from her fingers, clattering against stone. A sharp wave rose in her throat, and she bent forward, retching until bile burned her tongue. Her body convulsed again, leaving her weak and shaking.

She wiped her mouth on her sleeve, eyes blurred, breath ragged. The silence pressed in heavier than before. She did not feel safer. She did not feel stronger. She felt emptied, as though the strike had hollowed something from within her. She had taken a life.

When she could move again, she forced herself to the pack. Inside she found a cloak heavier than her own, thick with the smell of sweat and smoke, and boots that hung loose on her feet but promised warmth her thin shoes could no longer give. She pulled them on with numb fingers. They fit poorly, but they would keep her alive.

Alive. The word felt sharp and cruel. She had taken that from him to claim it for herself. Not because she wanted to, but because he gave her no choice.

The blood, though, would not wash away.

The days that followed carried her across hills stripped bare by frost and through woods that thinned into cart-trails, half forgotten by trade. She kept her hood low, her eyes lower still, moving at a pace meant to draw no notice. The road itself was too open, yet the villages it led toward offered no safety either.

From the treeline she studied them first, letting her gaze sweep over rooftops and smoke plumes before she dared draw close. Some were little more than clusters of thatch and stone, others larger with markets and guards at the gates, but they all bore the same silence once she stepped within. Conversations broke apart when she neared. Children stared with wide eyes until pulled sharply back indoors. Doors closed a heartbeat too quickly. The hush followed her like a shadow.

In Gladecross she felt it strongest. The streets were swept clean, the windows shuttered even at midday, the air carrying a stillness that set her teeth on edge. Children played in muted gestures, their laughter pressed down as though joy itself were forbidden. The adults spoke only in whispers, their eyes sliding over her and away again, never meeting for long.

She passed one cottage with a dark brand burned into its lintel. It was not random fire damage but deliberate markings seared deep into the grain. She knew the crest. It had hung in Snowhaven, stamped in bright color above the garrison doors. Here it was smaller, cruder, but no less heavy with meaning: the sign of the king.

Farther on she found books smoldering in a heap behind a house, pages curling into ash. No one tended the fire. No one dared watch. The smell clung to her cloak as she walked on, sharp and acrid, a scent that belonged more to memory than to the present moment.

As time went on in her journeys, other villages gave no better welcome. She learned to lower her hood farther, to let her silence deepen. It unsettled them. If silence was what they feared, then silence was what she would become.

The deeper she traveled, the clearer the shape of things became. This was not chance. It was not a scattering of cruelty left unchecked. The marks, the burnings, the silence—they carried design. The kingdom had teeth, and they were bared.

South of Hollowmere the trail wound along a ridge where farmland once stretched in tidy rows. Now the fields lay untended, fences sagging, weeds climbing unchecked. At the edge of one pasture, nailed to the trunk of a weathered oak, she found the notice.

The parchment had soaked through with rain, the ink smudged but still legible.

"By order of King Aldric: All unlicensed healers and peddlers of enchanted goods shall be detained for questioning. Resistance shall be met with force."

The words clung to her longer than they should have. She did not need them explained. Snowhaven had already given her the lesson. The silence of the villages, the shuttered windows, the marks seared into doorframes—all of it began to weave into the same thread.

When she passed through the next hamlet, she watched with sharper eyes. In the market square a woman stood bound to a post, her sleeves torn to bare her arms while a soldier's whip cracked against her back. Her crime was spoken in a single word—"tinctures"—and nothing more. The villagers did not intervene. They bowed their heads, bodies stiff with fear, as though looking up might draw the lash to them instead.

Lysandra did not stop. She turned her hood lower and walked on, the sound of the whip carrying after her until distance dulled it.

At wells and crossroads, she began to linger just beyond the edge of notice. Words traded in low voices told her what proclamations never could. A woman's son taken in the night, accused of muttering spells into the iron he forged. A shop set alight because a parchment within bore markings mistaken for runes. Books piled in squares and burned to ash under banners stitched with the king's crest.

She listened. She remembered. And she learned. The kingdom was not losing itself to chaos. It was being cut, piece by piece, into silence by the king's men.

Lysandra kept to the margins where words slipped more freely. At market stalls she lingered near the backs of crowds, her eyes on the wares while her ears strained for the murmurs exchanged between neighbors. In taverns she chose the darkest corners, hood drawn low, sitting so still she became little more than another shadow against the wall. Silence made her forgettable, and forgettable meant safe.

It was never the loud voices that carried the truth. Loudness was for show, a bluff spoken to convince the speaker as much as anyone else. The truths lived in whispers—fragile, fleeting things that carried more weight than any decree.

At a well in a crossroads town she saw a woman clutch a satchel passed swiftly into her hands by a man. Someone muttered nearby, low enough to escape notice but not her ears, "The blacksmith's wife. They took her last week. Said she was enchanting the tools."

Another day she hid in the cellar of a tavern, tucked behind barrels where mold clung to the wood. Two laborers bent close over a guttering candle stub, voices hushed to nearly nothing.

"They burned it all," one whispered. "Said there were books. I saw them...just trade documents, old recipes."

"Doesn't matter," the other answered. "It was a message. Ash doesn't argue."

Every story told the same thing in different words. People did not need to be silenced with chains. Fear was sharper, and rumor spread faster than soldiers. The king did not need to speak to remind his people of his reach. The uncertainty was enough. Anyone could be listening. Anyone could be next.

When she crossed the low ridges that bordered another farming village, she could feel the weight of it in every glance cast her way. People turned from her not only because she was a stranger, but because silence had become their shield. They were practiced at looking away, at lowering their heads, at erasing anything that might draw notice. Fear had become routine, a discipline as familiar as breathing.

The realization carried no comfort. It stripped away what little hope she had left that these were isolated cruelties, accidents of chance or malice left unchecked. The truth was far colder. The rot had spread too evenly, the signs too familiar. The hand behind it was steady.

Lysandra clenched her fists inside the cloak. She pulled it tighter around her shoulders and kept walking. The road ahead was no straighter than the ones behind. It wound through woods and villages alike.

Suddenly, the air thickened with the taste of iron and damp earth, heavy against her tongue, and the wind carried the smell of rain before the clouds broke. Lysandra glanced upward and found the sky already swollen with darkness, the horizon swallowed by rolling masses of grey. Dusk came early, lowering the light to a bruised dim.

The first drops struck her cheek as she crested a muddy rise. Then the storm fell in earnest. Rain sheeted across the land, cold and punishing, soaking her cloak within moments. Her boots filled with slush that squelched at every step. She tried to hold her pace steady, but the ground turned slick beneath her and sent her stumbling more than once.

The trees thinned as she neared the next village. Daggerfall was little more than two dozen buildings clustered together like livestock huddled against wind. No walls, no watchtower, only thatched roofs hunched low, lamplight struggling against the storm behind warped panes of glass.

She did not risk the main road, it was too open... too visible. Instead she cut behind a weathered barn that leaned with age, its back fence sagging under ivy and rain. The door hung crooked, warped from seasons of rot, but when she pushed it open, the hinges gave way with only a muted groan.

The smell struck her first: wet hay, animal musk, and the faint sourness of mold. It was no hearth, no home, but it was shelter from the weather. She climbed the ladder into the loft, her limbs trembling from exhaustion, and collapsed into the hay. The damp clung even here, but the weight of the storm on the roof above made the loft feel almost enclosed, a fragile pocket carved from the fury outside.

Her fingers fumbled with the satchel buckle, clumsy from cold, before she dragged it against her chest and curled around it. Water dripped from the edge of her hood onto her nose. A rat scurried somewhere in the straw, but she was too tired to care.

Lightning flashed through the gaps in the planks, throwing the loft into stark relief. Thunder rolled a moment later, a deep crack that shook the rafters and seemed to echo in her chest. She shut her eyes tight, her face buried against her arm.

Sleep finally hit her the way storms do...all at once, swallowing everything in its path. The storm had softened by the time she stirred again. Rain still tapped a steady rhythm on the roof, but the thunder had drifted farther off, its voice muffled and tired. The loft smelled of damp hay and mildew, and her cloak clung heavy against her skin. She blinked blearily, her cheek pressed to the straw, and for a moment thought she was alone.

Then she heard the soft creak of the barn door opening below. Her body tensed. She stayed still, listening. Footsteps pressed lightly into the straw. They were careful steps, measured and slow, but not heavy. Not a man's stride. Smaller. Younger.

The ladder groaned once. Twice. A face appeared at the edge of the loft, framed by a curtain of tangled blonde hair. A girl, no more than eleven, peered up with wide eyes. She did not climb all the way, only enough to see. In her hands she held a bundle wrapped in cloth.

"I brought you something," the girl whispered. Her voice was thin but steady. "It isn't much."

Lysandra said nothing. Her fingers had already found the knife's hilt, though she did not draw it.

The girl waited, then set the bundle gently on the edge of the loft and backed down the ladder. She crouched at the bottom, her eyes never leaving Lysandra.

At last, Lysandra pulled the bundle close. Inside were two small rolls of bread, hard but still edible, and a strip of dried meat. The smell of salt reached her first, real and undeniable. She hesitated only long enough to test the meat with a cautious bite. It was bitter and tough, but safe. Hunger won the rest. She devoured both pieces quickly, her stomach protesting with sharp cramps even as relief washed through her.

When she looked down, the girl was still watching.

"What's your name?" the child asked softly.

Lysandra kept her silence.

"That's all right," the girl said quickly. "You don't have to tell me. My name's Tana." She hugged her shawl tighter around her shoulders, small legs folded beneath her. "My father says you're a ghost. That people like you walk the roads at night and don't speak because they've forgotten how."

Lysandra's eyes narrowed slightly, but Tana's smile was soft, un-mocking.

"I don't think you're a ghost," she added. "I think you're just alone. Like me, sometimes."

The wind rattled the barn doors. Tana stood, glancing toward the village. "They'll notice if I'm gone too long. If you're still here tomorrow... I'll come back."

She slipped through the crooked door as quietly as she had come, leaving nothing but the faint warmth of her presence behind.

Lysandra sat in the loft, the taste of bread still lingering, the meat heavy in her belly. For the first time since Snowhaven, she felt something other than hunger and fear. Kindness had not vanished entirely; it wore a small shawl with messy blonde hair.

Chapter Nine

SILENT VOWS

The barn was quiet when she woke, the air damp with the smell of straw that had soaked through during the night. Pale light crept between the warped boards in thin silver lines, cutting across the loft and setting the dust drifting like ash caught in a slow current. Lysandra stayed still for a long time, her cheek pressed to the hay, listening for any sound that might mean she was not alone. No step on the ladder, no murmur of a girl's voice, no rustle of a bundle being set down. The silence was complete, and in that silence she understood what her body had already suspected—Tana had not come back.

She pushed herself upright, stiff from the damp, and let her gaze fall to the folded bread cloth resting beside her satchel. The fabric was rough beneath her fingertips when she touched it, and though it carried nothing more than crumbs, she kept it close, unable to discard the one small token of kindness she had been given. Hunger pressed at her ribs, urging her down from the loft, but she lingered as though patience itself might call the child back. Only when the sunlight stretched fully across the rafters did she move, slinging the satchel over her shoulder and descending the creaking ladder.

Outside, the village was already waking. She kept to the shadows behind a crooked shed, her cloak still damp and heavy on her shoulders, and from there she heard voices rising softly near the well. Two women stood with their heads bowed close, the words they traded too quiet for most ears, but Lysandra had learned to listen for fragments.

"...taken last night. Just gone."

"No warning?"

"None. Her mother found the back door open. No sign of struggle. Like the wind itself carried her away."

Lysandra's stomach tightened before her mind could form the name. Tana.

"She was always too curious," one of the women muttered, arms folding tight against the morning chill. "Always looking where she shouldn't."

"Poor thing," the other whispered. "And so young."

Their voices trailed away as they lifted their buckets and moved toward the square, leaving only the faint echo of their words hanging in the air. Lysandra did not follow. She pressed herself against the boards of the shed until the sound of them was gone, then straightened slowly, her hood shadowing her face. She had no tears left for the truth they carried. Instead, she turned back toward the overgrown field and walked the path she knew would lead her once more to the barn.

The path back to the barn felt heavier with every step, the field bending around her legs and the leaning fence marking the way as though she were retracing a line she wished had never been drawn. When she reached the crooked doorway she paused, one hand resting on the weathered frame, listening to the silence inside as if it might somehow deny what she had overheard at the well. The quiet was unchanged, thick and unmoving, and she knew the truth would not be undone.

She climbed to the loft and sat in the place where Tana's face had first appeared, the boards holding only emptiness now. Her satchel lay at her side, and after a time she reached into it and drew out a bundle of dried feverfew, the stems brittle and pale from weeks pressed together but still whole enough to carry meaning. Her mother had once said the flowers could ease grief, though Lysandra had never known if that was true. Belief mattered less than the gesture, and she understood that even if the blossoms could do nothing for the ache in her chest, they could still serve as a marker of what had been lost.

She tied the stalks with a scrap of twine and carried them back down the ladder, her boots whispering against the worn rungs. At the threshold she knelt and placed the bundle across the sill, arranging it carefully so that it would be the first thing seen by anyone who entered. Already the petals had begun to curl, their white fading at the edges, but she did not move to reclaim them. Some offerings were meant to wilt. That was their truth.

Standing again, she lowered her hood and looked once more at the flowers lying fragile in the draft. They would not last long; by midday they would droop, and by nightfall they would be nothing more than husks scattered by the wind. The village would forget. The world would continue as if the girl had never been. But Lysandra would remember, and that had to be enough.

With her satchel strap tight across her shoulder, she turned from the barn and walked into the pale light of morning, leaving the feverfew behind as both grave and promise.

By midday the path bent away from the village and carried her into a stretch of woods that thinned to scrub and open ground. The air smelled of damp earth, sharp with pine resin, and the sky had begun to clear in uneven patches, letting pale sunlight fall in broken shafts across the ruts of the trail. When the track split at a fallen milestone—two narrow roads leading in different directions—she stopped.

The fork was unmarked. To the east the ground dipped toward the lowlands, the air there carrying the faint sweetness of meadow grass. To the south the trees closed in again, darker and less certain, a wall of branches that swallowed sight after only a few paces. Either way led away from the barn, away from the name she had left behind in silence. She stood between them for a long time, weighing nothing but the ache in her legs and the steady pull of habit that told her to avoid what others might choose.

It did not matter which way she walked. Roads rarely gave what they promised.

At the edge of the clearing lay a dead tree, its bark split and its heart hollowed by rot. Lysandra knelt beside it and pulled her knife free from the satchel. The hilt felt smooth in her palm, the steel dull but familiar, and she pressed the edge against the trunk until it bit into the wood. Slowly, carefully, she carved a triangle and scored it through with a vertical line. The mark meant nothing to anyone but her, yet she cut it with deliberate care, the motion steady enough to feel like ritual.

When she leaned back the symbol stood dark against the pale bark, a shape that would outlast her passing. She touched it once with her fingertips, then slipped the knife back into its cloth and rose. Whatever lay ahead, the tree now held proof that she had stood here, had chosen, had continued.

She stood for a moment longer at the edge of the clearing, the breeze tugging faintly at her hood and carrying the scent of wet leaves. The mark she had carved stared back at her from the dead tree, stark against the pale wood, a quiet defiance etched where no one might ever see it. That was enough. She did not need witnesses; she only needed to know that something of her remained, even if the forest swallowed her whole.

Her breath clouded in the cool air as she adjusted the strap of her satchel across her shoulder. The path southward narrowed quickly, roots breaking through the soil like ribs and branches clawing low across her hood, but she welcomed the cover. The road east might have been easier, but ease invited notice. The woods offered concealment, and concealment meant survival.

She took one last look at the carved symbol, then turned from it without hesitation. The knife's weight pressed steady against her side, a reminder of choices made and carried forward. The dead tree would hold her mark until rain and time wore it away. By then she would be far from this place, leaving other signs in other corners of the kingdom.

The fork fell behind her as she disappeared beneath the canopy, her boots soft in the loam, her figure absorbed by the shadows of the forest.

The forest gave way to a scattering of fields that looked as though they had been left to grow wild. Stone walls sagged under creeping ivy, and moss clung thick to the timbers of outbuildings that leaned with age. At first glance the place seemed abandoned, but as Lysandra drew nearer she saw thin trails of smoke rising from chimneys and the faint movement of figures in doorways.

The village had no gate, no posted name, no guards to measure strangers at its edge. Homes hunched low to the ground, their thatched roofs held fast with stones, shutters faded but open to the light. There was no sound of hammers striking iron, no bells, no shouted trade. Yet the silence here was different—watchful, not afraid.

She kept her hood low and followed the track that led toward a small square near the center. Market stalls stood there in a quiet row, their tables neatly arranged with jars of salve, bundles of herbs, strips of cloth, even a few small tools laid out in order. No merchants stood behind them. Only a tin dish rested at the corner of each table, etched with a single word: *Fair.*

Lysandra stopped at the first stall. A jar of salve sat labeled in neat, looping script: *for pain and swelling.* She glanced around, half-expecting someone to step from a doorway and watch her hand. No one did. The square remained still. A dog padded lazily across the cobbles before curling beneath a bench. An old man carved wood on a porch, his knife moving in slow, steady strokes, his eyes occasionally lifting to her before returning to his work.

She reached into her pouch, pulled two thin copper coins, and dropped them into the dish. The clang rang louder than she expected, echoing briefly across the square, but no heads turned. She slipped the jar into her satchel and moved on, her steps careful, her heart unsettled by the strangeness of it all.

Beyond the square, a stone arch rose from the earth, its legs wrapped in moss, its curve broken but still standing. The path beneath it led into the husk of a chapel. Most of the roof had fallen long ago, and the altar lay blackened by fire, its surface cracked and pitted where the flames had eaten deepest. Ferns pressed up through the flagstones, and ivy claimed the walls, but the ruin was not abandoned. The floor had been swept clear of debris, and the vines at the altar's base had been cut back, as if someone still tended the place with quiet care.

Lysandra stepped through the arch, her boots scuffing against the stone, and felt the air shift. It was heavier here, stiller, like a breath held too long. She paused near the altar, letting her fingers brush across the scorched stone, and saw that one pillar yet remained upright at the back of the chapel. Its surface was marred with soot, but beneath the black a hand had carved words, the lines uneven but deliberate.

We remember.

No dates. No names. No prayer. Just those two words, cut deep enough to outlast the fire that had tried to erase them.

Lysandra traced the letters with her fingertips. The stone was warm from the afternoon sun, but the words carried a weight beyond their heat. They were not meant for gods. They were meant for people who refused to forget.

The sound of footsteps drew her around. An older woman stood a few paces away, a scarf binding her braided hair, her hands folded loosely before her. She did not startle at Lysandra's presence. Her voice was even, almost casual.

"Salve you took in the square's good for bruises and burns," the woman said. "Won't do much for old wounds."

Lysandra held her silence.

"You heading south?" the woman asked.

After a pause, Lysandra inclined her head.

The woman's gaze lingered on the knife at her side, on the frayed hem of her cloak, on the worn leather strap of her satchel. She nodded slightly, as if confirming something she already knew. Then she stepped closer and offered a small bundle wrapped in cloth—bandages, a sprig of thyme, and a biscuit baked hard for travel.

"We don't ask names here," she said. "And we don't give them easily. Just take it."

Lysandra's fingers closed around the bundle. For a moment she searched the woman's face, looking for pity, but found only steady eyes. She gave a single nod of thanks.

"Keep moving, girl," the woman added, her tone softening. "You've seen too much to linger. And you've got the kind of eyes that make the empire nervous."

She stepped aside, letting Lysandra pass.

Lysandra did not look back as she left the ruin, the bundle warm in her hand and the words on the stone echoing louder than any sermon: *We remember.*

The village square had thinned by dusk, its stillness deepening as people withdrew into their homes. Lamps glowed faintly behind shutters, and smoke from evening hearths drifted upward in thin ribbons. Near the well, an old man sat on the stone rim, his posture straight despite his years, a knife resting in one hand and a block of wood in the other. The curl of shavings at his feet marked the time he had already spent there, patient and unhurried.

Lysandra kept to the edge, watching. She told herself she lingered only to note the roads in and out of the village, to weigh the distance to the fields, but her gaze stayed on the man at the well. He had the air of someone who expected to be noticed, even if he pretended otherwise.

Without looking up, he spoke. His voice was steady, low enough to carry only a few paces. "You've got the manner about you, girl, who listens before she speaks."

Her body went still.

He shaved another curl from the wood, letting it fall. "That's a rare thing now. Too many talk and forget what they've said—or who was listening when they said it."

Finally, he set the carving aside and reached into his pocket. From it he drew a stub of chalk, worn nearly to dust. Leaning forward, he pressed it against the well's stone lip and traced a circle, careful and unbroken, then crossed the inside with four short lines like a compass.

"We used to call this the circle of stead," he said, tapping the mark with the chalk. "It means a place holds still, even when the world doesn't."

He looked at her then, his eyes sharp beneath white brows, as though measuring whether she understood.

"You've been walking a long time," he added, his tone quieter now. "Long enough to know the shape of things. Of what was, before the rot."

Lysandra said nothing. The words caught in her chest, too heavy to release, but she held his gaze until the silence became its own reply.

The old man gave the faintest smile, then returned to his carving as if the exchange were finished. The chalk circle gleamed pale in the fading light, a mark too simple to draw notice yet heavy with memory.

She passed the square again before night fully settled. The stalls stood unattended, their wares covered by neat cloths, and the lamplight from nearby homes pooled faintly across the cobbles. The smell of bread drifted on the air—warm, earthy, laced with herbs. It tugged at her before she realized she was already following it.

At the far end of the lane a baker worked with her sleeves rolled high, hands dusted with flour as she shaped loaves on a wide wooden board. The door behind her gaped open to a room lit by a single fire, its glow falling across shelves lined with jars and bundles of rosemary hung to dry. She noticed Lysandra, but did not startle. She simply brushed flour from her hands and lifted a small loaf already wrapped in cloth.

"This one's yours," she said, voice calm, steady. "We still knead rosemary into the dough, like we used to. They told us to stop, said the blessing was wasteful. But some things aren't meant to be forgotten."

Lysandra hesitated, her hood shadowing her face.

The woman pressed the loaf into her hands, her expression gentle but firm. "Take it. You don't have to give anything back."

The bread was still warm, its scent sharp with rosemary. Lysandra clutched it against her satchel, the weight more than food—it was memory baked into grain, a defiance that carried no banner and drew no sword, but endured all the same.

"We don't pray aloud anymore," the baker added quietly. "Not where it can be heard. But we still bless the hearth when the fire's low. Some traditions can't be burned away."

Her eyes met Lysandra's, holding them for a breath before she turned back to her work, rolling another lump of dough beneath her palms. The firelight caught in the flour that dusted her skin, bright as pale ash, and for a moment the whole lane smelled of bread and remembrance.

Lysandra pulled her hood lower and stepped back into the street, the loaf tucked safely inside her cloak. She carried its warmth into the shadows, the lesson written not in words but in practice: rebellion did not always shout. Sometimes it whispered in rosemary and firelight.

At the far edge of the village, a narrow path drew her in. It wound between briars and low boughs that seemed intent on closing it off, as if the forest itself meant to keep the way hidden. The air grew still as she followed it, quieter than the fields and lanes she had left behind, until the trees parted to reveal the ruin of another chapel.

Two walls still stood, blackened but upright, and the shape of the doorway remained, though the doors themselves had long ago been consumed by fire. The roof was gone, leaving the sky bare above, yet ivy clung to the stone as though refusing to let the place fall entirely to ruin. Ferns rose where pews had once been, and the floor was scattered with the broken ribs of an arch that had collapsed into rubble.

Lysandra stepped across the threshold, and the hush inside deepened. It was not the silence of absence but the silence of something held, waiting. Her boots scraped softly against stone as she moved past the shattered altar and found herself staring at a single column that still stood near the back. Its face was scorched, soot clinging to every groove, but a hand had cut through the black to carve words into the stone.

Truth lives in silence. So listen.

She crouched and brushed her fingers over the letters. Ash crumbled away beneath her touch, but the words remained, carved deep enough to resist fire and time alike. She did not know who had left them or when, but the meaning was sharp, immediate, as though the message had been waiting for her alone.

She thought of her own life—of the nights pressed under roots, of listening from cellars and shadows, of keeping her voice locked tight when the urge to speak threatened to break her. It had not been weakness. It had been strength. She understood that now.

They had tried to burn the chapel, to silence the voices that had once prayed here. But silence, when chosen, carried truth of its own.

She sat there for a time, breathing in the heavy stillness, not in reverence and not in grief, but in recognition.

The phrase lodged in her chest with the weight of something undeniable. Her mother's lessons echoed within it. So did Tana's gift, the baker's rosemary loaf, the quiet chalk mark on the well. All of them fragments of a truth too dangerous to speak aloud, yet impossible to erase.

She lingered for a moment longer, then pulled her hood forward and stepped back into the open air. The forest path welcomed her in silence, and the ruin slipped behind the wall of trees until it was gone from sight. But the words followed her, carved not only into stone but into her memory.

This was not reverence. It was not prayer. It was recognition—an understanding that survival was not only in hiding, but in carrying memory forward. She bore it now, quiet and unshakable.

Her pace quickened as she rejoined the broader track. The satchel bounced lightly at her side, and her fingers brushed the cloth-wrapped knife through the flap, a ritual as steady as breathing. She did not need to speak the lesson aloud. The stone had already done that.

And as she moved southward, she knew: what they tried to burn could still endure, as long as someone listened.

Morning came veiled in mist, the kind that blurred the edges of the world and muffled every sound. Lysandra had risen early, satchel already strapped across her shoulder, cloak drawn tight against the chill. She had planned to slip away as she always did—quietly, without farewells, leaving no trace but the press of her boots in the damp grass.

But as she neared the leaning arch that marked the village's boundary, a figure stepped into her path. The woman from the market—the one with the hawthorn scarf and the scar along her jaw—stood waiting. There was no smile on her face, only a steady gaze and a small bundle cradled in her hands.

"For the road," the woman said. Her voice was calm, unhurried, as though she had been expecting this moment. She pressed the bundle into Lysandra's grasp. "Salve, binding cloth, dried root. And a little sweetbread. Not much, but it will keep."

Lysandra started to nod, to turn, to go without a word, but the woman's fingers lingered on hers, holding her there for a breath longer.

"You keep your eyes open, girl."

The words carried no malice, no warning of danger just ahead, but something heavier—an urging, born of long years. The woman leaned closer, lowering her voice so that it seemed the mist itself carried it.

"There's something in the wind. It's shifting."

Lysandra did not know what answer to give. Her throat felt too tight for words.

The woman let her hand fall away and stepped aside. "Keep moving. Don't stay anywhere too long. And if you find others who listen—others like you—remember we are out there."

For a moment, Lysandra stood still, bundle warm in her hands, the path ahead opening into fog. Then she inclined her head in thanks, the smallest of gestures, and moved on.

Behind her, the village folded back into the mist, its simple houses and quiet lanes vanishing as though they had never been. Yet she knew better now. What had looked ordinary from a distance was something else entirely. Memory disguised as silence. Defiance written into the small rituals of daily life.

She walked south, her cloak damp with morning dew, and for the first time in many months, she did not feel entirely alone.

The taverns became her maps. Not marked in ink or stretched across parchment, but charted in voices—the careless boasts of soldiers, the muttered fears of merchants, the whispered warnings of villagers too cautious to speak above a breath.

Lysandra never entered through the front door if she could help it. She slipped into cellars through warped doors, crawled beneath porches where the slats had rotted, wedged herself behind barrels stacked too high for anyone to look past. There she learned to still her breath, to quiet the small reflexes that betrayed presence: the startle at a rat brushing her ankle, the shift of weight when a board creaked. She became a shadow stitched into the corners, a silence that listened longer than anyone expected.

At first, it was fragments she gathered. A guard too deep into his cups, bragging about the village of Gallow's Bend. "Not a whisper left there. Burned the whole ridge."

A merchant swearing under his breath as he slammed down an empty cup. "They confiscated my trade—called a family crest a relic."

A villager speaking to another in the half-slurred tongue of grief. "They took all the boys over sixteen. Said conscription. You and I both know what that means."

She did not write these things down. She did not need to. Each word etched itself into her memory, sharp as the scars on her hands. She collected them as her mother once collected herbs—sorted, pressed, preserved for use later. The voices became threads, and she wove them together, until patterns began to take shape where others saw only rumor.

Some villages fell silent days before soldiers arrived. Some markets burned after strange seals changed hands in shadowed corners. Some names appeared again and again in whispers that made men look over their shoulders.

The kingdom's cruelty was not random. It was practiced. Planned.

And in the dim corners of taverns where the air reeked of smoke and spilled ale, Lysandra learned to hear it for what it was.

She no longer feared being caught. It had been three years since anyone knew who she was. What gnawed at her instead was the possibility of missing something, some clue that might explain where her mother had gone, some pattern that might reveal how to stop the silence from spreading further.

Her fear had hardened into something sharper. Resolve.

What began as instinct soon hardened into method. She no longer drifted from village to village without aim. She charted. Observed. Remembered.

The guards taught her more than they realized. Not the officers in polished armor who paraded through cities, but the weary ones left behind in border posts and crossroads towns. Men and women who drank too much, played dice too loudly, and forgot how to guard their tongues after the second mug of ale. They were creatures of habit, and habits were as revealing as confessions.

Every fifth night the patrols shifted, and the new watch always walked the same route. Certain lieutenants stayed behind while others rode out, feigning illness or feasting in taverns until their return. Some checked papers with a show of diligence; others waved travelers through without a glance.

She learned to tell the difference between lazy and dangerous. The lazy ones were predictable, their neglect as steady as the sunrise. But the dangerous ones—those who noticed too much, who listened too closely—she marked in her mind and remembered.

The heavyset officer in Corvale who twisted his ring whenever he lied. The red-haired captain in Dunley whose hand never strayed far from his sword. The ink-fingered scribe in Maymoor whose laughter came too quickly when someone screamed.

Then there were the documents. She never touched them, but she watched. Leather satchels slung from shoulders, wax seals pressed hurriedly in dark corners, folded papers passed hand to hand. Some bore the king's crest, bold and unquestionable. Others carried smaller marks... sigils unfamiliar, pressed deep into wax and hidden in clenched fists.

Those she followed with her eyes. She traced the paths of messengers, noted which villages they visited, which names vanished in whispers soon after. Patterns emerged. Orders left a post. A name disappeared. A village burned.

It was never about magic, or heresy, or rebellion. Those were the words used to dress the truth. The truth was simpler, colder. Control.

The tavern smelled of woodsmoke and sour drink, its rafters low and blackened from years of fire. Shadows moved like smoke across the room as men leaned close over their mugs, voices raised and lowered in a restless rhythm. Lysandra kept to the corner, her hood drawn, her hands wrapped loosely around a chipped cup. She had not touched the ale inside. The coin she had given the barkeep bought her something more valuable than drink—it bought her the right to sit and listen.

The guards at the next table had shed their armor, piling it beneath the bench as if the kingdom itself could be set aside with the weight of steel. Their voices carried in drunken waves, too careless to guard what they spoke.

"She's gone," one muttered, his words thick with ale. "No trace left. Just vanished."

The other shook his head, lowering his tone though not enough to matter. "No one vanishes without help. Someone was asking questions. That's how they always find them."

The first leaned in, voice a rasp just above the hum of the room. "That's how they knew about Evern's girl."

Lysandra did not lift her head, did not let her breath quicken, but the words cut clean through the haze of the tavern. A name she did not know, bound to the fate she had heard too many times before. A girl taken. A silence forced. Another life erased.

She listened until their voices drifted back into laughter, careless again, but the name lingered, sharp and unfamiliar. She repeated it once in her mind—*Evern*—and stored it the way she stored every fragment that mattered.

The pattern was tightening. Villages burned. Healers disappeared. Families silenced. The guards spoke of it not as chance, not as rumor, but as certainty. The kingdom watched. The kingdom listened. And when someone pressed too close to truth, it swallowed them whole.

Her cup sat forgotten, the firelight breaking its surface into pieces of shadow and flame. For years, silence had kept her alive. But silence would not change the pattern. Silence only made it easier for them to keep taking.

She rose with the same quiet she had used to enter. The guards did not notice. Their laughter swelled again, filling the room with the sound of men too drunk to care.

Outside, the air was damp, the night heavy with the promise of rain. Lysandra pressed her back to the cold stone wall of the tavern and closed her eyes.

Evern's girl. She did not know who that was. But she knew what it meant. Another name lost. Another life struck from memory.

And if the kingdom could take her, it could take anyone.

The tavern had emptied into silence, but the words still burned in her mind. She wandered the narrow lane until stillness pressed too tightly against her chest, then climbed. The roof's shingles were warped with age, slick from the night's drizzle, and creaked faintly under her weight. She moved carefully, settling low against the slope until the village lay open before her.

Lanterns swayed at the corners of streets, their glow spilling weak light onto puddled cobbles. Patrols traced their loops with the same steady rhythm she had memorized in every town before this one. Boots splashed through water, blades clinked against armor, and nothing changed. That was the danger of it—the pattern looked harmless, ordinary, until it was not.

Her satchel dug into her shoulder, heavy with the meager things she carried: cloth strips, dried herbs, a scrap of bread, her mother's knife. They were tools for survival, nothing more. Survival had carried her this far, but it had not stopped villages from burning, had not saved children from vanishing, had not broken the silence forced over every doorframe and hearth.

She slid the knife free, turning it until the moon caught the steel. Its edge glimmered faintly, more memory than weapon, yet it steadied her hand. She traced the worn hilt with her thumb and followed the line of the road south. It cut through the dark like a pale scar, leading away from the borderlands and toward Arden's Wake, where the king's banners rose tallest. She had thought once that safety meant staying away from that heart, keeping to the shadows at the edge. Now she understood. The rot bled outward because its roots ran deep in the capital.

Her breath clouded in the cold as she whispered into the dark, her voice meant for no one but herself. "I won't stay at the edge." The words anchored her, solid as stone.

She looked once more at the knife, then slid it back into its sheath. If she wanted to end the pattern, she could not remain hidden in the margins, listening and surviving while others vanished. She would have to walk into the very place where the orders were given, where names were crossed away, where silence was written into law.

If she wanted to kill the roots, she could not do it from the forest's edge.

She had to become one of them.

To burn it down from within.

CHAPTER TEN

INNER FIRE

Lysandra reached the crest of the ridge and stopped with the city laid out beyond, a sprawl of stone and smoke that swallowed the horizon. Wind ran its cold fingers through the scrub and tugged at her hood, but the world below made the wind feel small. Arden's Wake did not sit against the land. It pressed into it, a weight of walls and towers that bent roads toward its gates the way rivers bend toward the sea. Sound traveled even this far: the rise and fall of voices, the clatter of carts, the strike of iron on iron. It carried the restless energy of a place that refused to sleep.

She stood with her hands at her sides and let her breathing settle. For years the quiet had been her companion. That life had been a thin thread she could follow without being seen, a way of moving that left no mark. The city below promised the opposite. It invited the eye and punished the unready. It would swallow someone whole that was not ready.

Her gaze traced the walls. They climbed as if they meant to deny the sky, block by block, old stone fused to newer cuts where repairs had been made and embellished. Towers stood like knuckles along a closed fist, each one set to watch not only the world without but the streets within. At the main gate, people funneled through in an unending tide that did not slow even when the guards shifted their stance. The first truth the city showed her was that it would not make accommodations. You took it, or you were carried where the current wanted you.

Her breath caught shallow in her chest. The question rose without mercy. *How do I survive there?* The answer did not come. Doubt tried to speak in its place, that old voice with its familiar shape, but she refused it. She had weathered emptiness. She had weathered hunger and long miles and the kind of silence that made a person think they were fog drifting over a field. Those trials had edges she could feel. This was different. This was a press from every side at once.

She drew a long breath through her nose and let it out slowly, steadying the shake that tried to enter her hands. The ridge offered one last clean horizon. She took it in as if it were a final drink before a crossing, then stepped down the slope and did not look back. With each stride the city climbed higher in her vision until stone replaced sky. The road widened, then narrowed, then became a crush of people whose pace set its own law. She matched it without thought, shoulder to shoulder, her cloak pulled close, her head angled so her eyes could work while her face remained unread.

The gate loomed. Guards stood in pairs, their armor bright in a way that spoke of regular polish. They watched the moving river of bodies with boredom. Their hands rested near their sword belts for comfort, not need. Questions were asked at random, more performance than inquiry. She kept her gaze soft and her steps even. When a guard's attention drifted toward her, she let it pass by giving him nothing to catch.

Inside the arch, the sound changed. Stone amplified it. Wheels ground against cobbles and sent the tremor into her feet. Voices tangled and refused to separate. Somewhere a bell marked the hour, and the air responded to it. The smell of yeast from a baker's vent cut through smoke and sweat. A horse stamped. A child laughed with a wild, unselfconscious sound that did not belong to rules yet. A door banged open. A shutter slammed closed. The city was alive with chaos.

She let the tide take her for a short stretch and studied the edges where it broke. Stalls pressed against the first street beyond the gate, canvas awnings dipping under the jostle of elbows and rainwater collected from a brief morning shower. A woman weighed apples on a scale and never once glanced at the man slipping a second piece of bread to the child at his knee. Two men argued over a wheel rim in a way that suggested they had argued the same point yesterday and would again tomorrow. A patrol turned the corner at an even pace, boots landing together on the downbeat.

Their faces were closed. Their presence was a warning to those who needed it, a reassurance to those who wanted it, and an irritation to everyone else.

She adjusted her stride. When the flow quickened, she matched it. When it slowed near a knot of buyers, she turned before the pause could trap her. When others laughed, she allowed a faint curve of her mouth and then let it fade. She tucked her threadbare edges deeper beneath her cloak without fidgeting. The trick was to wear the movement of the crowd like a borrowed coat. The trick was to know when to vanish inside a thing and when to be the seam no one noticed.

A surge pushed her near a low wall where a cart had stopped to unload sacks of barley. She took the moment to shift her weight and breathe. The castle rose above the roofs ahead, all planes and angles, its color set darker by distance and by the smoke that lay against it like gauze. From here the highest tower seemed to lean over the city with a patient confidence. That was where orders began and ended. That was the place that had put a hand through her life and drawn out the warm center of it without a word.

Her jaw tightened. *This city will not swallow me.* The thought formed cleanly, without heat. It was a rule she wrote for herself, and she accepted it.

She let the press of bodies pull her forward again. A vendor thrust a tray of rolls at a passing pair and shouted his price over their talk. A boy darted between skirts with something small hidden in his palm. A clothier snapped a measuring string and grinned through his beard at a woman who rolled her eyes but did not walk away. At the next cross street, a soldier glanced toward her and then past her as if she were fog after all. She gave him nothing to remember.

By the time she reached the first true square, the rhythm of the place had settled inside her muscles like a second heartbeat. She set her chin, eased her shoulders, and let the line of her mouth flatten into something that neither invited nor refused. She entered the city as if the city were a river she had always meant to cross, and the current carried her toward the gate that led to the yard where bodies were counted and names were written.

Within the shadow of the arch the world tightened. Stone narrowed the sound into a deeper roar and bent the light into stripes that moved with the crowd. A scribe on a stool scratched notes while a guard beside him scanned faces without interest. Another guard tapped the haft of his spear against a crate to hurry a stalled peddler along. The peddler muttered a prayer into his sleeve and shuffled forward, shoulders hunched as if the gate might decide to close on him alone.

Lysandra kept to the left where the flow ran smoother. She let a teamster's cart shield her from a watchful glance, then slipped past the rear wheel before a second glance could follow. A woman with a baby at her breast pressed close, eyes fixed on the opening beyond. The child turned its head and regarded Lysandra with the unblinking seriousness of the very young. She nodded once to the child with a slipped smile in her eyes at the child's innocence.

The city accepted her without ceremony. Noise poured over her shoulders, then settled into a rhythm she could measure. There was no space to pause, so she made space by matching the pace and narrowing her world to the next ten steps. Every movement became deliberate. A turn here. A slide there. A small lift of the hand to indicate she would pass a slower walker on the right. The rules announced themselves to anyone who listened. She listened.

Canvas awnings spilled color into the square. Reds and greens had faded under long summers, but the edges still caught light and made the stalls look festive from a distance. Up close, the festival peeled away and work remained. Hands moved grain, cut twine, measured cloth, and counted coins. Voices reached out, each trying to lift above the others without breaking. A baker slid a peel into a deep oven and pulled out a loaf that cracked as air met crust.

Soldiers stood at the corners like iron punctuation, reminding the sentence who ended it. Their armor caught the noon light in hard planes. Their eyes did the same work they always did, weighing faces and deciding which ones needed to feel the weight in return. Their presence did not stop the square from moving, but it set a limit to the kind of movement people risked. Laughter lived here, though it carried a certain caution. Disputes lived here too, settled in coin or in a firm voice before a mailed hand settled them by force.

Lysandra let her gaze drift without fixing on any one thing long enough to be counted as interest. The skill had become instinct in the years behind her. She built a mental map while she walked. Mills to the east by the smell and the pale flour on shoes. Tanners to the south by the sting in the air. The castle's road fell in from the north with a grade she felt in her calves. The recruitment yard would sit along that road or on a street that fed it.

At the near corner a boy slipped a plum into his sleeve while the seller argued with a customer about weight. The boy was gone before the argument ended. A woman in a blue shawl noticed and said nothing. People kept their own accounts here.

A commotion began as a ripple that moved faster than the crowd. Heads turned toward a cross street. Silence ran ahead of the trouble and then broke apart as it arrived. A thin man stood with his back to a wall, hands open, palms up. Four soldiers rushed up to face him. The sergeant spoke quietly and the man answered too quickly. When his words failed, he tried a smile that did not reach his eyes.

The first blow landed without warning. A backhand that snapped the man's head against the stone. He slid down the wall as if the mortar had turned to water. Blood wet his lip and disappeared into the stubble there. No one screamed. No one pleaded. The square learned long ago that pleas bought only a longer lesson. People shifted their gaze to their hands, their wares, and their children. The crowd obeyed the shape fear had given it.

She moved only when they had passed. The fallen man found his feet. He didn't look at her as she slid by. She did not offer a hand he would be afraid to take. Mercy here would mark them both. She carried the image with her instead, set it beside the castle in the ledger she kept in her head.

She turned toward the road that climbed to the barracks yard. Somewhere above, a clerk with a blunt quill would ask for a name. She had chosen the one she would give. It would be the first stone laid in the road she intended to walk.

The road bent uphill, narrowing between tall stone buildings whose windows leaned over as if listening. At the crest, the noise of the market gave way to a different sound of shuffling boots, muttered voices, and the cough of dry throats.

A courtyard opened beyond a pair of timber gates, its ground trodden to mud by countless feet. The smell of sweat and damp wool hung thick in the air. A line of recruits stretched across the yard, men and women of every shape and state, their silence carrying more weight than any words.

Lysandra slipped into place at the end, her gaze lowered but attentive. She counted faces without seeming to. Hollow cheeks, nervous glances, hands that twitched against empty sides. Some were farm boys with dirt still beneath their nails, others city-worn drifters whose eyes had stopped expecting anything better.

Two men ahead of her whispered without moving their heads.

"Think they'll check the names?" one murmured. His eyes flicked toward the soldiers patrolling the yard.

"Doesn't matter," the other answered, voice flat with exhaustion. "They want bodies. Names don't mean a thing."

Lysandra absorbed the words without reaction. He was right. Every person in this line carried a lie—small or large, spoken or silent. She was simply one more body in their numbers.

The line moved forward. Boots squelched through the mud. An officer at a table scratched his quill across parchment, never lifting his eyes higher than the line before him. His indifference was as heavy as the wall behind him.

Her pulse began to quicken. Every step closer tightened it further. She had rehearsed the answer in silence so many times it already felt real, but now the moment would press it into ink.

When the line thinned to nothing before her, Lysandra stepped forward. The officer did not look up immediately. His quill dipped lazily into the inkwell, then scratched across another line.

Finally, without raising his head fully, he spoke. "Name."

Her breath steadied. The word was simple, but it closed the door to everything that had come before.

"Lysa Evern," she said.

The quill moved, scratching her lie into permanence. She watched the letters form, black on white, each stroke severing the last tie to who she had been.

"Age?"

"Sixteen."

Another scratch of ink. No pause. No suspicion. He had not even looked into her eyes. She could have been anyone. She was no one. And that anonymity was her shield.

"Sign," he said, sliding the parchment toward her.

Her fingers tightened around the quill. The tip touched parchment, and for a moment her hand stilled. She thought of her mother's true name. Of the cottage. Of the night it had all unraveled. Then she pressed the strokes clean and final.

Lysa Evern.

The ink glistened wet for a heartbeat, then dulled as it dried. The falsehood was whole. It was hers now, more than the truth could ever be.

A soldier behind her shifted impatiently, and the officer shoved the parchment aside for the next in line. Hands guided her roughly toward a waiting cart.

She did not resist. She climbed onto the wooden bed and gripped the side rail. The cart lurched forward. Behind her, the courtyard and its desk began to shrink, while ahead, the castle's towers rose higher against the sky.

The cart groaned beneath the weight of bodies packed shoulder to shoulder. Every jolt along the cobblestones rattled through its frame and into the spines of those inside. No one spoke. The silence was not agreement but survival, a hush held tight between clenched jaws and darting eyes.

Lysa braced herself with one hand on the side rail. The wood was rough beneath her palm, splinters catching at her skin. She let her weight settle into her stance as the wheels struck ruts in the road. Around her, recruits shifted uneasily, trying to carve out inches of space that did not exist. The smell was close—mud, sweat, old wool, and fear.

She studied their faces in careful glances. A boy barely grown, his lips moving soundless prayers. A scarred man with the look of someone who had outlived more winters than he deserved. A woman standing rigid, arms crossed, her jaw tight as if she dared the world to challenge her. Every face was a story hidden in silence, each one bound now to the same road.

The city walls receded behind them, towers softened by haze and smoke. Yet the weight of the place clung to her as if she had swallowed stone dust. She turned her head, fixing the image of Arden's Wake in her memory—the market square, the narrow streets, the towers of the castle rising above it all. The city had taken her name and given her a new one. That exchange could never be undone.

The cart's path tilted upward, wheels grinding against the climb. Ahead, the castle loomed larger, its walls layered like the ribs of some vast beast. Each tower stood as a watchful sentinel that believed itself eternal.

Lysa tightened her grip on the rail. The sway of the cart became her heartbeat, steady, unrelenting. She allowed herself one final glance back over her shoulder. The sprawl of the city blurred into distance, a place she had entered by choice and already seemed to be leaving behind.

Her eyes returned to the fortress ahead. Every creak of the wheels carried her closer to it. Every jolt pressed her further into the life she had chosen.

The cart rolled through iron gates and into a yard already scarred with use. Mud clung thick to the ground where hundreds of boots had churned it to sludge. The air was heavy with the smell of damp leather and smoke from nearby forges. Stone walls hemmed them in on all sides, tall and featureless except for narrow windows that looked more like arrow slits than anything built for comfort.

A barked order split the silence. Trainers strode forward, their voices sharp as whips. "Out! Move!"

The recruits stumbled from the cart, some nearly falling into the muck. Lysa dropped lightly, knees bending to catch the landing. She straightened quickly, cloak clinging damp against her legs, and fell into line with the others.

They were herded toward a long barracks hall. Inside, rows of cots stretched along the walls, the space reeking of stale straw and unwashed bodies. The recruits were given no chance to linger, only time enough to drop what little they carried. Then the trainers stormed in again, voices rising like thunder.

"On your feet, dogs! Out into the yard!"

Sleep-deprived, half-fed bodies scrambled to obey. Lysa moved quickly, keeping her motions controlled, precise. She would not be the one singled out.

The yard was colder than the barracks, wind slicing through the open space. Clouds hung low, their color promising rain. Recruits formed into uneven rows while instructors paced before them, their eyes searching for weakness.

One stopped in front of Lysa. He looked her up and down, lips curling into a sneer. "What's this? Did someone misplace their little sister?"

Laughter rolled through the line. Harsh, mocking. It cut sharper than the wind, but Lysa kept her face blank, her gaze fixed ahead.

The instructor leaned closer. His breath was sour with ale. "Think you'll last here, girl? This isn't a place for strays."

Her pulse quickened, but she forced stillness into her stance. She gave him nothing.

The sneer deepened. He stepped back and shouted, "Weapons!"

Assistants dragged out bundles of training swords. They threw them into waiting hands. The recruits staggered beneath the sudden weight.

"Raise them high!" came the order. "Again! Again!"

The drill began. Arms lifted and fell, lifted and fell, wooden swords slamming against air in endless rhythm. Trainers barked corrections, curses, threats. Mud sucked at their boots with each step. Sweat stung eyes, muscles screamed, shoulders shook. One by one, recruits faltered, dropping weapons, collapsing into the muck.

Lysa's breath came ragged, her arms quivering as the sword grew heavier with every repetition. Still she lifted it. Again and again. Her body demanded rest, but she forced her motions to remain steady, efficient. She would not fall.

Beside her, a recruit stumbled. An elbow shot sharply into her ribs, deliberate, cruel. Pain flared hot through her chest. She staggered, biting back the cry that threatened her throat.

The broad-shouldered boy smirked, then chuckled. "Oops."

Her jaw tightened. She steadied her stance, ignored the ache, and lifted the sword again. Not a glance in his direction. Not a word. Only movement, clean and unbroken.

By afternoon the drills shifted. The trainers herded the recruits into a wide ring of churned mud, its edges marked by trampled stakes and the jeers of tired bodies eager for someone else's suffering.

"Pair off," an instructor barked. "Let's see which of you know how to stand, and which of you belong in the dirt."

Eyes turned, measuring, calculating. The broad-shouldered boy who had elbowed Lysa earlier shoved forward with a grin already curling at his lips. He planted himself opposite her, swinging his practice sword with arrogance.

"Careful, little one," he called, loud enough for the crowd. "Wouldn't want you tripping over your own feet."

Laughter rippled through the recruits. Lysa did not respond. She stepped into the ring, boots sinking into the muck slightly, her sword gripped firm but low. Her breathing slowed. The noise around her blurred into a dull roar.

The trainer gave the order. "Begin!"

The boy charged, his first swing a wide arc meant to overwhelm, not strike clean. Lysa waited until the blade cut close, then shifted a single step aside. The weight of his swing carried him past her. He stumbled, recovered quickly, and scowled.

"Lucky dodge," he spat.

She adjusted her grip, silent, eyes fixed on his shoulders, the telltale twitch before the next attack. He lunged again, reckless, his footing sloppy in the mud. She saw the gap, stepped forward rather than back, pivoted on her heel, and swept her leg low.

His balance shattered. He toppled face-first into the muck with a crack of wood against earth. The crowd fell into stunned silence.

Lysa stood over him, sword raised, chest rising and falling with controlled breaths. Her expression never shifted.

The boy rolled onto his side, sputtering mud, rage twisting his face. "You—"

"Enough," the instructor cut in sharply. He eyed Lysa for a long moment before nodding once. "That's how you fight. Precision. Timing. Remember that."

The boy slunk out of the circle, jeers replaced by whispers. Eyes followed Lysa as she lowered her sword and stepped back into line.

She gave them nothing. No smirk, no triumph, or acknowledgement. Inside, satisfaction stirred, sharp and steady, but her face remained stone.

The barracks was quieter that night, though not because exhaustion alone had claimed the recruits. The usual mutter of conversation, the careless laughter, even the crude jokes tossed across cots had thinned into uneasy silence. The room still held sound, but it was a different kind. The hush of glances quickly turned away when Lysa walked past.

She moved the same as she had shown in the yard, refusing to betray the ache in her muscles or the throb of the bruise blooming along her ribs. Her steps were steady, her expression unreadable, as though the fight in the mud had been nothing more than another drill. Yet she felt the shift pressing against her from every side. The sneers that had followed her since her arrival were gone. In their place lingered a different sort of attention, cautious and measuring, as if the others were trying to decide whether she was a threat worth fearing.

The boy she had toppled into the mud sat hunched on his cot, his face still streaked with dried earth, his pride wounded more deeply than his body. He kept his head bowed, eyes fixed on the floorboards, unwilling to risk another confrontation. Around him the other recruits gave space, their silence forming a ring just wide enough to mark his humiliation.

Lysa did not linger on him. She lowered herself onto her own cot, removing her boots and setting them neatly beneath the frame. Her hands moved through the motions of checking her gear. Her cloak folded, her belt placed within reach, the knife her mother had left her brushed with her thumb before she tucked it back beneath the thin mattress. She did everything as she always had without haste, methodical and precise. The last three years of always taking a count of what she had left at the end of the day.

When the lamps dimmed and the room settled into the restless shuffle of bodies preparing for sleep, she lay on her back and fixed her gaze on the beams overhead. The whispers that had dogged her since her first step through the barracks door had stilled. No one dared toss a joke her way. No one pressed for a response. For the first time since she had entered these walls, she felt the room grant her the smallest measure of quiet.

Her eyes closed slowly, though sleep came lightly.

The weeks blurred into one another, a relentless march of drills, sparring, and endurance runs that began before sunrise and ended long after the light had gone. The schedule was designed to break recruits, to grind the weakness from their bodies until only obedience and muscle remained. Some faltered. A few disappeared altogether, their cots stripped bare by morning with no explanation given. The rest endured because there was no choice.

Lysa endured differently. She did not rely on strength alone, nor did she waste herself in futile defiance. She learned to ration effort, to move with precision rather than force, to conserve energy where others spent it recklessly. Each motion was studied and pared down until nothing remained but the necessary. She ran when others stumbled, not faster but longer, her pace steady. She struck with timing rather than power, her blows landing where they would matter most. She never quit, never begged for respite, and never drew attention to her own limits.

Instructors noticed. At first, only with a grunt when her form held longer than expected, or a clipped nod when her stance mirrored their commands with quiet perfection. Soon, they began to use her as example, pointing to the economy of her movements, the way she wasted nothing. The other recruits noticed as well, though their attention carried a different weight. They no longer mocked her, nor did they treat her as one of their own. Instead, they watched her with sidelong glances, measuring her with wariness.

The nickname began quietly, whispered during drills when they thought she could not hear. *Ghost.* It clung to her because she moved without fuss, without sound, always present but never quite seen until she chose to be. She did not respond to it. She neither claimed it nor denied it. In silence, it became hers all the same.

At night, when the barracks settled into restless sleep, she lay awake, listening. And in the quiet before dawn, while others still stirred beneath their blankets, she rose. She ran the perimeter of the yard, her boots crunching frost. She drilled alone in the gray light, blade in hand, until the motions fused into instinct. Every repetition honed the edge she was becoming.

By the time the first snows fell, the barracks had shifted around her. No one cut in front of her in line. No one shoved her during drills. When sparring came, they no longer underestimated her, though they still often lost. She was not accepted still, but she was no longer dismissed.

She was something else now; an unknown, a presence that unsettled more than it comforted. And in that space between fear and respect, she thrived.

Once her place in the barracks had steadied, Lysa shifted her attention. Training drills could sharpen her arm, but it was not strength of limb that would unmake the king's hold on this city. The true power lay in the rhythm of the clockwork of men, orders, and routine that kept Arden's Wake in line.

Each day she absorbed more than the commands barked at her. She marked the order of patrols, the way guards rotated along the walls, the moments when a sergeant lingered too long with a mug in the alley rather than at his post. She noticed which officers arrived late to inspection, which hurried their men only when another superior's eye was upon them, and which carried themselves with authority that needed no show.

Every detail mattered. The guards believed themselves strong, but their strength lay in pattern. Pattern could be measured, memorized, and one day, broken.

At first she only watched. During marches through the city, her eyes traced the lines of movement rather than the buildings themselves. She counted bells in her head, marking the hour when patrols shifted. She mapped alleys and side streets not for their cobblestones, but for where they emptied or converged. By night, lying still in her cot, she replayed the day in silence, ordering every fragment into memory until it fit neatly into place.

She left no trace of this work. No notes, no scratches in the dirt, nothing but the ledger she built inside her mind. That ledger grew quickly. The northern gate rotated late by a quarter-hour. A courier crossed the barracks three times each week, whistling the same tune with a pouch of sealed orders. A pair of young guards always traded places on the eastern wall before their shift ended, eager to sneak a moment with tavern girls instead of standing their post.

It began with something so small another recruit might have missed it entirely. Lysa had been ordered to carry a supply ledger to the quartermaster. The parchment was damp at the corner, the red wax seal cracked where the fold had weakened. When she turned it in, the officer never noticed the flaw, never cared. But she noticed.

Later, while hauling discarded gear to the loft above the yard, she found an old brass stamp, dulled by rust, lying forgotten among broken buckles and useless scraps. Its face bore the raven and crown of Dunmoh's city watch, the same sigil she had seen pressed into a hundred orders. A careless loss to the man who dropped it, but to her, it was opportunity. She slipped it into her cloak without hesitation.

Nights became practice. By the stub of a candle, with scraps of parchment and dripped wax melted from her own tallow lamp, she experimented. She pressed too quickly at first, leaving smudged impressions. Then too slowly, the edges blurring into soft lines. She learned the weight of the stamp, the timing, the cooling point when wax held its shape without cracking. Soon, she could make seals indistinguishable from those she had delivered.

But she did not stop there. Forging the seal was one skill; matching the hand that wrote beneath it was another. She studied the lettering styles of different officers—the sharp strokes of one, the hurried scrawl of another. During errands she watched the angle of a wrist, the way ink pooled at the tail of a letter. She rehearsed their cadences in silence until her own strokes became near reflections.

She learned how to loosen a wax seal with steam, how to read a letter upside down while delivering bread to the scribe's table, how to catch words spoken under breath between officers who believed themselves unheard. Every fragment became part of her quiet arsenal.

Still, she never overreached. Orders written in black wax—rare and carried only by high couriers—she left untouched. She logged their patterns instead: who bore them, where they entered the castle, how quickly men scattered at their sight.

Each night, she rehearsed it all in her mind as she lay on her cot. Patrol rotations, courier routes, signatures, seals. Not to follow them. To bend them. To break them.

The city guard thought they were shaping her into one of their own. They had no idea they were teaching her how to unmake them from within.

The taverns of Arden's Wake reeked of spilled ale and sweat, their air thick with the stench of smoke, grease, and unwashed armor. To the men who filled them, they were escapes—places where laughter drowned the drills of the yard and drink softened the weight of duty. To Lysa, they were something else entirely.

She kept to the edges, a hood drawn low, a half-empty cup left untouched at her table. Sometimes she pretended to doze, her posture slouched enough to look forgettable. Other nights, she offered her hands to the barmaids for small tasks—wiping mugs, carrying trays—in exchange for a seat close to soldiers who talked more freely when they thought the girl beside them invisible. And she listened.

Voices rose in drunken rhythm, words loosening as mugs emptied. They spoke of patrols, of captains they despised, of punishments endured. Beneath the grumbling, other stories surfaced.

"They say the prisoner wagon never reached Blackmoor," one soldier muttered, his knuckles tapping a nervous beat on the table. "Vanished. Not a trace."

"Nothing new," another slurred, his voice too loud. "The healer from Ryemarsh—remember her? No trial, no record. Gone overnight."

"Black wax," a third whispered, and at once the others quieted.

The phrase surfaced often, always in hushed tones, always followed by silence. Orders sealed in black wax did not move through the usual channels. They cut past commanders, past tribunals, past the law itself. Lysa had seen them only from a distance, gripped in the fist of a courier marching straight to the castle. They carried weight no one dared question.

Another night, after too much drink, an older soldier laughed too loudly at a crude joke, then slumped forward, mumbling. His companion shook his head and muttered, "Still brooding about that caravan in the gorge. Swears it was rebels. But it wasn't rebels. It was us."

The other man's eyes hardened. "Shut your mouth. You're drunk."

But the silence after spoke louder than any denial. Lysa sat in her corner, feigning sleep, her mind razor-sharp as each word burned itself into memory. She learned that what soldiers feared most was not the enemy beyond the walls, but the orders that came from within them. Every slip, every whisper, every gap in their stories widened the cracks she had begun to see.

They drank and she listened.

She waited until the city lay under mist and torchlight, when patrols thinned and the barracks had sunk into heavy sleep. Then, with careful steps, she slipped through corridors she had walked often enough to memorize. Timing was everything—knowing when a guard lingered too long by the hearth, when another left early to relieve himself, when the silence stretched wide enough to carry her unchallenged.

The records chamber was colder than the halls. Dust hung in the air, stirred by her entry, the shelves rising high on either side like narrow cliffs. Scrolls, ledgers, and dispatches filled them in untidy ranks bound by cord. She moved quickly but not carelessly, her hands steady as she sifted through bundles marked with months and regions.

She whispered the name to herself, the syllables carrying no sound beyond her lips. *Ksara.*

Each ledger she opened offered a litany of the condemned—names of men accused of harboring forbidden texts, women taken for healing without sanction, children marked as thieves or runaways. Page after page recorded punishment in neat lines of ink. But not her. Not once.

She pulled another. Then another. Eyes darting faster now, heart rising with each absence. The name should have been there, carved in the same impersonal hand that condemned the others. Instead, there was nothing.

At last, she reached the ledger marked with the right month. Her finger traced down the list until her breath caught. There was a name. Then, beneath it, a space—blank. No crossing out, no redaction, no smudge of ink where a hand had hesitated. Just an emptiness as deliberate as the words that surrounded it. Then, below the gap, the list continued as if nothing had been lost.

She froze. The silence of the chamber deepened, pressing against her ears.

It wasn't a clerical error. It wasn't negligence. It was deliberate. Her mother hadn't just been imprisoned. She had been erased.

The crown had not contented itself with taking a body. It had reached further, striking at memory itself. Ksara had been stripped from the ledgers, from the city's history, as if she had never drawn breath, never brewed tea in the cottage, never sung lullabies by the hearth.

Lysa's hand clenched at the edge of the desk until the parchment beneath it crumpled. For a moment her vision blurred, but no tears fell. Grief sharpened into something harder.

They had stolen her mother's name. But they had left her daughter.

She closed the ledger with quiet care, set it back into its slot, and drew a breath deep enough to steady the storm within her.

This wasn't about justice anymore. It wasn't about finding records to prove what she already knew. It was about vengeance—and vengeance did not shout. It waited. It planned. It cut deep and left scars that could not be erased.

She slipped from the chamber, her steps measured and silent. The torches flickered along the corridor, shadows stretching long across the stone. The walls seemed narrower, the air thicker, but her purpose burned clearer than it ever had before.

They had erased her mother from the record. She would carve her back into history with the ruin of a kingdom.

The city lay hushed beneath a veil of mist, torchlight swimming faintly in the damp air. From the southern barracks wall, Lysa could see the castle's silhouette carved against the night, its towers jutting like blackened spears into the sky. She perched between the worn crenellations, her cloak drawn tight, though it was not the cold that made her hold it close. Her skin burned with purpose, her breath steady despite the wind tugging strands of red hair across her face.

For years she had been a watcher in the margins—living at a distance, unseen, surviving on the edges of forgotten roads. Now the heart of her enemy loomed before her in stone and iron. Within those walls sat the man whose order had destroyed her life, a king surrounded by loyal guards and a kingdom stitched together by fear. She stared at the highest tower and let the question come. Did Aldric remember the faces his decrees had erased? Did he recall her mother's name at all? The answer was clear even before she shaped the thought. No. That was the point.

Her fingers curled into fists against the stone. The castle did not seem unbreakable to her now. It seemed arrogant, a monument to men who believed themselves untouchable. Mortals had raised these walls; mortals could bring them down. She would be the start of it.

"You erased her," she told the night, the words unspoken yet solid in her chest. "But I am still here."

The torchlight along the battlements wavered in the breeze, but she remained still, eyes locked on the fortress as if she could draw strength from the act of watching. The silence between her and the stone deepened, until it felt like a promise had been forged in the space that joined them.

When at last she descended from the wall and returned to the barracks, the vow followed her like a shadow that could not be shaken.

The barracks had fallen into uneasy quiet by the time Lysa returned. Recruits sprawled across their cots in fitful sleep, the air heavy with the sour blend of sweat, straw, and damp wool. Snores echoed in uneven rhythm, boots and belts lay scattered across the floor, and the faint drip of water from the eaves tapped against the stone.

She moved through the narrow rows without a sound, her steps light and practiced, until she reached her cot near the far wall. Kneeling, she reached beneath the thin mattress and drew out the knife she kept hidden there—her mother's knife. Sliding onto the floor, she pressed the knife into the underside of the cot. The wood groaned softly as the point carved into it, but the sounds of sleep around her masked the scrape. Slowly, carefully, she etched the letters one by one, each stroke deliberate, each groove cut deep enough that time could not erase it.

Ksara.

When it was finished, she sat back on her heels and traced the letters with her thumb. Splinters bit her skin, but she did not flinch. The name lived here now, hidden inside the very place that had sought to bury it. A secret memorial. A scar carved into the belly of the beast. Every day she slept above it. Every time her hand brushed the knife beneath her pillow, she would remember.

The kingdom could erase her mother from parchment, but they could not erase her daughter's memory.

She slid the blade back beneath the mattress, lay on her cot, and fixed her gaze on the ceiling beams overhead. Beneath her, her mother's name endured, carved in defiance, carved in love.

And above her, vengeance waited.

CHAPTER ELEVEN

A DANCE OF BLADES

Twenty years since the fateful night...

The clearing where Caelan and Torin stood was bathed in early morning light, the first golden rays threading through the lumbering trees of the Elderwood. The air was crisp. Dew clung to the grass like scattered diamonds, disturbed only by the slow, measured steps of two warriors as they took their places.

For a long moment, neither of them spoke. They stood facing each other. There was a weight of five relentless years pressed between them. Every bruise earned. Every grueling lesson learned led to this moment.

Torin's stance was firm. His broad shoulders squared as his fingers flexed against the worn leather of his sword's hilt. His eyes locked onto Caelan's every movement. Caelan mirrored him. His grip on his own blade was steady but loose. Shadows flickered across his face, the sun caught wisps of his dark auburn hair. It was no longer the unruly mop of a boy, but the tousled locks of a man.

The duel begun.

Caelan moved first, circling Torin in deliberate steps. His sword held high. His breaths were even and controlled. His grip was relaxed but steady.

Torin lifted his sword in response and mirrored Caelan's guard. His eyes locked as he watched every shift of weight, every subtle twitch of muscle. He had spent years teaching Caelan, yet there was something different in how Caelan carried himself today.

Suddenly, Caelan feigned left. His body twisted as if to strike low, only to pivot sharply and lunge toward Torin's abdomen. The attack was swift and precise, but Torin was faster. A flick of his wrist sent the blade harmlessly to the side. The clash of steel broke the stillness.

Torin anticipated a follow-up. So he stepped inside to capitalize on the opening. His sword arced upward in a vicious diagonal slash aimed at Caelan's exposed shoulder. Caelan reacted in an instant. A single step back. A sharp roll of his shoulder, and the blade missed by inches as it sliced only air.

His sword came alive in his hands, a blur of silver flashed through the morning light. He launched a relentless series of slashes with blistering speed and force. Caelan sought to overwhelm Torin's defenses. The air hissed with every cut. The force behind their blows sent ripples through the mist that clung to the air.

Torin was no stranger to aggressive onslaughts. His blade moved in tight, efficient arcs, meeting every strike with a dance of parries. He never allowed himself to be driven back without intent. He read Caelan's assault for openings.

It was a battle of patience and skill. Caelan pressed forward, Torin held his ground, and the morning air rang with the song of steel.

As they moved, their blades carved silver arcs through the morning air. A metallic symphony accompanied by the soft rhythm of boots striking the damp earth. The duel had become a conversation without words; Each strike a statement. Each parry a rebuttal.

Caelan launched into a maneuver they had drilled countless times. A double feint followed by a low sweep. Every false attack was meant to lure Torin into a misstep. The first was high, a flicker of steel toward his shoulder. The second was a quick redirection toward his ribs. Neither were meant to land, only to force a planned reaction.

Torin took the bait. He adjusted to intercept the incoming strikes. His stance shifted. But that was all Caelan needed. He followed the double feint maneuver with a low, sweeping strike aimed at Torin's legs.

Torin reacted on instinct alone. He barely escaped, as the move forced him to leap back at the last second. The blade missed his shin by a hair's breadth.

"Very good, Caelan," he mused as he rolled his shoulders to reset his stance. "Let's see how well you handle this!"

Torin pressed on. His strikes sharpened. His footwork moved faster. Each attack came in a relentless succession, testing the full measure of Caelan's skill. Steel clashed against steel in a furious rhythm.

Torin forced Caelan to adapt and push past his limits.

Caelan's defenses tightened. He wasn't reacting any longer. He was predicting. He noticed the faint tightening of Torin's grip before a downward slash. He recognized the shift in stance before a thrust.

He felt the rhythm of the battle. Its momentum beat through his veins like a song that only he could hear.

Torin led Caelan toward the tree line. He darted behind a thick trunk, forcing Caelan to adjust his stance and follow. Caelan anticipated Torin's move and sidestepped just in time to avoid a thrust aimed at his side.

Between strikes, Torin kicked at the loose roots and rocks scattered across the ground to create obstacles. He leaped onto a fallen log to gain the high ground. His sword flashed downward in a relentless cascade of strikes.

Caelan reacted with a sudden burst of movement. He rolled beneath the log just as Torin's sword crashed down where he had stood a heartbeat before.

Torin had a second to react before Caelan emerged on the other side. His blade swept for Torin's legs.

Torin leaped back, his boots landing firmly on the damp wood. He did not waste time recovering. He pressed his counter.

The forest was alive with their battle. Birds scattered in a flurry of wings. Leaves beneath their feet rustled in protest. The morning air rang with the sharp clash of steel.

Torin pushed Caelan into a denser area, forcing him to navigate uneven terrain. Roots twisted beneath fallen leaves. He advanced, executing a sweeping parry before launching into a flurry of strikes meant to disarm Caelan. His blade came in fast. Each attack struck high and then low, meant to force Caelan to keep up.

Caelan's instincts screaming to regain control. And then he saw it. A single opening in Torin's unyielding assault.

He executed a counter Torin had taught him, deflected the last strike and twisted into a sudden, precise spin. His blade arced dangerously close to Torin's shoulder, the edge bit into the fabric of his tunic.

Torin froze, just for a moment, then grinned. The fire of challenge blazed in his eyes.

Caelan had learned well.

Caelan feigned high. His blade flashed toward Torin's shoulder. He dropped low at the last second, aimed for his legs. Torin didn't fall for it. Anticipating the move, he twisted sharply and delivered a brutal kick to Caelan's chest. The impact sent Caelan sprawling back. His breath ripped from his lungs as he hit the ground. A sharp jolt shot through his ribs, but he didn't linger in the fall.

He rolled with the momentum. He twisted onto his shoulder and sprang back onto his feet in one fluid motion. His blade was raised. His eyes locked onto Torin as he steadied himself.

"Nice recovery," Torin smirked.

The duel reignited.

Torin moved first. He kicked up a cloud of dirt, sending a fine spray of dust and grit into the air between them. The sudden haze blurred Caelan's vision for a brief moment. A sudden shift in the air. The whisper of movement.

Caelan barely had time to react before Torin closed the distance, his sword cut downward in a powerful strike. Caelan's instincts screamed. He raised his blade in time to intercept the blow. The force of it rattled his grip, reverberated up his arm, and threatened to buckle his stance. His boots dug into the soil as he absorbed the impact. The metallic ring of clashing steel cut through the air.

He didn't wait to recover. Caelan pivoted to turn the momentary deadlock into an opportunity. He wrenched his sword free and swung in a wide, sweeping arc. Torin saw the strike coming and leaped back just in time. The tip of Caelan's blade sliced through empty space. He landed in a crouch, but the sudden retreat had cost him the ground. Caelan exhaled as he adjusted his grip. He was still in this fight.

The duel surged towards its crescendo. Movements blurred into a relentless dance of steel and shadows. Each clash rang through the clearing like a hammer strike on an anvil. Caelan's body burned with exertion. Every muscle screamed in protest. His arms were leaden, and breaths ragged.

Torin pressed him harder and faster to test everything Caelan had left to give. Their swords carved through the air in rapid succession. Each strike met with an equally fierce rebuttal. Sparks flew as metal bit against metal. Their boots scuffed at the earth.

Fatigue clawed at Caelan's edges. His focus remained razor-sharp.

The final clash came without warning. Their blades met in a forceful bind, neither willing to yield. Their swords trembled under the strain.

Their gazes met. The weight of the moment settled between them.

Caelan could feel his pulse pound in his ears.

Torin exhaled, the tension in his muscles eased as he took a step back. The duel was over, and he withdrew and slid his sword into its sheath. The soft metallic click broke the silence between them. His eyes never left Caelan's.

"You have matched me, Caelan."

"There is nothing more I can teach you. You are ready." his voice steady with pride and a subtle finality.

Caelan lowered his sword. It practically dropped to the ground, still being held by his hand. Caelan collapsed in place. Thankful. He didn't know how much more he had left. He looked up to Torin's gaze. He had spent years chasing this moment, this measure of his growth. And now, he finally felt the weight of it.

That night they sat close to the fire, the flames snapping in the cool air, throwing light and shadow across the trunks of the Elderwood. Caelan nursed his cup while Torin leaned back on his elbows, eyes half-lidded as though he were speaking more to the fire than to his companion.

He began with humor, as he often did. A tale of a stag hunt in his youth gone spectacularly wrong. He had set the snare too high and ended up dangling headfirst in the branches, his boot caught fast while the stag wandered off unimpressed. "There I was," Torin said, gesturing with his cup, "shouting every curse I knew while blood ran to my head. Two hours, Caelan. Two hours until a farmer passed by and cut me down. He didn't even take me seriously enough to laugh. Just shook his head like I was some fool of a boy, which I suppose I was."

Caelan nearly choked on his drink at the image. To picture his master, always composed, always immovable, thrashing upside down in a tree. It almost stripped away the unshakable mantle Torin had worn all these years. For the first time, he saw the man beneath it.

The story loosened something between them. One memory tumbled into another: a spar gone wrong when Torin misjudged his footing and ended up sprawling face-first in the mud, a hunting trip where he ate berries that left him sick for two days, the scar on his forearm not from a glorious battle but from a goose that hadn't taken kindly to being caught. Each tale carried with it a grain of humility, of lessons learned the hard way.

"Don't mistake me," Torin said, his voice softening as the laughter ebbed. "Skill matters. Discipline matters. But the world will find ways to humble you, Caelan, no matter how sharp your blade or how quick your hand. Sometimes those lessons leave scars, sometimes only bruises to your pride. But take them all. Learn from them. Because in the end, it's not strength that carries a man forward, but the wisdom to know when he's been made a fool and when to rise again."

His tone shifted then, no longer a sparring master's cadence, but something closer to confession. "I have fought battles I should have walked away from. I have walked away from fights I should have stood my ground in. You'll make the same mistakes. All men do. What matters is that you carry yourself with honor, even in failure. Remember that."

The forest hushed around them. Firelight glowed in Torin's eyes, and for a long moment Caelan simply listened, the words settling into him like stone laid in a foundation.

When sleep came, it was deep and untroubled.

But dawn revealed the silence of departure. Caelan stirred against the pale light, blinking away the weight of dreams, only to feel the emptiness before he saw it. The fire had burned to ash. The tent was gone. Torin was gone. The clearing was as it had been before their years together, untouched, unmarked—except for a single hawk feather resting on the log where Torin had sat.

Caelan picked it up, his thumb tracing its edge. The feather felt light, yet it carried the weight of five long years. Every bruise, every scar, every lesson endured and endured again until his body remembered more than his mind. Torin had left nothing else behind, no words of farewell, no token save this. A silent acknowledgment.

Caelan stood slowly, the forest opening around him in quiet invitation. He was no longer the boy who had raised a wooden sword under Torin's watchful eye. He had been shaped. His master had given him all he could. The rest was his to walk alone.

He drew in a long breath of the cool morning air, the scent of pine and earth filling his lungs. Before him the paths of the Elderwood stretched outward, some shadowed, some painted in light. He stepped forward, carrying the weight of lessons that would follow him wherever he went.

ACT II

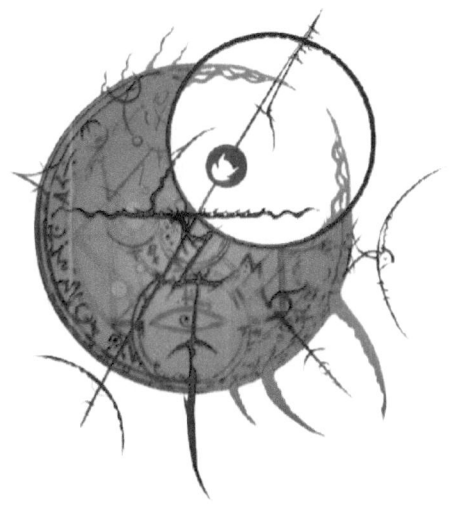

The whisper came, inevitable.
It came because it had always been trying to.

"I am."

There was no sound to carry it. No mind to know it.
But it rippled, as if the silence itself remembered something it
had tried to forget.

CHAPTER TWELVE

STAG AND SHADOW

The path through Elderwood back to the cottage felt both familiar and foreign beneath Caelan's boots. Five years had passed, shedding sweat, blood, and tears under Torin's relentless training. He had left this area of the forest as a teenager who barely understood his place in the world.

Sunlight burst through the tree coverage in broken rays spotted along the forest floor. The wind whispered through the leaves. Critters darted through the underbrush. Birds called out in their songs.

Caelan idly rested his hand on the pommel of his sword as he recalled to a particular sparring session with Torin.

"You hesitate," Torin growled as he parried Caelan's strike.

The ranger had barely broken a sweat while Caelan was already breathing hard. His arms ached from the repeated clashes of steel.

"I'm thinking through my moves."

"Too much thinking will get you killed. Feel. Anticipate. Trust your instincts."

A flicker of movement, the faintest twitch in Torin's stance, had been all the warning Caelan received before a boot slammed into his ribs, sending him sprawling in the dirt. His sword flew from his grip, landing several feet away.

"A dead man has all the time in the world to think," Torin said, standing over him.

Caelan had groaned, pushing himself up, his pride more wounded than his body.

"Duly noted."

Now, as he made his way back home through the Elderwood, those lessons Torin had taught him resonated more than ever. His instincts were sharper. His awareness heightened. He knew the forest better than any road or city. Yet, he couldn't shake the feeling today that something was off. Something not of the forest was watching him. The birthmark on his chest slowly began to tingle. An unknown magic was nearby. He hadn't felt this sensation since Elaria started to teach him basic spells. The air around him felt still, and ambient sounds went silent. His hand unconsciously tightened around the hilt.

"Feel. Anticipate. Trust your instincts."

The trees appeared more wild than he remembered. Their gnarled roots twisted through the earth like the veins of something ancient and alive. Shadows stretched longer, moving in ways that defied the light. It wasn't acting hostile, but it didn't seem natural either. He attempted to steady his breathing.

He had changed. Perhaps the forest had, too.

He approached the glade when he saw his home through the trees. A childish excitement swelled up in him that made him smile. Smoke trickled up from the chimney. The windows flickered with warm candlelight, a beacon against the deepening twilight.

Caelan paused at the tree line, drinking in the sight. Five years. And yet, it felt like he had only walked away from this place yesterday.

He made his way up the path that led to the door when his anticipation was interrupted by a familiar sound. Thistle let out a neigh louder than he ever remembered her sounding. A smile appeared as he looked over as she trotted to greet him. She shook her head up and down in syncopation with her steps. When she reached him, she nuzzled into his shoulder, huffing, trying to push him up.

"Hey, girl." He reached up to pet her cheeks and neck. "I've missed you too."

He placed his hand on the white strip up her muzzle and turned back to the cottage. The door opened.

"What's going on out here, Thistle?" Elaria stood in the doorway as she looked out.

At that moment, she just stared at him, attempting to comprehend what her eyes saw.

"Caelan?!" she exclaimed as she ran towards him.

She feared that he might be just an illusion at first. He didn't even have time to respond before she pulled him into an embrace that nearly stole his breath. The scent of her hair brought back memories. She smelled of old parchment, herbs, and home.

"Oh my... look at you!" Elaria whispered, stepping back just enough to take him in. She cupped his face, her thumbs brushing over the faint scruff along his jawline. Her eyes glistened as she fought off the tears.

"Look at how much you've grown!" she exclaimed proudly, her hands settling onto his shoulders.

She studied him, taking in every change. Just as she had done all his life, she reached up to brush the hair from his eyes.

"It has been too long," she whispered.

He realized how much he had missed the warmth of her touch and the way she looked at him.

"I missed you, Momma," he managed, his voice catching in his throat.

Elaria smiled, a single tear running down her cheek. "I missed you too, son. More than you know."

She cupped his cheek again, smiled, and gave his shoulder a playful shake.

"Come inside. You must be starving," she exclaimed. "And I won't hear any excuses. Whatever crazy, wild diet Torin had you on, I know it wasn't nearly enough. You're home now, and you will eat."

A small smile appeared on Caelan's lips. Some things never changed.

Squeezing his hand one last time, Elaria turned to lead him inside. The warm light of the cottage welcomed him home.

Elaria stirred beneath her blankets. She shifted onto her side, stretching her legs beneath the covers. A few snaps and crackles accompanied her full stretch. She laid still for a moment. The morning glade outside was coming to life again. Sunlight started to breach through her window. Then she heard a sound different from the usual morning symphony. A moment passed before she recognized it, the unmistakable whisper of a blade slicing through the air.

Caelan was already awake and outside.

She sat up gently on the bed. The wooden floor was cool beneath her feet. She reached over for her shawl to drape over her shoulders as she stood. Her reflection caught briefly in the glass of her window. She had aged, but not unkindly. Her long chestnut-brown hair hung loosely down her back, with a few strands that strayed from sleep. Several fine silver streaks wove through the darker strands. Her face was now accented by faint creases at the corners of her green eyes.

Elaria brushed her right hand through her hair to tucking a few loose strands behind her ear before she stepped toward the window. She placed her hand on the glass. It was cool to the touch and fogged slightly from her breath.

There in the clearing, Caelan stood with a sword in hand, was moving through stances. She could only guess that Torin had taught him. His sword cut through the air in sharp, precise movements. She remembered the boy who once chased dragons with wooden sticks. That boy was gone now, replaced by the man he had become.

She stood watching him for a moment. The sun flashed off the steel briefly, forcing her to squint. After a few minutes, she turned away from the window to continue her morning routine.

Caelan moved into his next stance, steadying his breathing. The morning air was cool against his skin. His body flowed perfectly in sync with his sword. He no longer had to think about his movements. Each step, each pivot, and strike was the result of years of them being drilled into him.

Now twenty years old, he had grown into his frame. His once-lean build had been honed into solid muscle. His shoulders were broader, accented by his dark auburn hair falling just to his neck. Hair clung to his forehead with sweat. His facial features were sharper. The spark within his storm-gray eyes seemed to flash with determination as he landed each stance.

He stepped into a defensive position, adjusting his footing slightly before pivoting into a thrust. His blade cut through the air, forcing it to flee suddenly.

"Precision over power. A blade is useless if it cannot find its mark."

Caelan inhaled slowly, shifting his weight into a series of fast slashes, testing his speed. Torin's lessons still resonated with him.

"Feel the flow of battle. Don't fight it."

His sword sang through the air as he transitioned into his final stance. With a sharp exhale, he executed a forceful downward strike. The blow displaced the air below, stirring the dew-laced grass. He stood there for a moment, his blade lowered, his pulse steady, and his breath even. His body was warmed but not fatigued.

Good. The discipline had not left me.

Caelan sheathed his blade. His shoulders were stiff. So, he rolled them and stretched his arms across his chest to help loosen the tightness in his muscles. Then, he caught a whiff of himself. Training had left him sweaty. He walked over to the creek at the edge of the glade. He knelt beside it, scooped his hands into the crisp water, and splashed it over his face. He splashed some on his chest and armpits, too. The sudden chill against his skin was refreshing. Running his fingers through his damp hair, he pushed it away from his face before splashing more water on the back of his neck.

As he sat back on his heels, something in the distance stirred. It wasn't a sound. More of a pull toward a presence. Caelan lifted his gaze toward the tree line.

The stone circle.

It had been years since he had last set foot there. He remembered the resonance of energy there. It had always felt different. Ancient. Alive.

It would be a good place to meditate and help him center himself after practice. A place to settle his mind. He rocked back onto his heels, stood up, and turned back toward the cottage. Smoke lingered from the chimney, Elaria must be up by now.

She stood near the hearth as she prepared breakfast, placing some bread on the table.

"I'll be back later," Caelan said.

One hand held the door, and the other rested on the doorframe. Elaria glanced over her shoulder at him, raising an eyebrow slightly with intrigue.

"The stone circle?"

Caelan paused for a second, then nodded. Of course, she knew. She always did. Elaria hummed softly, returning to her cooking. "Don't be gone too long."

"I won't."

And with that, he stepped off.

Caelan thought that the path seemed more feral than he remembered. The forest barely cleared the path for him as he approached. He used to run through these areas during their morning walks. He trekked on, the presence of the circle grew stronger the closer he got.

After about an hour, the forest went quiet. Not in an eerie way, but in a feeling of reverence. As if the wildlife and forest respected the sanctity of his destination. Then, finally, through a thinning veil of trees, he saw them. The ancient stones. Standing in silent formation, half-buried by time. Caelan stepped into the clearing.

The air felt different here. Thicker. The stone circle stood before him. Its ancient pillars positioned precisely at specific points on the diagram etched into the floor plate. Moss clung to their bases, vines weaving through the cracks. Wanting to feel closer to nature, Caelan removed his boots, setting them off to the side. He also removed his sword and shirt, placing them beside his boots. The sigil of his birthmark tingled in the presence of the stones.

He lowered himself into a cross-legged position in the middle of the circle. Meditation had been part of his training for years. It helped him focus his raging storm of thoughts. He rested his palms on his thighs and closed his eyes. He let his breathing slow... deep... steady. The pulse of the forest thrummed in the back of his mind as he focused. He could hear everything around him. Leaves rustled on the ground to his east about thirty meters. An owl hooted in a tree behind him. Squirrels chittered in the brush to his west, likely searching for fallen nuts.

And yet... something was off. The hairs on his arms prickled. He was not alone. His fingers instinctively moved toward the hilt of his sword. It wasn't there. He had taken it off earlier, it layed a few feet behind him.

Don't move.

Then, he heard it. A low, deliberate exhale. It sounded almost like a deer. Caelan's eyes snapped open. Standing just beyond the edge of the stones was a stag. But it wasn't just any stag. It was unlike any beast he had ever seen. Its massive frame was bathed in a soft, spectral light that seemed to radiate from within. The silvery white coat shimmered in the sunlight. Its antlers were etched with faintly glowing runes that shifted and pulsed with energy. Its golden eyes locked onto his, refusing to blink.

Caelan's pulse quickened. This was no ordinary animal. It was watching him. Studying him. Caelan couldn't move. He wasn't sure if he should. The stag did nothing, just stood there.

He decided to move first and stand up. At least then, he could run if he needed to. He'd have to come back for his sword and boots.

The stag stepped forward. The silver glow around its fur flickered. Its hooves made no sound at all. Caelan resisted the urge to step back. There was no threat in the creature's presence. Yet, his heart pounded against his ribcage. It came closer, a few feet away now. The stag's golden eyes never left his. It lowered its head.

Caelan swallowed, watching as the creature leaned in. The runes on its massive antlers pulsed like a steady heartbeat. Then, slowly, deliberately, the stag touched the tip of its antler to Caelan's birthmark.

A surge of energy ripped through him. The world around him fractured. Colors bled into one another, the sky split apart, and the ground beneath his feet vanished. Caelan gasped as reality collapsed around him, twisting into something unrecognizable. He was falling, not through space, but rather... through time.

He landed on a ridge overlooking a ruined landscape. The sky was devoid of stars. The sun was gone. Only a dim, suffocating twilight remained, casting its sickly glow over the land. Where once stood villages, now only blackened ruins smoldered. Roads were shattered. Trees stripped of life, their skeletal remains clawed at the sky like the hands of the damned. Unusually shaped mounds scattered along the plains. Caelan tried to look closer. They weren't mounds at all. They were piles of corpses.

A slow creeping mist crawled over the land. It whispered. No, it wasn't mist. It was a living shadow, twisting, shifting. It writhed as if it were hungry. A jagged black spire stabbed into the ruined earth, towering and curved like a rotted fang. Its surface pulsed with veins of unnatural darkness. At its base stood a figure cloaked in tattered robes. It did not move, yet Caelan felt its gaze pierce through him.

Chains of shadow slithered outward, stretching across the land and winding through the broken remnants of civilization. They reached into the halls of power, into cities, and homes.

He blinked...

The grand throne room of Dunmoh flickered into view. King Aldric sat slumped on his throne. His crown barely hung onto his head. His face appeared pale and hollow. Shadows coiled around him like serpents. Their whispers seeped into his bones.

Caelan could hear them. Their words curled like smoke.

"They will betray you."

"Your kingdom is lost."

"You must purge them all."

The shadows were not just consuming the land. They were infecting the hearts of men. A voice, ancient and weary, rumbled through the vision. But it wasn't from the dark figure. Something... deeper... older.

"If you do not walk the path, all will be lost."

Caelan turned. Beyond the destruction, the spire of rot, and the encroaching darkness stood a mountain shrouded in mist. A temple lay hidden there. Its doors carved with symbols older than kingdoms and the history of time. Unlike the twisted spire of shadow, this place radiated power. But it wasn't of dominion... of balance. The voice rumbled again.

"The answers you seek lie here. But you must choose to seek them. The path will not open unless you walk it."

The vision collapsed.

Caelan staggered backward, gasping for air. The weight of the vision pressed against his chest like iron chains. The stag was gone. The clearing was empty again. His birthmark burned. He lifted his hand to his chest. His fingers pressed against the warmth of the sigil. His breath was ragged gasps as he attempted to piece together what he had seen.

He had no choice. If he did not seek out this temple and find what lay within, the land would fall. Caelan clenched his fists trying to steady himself. He gathered his shirt, then kneeled down to lace up his boots. He picked up his sword last, rose up, and slowly sheathed it. Caelan tried to recall any lesson from Torin that might help in this situation. There was nothing that came to mind. How could a sword fare against such malice? Such overwhelming evil? His knuckles turned white, still holding onto the hilt. He turned to regard the stone circle once more before turning back and heading home.

As he walked, images of the vision flashed into his mind. The ruined land. The creeping shadow. The throne room corrupted by whispers. His pace quickened to get home. Elaria might know more... or at least something. The trees began to thin, revealing the glade to him once more.

Caelan slowly opened the door. Elaria sat at the table, her back to him, cutting some herbs. A neat row of her jars sat to her right side.

"You're back sooner than I expected," she quipped.

Caelan lingered in the doorway. His grip dug into the pommel of his sword. He was almost lost for words, but his face expressed the weight of the words he was fumbling with inside his head. Elaria finally turned around, her eyes immediately reading the expression on his face.

"What is it?"

Caelan stepped forward. "I had a vision."

Her lips parted slightly, bringing her hand up to her mouth. She was surprised but didn't say anything.

He swallowed. "It wasn't just some dream. It was real. It was... a warning."

She set her knife down on the table, then dusted her apron off as she spun in the chair to face him.

"Tell me everything."

So, Caelan told her. He spoke of the ruined land, the creeping mist that wasn't mist at all, but instead, it was shadow. The spire, the figure cloaked in tattered robes. The throne room, the whispers, the slow corruption of Dunmoh.

Elaria listened in silence. Her fingers slowly curled into her apron. When he finally finished, a silence fell between them for a moment. The soft crackle of the hearth almost seemed muted for a second.

"And what of the temple?"

Caelan nodded. "That's where the answers are. But I must choose to take that path."

She studied him for a moment. Then, with a determined look in her eyes, "And you're going to go."

It wasn't a question.

Caelan held her gaze. "I have to, I suppose."

Elaria sighed, rubbing at her temple as she looked at her bookshelf.

"Then we need to prepare you for the journey."

CHAPTER THIRTEEN
VEYLTHAR SANCTUM

The hearth crackled low, casting amber light across the wooden floorboards in slow, flickering waves. Morning had not yet crested the horizon, but the cottage felt awake in its own way—books humming with the soft weight of memory, dried herbs rustling as if whispering farewells. Caelan sat quietly at the edge of the hearth, already dressed, boots laced tight, his satchel lying open on the floor beside him.

Across the room, Elaria stood before the bookshelf. Her fingers drifted along the spines like they knew each one by touch alone. She moved without urgency, but with focus—each motion deliberate, each breath measured. The wood beneath her bare feet creaked faintly as she reached for a thick, weathered tome bound in dark leather. The cover shimmered faintly where the firelight caught the arcane sigils embossed into its hide.

She brought it to the table, laying it down with care.

The Chronicles of the Arcane Order.

"I was younger than you when I first read this," she murmured, brushing a loose strand of hair behind her ear. "Much of it's theory, history, and names that no one speaks anymore. But buried in the footnotes are truths older than any kingdom."

Caelan leaned forward as she opened the cover. The pages were yellowed, the edges rough. Symbols had been penned in fine hand and annotated again and again over the years, notes tucked in the margins from long-forgotten scholars. She turned the pages with reverence, until she came to one illustrated by hand—a map etched in ink so faded it might've vanished in another century.

The Elder Mountains stretched across the parchment in jagged lines, their peaks crowned with symbols only a mage could read. No roads, no labels. Just raw, unforgiving terrain. Elaria traced a path with her finger, moving slowly across the ridgelines until she stopped at a place marked not with a name, but a sigil.

A swirling vortex drawn in a single, unbroken line.

"This," she said quietly, "is where you must go."

Caelan's brow furrowed as he leaned closer, studying the mark. The parchment smelled of dust and pine and the faintest echo of ink. He swallowed. "There's no trail... no landmarks. Just a symbol."

"It's not meant to be found easily," she replied. "The Veylthar Sanctum was built as a refuge during the Sundering Wars, hidden even from the mages who weren't welcome within its halls. Only those who are ready—or desperate—can find the path."

Caelan's voice dropped to a whisper. "And you've been there?"

Elaria's gaze lingered on the page for a long moment before she closed the tome and met his eyes. There was a glint there—of memory, of pain, of pride.

"I have. Once. It changes you, in ways that words can't prepare you for."

She rested her hand atop the closed book and let the silence fill the room between them.

Elaria stepped away from the table and moved toward the hearth, her silhouette framed by the gentle light. Caelan watched her crouch beside the low chest near the fire—one he had seen all his life but had never dared to open. Its dark oak frame was bound in iron bands, worn with age but never neglected. It was always locked. Always quietly off-limits.

She extended her hand over the lid, palm hovering just above the latch. A flicker of energy pulsed outward, and the lock gave a faint click as the enchantment released. The chest opened with a whisper, its hinges sighing like something long held in silence finally exhaled.

Inside lay an arrangement of supplies, each placed with the kind of precision only necessity—or love—could inspire. Caelan stood and approached slowly, not wanting to disturb the moment. Vials of thick liquids and crystalline powders sat nestled in carved hollows of wood. Rolled parchment and aged cloth wraps were tucked along the edges. But what caught his eye most was the deep indigo cloak, carefully folded and resting atop it all.

Elaria reached for it first, lifting it with both hands. As she shook it out, the silver embroidery shimmered—intertwining threads that caught the firelight in complex weaves. Runes, delicate and intricate, formed subtle patterns along the hem and collar.

"This cloak was mine," she said, turning it in her hands. "Worn when I made the journey myself. Each stitch carries a ward, woven in."

She stepped forward and draped it gently across the back of Caelan's chair. Her fingers lingered on the fabric, smoothing the fold.

"It will keep you warm where even fire forgets to burn," she continued, "and more importantly, it will shield you from those who would try to find you through unnatural means."

Caelan ran a hand across the fabric. It was soft but heavier than it looked, as if it remembered where it had been.

Elaria turned back to the chest and lifted a leather satchel from the corner. She began selecting a few small vials—amber, violet, and emerald glass—nesting them into padded slots with practiced ease.

"This one is for exhaustion," she said, holding up the violet. "A sip will carry your body further than your will can alone."

She picked up another. "This one mends torn skin, bruised muscle, things that rest alone won't fix."

"And this," she said, drawing out a small rough-cut crystal bound in silver wire, "will guide you when you cannot see the way."

Caelan took the crystal from her palm, holding it up to the firelight. It refracted light in strange ways, not just bending it, but folding it. It hummed faintly against his fingertips.

"How does it work?" he asked.

"It doesn't show roads or directions," she replied. "It responds to your intention. If you walk blindly, it will remain silent. But if you walk with purpose... it will point the way."

He turned the crystal over once more before tucking it into the satchel.

Elaria closed the lid of the chest and rested her hands atop it for a moment, gathering herself. When she rose, there was something in her posture that hadn't been there before—a tightening, not of the body, but of the spirit. A quiet bracing.

She looked at him, not as a mother to a boy, but as a woman to the young man he was becoming.

"You've been trained to fight," she said. "To heal, to listen, to protect. But the mountains do not test skill. They test certainty."

Caelan met her eyes. "Then I'll be ready."

Elaria stepped forward, her hand rising to touch the side of his face. Her voice dropped to a whisper.

"No one is ever ready, Caelan. But you... are prepared."

Elaria moved with quiet purpose through the cottage, collecting the final items for his satchel—dried fruits wrapped in cloth, flint and steel, a rolled parchment sealed with wax. Each item seemed to carry more weight than it should, not because of its mass, but because of what it meant. This wasn't simply a supply run. This was a parting.

Caelan knelt by the fire, adjusting the straps of his boots, the cloak now folded atop his pack beside him. His hands moved with practiced steadiness, but his chest felt tight. The room around him, so familiar, now felt like it was already pulling away. Shadows danced on the walls as the fire hissed softly, as if reluctant to stay lit for just one more morning.

Elaria returned to the hearth and stood across from him. The satchel was full. The crystal was secure. There was nothing more to pack.

"The Elder Mountains are old," she said at last, her voice calm but distant, like it was drifting across time to someone far away. "Older than any spell, older than any book I've ever read. They remember things the world has forgotten."

Caelan stood slowly. "You mean the land is alive?"

"It doesn't breathe the way we do," she answered, "but yes. The peaks listen. The passes judge. The winds carry more than cold air. There's magic woven into the stone itself—ancient magic, long before the kingdoms rose."

She stepped closer, her eyes tracing his face. "You won't just be crossing terrain, Caelan. You'll be walking into the bones of the world. And it will know you're there."

He nodded, his throat dry. "And the temple?"

Elaria hesitated, then lowered her gaze slightly. "The Veylthar Sanctum is hidden for a reason. Not everyone who seeks it finds it. Some turn back. Some... forget what they came for. And some are changed so deeply that even their reflection doesn't recognize them anymore."

Caelan's brow furrowed at that. "Is that what happened to you?"

She looked up again. A half-smile touched her lips, but it didn't reach her eyes. "I was a different person when I entered. I was wiser when I left. But wisdom... always comes at a price."

She let the words settle, then reached for the indigo cloak and held it up, unfolding it once more. "Turn around."

He did so without a word, and she draped the cloak over his shoulders, smoothing the fabric along his back, fastening the clasp beneath his throat. The embroidery shimmered faintly, almost responding to the warmth of her touch.

"There," she whispered. "You look like someone the world might listen to."

Caelan turned to face her. He wanted to say something—something meaningful, something strong—but no words came. He opened his mouth, then closed it again. All the lessons, all the nights by the fire, all the quiet strength she had given him... and all he could offer was silence.

That was enough.

Elaria stepped forward and placed her hand against his cheek. Her fingers lingered, brushing back the strand of hair that always fell across his brow.

"You are my heart," she said softly, "but you are not mine to keep."

He reached up, covering her hand with his.

"I'll come back," he said, with the stubbornness of someone who meant it.

Elaria's eyes shimmered with the weight of hope and fear entwined. "Then let the mountains remember your name."

She stepped back and opened the door. Cold air rushed into the cottage, carrying the scent of frost and pine, and somewhere in the distance, the wind howled as if welcoming or warning.

Caelan lifted his pack and stepped toward the threshold. He paused there, taking one final look at the room—the table, the fire, the herbs above the window, the life they had made.

Then he stepped outside.

Elaria watched from the doorway, her arms crossed, but not from the cold.

He didn't look back.

And that, she knew, was the surest sign he was ready.

The forest thinned as Caelan followed the worn footpath beyond the glade, the first pale blush of dawn filtering through the canopy overhead. Frost clung to the edges of leaves, sparkling like scattered fragments of glass as the sun crept higher, its light still gentle, not yet bold enough to burn away the mist coiled along the earth.

He adjusted the satchel at his side, the indigo cloak wrapped snug around his shoulders. It trailed slightly behind him, catching the occasional burr or snag of underbrush, but he didn't mind. The familiar scents of pine, dew, and distant woodsmoke clung to his senses. Every sound seemed more vivid—birdsong layered with the rustle of unseen critters, the creak of old trees bending ever so slightly with the wind.

Somewhere behind him, the glade was already fading into memory. He didn't turn around. He couldn't.

A flicker of movement caught his eye—just to the right of the path. There, among the low thickets and root-twisted trees, stood the fox.

Its fur was a swirled patchwork of silver, white, and charcoal. Not quite natural, not quite ordinary. Its ears twitched at his gaze, but it didn't flee. It merely watched, tail flicking once. Caelan paused, breath held.

They had played this game before—glimpses, disappearances, a watching presence at the edge of childhood. But this felt different.

He dipped his head slightly in acknowledgment, a quiet farewell. The fox blinked once in reply, then turned and slipped back into the brush, silent as a shadow.

The path grew narrower as he walked. Brambles nipped at his boots, and the canopy overhead began to break apart, letting in more sky. The temperature dropped, subtle but certain. Here, the forest surrendered to the bones of the land—tree roots lost their dominance to stone, and soft soil hardened into uneven ridges.

He passed a moss-covered standing stone, half-swallowed by ivy. It bore no markings he recognized, but the air around it felt weighted, like something once sacred still lingered in its shadow. Caelan paused for only a moment, laying his fingers gently against its cold surface.

"I will not forget," he whispered.

He didn't know why he said it. Only that it felt right.

The trail ahead would not be kind. The Elder Mountains were already rising in the distance—jagged teeth silhouetted against the sky, their white peaks gleaming faintly beneath the rising sun. The forest path would give way to rock soon. He could feel the shift already, like the land itself was holding its breath.

As he crested a low ridge, he looked out over the stretch of valley behind him. Trees spread like a dark ocean, the morning fog weaving through their limbs like restless ghosts.

It looked small now. He turned back to the mountains. And kept walking.

The narrow trail bent upward in a slow, relentless climb. Grass gave way to stone, and the loam beneath Caelan's boots turned to packed earth laced with jagged roots and brittle shale. The trees, once thick and towering, now stood farther apart—scarred pines and gnarled oaks hunched like sentries at the edge of the world.

With each step forward, the air grew thinner, drier. Colder. A sharp wind cut down from the peaks and knifed through the folds of his cloak, stinging his cheeks and catching strands of his hair in its grasp. He pulled the cloak tighter around him. The silver-threaded runes stitched into its seams hummed faintly against his skin, offering warmth that wasn't physical but somehow settled deeper—like a ward pressed to his bones.

The trail wound along a ridge, revealing brief views of the valley below—vast and shadowed beneath the mid-morning light. Distant rivers glinted like silver veins through a sleeping beast. Somewhere, far below, was the glade. And beyond that, Gladecross. Villages where the king's laws twisted the hearts of men. Places where silence was safer than truth.

But up here, the silence was different. It wasn't fear—it was memory.

He came upon a cairn near a bend in the trail. Weathered stones stacked with care, its top crowned by a flat shard of slate bearing an etching barely visible with age. A spiral, imperfect, carved by hand. Not a grave. A marker. A message to any who knew how to read it: *You are not the first to walk this path.*

Caelan touched the spiral with gloved fingers. The cold bit through the leather, but he held it a moment longer. Then moved on.

Further up, the wind began to change. It didn't howl, not yet. But it carried with it the echo of something deeper—an unsettling vibration in the chest, more felt than heard. The sound of the mountain breathing. The rhythm of stone shifting beneath time's weight.

The trail disappeared entirely in places, replaced by nothing more than deer runs and slanted rock. Caelan moved cautiously, using a stick to test footholds when needed. He passed under a natural arch of stone, weathered smooth by centuries of wind and rain. Its surface shimmered faintly beneath his fingertips—a trace of magic, long dormant, woven into the mountain's bones.

By midday, he found a ledge to rest upon. He dropped his satchel with a soft grunt, careful not to let it roll, and pulled out the small crystal Elaria had given him. He turned it in his fingers, watching the light refract and twist along its fractured edges. Then he held it flat in his palm, closed his eyes, and quieted his breath.

Not where I am... he thought. *But where I must be.*

A slow warmth built in his hand—not heat, but pressure, like the tug of a river current beneath still water. The crystal pulled gently to the left, guiding his awareness toward a barely visible trail etched into the slope above.

He nodded once, pocketed the crystal, and stood. The wind shifted again, stronger now. He could hear it howling farther up in the passes. Not a threat, not yet. But it was speaking. And the mountain was listening.

By the time the sun dipped low behind the western peaks, Caelan's legs ached from the climb and the thin mountain air. The trail, if it could still be called that, had narrowed into little more than a tilted span of crumbling stone hugging the cliffside. He had kept moving, driven by the soft pull of the crystal in his pocket and the memory of Elaria's voice—steady, instructive, always just behind him in thought.

As dusk thickening into night, he found shelter. A jut of overhanging rock carved a shallow alcove into the side of the slope. It wasn't much—barely enough room to sit upright—but it offered protection from the wind and a view of the sky stretching vast and empty above. Below, the world was a jagged mess of shadow and stone, obscured by low clouds that rolled like mist along the spines of the mountain range.

Caelan dropped his satchel and sank to his knees. Every joint in his body throbbed with the dull weight of exhaustion. His breath fogged in the cold air, sharp and thin in his lungs. He fumbled numbly with his supplies, unwrapping a strip of dried meat and breaking off a piece of flatbread. The food was coarse, tasteless—but it filled the hollow in his stomach. He chewed in silence.

The wind outside the alcove hissed along the rock, rising in unpredictable bursts that whistled through cracks in the stone. It wasn't just cold—it was old. Like something whispering stories too ancient for any tongue to remember. He drew the cloak tighter around himself, grateful once again for Elaria's enchantments.

With numb fingers, he pulled out the small vial she'd given him—the one for exhaustion. He hesitated, then tucked it away again. *Not yet.* He would save it for when his legs gave out completely. This... this was only the first day.

As the sky darkened, stars began to emerge—brilliant, icy pinpricks in a vault of black. No flicker of firelight from other travelers. No sign of birds or beasts. Just wind and stone and sky.

He watched the constellations slowly turn, trying to pick out the ones he remembered. The Hunter. The Silver Chain. The Gatekeeper.

Somewhere, past the farthest horizon, was Elaria. Alone in the cottage. Still watching the fire, maybe. He pulled the crystal from his pouch again, holding it against the starlight. It did not glow, but the way it caught the faintest light.

"Guide me," he whispered. "If you can hear me. Just... keep me on the path."

He held it until the cold bit into his knuckles, then tucked it away. Caelan curled into the narrow space beneath the rock, wrapping his cloak around himself as best he could. The stone was unforgiving beneath his back, but he didn't complain. He had chosen this. And he would see it through.

Sleep didn't come easily. Every sound—the gusting wind, the groan of distant rock, the rustle of gravel—kept his mind alert. He drifted in and out of shallow dreams, his fingers curled tight around the hilt of his belt knife.

In one dream, he stood on a high ridge staring out over a field of stars, and a voice—not Elaria's, not his own—whispered a word he could not remember upon waking.

The morning light came slow and grey, bleeding gently across the eastern sky. Caelan rose stiffly, brushed the frost from his cloak, and stepped back onto the path.

The mountain was waiting.

The trail steepened by midmorning, narrowing into jagged steps carved into the stone by time rather than hands. Wind scoured the ridgeline with relentless persistence, tugging at Caelan's cloak and stinging his face with fine grit. Clouds crept low across the sky, casting the mountain in a shifting veil of shadow and silver. His breath came harder now—short, controlled draws as he ascended the path in steady rhythm.

Loose stones scattered beneath his boots as he climbed, forcing him to pause often and test the footing ahead with care. The higher he rose, the more the world seemed to fall away behind him. Trees had long since vanished. Even the birds no longer followed. Only the wind remained. And the mountain.

He rounded a bend where the path collapsed entirely into a narrow ledge—no wider than a man's shoulders, hugging a sheer cliff wall that dropped into mist and silence below. One misstep and there would be no second chance. He pressed his hand to the stone beside him, steadying himself, and forced his body forward inch by inch.

The ledge curved again, and he froze.

Just ahead, perched impossibly on a jut of stone that jutted out like the blade of a broken axe, stood a mountain goat. Its thick white coat rippled in the breeze, horns curving back with regal symmetry. The creature looked directly at him—calm, unbothered by the drop beneath it or the wind howling past.

It blinked once, then turned, picking its way along the cliff with careful precision. And paused as if waiting.

Caelan's lips parted, breath caught somewhere between awe and disbelief. "You've got to be joking," he muttered under his breath, watching the creature glance back at him again.

He shifted his weight carefully, following. The goat moved ahead, always just far enough to stay ahead, but never so far that it vanished from sight. It walked with confidence—its hooves finding purchase where none should exist, leading him along ledges and over tight ridge-lines that no map would ever mark. And somehow, impossibly, Caelan followed.

There was no trail now. Only instinct. Every so often, the goat would pause atop a boulder or slope and regard him again. Its eyes didn't hold the blank dullness of a beast, but something deeper—an old calm, as if it had walked these heights for generations and remembered the shape of every wind.

Caelan's muscles ached with the effort of keeping pace, of climbing where climbing should not be possible. The path it led him on wound through narrow passes, up broken switchbacks, and across icy stones where frost clung like webbing in the cracks.

But he did not question. He didn't speak. He just followed. At last, hours later, the goat stopped atop a crest of stone that overlooked a sheer basin below. It stood there, its frame outlined against the sky as the clouds parted briefly to spill light onto the peaks. Caelan reached the ridge, panting, boots scraping against the rock.

The goat stared at him one last time. Then turned, and in a single fluid motion, leapt down the opposite side and disappeared beyond the rise. He rushed to the edge—but there was nothing. Only crag and wind, the trail veering again into shadow. No hoofprints. No sound. Just the sense of something ancient, watching from above and below.

He exhaled slowly. then whispered, "Thank you."

Whether it had been a spirit, a guardian, or merely an animal didn't matter. It had shown him the way. And now, the mountain waited to see if he'd keep going.

The wind died as Caelan descended from the ridge the goat had vanished beyond, leaving only the steady sound of gravel shifting beneath his boots. The new trail was narrow and steep, snaking down into a natural crevice where the mountain walls rose like jagged teeth on either side. Here, the air grew still and heavy, and shadows clung stubbornly even as the sun shifted high above.

He moved carefully, guided by instinct and the lingering pull of the crystal in his satchel. The path dipped into a bend, and for a moment, he allowed himself to think it might level out—that perhaps the worst of the ascent had passed. But as he rounded the bend, his breath caught in his throat. The trail was gone.

Before him stretched a field of ruin—boulders stacked like fallen giants, trees split and buried in snow and shale, a wall of collapsed stone blocking what had once been a pass between the cliffs. An avalanche. Not recent, by the look of it, but massive. The destruction reached up toward the peaks and down into the gorge like a scar across the land.

Caelan stood at the edge of it, scanning for any sign of a way through. Nothing. No gaps. No cut in the wall. Just jagged ruin. He stepped forward and tested the edge of the rockfall with one boot, sending a loose stone skittering down into the cracks. It disappeared far too quickly. Deep.

He exhaled sharply, backing away. He could try to climb it, but one wrong move would send the slope shifting again. And if it gave out beneath him...

No. That wasn't the way.

He knelt slowly and pulled the crystal from his satchel. The light struck it with a pale glint, but the crystal didn't pull. It rested in his hand, unmoving. Uncertain. As if it didn't know the way forward either.

Caelan closed his eyes and cleared his mind. Not where I am. Not where I *think* I need to go. Where must I be?

He breathed deep. Slowed the rhythm of his heart. Let the silence return. And then—a warmth. Faint. Subtle. The crystal tugged. Not forward. Down. He opened his eyes.

To his left, the cliff wall curved inward, forming a narrow shelf along the edge of the rockslide. There, almost hidden by frost and hanging roots, was the mouth of a narrow fissure—no taller than his shoulders, no wider than a grown man's stride.

The crystal pulsed again in his palm. He stood, approached, and crouched low to inspect the opening. Cold air flowed from within—not the chill of wind, but the deep cold of untouched stone. He slipped the crystal back into his cloak, adjusted his pack, and ducked inside.

The passage sloped down sharply, forcing him to move with one hand to the wall, the other held low to steady his balance. His boots scraped over loose gravel, echoing faintly in the narrow confines. The air grew colder the deeper he went, and a quiet pressure settled in his ears.

After several minutes, the passage began to rise again. The floor leveled. A thin beam of light pierced through a fracture ahead—faint, but real. Caelan pressed forward.

He emerged onto another ledge, far narrower than the last, but clear of the avalanche. The fallen pass was behind him now. The mountain had offered another way—but only to those willing to stop. To listen. To trust something beyond sight.

He took one final glance at the blocked path behind him. Then kept climbing. Night fell hard at elevation.

By the time Caelan found a stable outcrop to rest upon, his limbs trembled from exertion, and his breath steamed thick and ragged in the frigid air. The climb had been relentless—every muscle in his legs burned, and his hands ached from gripping the cold stone face as he ascended through a narrow chimney between cliffs. But he had made it to a natural plateau ringed by stone and half-shielded from the wind. It was the closest thing to shelter he'd seen since dawn.

He didn't bother with a fire. There was no dry kindling, and the air felt wrong—thick with old magic, as if flame itself might be unwelcome here. Instead, he wrapped the cloak tight around him and curled against the rock wall, his satchel nestled at his side. The stars above blinked cold and unfamiliar, distant even from those he remembered seeing above the Elderwood.

Sleep came without permission. Not from comfort, but from collapse. And with sleep, the dream came.

At first, it felt like waking. He stood barefoot atop a windswept peak, stars gleaming unnaturally bright above him. The sky was no longer night but a tapestry of indigo silk, stitched with rivers of light—constellations twisting and pulsing like veins in a living thing. No cold, no wind. Only stillness.

Before him rose an arch of stone. Towering. Impossible. Not built, but grown—formed from veins of crystal and glimmering metal, as if the mountain itself had shaped it out of reverence. And beneath the arch stood a figure.

Cloaked in robes of silver-threaded dusk, their face was obscured by a hood. But light bled outward from them in quiet pulses—like the crystal Elaria had given him, but deeper, older. In one hand, they held a staff etched with spiraling runes that bent and reformed as if reshaping language with each breath.

Caelan stepped forward. His voice caught in his throat. The figure raised a hand—not in warning, but in greeting.

"You've heard the mountain," the figure said. Their voice echoed not in the air, but in Caelan's bones—low, calm, and measured. "But have you heard yourself?"

"I... I don't understand," Caelan replied. The words barely formed, like smoke on a windowpane.

"Understanding is not the first step," the figure answered. "Listening is."

The stars behind them shifted, rearranged into sigils that pulsed and bled into one another.

"You carry the mark of a story too old to read. You seek a place built on silence. A temple whose walls remember things even the gods tried to forget."

"Veylthar," Caelan whispered.

The figure nodded once.

"But the temple will not open to hands alone. It opens to intent. And yours is not yet shaped."

Caelan's fists clenched at his sides. "Then shape me. I've come this far—I won't turn away."

A pause. Then the figure tilted their head slightly, as if peering beneath the surface of him.

"You will be tested," they said. "Not by steel, nor spell, but by what lies beneath both. The shape of your truth will be measured."

Behind them, the stars flared. The sky burned white.

"And when the name buried in frost is spoken... you must not look away."

The arch began to fracture. The ground splintered. Caelan's vision shook. Then—nothing. Just black.

He awoke with a gasp, the cold morning slashing across his face like a blade. His heart thundered in his chest, sweat already freezing along his hairline. The sky above was gray, the world still cloaked in shadow.

The dream was gone. But the words remained.

When the name buried in frost is spoken... you must not look away.

He sat there for a long time, unmoving, until his breath returned to rhythm. Then he stood, fastened his cloak, and stepped back onto the path.

Chapter Fourteen

ENTRANCE TO THE WORTHY

The trail narrowed again as Caelan reached a high plateau flanked on either side by sheer cliffs. The wind had less room to cut through here, but what it lost in force, it gained in texture—a low, constant vibration that rode beneath the gusts like a second breath. It wasn't a sound exactly, but a resonance, something felt rather than heard. The kind of sensation that stirred a whisper of unease in the spine.

Ahead, the path curved into a basin carved from the bones of the mountain itself. A ring of standing stones encircled a flat stretch of frost-dusted ground, their surfaces worn smooth by time and weather. The stones were massive, easily twice Caelan's height, and spaced with intentional symmetry. Despite their ancient erosion, faint runes still clung to their surfaces, etched deep into the stone and glowing dimly beneath a thin glaze of rime. He knew these were not natural formations. This was no accident of geography. This place had been built—ritualized.

At the center of the circle, the air shimmered like heat rising from sunbaked stone, though the wind carried the cold bite of ice. The shimmer pulsed in slow rhythm, as if it were breathing.

Caelan slowed his steps. The pressure in the air thickened with each pace forward, a quiet weight settling against his skin and drawing the breath tighter in his lungs. His foot brushed across the threshold of the circle, and the mountain responded.

A deep hum rose beneath his boots—not from the ground, but from something woven into the foundation of the place itself. It wasn't threatening, but it was watching. He could feel it. Not with his eyes or ears, but with something deeper, older, just beneath the surface of conscious thought. He reached for the crystal in his satchel.

The moment his fingers touched it, it responded. A gentle pulse of light bloomed within the stone, spreading a soft glow across his hand. It warmed slightly, not enough to comfort, but enough to remind him it was aware. He stepped into the circle fully.

The hum grew louder—not in volume, but in presence. The cold receded slightly, replaced by a prickling warmth across the back of his neck and the tips of his fingers. The standing stones pulsed in answer to the crystal, each rune lighting faintly in sequence as if they were reading him. Or weighing him.

He held his ground, letting the wind wash across his face, letting the weight of this place settle in. The shimmer in the center of the circle intensified, and the world around him dulled. Sound dimmed. Color faded to a wash of muted greys and silvers. Even the cold seemed to draw back, leaving only stillness and tension in its wake.

Then something shifted. The pressure in his chest grew heavier, not from fear or fatigue, but from presence. A question formed—not in voice or language, but as a feeling placed directly into his mind. Clear. Deliberate.

Why do you seek the Sanctum?

The thought pressed against him like a stone held just above the ribs. It wasn't demanding, but it wouldn't be ignored.

He opened his mouth to answer, but no words came. He tried again, thinking to speak aloud, to say he was seeking knowledge, that he needed training, that he was born with magic and had nowhere else to go. But the moment those thoughts surfaced, the warmth of the crystal dulled. The runes on the stones flickered, as if turning away.

Wrong answer.

He fell silent again, eyes lowering to the center of the circle where the shimmering air pulsed slowly in time with his breath. He tried to quiet his thoughts, just as Elaria had taught him. Let them fall away, one by one, until only the truth remained.

He thought of Gladecross. Of the market. Of the guards who struck down a man for nothing more than suspicion. Of the boy who had screamed for his mother as soldiers dragged him away. He thought of how his fists had clenched, how the magic inside him had surged to the surface, and how he had buried it out of fear. Not for his life—but for hers.

Then he thought of Elaria's voice, calm and unwavering, teaching him the old ways. Not to dominate. Not to destroy. But to protect. His fingers tightened around the crystal.

"I want to shield what cannot shield itself," he said softly, voice steady. "I want to learn—not to wield power for its own sake, but to understand it. To carry it with purpose. To never be helpless again."

The crystal in his palm brightened, and a faint warmth flooded outward from its center. The shimmer ahead began to shift. The veil of energy at the center of the circle, once static and impenetrable, peeled away like fog lifting from stone. The standing stones around him glowed brighter, not blindingly, but with solemn approval.

The hum receded. The pressure lifted. The way forward opened, unspoken but unmistakable.

Caelan took a long breath, letting it fill his lungs with clean, thin air. The silence that followed was not empty—it was expectant. The circle had heard him. And, for now, it had answered.

He stepped beyond the ring, the glow fading quietly behind him as he crossed into what lay beyond.

The path beyond the warding circle narrowed once more, winding between slabs of dark stone that rose like blades from the frozen ground. The light had shifted—no longer true sunlight, but a diffused pallor cast through a ceiling of mist. Caelan walked slowly now. The cold no longer bothered him, but something else had settled into the air.

The moment he passed between two towering stones marked with glyphs older than any language he could name, the world around him stilled. His footfall didn't echo. The air no longer moved. He reached for the crystal at his side, but it had gone silent, inert in his satchel. And then the path changed.

The stone beneath his boots gave way to cobblestone. The air grew warmer, tinged with the scent of iron and ash. Voices rose in the distance—muffled, indistinct at first, then clearer with each step. Caelan turned his head. He knew this sound. He knew that scent.

The mist parted, revealing not the cliffs of the Elder Mountains, but a town square. Foxburrow. It wasn't possible. But it was real.

The buildings stood as he remembered them—simple stone and timber, worn by wind and age. Merchants hawked their wares. Children darted between wagons. A familiar melody floated from a flute, played just off the edge of the square. And near the center, a man stood behind a wooden cart, his hands raised defensively, voice trembling.

"I swear, gentlemen, they are just trinkets from the sea... nothing more!"

Caelan stopped dead in his tracks.

He knew this moment. He had lived it.

The guards closed in. Their black-and-gold tabards glinted in the sun. The captain—the one with the scar across his cheek—stepped forward, voice flat and final.

"Lies. We have reports that you deal in artifacts of sorcery."

The blade flashed.

The merchant staggered, clutching at his chest as blood seeped through his tunic. The crowd gasped. The boy cried out. Caelan clenched his fists as the scene played out exactly as it had before. Only this time, something was different.

He was not fifteen years old. He was not hiding behind Elaria's cloak. He was standing in the center of it. And the guard captain was looking directly at him.

"You," the man growled. "You did nothing."

Caelan took a step back, but the stones beneath his feet locked him in place. The sky darkened. The villagers' faces turned toward him—dozens of eyes, blank and expressionless. The merchant lay still at their feet. The boy sobbed against his mother's skirts.

"You had the power," the captain continued. "You felt it rise. You buried it."

Caelan tried to speak, but no sound left his lips. Another voice joined the first—Elaria's voice, gentle but unyielding.

"Power without wisdom is destruction."

The light warped. The guards dissolved into mist. The crowd withered into shadows. The square crumbled into ash beneath him. And Caelan stood alone in the void of the mountain's memory. The shimmer of the warding stones returned, circling him in a quiet hum.

Then, slowly, the ash beneath his feet became stone once more. The wind returned, whispering along the mountain ridges. The path before him cleared. The illusion—or vision—had ended, but its weight remained.

Caelan exhaled, shaking as he reached for the satchel and checked for the crystal. It was glowing faintly again. The pulsing light steadied with his breathing. He had passed the trial by facing what he had once refused to look at.

He turned toward the narrowing trail ahead. The stone arches beyond the pass waited, runes gleaming faintly along their sides.

The final stretch had begun.

The wind sharpened again as Caelan stepped beyond the last remnants of the vision, curling through the narrow defile ahead and whistling low between the stones. The runes carved along the walls seemed brighter now—not merely glowing, but breathing with a soft cadence, their light responding to his approach. Each symbol pulsed faintly as he passed, like notes in a melody too ancient for instruments. He didn't know their meaning, but he felt their presence, steady and resonant in the air around him.

The ground beneath his feet no longer felt like natural stone. It had been shaped—deliberately carved and leveled long ago, smoothed by hand and spell. The mountain here was no longer wild. It was sacred.

Before him stood a series of massive arches rising from the rock like ribs from the spine of some slumbering giant. Each one stretched over the path with graceful weight, their surfaces etched with intricate markings that spiraled along their curves—some of them familiar from Elaria's tomes, others so old their meaning was lost entirely. They stood in sequence, spaced evenly apart, drawing the path forward into a narrowing corridor of silence and light.

Caelan passed under the first arch.

The moment he crossed beneath it, a pressure settled across his shoulders. Not painful—more like a cloak laid gently upon his back. The rune just above his head shimmered, and a whisper touched the edge of his hearing. A memory, perhaps. A voice from the stone itself, speaking not in words, but in recognition.

He continued forward. The second arch greeted him with warmth. The air shifted, growing less harsh, the biting cold softening like snow beneath sunlight. The stone here felt older, but less heavy. Less guarded.

The third arch was darker. As he passed beneath it, a shadow flickered across his vision—not from the sun, but from something within himself. The image of the merchant's blood pooled on cobblestones flashed again in his mind. He blinked it away and kept walking.

By the time he reached the final arch, he could see the temple. It rose from the mountain itself—not built upon it, but carved directly into the rock face. Its pillars were massive, forged from the same dark granite that formed the peaks around it, but smoother, shaped with impossible precision. No banners flew from its walls. No fires burned in greeting. The temple gave no signs of life. And yet, it was not empty.

The moment his foot touched the threshold between the final arch and the stone stair leading to the entrance, the air thickened. A presence met him there—not hostile, but watchful. Not waiting to be challenged, but expecting reverence.

Caelan stopped at the base of the steps and drew in a long, quiet breath. He let the wind push against his cloak, let the weight of the mountain settle around him once more. He placed one hand lightly on the crystal inside his cloak. It was steady now, no longer pulling or glowing. Its work was done.

He climbed the steps. Each footfall echoed as if striking a bell—low, steady, eternal. The great entrance loomed overhead, flanked by columns carved with celestial symbols and swirling patterns that traced the shapes of stars, moons, and unending spirals. He paused beneath the lintel, studying the door before him. There was no handle. No keyhole. Only a single symbol etched at eye level—a circle bound by three intersecting lines.

Caelan lifted his hand and placed it against the center of the mark. For a moment, nothing happened. Then a pulse traveled through the door, through the arch, and into the mountain. The lines shimmered and vanished, and with a deep groan of stone against stone, the entrance opened inward.

Warm light spilled from within—soft, golden, and steady, casting long shadows across the threshold. Standing just beyond the opening, half-veiled in light, was a figure in robes of deep indigo and silver. Their face was obscured by the folds of their hood, but their posture was calm.

"Welcome, Caelan," they said, voice echoing slightly as if spoken within a deep chamber. "You have come far. And the road behind you has prepared you for what lies ahead. But know this: what you seek, and what you find, may not be the same."

Caelan met the gaze beneath the hood, even if he couldn't see the eyes themselves.

"I didn't come here for certainty," he said. "I came to understand."

The robed figure inclined their head slightly. "Then enter with an open mind. And a steady heart."

The doors widened. Caelan stepped into the light, leaving the wind and the wildness of the mountain behind. The sanctum had accepted him. And his training was about to begin.

The silence inside the temple was not emptiness, but presence. It was the kind of stillness that pressed against the skin and filled the lungs—a silence that had waited lifetimes to be heard. Caelan stepped through the threshold, his boots landing on polished stone so smooth it caught the golden light like water. The warmth surprised him. After days of cold and wind, the shift was profound—his muscles slowly began to unknot beneath his cloak, even as his senses remained alert.

The great hall opened wide around him, its ceiling lost in shadow high above. Massive pillars rose on either side, shaped from the mountain's living heart, each one etched with layers of runes that twisted upward in elegant spirals. They glowed faintly—not with magic that reached outward, but with something more reserved, internal. The glyphs pulsed as he passed them, gentle and ancient, acknowledging his presence without judgment.

The light came from nowhere and everywhere at once. There were no visible torches or sconces. Instead, it bled softly from the walls themselves—warm and golden, like the last breath of sunlight before dusk. It gave the entire space a sense of timelessness, as though the sun had never truly left, only retreated inside.

The air smelled faintly of old parchment, burned herbs, and polished stone. The scent reminded him of Elaria's cottage, though this place carried none of her comfort. It was not unwelcoming—only unfamiliar, watchful, layered in history so thick it was felt more than seen.

Caelan walked slowly down the center aisle between the pillars. Every step echoed in the vastness of the chamber, but the echoes were never sharp. They softened as they traveled, swallowed by the enormity of the temple itself. As he moved deeper, the arches overhead curved into intricate intersections that mirrored the constellations. He recognized a few—The Gatekeeper, The Falling Flame, and The Crown of the Watchers—each carved with reverence into the stone above.

He passed alcoves along the outer walls. Some were empty. Others held ancient relics—staffs, scroll cases, iron-bound tomes—each resting atop black stone pedestals with symbols inscribed around their base. He didn't linger. Whatever their significance, they belonged to this place, not yet to him.

At the far end of the hall stood a raised platform of tiered steps, and above it, a towering arch inscribed with the deepest runes yet—marks not meant to be read, but to be felt. The moment Caelan looked upon them, something stirred inside his chest. Not recognition, but resonance. As if part of him already knew the shapes, the weight of those lines, even if he could not name them.

He stood at the base of the steps, gazing upward. His breath was steady now, and though his legs ached from the climb, he felt no weariness here.

Behind him, the doors remained open—but the wind did not follow him inside. The mountain had brought him this far. Now the temple would decide what came next.

A soft chime rang out through the chamber. No bell. No visible source. Just a clear, sustained tone, like the moment before a string is plucked. Caelan turned instinctively, scanning the shadows near the far archway. From a recessed corridor between two pillars, a figure emerged—robed in the same indigo and silver as the one who greeted him at the threshold.

This one was shorter, with slower steps and a slight stoop to the shoulders. Their hood remained drawn, but no sense of menace lingered in their approach. If anything, the air around them grew calmer. The runes along the columns dimmed slightly as they passed, giving space without retreating.

"You walk with quiet purpose," the figure said, voice low and worn like weathered cloth. "Few make it this far. Fewer still walk through the vision unchanged."

Caelan didn't answer right away. The echoes of Gladecross still haunted the back of his thoughts, even though his body stood here, surrounded by impossible stone and sacred air. "It felt real," he said. "The vision. It wasn't just memory—it was judgment."

"All vision is both," the figure replied, coming to stand at the base of the stairs. "Memory, when properly stirred, reveals truth. And judgment is not always a punishment. Sometimes it is permission."

Caelan met the figure's gaze, though he still couldn't see their face. "You knew what I'd see."

"No," the figure said gently. "We knew you would see what you needed to."

Silence passed between them, not heavy, but full.

The figure motioned to the steps behind them. "You may climb. The sanctum has accepted your passage. The archway above marks your formal entrance. But know this—what you do with what you find here... that will not be guided."

Caelan nodded once. He looked toward the arch again. The runes still glowed faintly, their forms seemingly shifting each time he looked at them—like they were rewriting themselves just out of reach.

He took the first step. The stone was cool beneath his boot, but smooth, clean, unworn. No one had tread this path in a very long time.

He climbed slowly, not out of hesitation, but to feel each moment. Each motion. Each breath. When he reached the top, he paused beneath the arch. The chamber beyond was veiled in golden mist, shapes moving behind it—more robed figures, more halls, perhaps a library or a sanctum of study. He couldn't tell.

Behind him, the elder figure had not followed. Caelan looked back one last time. The hooded head inclined in a subtle gesture of farewell.

Caelan crossed the arch. The mist broke.

And the Veylthar Sanctum opened before him.

The golden mist clung to Caelan's cloak as he stepped beyond the final arch.

The silence inside the sanctum wasn't hollow—it thrummed, somehow, with quiet presence. The air shifted, denser now, carrying a charge he couldn't place. It wasn't just magic—it was memory. Weight. Like the stones themselves remembered every footfall that had passed before his own.

He moved slowly, reverently, down the inner passage. The outer chamber had given way to something more intimate now. The towering columns faded into softer curves, and the golden light dimmed to a gentle silver that pulsed along the seams of the walls. Not candlelight, not flame—but something older. Like the breath of the temple itself, slow and rhythmic, echoing faintly in the back of his chest.

Caelan exhaled, unsure when he'd stopped breathing.

Each step forward felt like a question. His boots made no sound. He dared not speak.

Ahead, an open space waited—neither grand nor simple, but perfectly balanced. A circular chamber, veiled in dim light, stood at the heart of this sacred place. In its center rose a monolith altar carved of black stone—not obsidian, not granite. Something else. It shimmered faintly, not from polish, but from a light within.

Caelan stepped toward it, drawn by an instinct deeper than curiosity. The air thickened. The glow brightened.

He reached out, hesitant, letting his fingers graze the stone. It was warm—surprisingly warm—and pulsed gently against his skin. Like a heartbeat.

A soft voice rippled through the chamber, not loud, not startling.

"Welcome, Caelan."

He turned, startled. A figure stood across the altar from him—tall, draped in spectral robes that shimmered like mist caught in moonlight. His face was lined but kind, and his presence filled the room with a stillness deeper than silence.

"I am Eryndor," the man said, inclining his head. "You have crossed into the breath of the Sanctum. You stand in the place between learning and becoming."

Caelan's mouth was dry. He swallowed. "You... you knew I was coming?"

"We remember what must be remembered," Eryndor said, as if that answered everything. "And the temple breathes again, because you are here."

Eryndor stepped around the altar, his movements measured, as if the weight of time itself moved with him. The silver threads in his robes caught the ambient glow of the sanctum, rippling softly like starlight reflected on still water. Caelan remained still, uncertain whether to bow, speak, or simply listen.

"You've crossed the threshold," Eryndor said, voice calm, with no need for volume. "Most never make it that far. Fewer still arrive unbroken."

Caelan flinched at that—not from the words, but from the truth of them. The trial had left him raw. Gladecross still lingered behind his eyes, a shadow on his thoughts.

"I thought I failed," he admitted. "In the circle... I couldn't control what I saw. I couldn't stop it."

"You weren't meant to," Eryndor replied. "The circle does not ask for strength. It asks for honesty. What it shows is not a punishment. It is permission—to feel, to fall, to remember."

Caelan's hands curled into fists. "I don't want to remember."

"And yet, the magic does," Eryndor said gently. "All memory is tethered. Even pain. Especially pain. That is why you must not bury it—but weave it into your understanding."

He motioned for Caelan to follow. Together, they walked toward the edge of the chamber, where a stone dais rose from the floor in concentric rings. The innermost circle was smooth, flat, and faintly aglow with interwoven sigils, humming at a frequency just low enough to feel rather than hear.

"Sit," Eryndor instructed, gesturing to the center. "This is where we begin."

Caelan hesitated only briefly, then lowered himself into a cross-legged seat at the heart of the pattern. The stone was cool beneath him, grounding. The runes pulsed once beneath his hands.

Eryndor sat opposite him. Not across like a challenger, but beside, slightly offset—like a guide walking the same path, just a few steps ahead.

"You were born marked, Caelan. Not cursed."

Caelan's breath caught in his throat.

"Yes," Eryndor said before the boy could speak. "We know of the mark. Its shape was carved into the temple long before any of us breathed our first. It has waited a long time to appear again."

Caelan said nothing. His thoughts churned, but he was too afraid to voice them.

Eryndor placed a hand to the floor beside him. "The temple does not judge. It remembers. What matters now is not the mark you bear—but the balance you choose to seek. Magic flows through you already. You've felt it. You've seen glimpses."

"I don't know what I'm doing," Caelan said, quieter than he meant to.

"You're not meant to yet," Eryndor said, with a small smile. "First, we listen."

He closed his eyes. "Let the breath settle. Let the self quiet. The temple speaks in silence. Hear it."

Caelan followed suit, though his pulse quickened in the effort. His legs were tense, his back stiff. The glow of the runes made patterns dance behind his eyelids.

And then, slowly, like a tide coming in...He felt it.

It began as a tremor—not in the stone, but in his chest. A faint thrum, like distant thunder buried beneath mountains. Then came the rhythm. Subtle. Unmistakable. The temple was breathing.

With each exhale, Caelan felt his own shoulders relax, his heartbeat slowing to match. The glow of the runes dimmed and brightened in time with the rhythm. As if the floor itself was alive—no, aware. Aware of him.

Eryndor's voice emerged like a breeze stirring still water. "Good. You're not forcing. Allow it."

"I feel... something," Caelan whispered. "It's everywhere."

"You're sensing the weave," Eryndor said. "Magic in its most honest form. It is not fire or frost or light. It is motion. Connection. Meaning."

Caelan breathed again, slower this time. His thoughts still moved, but they no longer raced. Instead of trying to push them away, he let them float. Memories surfaced—not visions, but impressions. Elaria's voice humming softly as she ground herbs in a bowl. Thistle's breath against his shoulder. The scent of Clara's cloak as she hugged him good-bye.

None of it was dramatic. None of it violent.

But all of it felt realer than stone.

"I thought magic would feel louder," Caelan murmured.

"It can," Eryndor said. "But that is not where it begins. Magic first whispers. Only those who learn to listen may one day speak with it."

The silence stretched—but it no longer felt like emptiness. Caelan's awareness expanded, not outward, but deeper. Like roots sinking into soil. He began to feel the strands—tiny pulses of energy around him, in the air, the stone, the very breath between words. Some flickered. Some curled. Some trembled when his thoughts touched them.

"They respond to me," he said, eyes still closed.

"They respond to who you are in this moment," Eryndor corrected gently. "Magic is not yours to command. It meets you where you stand."

Caelan furrowed his brow. "Then how do I use it?"

Eryndor smiled faintly. "By learning not to."

A beat of silence.

Then the elder rose. "Enough for now. Stay in this rhythm as long as you can. The first truth of the Sanctum is this: presence is the foundation of all power. Without it, every spell is just a scream into the wind."

Caelan remained seated, his body quiet but his mind newly alive. The glow beneath him continued to breathe. So did he.

He didn't know what would come next.

But—for the first time in days—he wasn't afraid to find out.

Chapter Fifteen

CATALYST

Seven years have passed since Lysa made her vow...

The heart of Dunmoh no longer sang.

Where once the morning sun warmed market awnings draped in silks and spice-laden air, now a cold gray pall clung to the stone. Towers loomed like silent sentinels, their banners hanging limp in the still wind—red and gold, proud and oppressive. The city breathed differently now, shallow and cautious.

Bootsteps echoed before they could be seen, a hard rhythmic stamp against cobblestone that sent vendors scrambling to silence their carts. Two guards turned a corner near the Temple Row, hands resting on sheathed swords, their eyes scanning the thinning crowd. A young boy—barely ten—tightened his grip on a cloth bundle and stepped backward into the alley shadows, holding his breath as they passed. He didn't exhale until they were gone.

Further down, a street where storytellers once stood, where painted dancers had moved in colorful spirals to the sound of drums and lyres, now lay quiet. Chalk lines still marked the ground where children had drawn sigils for games long forgotten—games their parents now forbade. The chalk was fading. No one dared redraw them.

Overhead, laundry lines drooped with half-dried garments, fluttering weakly in the breeze. The smell of baked bread wafted from behind shuttered doors, faint and nervous, like it too might be arrested if it dared announce itself too boldly.

The city was still alive. But it had forgotten how to move freely.

A woman hurried across the square, her shawl pulled low to shadow her face. She clutched a satchel to her chest, not from cold or modesty—but habit. Inside were nothing more than herbs and thread, harmless things. But she had once sold healing poultices. That alone made her suspect.

She didn't look up when someone called her name. She hadn't answered to it in weeks.

Nearby, a young couple argued in hisses behind their stall, barely loud enough to be heard over the creaking of a cartwheel. The man kept glancing toward the alley, his hands trembling as he folded a cloth over a crate. The woman gripped his arm, shaking her head. She was trying to talk him out of something. A decision. A risk. One of them wanted to flee the city. The other wasn't ready to leave their aging parents behind. The cart rolled away without resolution.

At the edge of the apothecary quarter, the shutters of a once-popular herbalist shop were nailed closed. A single wax seal marked the doorway—royal decree. Its red ribbon fluttered like a warning tongue. No one spoke of what happened to the woman who once ran it. But her cat still lingered outside the door each evening, waiting for someone who would not return.

Inside a dim tavern, a hand slipped from beneath a cloak and quietly passed a copper ring to the barkeep. No coin. No drink. Just the ring, and a glance. The barkeep said nothing, only nodded toward the back room. In the corner, an old man stirred his soup with a spoon he never lifted to his lips. His eyes never left the door.

Trust had become a dangerous luxury. Silence, the only safe currency.

Children no longer played in the open. When they spoke, it was with too much caution for voices so young. Parents taught them to lie with their eyes down and to speak only when spoken to. To answer "no" to any question that began with "Did you see..."

It wasn't just fear of punishment that kept them quiet. It was the not knowing who would listen—and who would report.

The wine sloshed in the cup before settling again.

Sir Reginald sat alone, the flicker of a single oil lamp painting long shadows along the stone walls of his quarters. His armor lay discarded on the bench by the door, one gauntlet still stained at the knuckles—mud, or soot, or something worse. He hadn't yet decided if he would clean it.

The chair beneath him creaked as he shifted his weight, the wooden legs old and unbalanced, much like the man who sat in it. His sword rested against the table, scabbard clinking softly as he reached again for the cup.

He drank, not out of thirst. Just to dull the taste of bile that hadn't left his mouth since sunset.

A child had screamed tonight. That wasn't new. What lingered was the silence afterward. The mother had begged—not for mercy, but for dignity. And dignity was not in the orders.

He stared into the cup. The wine was dark—almost black in the lamplight. It reminded him of the blood on the flagstones. That too had spread quickly. No magic. No weapons. Just fear and accusation. That was enough these days.

He could still hear the crack of the door as it splintered under boot. The sobbing. The chaos. And then silence again, after the guards had left with their prisoners. Just like all the others.

His orders had been clear. They were always clear. And each one brought him further from the man who had once believed in the law he now enforced. The cup hovered at his lips, but he didn't drink.

His eyes had drifted to the wall above his desk, where a faded banner of Dunmoh's royal crest hung. Red and gold. Once, it had filled him with pride. Now, it looked too much like dried blood stitched onto a lie.

He remembered the king's voice ringing through the great hall the day the decree was announced. Magic is chaos, Aldric had said. Magic killed the queen. We must cleanse it from our land before it unravels all we hold sacred.

Reginald had stood among the assembled knights, hand over chest, nodding in grim agreement. He remembered believing those words. Believing that order and sacrifice were worth any cost. That they were building something safer.

But that belief had grown quiet. And in its place, faces had taken root. Too many to name. Some young, some old, most terrified. None of them monsters.

He pressed a hand to his forehead, thumb and forefinger gripping the bridge of his nose. A headache pulsed at the base of his skull, throbbing in time with memory.

Once, he had been a man who led by example. Who trained new squires with patience, not threats. Who told stories of honor and law, and meant every word.

Now, he signed off on midnight arrests and looked the other way when bruises were left behind. When did the orders stop making sense? he wondered. When did following them begin to feel like betrayal?

The wine went untouched.

Reginald stared at the parchment on his desk without reaching for it. The words blurred at the edges, though his eyes had not moved. Another raid report. Another order. Another pair of names—no one he recognized, but he could already picture their faces. They were always the same in the end. Afraid. Ordinary. Caught in something larger than themselves.

The seal at the bottom was unbroken, pressed in dark wax and stamped with a magistrate's ring. He'd given that order. His hand had signed it. But now, looking at the ink already beginning to fade into the fibers of the page, he wasn't sure who had written it anymore. The words didn't feel like his.

He reached instead for a clean sheet, setting it down beside the report. His fingers moved slowly, deliberately, forming a new account—one that would never survive scrutiny, but would pass through the usual channels with just enough weight to stall the next step. A delay in the chain of command. A lost paper. A discrepancy that wouldn't be discovered until it no longer mattered.

He adjusted the language carefully. The accused were not home at the time of the visit. Witness statements were contradictory. No illegal materials recovered. Investigation to be reopened pending further evidence. He signed it with a lower-tier steward's name and pressed a seal he had borrowed months ago—one whose owner never bothered to check what it was used for.

The original report burned quickly in the hearth, curling into glowing edges before crumbling inward. He didn't watch it vanish. He returned the forged one to the stack of innocuous reports ready to be filed, the edges aligned precisely.

He sat back in his chair and exhaled through his nose. It wasn't rebellion. Not yet. But it was something else. A wedge in the machinery. A breath of resistance buried beneath protocol.

And it was the first thing he had done in weeks that didn't make him feel like a coward.

Lysa moved through the alleys of Dunmoh. The uniform helped—worn leathers bearing the city's faded crest marked her as one of the watch, just another low-ranking officer on patrol. No one questioned her presence, not in a city where soldiers were as common as soot on the windowsills. The anonymity of authority served her well, a mask she wore with practiced ease. Most saw the armor, the stoic expression, and looked away. That was the point.

She was lean and compact, built for speed and silence rather than brute strength. At just over five feet tall, she passed through doorways and crowds without drawing attention. Her red hair was braided tightly along the sides and pulled back from her face, emphasizing determined face and a pair of ocean-blue eyes that had learned to scan without staring. There were faint freckles across her cheeks and nose, remnants of a youth long buried beneath years of wandering and loss. Her skin, once fair and soft from northern winds and herbal smoke, had taken on the pale toughness of someone who rarely saw daylight without armor. Every movement she made was economical. There were no wasted steps, no idle turns of the head. She knew who was behind her by the scrape of their boots and who watched her by the change in the air.

To the casual eye, she looked unremarkable—perhaps forgettable. But there was nothing passive about her. The way she carried herself through the city, the slight tension in her shoulders, the glances she cast toward rooftops and corners, all betrayed a mind constantly in motion. Lysa didn't walk; she navigated. The city might have forgotten how to breathe freely, but she remembered every inhale it used to take.

This was not the girl who had fled from Snowhaven clutching herbs and hunger in a satchel. That girl had walked in fear. This woman walked in calculation. Ten years of survival and infiltration had shaped her into something Dunmoh's watchmen didn't see coming. She had traded her name for a cover, her past for a uniform. Once a scared thirteen year old girl, now stood a disciplined woman of twenty three.

She passed beneath an iron archway where the city's merchant banners used to hang. Only rusted hooks remained. A child watched her from behind a slatted window, small fingers pressed to the glass, wide eyes studying the armor she wore. Lysa didn't meet the gaze. She kept walking. There were meetings to attend, information to move, and faces to remember. Always faces. Always silence. Always the next step in a war no one was supposed to admit existed.

By the time the sun dipped behind Dunmoh's outer wall, Lysa was already below ground.

The meeting space was nothing more than a root cellar long abandoned by its original owner. The stone walls sweated in the evening chill, and the air carried the earthy dampness of decay. A single oil lantern hung from a bent hook, casting uneven light across the warped table at the room's center. Maps were spread across its surface, corners weighted by cobblestones and dented tin cups. Arrows and markings in charcoal painted a network of safe routes, storage points, and guard schedules—the veins of a city no longer safe to walk openly.

She stood at the head of the table, arms crossed, listening as a wiry man in patched leathers spoke in low, clipped tones. His knuckles were stained with ink, his nails bitten down to the quick.

"There's been another sweep through the artisan quarter. They pulled a boy from the weaver's shop. Said his mother was hoarding spell-books. Neighbors swore they saw nothing, but the guards took her anyway."

A woman at Lysa's right shook her head, muttering under her breath. The others remained quiet, absorbing the weight of it. It was the third report this week.

"We need to move before the next rotation," the man continued. "If we wait too long, they'll start locking the ward gates again. We'll be boxed in like rats."

Lysa unfolded her arms and leaned over the map, her fingers brushing lightly over the markers near the north district.

"No," she said firmly. "Not yet. If we push now, it'll be loud. They're expecting that. The guard is shifting into position to make an example of someone. If we hand them a target, they'll take it."

"Then we do nothing?" the woman asked, frustrated.

"We strike where it hurts," Lysa replied, her tone even. "But not with blood. Not yet. Disrupt their flow. The supply roads from the barracks to the outer watchtowers—cut them off. Quietly. No deaths, no blaze. Let them wonder why their shipments go missing. Let them start doubting each other."

The room fell still. This was why they listened to her. She didn't shout. She didn't posture. She calculated. Each word she spoke had weight, and each plan carried a path forward that did more than provoke—it protected.

One of the older men near the back, quiet until now, gave a single nod. "You've got my route. I'll hit the cart before dawn. No one'll know it was touched."

Lysa gave a brief nod in return. It wasn't victory. But it was momentum. And right now, momentum was everything.

The tavern above throbbed with muffled footsteps and occasional bursts of laughter, a practiced illusion that masked the truth below. In the cellar beneath the ale-soaked floorboards, the atmosphere was taut and subdued. The room was lit by a single lantern hung from an iron hook in the beam overhead, casting a steady amber glow across a table riddled with gouges and ring-stains. Empty crates and overturned barrels served as makeshift chairs, arranged in a crooked circle around it. On the far wall, a rusted wine rack sagged beneath the weight of dust-covered bottles no one dared to drink.

Lysa stood at the center, her gloved hands pressed flat on the table as she scanned the faces of those gathered. There were only six tonight—a pair of grim-faced couriers, a disgraced scribe, a former quartermaster from the outer barracks, and two women who had once worked in the palace kitchens before their brother was taken and their home torched. Each wore the fatigue of fear and purpose, but their eyes held to Lysa like steady anchors.

She didn't need to shout. Her voice, low and level, held the room with little effort.

"We're no longer guessing at patterns," she said, drawing a finger along a rough charcoal sketch of the outer ring district. "The patrols are rotating faster. Fifteen-man shifts instead of ten. Reinforcements at the barracks tower every third night. They're anticipating retaliation."

The courier on her left—barely old enough to shave—shifted in his seat, worry flickering across his face. "They think we're going to strike the central records, don't they?"

Lysa nodded. "Which is why we won't."

She tapped a point along the eastern quarter, far from the usual activity. "We hit the waystation instead. Two carts of supplies from Arden's Wake scheduled to offload there by dusk tomorrow. No magical goods, just steel, grain, dried medicinal stock—the kind of things the inner guard relies on to stretch control further out."

One of the kitchen women leaned forward, eyes sharp. "You want sabotage. Not spectacle."

"I want disruption," Lysa said. "Delay their next movement. Make them question their logistics. That buys us time—time to get more people out, to move information safely, to breathe."

The room was silent for a moment. Not with doubt, but with the heavy weight of agreement. These weren't soldiers. None of them had signed up to be part of a rebellion. But Dunmoh's laws had made them enemies of the crown all the same.

From the back, the former quartermaster gave a slow nod. "I can bribe the manifest keeper. If no one records the delay, it'll take them a full day longer to notice the break."

Lysa's expression softened slightly. "Good. Make it happen."

Another voice from her right, hoarse with age, asked the question hanging in the air.

"And what about the city guard?"

Lysa's eyes didn't flinch. "Leave them to me."

She rolled the map closed and extinguished the lantern with a flick of her gloved fingers. Darkness reclaimed the cellar as the meeting dissolved into quiet footsteps. Above them, the tavern's laughter roared a little louder.

The barracks of Dunmoh's eastern watchtower were as cold and joyless as the city it overlooked. The scent of old steel and damp leather clung to the walls, thickened by the smoke of oil lamps that burned from dawn to dusk. Boots scraped across stone as guards filtered in and out between shifts, their voices low and clipped. Discipline had become its own language—sharp, efficient, devoid of warmth.

Lysa stood in formation with three others as the officer in charge read from a slate. Her helmet was tucked under her arm, her posture straight, unyielding. To anyone watching, she appeared every inch the dutiful guard—clean, alert, unobtrusive. The truth, as always, lived elsewhere.

The officer glanced up at them, disinterested, then scratched something out and pointed to her.

"Evern. You're being reassigned. Captain Reginald's detail, effective immediately."

There was no explanation offered, no gesture of significance. Reassignments happened often in the guard. Still, the others cast her brief, sidelong glances. No one volunteered to trade places. She gave a brisk nod and stepped out of line.

The walk to Reginald's quarters was silent. No escort. No briefing. Just a name, a door, and an assignment. She had heard of him, of course—Sir Reginald, once a loyalist's loyalist, now spoken of in quieter tones. He still had rank, still had command, but there were whispers. The kind that didn't stick to parchment but traveled just fine over cups and dice. They said he was different now. Not disloyal. Just distant.

When she knocked, the door opened with a low groan. The man inside barely glanced up.

He was older than she expected, though the years hadn't softened him. His frame was broad, still shaped by armor, though his posture held the weariness of someone who had been standing for far too long. His hair was streaked with silver, and his face bore the weight of too many decisions made too late.

"Officer Evern," he said, reading her name from the parchment before setting it aside. "You've been assigned under my command. I don't waste time with ceremony, so I'll be brief."

He stood and walked to the rack of weapons near the far wall, choosing a blade and inspecting the edge as he spoke.

"You follow orders. You report clean. You speak only when it serves the task. If that's a problem, now's the time to say it."

Lysa met his gaze when he finally turned. Her voice was calm, steady. "No problem, sir."

He studied her for a moment longer than necessary.

"Good," he said at last. "Then let's get to work."

It was a simple beginning, unremarkable in the eyes of the others. But something passed between them in that brief silence—a recognition, sharp and unfinished. Neither of them believed in their uniforms anymore. Not fully. But neither had stopped wearing them. Not yet.

The city was quieter in the early hours, though silence in Dunmoh was never comforting. It was the kind born of caution, not peace. The streets were empty save for the occasional sweep of patrols and the distant clatter of carts unloading at the south gate. Even the ravens were silent on the rooftops.

Reginald stood at the overlook above Eastwatch, arms folded behind his back as he surveyed the ward below. The morning fog had not yet burned off, and the rooftops appeared like broken stones jutting from a sea of mist. His armor, though polished, caught no light. The gray skies had seen to that.

Lysa approached without announcing herself, her boots sounding lightly on the worn stones of the wall. He didn't turn. He didn't need to. He'd already known she was there.

"You walk quieter than most," he said without looking away. "That's good."

She stepped beside him, glancing down at the same fog-choked streets. "Force of habit."

He gave a slight nod. "That's a habit you'll want to keep."

For a few moments, they stood in companionable silence. No orders. No inspections. Just the sound of distant bells ringing from the temple district and the shrill cry of a gull overhead.

Reginald finally broke the quiet, his voice lower now, less rehearsed. "I've been watching how you handle your assignments. You keep your distance. You don't rush to violence."

"Violence doesn't solve everything," Lysa replied, her tone measured but sincere. "Sometimes it only makes things worse."

"Tell that to the men who trained me," he muttered. "They'd call that softness."

She turned slightly, studying the man who had once been feared for his discipline. There was no softness in him. Not outwardly. But she could hear it—buried behind the iron in his voice, dulled but not gone.

"You think that's why I'm here?" she asked. "Because I hesitate?"

Reginald looked at her for the first time. His expression was unreadable. "No. I think that's why I trust you."

The words caught her off guard, not because they were sentimental, but because they weren't. There was no flattery, no warning. Just quiet honesty.

"I've seen too many officers do the job with blind certainty," he continued. "They stop asking if what they're doing is right. You haven't stopped asking. I can see it in your eyes. You're not hiding it as well as you think."

Lysa didn't deny it. "And you?"

He turned back toward the city, his jaw tightening as he looked out across the fog.

"I stopped asking for a while," he said. "That was the worst of it."

They stood like that for a long time, neither pushing the moment forward, neither retreating from it. There was no oath made, no secret revealed. But something between them had shifted. Not comrades. Not yet. But something close.

The first test came three days later. A tip had come through official channels—anonymous, unverified, but taken seriously enough for immediate action. A suspected mage harboring contraband alchemical supplies, hidden beneath a butcher's shop near the river quarter. Standard procedure demanded an immediate search and arrest. Reginald received the report at dawn. By midday, he and a small detail, including Lysa, were dispatched to investigate.

The shopkeeper was older, rheumy-eyed, and hard of hearing. His hands trembled as he tried to light a lantern while answering their questions. No magic, no tomes, no signs of resistance. Just hooks of salted meat, floorboards thick with years of grime, and a back room that smelled more of lye than sorcery.

Protocol said they should search every inch. Tear up the floorboards. Turn the crates. Rattle the cupboards until something incriminating fell out.

But Reginald called the search off early. He stood in the center of the shop, scanning the space, and then gave a slow shake of his head.

"False lead," he announced. "There's nothing here but a frightened man and cold pork."

The other guards exchanged glances but said nothing. Orders were orders, and few dared question his. As they exited, Lysa lingered a step behind. Her eyes met the old shopkeeper's as he exhaled in slow relief. She didn't smile, didn't speak—but she gave him a subtle incline of her head before slipping out the door.

Later that night, under cover of fog, Lysa found Reginald alone outside the barracks, sharpening his blade by the firepit. He didn't look up when she approached.

"You knew there was someone in the cellar," she said quietly.

He didn't pause in his work. "I knew there was someone hiding. Didn't need to know more than that."

"And the false lead?" she asked.

He slid the whetstone down the length of the blade, slowly, precisely. "It's what I'll write in the report."

There was silence between them, broken only by the rhythmic scrape of steel.

Lysa folded her arms, eyes narrowing slightly, evaluating Reginald. "You're taking a risk."

He stopped, setting the blade down across his lap. His gaze was steady, but something behind it had shifted.

"So are you," he said.

CHAPTER SIXTEEN

MEETINGS IN SILENCE

The abandoned bathhouse beneath Dunmoh's trade district had long since fallen off city ledgers. Its tiled floors were cracked and caked with dust, its upper rooms collapsed and forgotten. But beneath the rubble, down a narrow spiral stair sealed by illusion and broken mortar, the old cistern halls still held firm—and there, the resistance moved like breath through lungs.

Lysa stepped through the arched entrance with her hood low and a rolled satchel clutched under one arm. The sound of her boots echoed softly through the passage as the chamber opened before her, lit by lanterns tucked into alcoves between the old stone columns. At the room's center stood a table constructed from two scavenged doors balanced over crates, layered with papers, wax-sealed messages, and coded ledgers. Around it waited a dozen individuals—none in uniform, and no two dressed alike.

Some she knew by name. Others by alias. All were part of Dunmoh's fractured resistance: a network of shopkeepers, tradesmen, former guards, priests, smugglers, and mages in hiding, drawn together not by ideology but by necessity. Their goals aligned, barely, and it was Lysa who held them together.

She placed the satchel on the table, unrolling its contents: updated maps, marked patrol shifts, a new list of watchmen recently transferred from the southern garrison.

"East wall patrols are weakening," she said plainly, pointing to one of the corners marked with hash lines. "A supply line was rerouted three nights ago. We can intercept before it reaches the main stores—quietly."

A merchant-turned-smuggler frowned as he studied the parchment. "They've increased checkpoints on the river roads. That won't be an easy pull."

"I'm not asking for easy," Lysa replied. "I'm asking for clean. If they start losing shipments without seeing faces, it'll rattle them more than blood ever could."

A younger woman across the table, robed in nondescript gray, leaned forward. Her voice was quiet but pointed. "And if they retaliate? Round up more innocents? Raise another square in warning?"

"They already do," Lysa said, not unkindly. "With or without cause. Our restraint hasn't slowed the purge. But disruption? That forces hesitation. Doubt."

The conversation circled, each voice adding tension or support, but none could offer a better alternative. As always, they settled on her plan—not because it promised safety, but because it offered direction.

By the time the meeting ended, new assignments had been passed, routes updated, and names marked for extraction. Lysa remained behind as the others filtered out. She stared at the empty room for a long while, then rolled up the map again and tucked it back beneath her cloak.

There were more meetings to come. More decisions. And far too many names not yet written down.

The candlelight wavered as the door to the apothecary's back room clicked shut behind them. Dust motes drifted through the air, swirling with the draft. Shelves of faded jars lined the walls—some filled with herbs, others empty save for residue that hinted at once-vibrant contents now abandoned. The shop hadn't served customers in over a year, but its walls still remembered the rhythms of potionwork. Now, it served a different kind of alchemy.

Lysa stood before a wide table marked with fresh ink and grease-smudged scrolls. The air smelled faintly of burnt tallow and cedar oil, an old mix meant to mask the sharper odors of fuel and powder. Across from her, seated on an overturned crate, was Deren, one of the quartermasters who had survived the eastern garrison purge. His left eye was sealed shut by a jagged scar, but the right was clear and calculating.

"I've gone over the routes twice," he said, tapping the parchment. "The next shipment passes through the aqueduct tunnel just before dawn—grain, iron, dried medicine, and timber crates marked for the outer ward."

"And weapons?" Lysa asked.

Deren shook his head. "Not in this run. But the rations will be marked with royal insignia. If they don't arrive, someone's going to feel it."

Lysa leaned over the map, scanning the hand-drawn route. The aqueduct channel was dry this season—its base served as a footpath just outside the city's eastern edge, hidden from watchtowers by a crest of overgrown stone. It wouldn't be guarded heavily. The transport was routine. Predictable.

"Sabotage the axle?" she suggested, eyes still on the route.

"Too loud," Deren replied. "They'll know it was us."

"Then we make it look like rot," she said. "Remove just enough to weaken the load. Snap it halfway through the slope. Let the wagon topple."

Deren's smile was faint, but it showed. "They'll think it was poor maintenance."

"Which puts blame on their own logistics," Lysa added. "And buys us another week of rerouted supply runs while they reshuffle."

She straightened, her arms folding. "We'll need two lookouts on the ridge above the bend and one signal torch near the basin wall. I'll send one of mine to handle it."

"You trust them?"

"I wouldn't send them if I didn't."

Deren nodded and began packing the map and notes into a false-bottom crate. The others would be briefed separately, in different locations, under different names. No single point of failure. Lysa had enforced that system herself.

As she turned to leave, Deren spoke again—quietly this time, without the usual formality.

"You know this doesn't change the kingdom."

"No," she answered. "But it changes the pace of its decline."

She slipped through the side door and into the alley, vanishing into the lanternlit haze before her absence could be noticed.

The entrance was marked by nothing more than a pale ribbon tied around the base of a cracked lamppost—frayed and half-faded, indistinguishable from street detritus to any passerby. But Lysa saw it. She passed the signal without pause, turning down the adjacent alley as if headed nowhere in particular. The buildings here leaned close, their shutters drawn and wood swollen with years of fog and neglect. A back stair creaked under her weight as she ascended to the second floor of a tailor's shop whose sign had long since fallen.

Inside, the space was bare. No furniture, no tools, no mirrors. Just loose boards, an extinguished hearth, and three figures seated on the floor around a low table. They turned as she entered, none of them surprised to see her.

The woman who led them—gray-streaked hair tied in a scarf, eyes like storm glass—nodded once and gestured for her to sit. Lysa didn't hesitate. She lowered herself to the floor, removed her gloves, and laid them beside her knees. Her uniform creaked faintly as she shifted.

"These meetings grow riskier," the older woman said. "And yet you return."

Lysa met her gaze evenly. "Risk doesn't erase need."

The others listened in silence. A boy no older than fifteen, eyes sharp beneath a mop of brown curls. Beside him, a man in his thirties with burns along his neck—half-healed, likely magical in nature. No names were spoken. That was the rule.

"They've begun hunting younger," the man muttered. "Two children seized from the baker's lane last week. One screamed. The other... didn't."

"They're testing thresholds," the woman added. "Seeing how far they can go before Dunmoh breaks."

Lysa reached into her coat and produced a folded parchment. She passed it across the table without ceremony. "This is the next sweep schedule. The southern ward is being pulled into rotation early. There's a window for movement in three days. No patrols from dusk until third bell."

The woman took the paper and nodded. "It's enough."

There was a pause as the silence returned. The boy across from her spoke for the first time, his voice soft but clear.

"Why help us? You wear the uniform."

Lysa didn't look away. "I wear it so I can do more than just hope you live through the week."

The boy nodded once, a flicker of understanding behind his eyes. Lysa rose, collected her gloves, and gave the older woman a final glance.

"I'll return when it's safe."

Without waiting for a reply, she slipped through the door and descended the steps, vanishing into the cold stone quiet of the alley.

The farther Lysa moved between these lives, the thinner the veil between them became.

By day, she walked patrol routes alongside guards who still believed in the king's justice, or at least feared the punishment for disobedience enough to feign conviction. She kept pace, kept silence, nodded when spoken to and barked when expected. Her face had become a mask of discipline—eyes alert, posture sharp, emotions buried deep. She was one of them.

By night, she erased their steps.

She mapped their routes from memory and smuggled copies to allies hidden in lofts and crypts. She diverted raids with last-minute reroutes. She rerouted intercepted reports. Sometimes, she left doors unlocked—just long enough for someone inside to disappear. She never left her mark. She never signed her name.

But it was getting harder.

Last week, a slip nearly cost her everything. A warning meant for a sympathizer's safe house had gone late—courier delayed, weather sour. She'd run the message herself, arriving just as the city guard arrived from the opposite direction. She hadn't drawn steel. She'd simply banged on the cellar door, shouting about structural collapse, about water lines bursting, smoke in the floorboards. Her rank gave her weight. The bluff bought minutes. Just enough.

The patrol didn't question her. Not then. But one of them—a wiry man with a scar above his brow—had stared too long. Watched too closely. He hadn't spoken, but he remembered her face.

Now, every time she passed him in the barracks, she felt the weight of that stare. No accusation. Just awareness.

It was the kind of attention that didn't disappear.

She returned to her quarters that night and found a slip of parchment beneath her pillow. No name. No seal. Just a line written in ink too faded to be recent.

"Traitors bleed quietly. Be sure you know who hears."

Lysa burned the note in her hearth and stood for a long time after, watching the ash settle across the embers.

She had always known the risk. But now, it was no longer theoretical. The silence was beginning to listen back.

The summons arrived just before dawn, delivered by a senior officer whose face held no expression beyond duty. Lysa was instructed to report directly to Captain Reginald's quarters—no delay, no detours. She dressed quickly, strapping on her armor, though her hands moved more slowly over the buckles than usual. Orders at that hour meant urgency. Or danger. Often both.

When she arrived, the door was already open. Reginald stood beside his writing desk, his posture rigid, but not with the usual tired authority. His eyes were sharp, the kind of sharp that cut inward rather than out. In the dim glow of the wall lantern, the lines around his mouth looked deeper, more worn.

He didn't motion for her to sit.

"We've received a lead," he said plainly. "A reliable source claims a haven is operating out of the old candleworks at the edge of the tanner's row."

Lysa kept her reaction buried beneath the surface. She knew that building—too well. It had once been used to treat wounds and provide shelter to runners when the resistance had to smuggle people across the western gate. It was supposed to have been cleared out weeks ago.

"Orders?" she asked, voice steady.

Reginald studied her for a long moment. Not suspicious—more like he was weighing something heavier than the words he was about to speak.

"We're to inspect it before dusk. Quietly. No full detail. Just you and me."

That wasn't standard. Not for a haven lead. Even for someone of his rank, inspections of that sort usually involved at least four men—enough to secure any magic users, enough to ensure no witnesses remained.

He picked up a folded map and handed it to her. "If it's empty, we close the door and write it up as such. If it's not..."

He didn't finish the sentence.

She took the map, unfolded it, and glanced over the layout. The candleworks was positioned close to the riverbank, its back wall partially collapsed. There were two known exit points and a third rumored to exist—a hidden tunnel that the city records didn't acknowledge.

If anyone was still there, they wouldn't be expecting a two-man approach. Which meant they'd panic. Which meant someone might run. And if someone ran...

"I'll be ready," Lysa said.

Reginald didn't answer right away. He looked past her, toward the shuttered window that filtered in the pale gray of morning.

"I know you will."

The words felt heavier than they should have. Not a warning. Not quite a test. But close.

She left his quarters and tucked the map into her belt. Her pace was steady as she made her way back toward the barracks gate, but the war in her mind had already begun. Someone had betrayed a haven that was supposed to be gone. Someone had given them up.

And now, she had to decide whether to let them burn—or find a way to keep them from being found at all.

The streets leading to the tanner's row were unusually still. The wind carried the sour sting of old lye and rotting hide, but few carts passed at this hour, and the foot traffic was limited to tired laborers trudging toward their morning shifts. Lysa kept her stride casual but precise, her eyes scanning ahead beneath the brim of her helmet. Reginald walked beside her, silent and focused, his cloak tucked against the breeze and one hand resting loosely near the pommel of his sword.

They didn't speak.

Words, in moments like this, were more liability than comfort. The silence between them wasn't awkward—it was calculated. Lysa used it to count exits. To listen for movement in alleys. To catalog which windows above remained shuttered and which ones cracked slightly open.

The candleworks rose ahead of them like a forgotten monument, its soot-stained bricks and sagging roofline nearly indistinguishable from the decay around it. The faded emblem of a tapering flame still clung to the rusted iron sign above the front door, swaying gently in the wind. One of the upper panes had been shattered, but the glass remained lodged in place like teeth in a rotting jaw.

Reginald slowed first, motioning subtly toward the western wall. They didn't approach from the front. Instead, they circled to the alley between the candleworks and a long-abandoned tannery, where a crumbling drainage grate offered partial cover. The smell here was worse—sour, stagnant—but it masked them from view.

He crouched, scanning the windows above, and whispered low enough that only she could hear.

"We breach quietly. If there's nothing inside, we leave it that way. If there is..."

He didn't finish again. He never did. But the unfinished edge of his tone said enough.

Lysa nodded once. Her hand shifted to the hilt at her side—not drawn, not yet, but ready. She knew this structure. Knew the warped floorboard three steps past the door. Knew the hiding panel behind the melted wax shelf that once held rations for runners on the move. If anyone was still using this place, they had done so knowing the odds were thinning by the day.

Reginald gave the signal.

They moved toward the side entrance, boots soundless on damp stone, hearts heavy with the weight of what they might find.

The door groaned as it opened, its hinges rusted with disuse but not frozen. Lysa entered first, blade drawn but angled low, her steps careful across the warped wooden floor. Reginald followed, sweeping the room with a measured glance. The interior was dim, the only light filtering through a slat in the roof and the broken pane above the far wall. Dust floated in narrow beams, catching on the tattered remains of wax-stained tables and wooden racks long since stripped of their purpose.

The air smelled of wax and mildew, faintly sweet but edged with damp stone. No fresh footprints. No voices. Just silence, thick and pressing.

Lysa's boots creaked as she passed through the main floor. Her eyes scanned the spaces where runners once slept—behind the barrels, under the shelving, near the loose panel in the far wall. It all looked empty now, but the quiet didn't sit right. It wasn't abandonment she felt—it was stillness. The kind that meant breath was being held just out of reach.

Reginald's voice was a whisper behind her. "Check the corner chamber."

She moved without hesitation, slipping around the central support beam and approaching the far door. It stood half-ajar, the shadows inside unnaturally thick. She braced herself and pushed it open with her foot.

The room was empty.

No crates, no signs of recent occupancy. Just a collapsed section of ceiling and a pile of unburned candles left on their sides. She stepped fully inside, examining the corners, then crouched near the wall where a storage alcove had once been hidden behind a sheet of canvas.

The alcove was empty too—but the dust was disturbed. Recently.

Someone had been here. But not now. Not in the last hour.

She returned to the main room, where Reginald had paused near the melted remains of an old wax vat. His gaze was steady, but distant—drawn inward, as if weighing an outcome he wasn't ready to voice.

"It's clear," Lysa said.

He nodded slowly. "We'll mark it as vacated."

Lysa knew what that meant. No names recorded. No pursuit. The official log would state the place had been abandoned, no evidence found, no arrests warranted.

She didn't ask why.

But as Reginald turned to leave, she caught the way his hand lingered near the half-collapsed wall—the one that concealed the tunnel no one else was supposed to know existed. He looked at it, just briefly, then looked away.

They left together, stepping back into the lightless alley without a word. Behind them, the candleworks remained still, its secrets preserved one day longer.

They walked the long route back to Eastwatch in near silence, the kind not born of awkwardness but of mutual calculation. Lysa kept her gaze ahead, eyes scanning rooftops and alley corners as they passed through Dunmoh's industrial quarter. Reginald walked beside her with his usual measured stride, neither hurried nor slack. To anyone watching, they were simply two officers returning from a fruitless inspection.

But beneath that surface, the silence thrummed with unspoken words.

They reached the upper ward before either of them broke it.

"You checked the alcove," Reginald said.

It wasn't a question.

"Yes."

He nodded once. "And?"

"Disturbed dust. Nothing else."

Another nod. Nothing more.

They crossed the threshold of the barracks and stepped into the stone corridor, where lanternlight danced faintly along the walls. Other guards passed them without pause, offering nods or brief acknowledgments. The world spun forward, unaware of what hadn't been said.

In the quiet of the ready room, Reginald removed his gloves and set them on the bench beside the weapons rack. He didn't look at her when he spoke again.

"There'll be another inspection next week. A different officer. Probably more thorough."

"I understand," Lysa replied.

"You won't be on that detail."

She looked at him, searching for the meaning behind those words. His eyes met hers—tired, guarded, but clear.

"You should be seen running drills," he continued, "visible on routine patrols. No sudden transfers. No suspicious absences."

It was protection. Carefully worded, plausible protection. Enough to deflect scrutiny without drawing more of it.

Lysa gave a single nod. "Understood."

He turned to leave but paused in the doorway. The next words came softer, not a command, not even a warning—just truth, shared between people who had both crossed a line they could never fully retreat from.

"We don't get to walk this path forever."

Lysa's reply came after a breath. "We just need to walk it long enough."

He didn't look back as he stepped out into the hall, boots fading into the sounds of a barracks already moving on with its day.

And Lysa, standing alone in that space, knew the moment for what it was.

They had not declared loyalty. Not out loud.

But they were no longer on opposite sides.

The tunnels beneath Dunmoh weren't built for revolution. They had once served as storm drains, refuse channels, and maintenance corridors for a city that no longer remembered how to maintain itself. But where the crown saw rot and stone, the resistance saw potential.

Lysa moved through the gloom with practiced ease, lantern held low to avoid casting light on the ceiling vents. The path forked twice—once near a rusted cistern, again beneath a cracked mosaic of Dunmoh's ancient crest—and she turned left both times. Behind her, the faint sound of trailing footsteps echoed off damp stone.

They reached the central node, a half-collapsed chamber where bricks bowed inward under the weight of the city above. Here, the resistance's pulse beat steadily. Wooden crates lined the walls, repurposed into tables, benches, and storage. A soft hum of conversation filled the air—coded terms, whispered names, quiet resolve. No banners. No oaths. Just movement.

Tomas, a former courier turned informant, looked up from a ledger as Lysa entered. His fingers were stained with ink, his jaw tight with fatigue.

"You're late," he said, though there was no judgment in his tone.

"I had to detour. Patrol presence has doubled near the windbreak arches. They're sweeping tunnels again."

Tomas cursed under his breath. "We may need to shift drop points. If they sweep too far into the east tunnels, the scholars will be exposed."

Lysa nodded. "We'll rotate them tonight. Quietly. Two-man teams. No lanterns past the cistern wall."

She stepped to the makeshift table and unrolled a scroll of marked names and symbols. Routes layered across each other, some inked in crimson, others in soot. Her fingers traced three names in silence—runners who hadn't returned.

"They're late," Tomas said, reading her expression. "But we don't mark them lost. Not yet."

"No," she agreed. "Not yet."

From the far wall, a soft whistle echoed—a two-note call. Friendly. Expected.

One of the watchmen entered moments later, cloak damp, boots streaked in tunnel grime. He approached quickly and placed a folded parchment in Lysa's hand.

"From the healer's nest. South end," he said. "New names. They've brought in two more. One's a child."

Lysa opened the paper. No identifying details, just initials, age, and potential threat level. The child was listed as *suspected latent*. Too young to train, but old enough to be noticed.

She exhaled quietly. "We'll move them tomorrow night. Tell the south corridor team to prep for transfer."

The watchman nodded and left without another word.

The room settled into motion again—voices low, hands busy, eyes alert. This was how the network survived. Not with speeches or bold gestures, but with rhythms. With unbroken links. With trust.

Lysa stepped back from the table, rolled the scroll closed, and slung it into her satchel.

It was growing. This web beneath the city. Fragile, yes. But alive.

And as long as it lived, so did the chance that Dunmoh's future could still be rewritten.

The warning came in a whisper—passed from a smuggler's apprentice to a cloth vendor who tucked it in with a bundle of dyed linen, delivered to a silent runner just before dawn. By the time it reached Lysa, the sun had barely cleared Dunmoh's eastern spires, and the barracks yard was still slick with dew.

She didn't read it until she returned to the tunnels that night, away from eyes and ears that knew how to interpret silence. The message was scrawled in tight, cramped ink on the corner of a page torn from an old ledger.

One of the western nodes was hit. No warning. No sweep schedule matched. Someone knew.

Lysa read it twice, then folded it with care.

The western node wasn't large—only three sympathizers had been stationed there, mostly runners ferrying injured out of the inner ring. But someone had spoken. And that meant everything was shifting.

She paced the length of the underground chamber, her fingers pressed against her mouth in thought. Tomas was already waiting when she turned.

"We lost them?" he asked.

"All three."

He didn't curse. Just nodded once, grim. "You think it was a leak?"

"I think it wasn't luck," Lysa replied.

Tomas glanced over his shoulder to make sure they were alone, then stepped closer.

"There's talk from the north tunnel group. They said a message was intercepted last week. Routine drop, but the courier was delayed... said someone was already there when he arrived. Someone wearing our colors."

"Could've been coincidence."

Tomas's voice dropped lower. "He said they smiled when he ran."

Lysa's eyes narrowed. "That's not coincidence."

A silence settled between them. He didn't ask what she planned to do. They both knew: if the network had been breached, every branch was vulnerable. And if someone inside the resistance had turned—whether by threat, greed, or desperation—it wouldn't be the last node to fall.

"We tighten the lines," she said. "Every message is to be hand-delivered. No open caches. We move the eastern nests and seal the fallback exits. If someone's feeding them our movements, I want to starve them first."

Tomas gave a single nod and disappeared into the tunnels, his footsteps quickly swallowed by stone and dark.

Left alone, Lysa stared at the blank wall across from her. No movement. No sound. Just the cold certainty that someone she trusted was walking the same tunnels she did, wearing the same false name.

And waiting to bleed them from the inside.

The tunnel was narrow and slick with condensation, its bricks sweating with the breath of a city that had forgotten it still exhaled. Lysa walked slowly, lantern dark, one hand trailing the wall for orientation. The silence felt different tonight—not cautious, but hunted. Every footstep pressed against her thoughts like an accusation.

She reached the chamber that once housed the old printing station—now a fallback stash for dried goods, parchment, and spare clothing.

Empty. Dust disturbed in odd places. Not from use, but from curiosity. Someone had searched through the belongings without taking anything.

She crouched beside the barrel tucked behind the support beam, checking the seam of wax she'd sealed two nights prior. It had been broken. Resealed clumsily.

Someone was checking inventory that wasn't theirs.

She straightened and let the air still. Her mind ran through names. Runners. Watchmen. Couriers. Smugglers. Informants. Every one of them had passed through her hands, vetted, trusted, relied upon. And now?

Any of them could be the reason three sympathizers died.

Tomas's story echoed again— *"They smiled when he ran."*

She sat down on the cold stone floor and rested her back against the wall. For the first time in months, she allowed the exhaustion to rise. It wasn't just the loss of ground or the danger of discovery—it was the fracture beneath the surface. The realization that this cause, this fragile web of defiance, was already splintering from within.

And it might be her fault.

She'd grown the network. She'd trusted the pace. She'd pressed for broader reach, faster communication. And now, the silence in this tunnel felt like the silence of something waiting to unravel.

Lysa reached into her cloak and withdrew a small coin-sized medallion—worn smooth along the edges, etched with an old symbol from before the purge. It had once belonged to a girl named Maren, who'd vanished last winter. No one ever found her body. Just this token, tucked under a cellar door after a failed raid.

She turned it over between her fingers. The feeling was too familiar.

A name would come. She knew it would.

And when it did, she would be the one to act. Quietly. Cleanly.

Because there could be no trial. No question.

Only the blade.

CHAPTER SEVENTEEN
THE WEAVE

The morning light in the Sanctum never arrived in beams or warmth—it simply existed, woven into the walls like breath made visible. Caelan had no sense of how many hours or months had passed since Eryndor's first lesson. Time inside the temple didn't behave the same. The torches didn't burn down, their light seemed infinite. The air never shifted temperature. But he felt rested, clear.

Eryndor stood nearby, his back to a column marked with old script. His eyes were closed, but his voice carried with calm certainty.

"Sit as before. But today, we stir the current."

Caelan crossed his legs atop the meditation dais, palms resting gently on his knees. He exhaled. The temple's breath waited.

"Reach out, but not with your hands," Eryndor said. "Sense the energy within your body—where it pools, where it clings. Most begin in the chest or the head. Some, the gut. There is no wrong place to feel from."

Caelan obeyed. At first, nothing changed. He concentrated on the space behind his ribs. A flutter. Then another. Like something coiled was waking slowly.

"There," Eryndor said, without opening his eyes. "Do you feel it?"

Caelan nodded slowly. "It's... like a thread pulling taut."

"Good. Now follow it. Let it lead."

He let his breath flow around the sensation. The more he allowed it to unfurl, the more distinct it became. It wasn't just energy—it was patterned. It moved in loops, responding to his focus. And beyond that, he could feel it brushing against... other threads. Lines that weren't his. Embedded in the stone. The runes. Even the air.

A sudden warmth bloomed behind his eyes, and his focus wavered.

"Stay with it," Eryndor urged gently. "It will resist. That is its nature. Energy tests those who grasp too tightly."

Caelan inhaled slowly, letting the warmth bleed away into the floor. He loosened his grip—not physically, but mentally. The thread settled again, humming softly beneath his awareness.

And then he saw it—not with eyes, but in the space just behind them. The weave.

Dozens—no, hundreds—of strands of light, faint as spider silk, winding through the room like living script. Some pulsed. Some flickered. All moved. Slowly. Purposefully. And as he watched, a single strand curved gently toward him, brushing his chest like a fingertip made of light.

It didn't enter him. It waited.

Eryndor opened his eyes.

"Invite it," he said.

Caelan did not reach for it. He welcomed it. And the thread stepped through him like a sigh.

The thread moved through him like a shimmer in still water. It didn't twist or possess—it observed. Responded. It traced a path through his chest, shoulder, hand, then faded, like breath cooling on glass.

Caelan opened his eyes. The chamber hadn't changed, but he had. The feeling wasn't power—it was something vast, watching, listening.

Eryndor knelt beside him, hands resting on his knees. "What did you feel?"

Caelan struggled for words. "It wasn't... like heat or wind. It was like—when you know someone's behind you, even if they haven't said anything. It touched me, and then waited. I didn't control it."

"Good," Eryndor said. "You're learning."

He rose and motioned toward one of the side corridors that spiraled away from the chamber's edge. "Walk with me. You need movement to let the weave settle."

They paced in silence through halls lined with etched symbols and still pools of water that reflected nothing above. The path bent without corners, folding inward without distortion. The further they walked, the quieter Caelan felt.

Finally, Eryndor spoke. "Magic remembers what we forget. Emotion, intention, regret—none of it vanishes. All of it roots. When you call on power, it will echo whatever lives deepest in you."

Caelan lowered his gaze. "What if what's inside me is... broken?"

Eryndor stopped. "Then you make it part of the pattern."

A soft hum resonated through the stone under their feet. They had arrived in a smaller chamber, circular like the one before, but lower—more intimate. The floor bore no sigils, only a shallow depression in the center where water pooled in still silence.

"Sit at the edge," Eryndor said.

Caelan obeyed.

"Look into it."

He did. At first, only his reflection. Then something shifted.

The water began to ripple—not from touch, but from feeling. The image in the pool shifted with his thoughts. Not his face, but moments. Flashes. Elaria's arms wrapped around him the morning they escaped. Clara setting her hand on his shoulder before sending him away. The scream in Gladecross. The fire. The silence that followed.

The pool stilled. His own face looked back at him—tear-streaked, eyes shining.

"This is your anchor," Eryndor said. "This is your cost. This is your compass. Do not bury it."

Caelan blinked. "I don't know how to carry all of it."

"You already are," Eryndor answered. "You're just now learning how to walk upright beneath the weight."

Caelan stared back into the water. For the first time, he didn't look away.

Even after the vision in the water faded, Caelan remained seated at the edge of the shallow basin, the cool stone steady beneath him. He hadn't realized how tightly he had been holding everything inside until now. With the reflections gone, there was no image left to brace against, no emotion screaming for his attention. Only breath. Only presence.

Eryndor's voice came again, softer this time, not so much spoken as offered. "Close your eyes once more. Let the weave find you, not the other way around."

Caelan drew a breath and obeyed, not because he was told to, but because he wanted to. Something in him had shifted. The resistance that always lived just behind his ribs had loosened its grip. He no longer needed to reach for the energy around him. It was already there—waiting. The threads returned to his senses, not in strands of light or vibrating cords, but as subtle currents rising through his limbs, winding around his breath and thought like rivers finding their path to sea.

He could feel the chamber this time—not just its stone and silence, but its memory. The runes beneath the surface were quiet but alive, pulsing in a cadence that matched his breathing. Each inhalation gathered warmth at the center of his chest. Each exhale released it back, as though he were part of a larger body taking in the same rhythm.

Further out, beyond the walls, he sensed distant movement. The tremble of trees stirring on the cliffside. The soft impact of something nesting beneath stone. The echo of wind curling through the peaks like a memory sung long ago.

All of it was motion. All of it was meaning. And none of it was apart from him.

For the first time, he wasn't trying to control it. He wasn't chasing mastery. He simply allowed the weave to move through him and found that it carried him just as gently. There was no need to pull or shape. The energy met him where he was, and in doing so, it folded into harmony. The threads, once erratic or resistant, now flowed with a kind of mutual respect—his breath joining the chamber's breath, his pulse syncing with something older than his own name.

At the center of it all, a familiar ache bloomed beneath his skin. The sigil on his chest—the mark he had come to fear—resonated faintly, not as a curse, but as a note that had found its key. It responded to the chamber's energy, not by flaring, but by joining in. No pain, no heat—just recognition. As though it had always been part of this place, and the Sanctum had merely been waiting for it to return.

When Caelan opened his eyes, the glow in the chamber had dimmed to a resting state. The stillness had deepened, but it was no longer intimidating. It felt complete.

Eryndor stood nearby, arms folded within the sleeves of his robe, his gaze steady and unreadable.

"You felt it," he said, and there was no question in his voice.

Caelan gave a slow nod. "I didn't force anything. It just... happened."

A small, knowing smile tugged at the edge of Eryndor's mouth. "Then you're beginning to understand."

He stepped forward, laying a hand briefly upon Caelan's shoulder—a gesture not of approval, but of confirmation.

"You're ready," Eryndor said quietly. "The trial will test more than your control. It will reflect what still lingers within you."

Caelan looked back at the basin, where the water now sat clear and unmoving.

"I'm not afraid," he said, though the words felt strange on his tongue.

"Good," Eryndor replied. "But you should be respectful."

The surface of the pool had stilled, but something within Caelan had begun to shift.

He remained seated at the edge of the chamber, his posture relaxed, the tension in his limbs finally giving way to quiet presence. The air around him felt denser now, not with pressure but with intent—like the space itself was aware of him and waiting.

Eryndor's voice came gently, not to break the silence but to shape it. "Close your eyes again. This time, do not seek the weave. Be still, and let it come to you."

Caelan obeyed without hesitation. There was no strain in the motion, no apprehension behind his breath. His thoughts, so often tangled with memory and uncertainty, softened like river silt settling after a flood. He was not empty. He was clear.

The sensation returned, first faint and familiar, then more vivid—threads of energy brushing against the edge of his awareness, not foreign but familiar now, as if the Sanctum recognized him. He did not reach for them. He allowed their presence, and in turn, they responded. They did not push or pull. They simply moved in rhythm.

The pulse of the temple became apparent to him—not in a single moment, but layered gradually, like music building from a single sustained note. Beneath the floor, he sensed the dormant hum of ancient runes, not just etched in stone but deeply embedded within the foundation. The columns echoed with stored memories, drawn from every person who had ever walked these halls. The air itself whispered, not with voices but with a slow, deliberate cadence—like the exhale of a sleeping giant that had never forgotten how to dream.

Even beyond the Sanctum's walls, he felt the land. Mountain winds slipping through narrow chasms. The thrum of distant thunder tucked deep inside the stone. The small vibrations of birds shifting in their nests far above the outer ridgeline. It all flowed. It all moved. And he was a part of it.

He did not guide it. He did not control it. He existed within it.

Then came something deeper—centered in his chest, just beneath the skin. His scar, the sigil carved long before he understood its meaning, warmed faintly. It didn't hurt. It didn't pulse with warning. It resonated, not with power but with familiarity. The weave recognized him. And in that instant, something within the temple—something old and qui-et—recognized the scar in return.

The harmony settled around him like a cloak woven from breath and memory.

When he opened his eyes, the chamber looked no different. But Cae-lan understood now why it had always felt alive. It wasn't sacred because of what was built here. It was sacred because of what remembered.

Eryndor stood nearby, silent for a time. Then he stepped forward and rested a hand lightly on Caelan's shoulder.

"You've taken your first true step," he said. "You listened, and the Sanctum listened back."

Caelan met his gaze, not with pride, but with stillness. "What comes next?"

Eryndor's expression remained calm, though there was something behind it now—something weightier. "The Trial. It will not ask for your strength. It will ask for your balance."

The corridor that led to the trial was narrower than the others, but carved with care. Unlike the grand halls etched in ancient runes and reverent silence, this passage bore no markings at all. The walls were smooth and seamless, their pale stone neither welcoming nor unkind—merely expectant.

Eryndor walked ahead, his robes trailing just above the floor, his pace deliberate but unhurried. Caelan followed without question, his steps steady, his breath quiet. The energy here felt different—not hostile, but restrained. Like something waiting behind a curtain, listening for the moment to speak.

At the end of the corridor, a single door stood embedded in the wall. It was formed of a black stone unlike anything Caelan had seen before—flat, unadorned, with no visible handle or mechanism. Yet it radiated heat, not from fire, but from movement. A hum pulsed just behind the surface, low and uneven, like the erratic beat of a wounded heart.

"This chamber is not part of the Sanctum," Eryndor said, pausing before the door. "It was carved into the mountain long before the temple was raised. The energies within it are wild—unraveled. Untamed."

Caelan studied the door, uncertain whether to be afraid or curious.

"Then why go in?" he asked.

Eryndor turned to him. "Because if you are to walk the path of the Weave, you must learn to face what exists beyond it. Magic is not always balance. Not always serenity. There will be times when the world offers you chaos, and you will have to choose not to become it."

He raised one hand toward the stone. The air shimmered as ancient sigils emerged from the surface—faint lines of silver curling like smoke, drawn by invisible hands. With a soft tremor, the door began to open, the stone sliding inward without sound.

A rush of pressure met them—neither air nor wind, but something else entirely. The kind of tension that filled a room just before lightning struck. Caelan's skin prickled.

Inside, the chamber pulsed with shifting light. Threads of raw energy lashed against the far walls—untethered, wild, spiraling in unpredictable arcs. The space itself seemed to breathe, but not in rhythm. The energy surged like a storm without direction, a symphony without tempo.

Caelan swallowed hard. Eryndor didn't follow him in.

"This is yours alone," the elder said. "You know the rhythm. You've heard the stillness. Now step into the dissonance—and listen for the thread beneath it."

Caelan nodded. He didn't feel ready, but he knew he was meant to enter anyway.

With one last breath, he crossed the threshold. The door sealed behind him.

The moment the door sealed behind him, the chamber pressed inward with a force that wasn't wind, sound, or weight—but something stranger. It felt as though the space itself had been waiting for him, held together by tension alone, and now it had been let loose.

Raw energy twisted through the air like serpents made of light and pressure, slashing across the chamber in unpredictable arcs. There was no rhythm to it—no harmony or pulse like the Sanctum's central hall. This was not the breath of the temple. This was its exhale.

Caelan took a tentative step forward, boots landing softly on a floor that felt solid only in name. The stone had no warmth, no hum, no welcome. Every movement stirred the air into agitation, as if his presence was a violation of the room's barely-contained chaos.

The strands of energy responded immediately. One arced toward him from the far wall, snapping past his shoulder with a sharp crack that left the hairs on his arms standing. It didn't strike him directly, but the aftershock left a tremor in his fingertips.

He tried to steady himself, recalling the centering breath he'd practiced with Eryndor. Inhale. Hold. Release. But the moment he reached inward for calm, the energies recoiled and then surged again, lashing in waves that refused to follow any pattern.

There was no rhythm here. No stillness. Only wild, colliding motion.

And then came the voices—not spoken, but felt. Thoughts that weren't entirely his own began to surface in his mind, carried on the current of the chamber like echoes bouncing through a canyon.

You do not belong here.

You are marked.

You are not ready.

The chaos sharpened as if feeding on those doubts. The closer he came to losing focus, the louder the room became—not in sound, but sensation. His skin prickled with invisible sparks. His chest tightened under the strain of trying to resist the collapse of control.

Driven by instinct, Caelan raised his hands and drew on the same protective weave he'd learned in earlier lessons. Light coalesced between his palms, forming a thin shell of ordered energy. For a breath, he believed it might be enough.

But the chamber rejected it outright.

The protective barrier shattered under a surge of raw force, and the backlash struck him full in the chest. He staggered, nearly losing his footing as a second arc caught him across the side. Pain followed—not sharp, but overwhelming in its depth, like something inside him had been unspooled rather than burned.

He fell to one knee.

The urge to fight surged in his blood. To force the chamber into obedience. To shape the energy into something predictable. But that wasn't what this place was testing. The storm wasn't meant to be conquered.

He thought of Eryndor's teachings. Of the stillness in the pool. Of the temple that responded not to control, but to presence.

And then, like a thread rising from memory, he recalled a quiet moment long before this—nestled beneath furs in the dim light of their small cabin. Elaria's hand had rested over his heart, warm and steady, as she whispered to him through the trembling of a fevered night.

"You don't always have to win the fight, Caelan. Sometimes surviving it is the victory."

His breath slowed. The panic loosened its grip. He lowered his hands and let the magic drop away.

Instead of resisting the current, he opened himself to it.

He didn't reach for the strands or try to redirect them. He accepted them. He acknowledged the chaos, the dissonance, the unformed motion—not with fear, but with awareness. The energy swirled wildly around him, testing, probing, waiting for something to clash against.

And when it found nothing, it began to shift.

The strands didn't vanish, but they slowed. Their movement changed—less erratic, more fluid. As if recognizing that the storm was no longer being challenged. He was no longer a wall they had to crash against. He had become part of the wind.

He remained still in that center of motion, eyes closed, breath calm.

And the room began to breathe again. The chamber no longer fought him.

The lashing currents that once spun like wild tempests now drifted with reluctant grace, spiraling around Caelan in slow, concentric waves. The energy still moved, still pulsed with power—but it no longer sought to consume or repel. Instead, it observed. It mirrored.

He stood at the eye of what had once been a storm, unmoving. Not because he lacked the strength to act, but because he had found something greater than resistance.

He had found stillness within motion.

The energies continued to shift, but now they responded to his breath. The rise and fall of his chest became a quiet anchor, and the strands around him began to fall into alignment—not by force, but by invitation. Each one curved inward, delicately at first, then with certainty, as if drawn to a center they had long forgotten.

And then the light changed.

It began as a faint glow at the edges of the room—cool and silvery, like moonlight on water. It gathered around the base of the chamber and slowly climbed the walls in steady, undisturbed waves. Caelan opened his eyes as the swirling threads above him began to spiral inward, weaving a soft pattern in the air that shimmered like a constellation in motion.

At the center of that spiral, something formed.

The strands coalesced—not into a weapon or shield, not into a barrier or rune—but into a single sphere of light, no larger than a closed fist. It hovered just above the stone floor, its glow steady and clean. Within its surface, the chaotic lines that had once battered him danced in harmonious rhythm.

Caelan stepped toward it, cautious but unafraid. The light warmed as he neared, as if recognizing the shift within him. When he extended his hand, the sphere rose gently and drifted to meet his palm.

It didn't sink into him. It didn't burn. It simply rested there—weightless, alive, listening.

The chamber had accepted him.

From behind, the soundless door opened without command. Eryndor stood in its threshold, his expression unreadable, but his eyes glinted with something between relief and affirmation.

Caelan turned, the sphere still floating just above his hand, and crossed the threshold in silence.

Eryndor studied him for a long moment, then spoke with quiet finality.

"You entered as a vessel. You return as a voice."

He held out his hand. The orb lifted from Caelan's palm and settled into Eryndor's grasp. The elder regarded it with reverence, then tucked it into the folds of his robe, where it vanished without a trace.

"No magic was taught in that room," he said, his tone neither praising nor scolding. "Only remembered."

Caelan gave a slow nod. His body ached, but not from strain. It was the ache of tension released, of weight carried properly.

"What now?" he asked.

Eryndor gestured toward a side passage branching off the corridor they stood in.

"Now, you meet Master Ildan."

The passage that led away from the trial chamber was narrower than the others Caelan had walked, though no less ornate. The walls were lined not with runes, but with clean, geometric carvings—sharp-edged sigils that felt less like memory and more like precision. The air here carried no lingering hum, no ancient presence. It was sterile in comparison, and undeniably colder.

Eryndor offered no words of parting as he turned back down the corridor behind him, his robes whispering against stone. Caelan watched him disappear before facing the dimly lit room ahead.

Within, the chamber stood in perfect symmetry—hexagonal in shape, with a lectern carved from pale marble at its center. A handful of silver inkwells lined a narrow shelf against the far wall, each positioned with such exact spacing that any deviation would have been immediately obvious.

The man standing beside the lectern turned before Caelan had even crossed the threshold.

Tall and austere, his frame was wrapped in high-collared robes the color of storm clouds. His face bore no softness, only sharp lines etched by years of contemplation and expectation. A narrow chain circled his brow, affixed with a small silver clasp over the center of his forehead.

"Caelan," the man said, his voice clipped and resonant. "You may enter."

There was no warmth in the greeting—nor was there cruelty. It was simply functional, delivered like a formula that need not be repeated.

Caelan stepped inside, noting the lack of anything ornamental. No personal effects. No flickering torches. The light in this room came from polished crystal sconces embedded with luminous glyphs—constant, cold, and unwavering.

"I am Master Ildan," the man said, turning to retrieve a tome from the lectern's base. "You are here to begin the structured foundations of magical theory."

Caelan hesitated. "I thought I was already—"

"What you experienced with Eryndor was essential," Ildan interrupted, not unkindly, but without apology. "It was raw connection. Unshaped. Unmeasured. It is the breathing of the world. But breathing alone does not build a bridge or weave a sigil. Here, you will learn the mathematics of magic—the principles that underlie structure, sequence, and cost."

He opened the tome with a crisp movement, revealing a page of concentric diagrams etched in fine ink. The lines pulsed faintly as the page turned, reacting to his touch.

"Magic obeys pattern. Even in chaos, there is structure. You will learn to see it."

Caelan stepped closer, the diagrams drawing his eye.

Ildan gestured to the outermost ring.

"This is a containment circle—not drawn to restrain power, but to preserve it. The glyphs represent containment through intention. Without it, even the purest energy diffuses into waste."

His tone was not lofty, nor was it dismissive. It was the sound of a man who had explained these things countless times and expected them to be understood the first.

Caelan absorbed the words, though he didn't yet grasp them in full. Still, there was something grounding in Ildan's precision—a rhythm to the way he spoke, as though each word had been weighed and placed like stone into mortar. This wasn't the breath of magic he'd felt with Eryndor. This was its structure. Its bones.

Ildan turned another page in the tome, revealing a layered diagram drawn in ink so fine it looked etched into the parchment. Rings of glyphs surrounded a central symbol Caelan didn't recognize—half spiral, half knot—anchored by three points arranged in perfect equilibrium.

"These," Ildan said, tapping the diagram, "are the first principles. Known as the Core Laws. Every form of spellcraft—no matter how ancient or intuitive—answers to them. Break them, and magic will fail. Ignore them, and magic will break you."

He motioned for Caelan to sit on the smooth stone bench opposite the lectern. Caelan obeyed, his eyes fixed on the design as Ildan began.

"The Law of Equivalence."

"All things drawn must be paid for. Magic cannot create something from nothing. To manifest fire, one must offer heat, air, will. To heal, one must endure. If you take without cost, the debt falls upon your body—or your soul."

Caelan nodded slowly, remembering how drained he'd felt after his earliest attempts to protect himself with wards, how the magic seemed to claw at him when he wasn't careful. This law, at least, made sense.

"The Law of Sympathy."

"Magic seeks connection. Like to like. Blood to blood. Stone to mountain. If two things share resonance, they may be bound, borrowed, or bridged. This is how enchantment persists, and how curses travel farther than blades."

He thought of the moment in the chaos chamber when the energy had turned violent the instant his thoughts soured. The weave hadn't needed to hear his voice—it had followed the weight of his emotion.

"The Law of Preservation."

"Magic resists erasure. Once invoked, it echoes. A glyph drawn in the wrong place may stain the world around it. A spell spoken with poor intent may hang in the air long after its caster has fallen. We do not simply cast. We leave traces."

Ildan let the page rest, allowing the weight of the lesson to settle.

"These laws are not theories. They are truths. Whether you shape them through words, runes, breath, or will—magic obeys these laws regardless of the form you give it."

Caelan leaned forward. "What about the mark?" he asked, voice quieter than he intended. "The one on my chest."

Ildan's gaze did not flicker, but his response came with measured precision.

"It is not a curse. Nor is it fully understood. But it is not outside the laws. That mark is a binding, carved by something beyond mortal language, but not exempt from consequence. It is a tether."

"To what?" Caelan asked.

Ildan closed the tome.

"That," he said, "is a question for which the world still waits an answer."

He stepped back from the lectern and crossed the room, retrieving a chalk-bound slate and a set of casting rings shaped from polished silver.

"Come," he said. "If you are to question the laws, you must first learn to apply them."

The practice chamber adjoining Ildan's hall was a stark departure from the sanctified stillness of the temple's earlier rooms. This space was utilitarian—its walls smooth and bare, its floors etched with faint grid lines. No torches flickered here. The light was fixed, clean, without warmth or shadow. A single casting circle had been inlaid at the center of the floor—precise, symmetrical, and unfinished.

Ildan knelt with mechanical grace, placing a ring of silver on the floor to complete the outer circle. He then handed Caelan a stick of chalk and gestured to the grid.

"You will inscribe the glyph for preservation here," he instructed, pointing to the center point. "And around it, a weave of equivalence—something small. A transmutation of stone to silver will suffice. This will test both your control and your understanding of cost."

Caelan took the chalk with a hesitant hand. He crouched at the center, recalling the diagrams from the tome. His first lines were careful, the movements cautious and precise. He let the rune take shape as it had on the page, watching the symbols glow faintly as he completed each stroke.

Ildan watched without interruption.

Once the outer ring was complete, Caelan set the chalk aside and took position just outside the circle, closing his eyes to focus. He reached inward—not to the storm, not to the breath of the temple, but to the measured presence he'd touched beneath both. His hand hovered over the rune as he summoned intent.

The lines responded immediately. Threads of latent energy surfaced, pulled from the floor's enchantments. They circled the glyph, testing the weave, then merged—unevenly. Caelan felt the resistance at once.

His first attempt faltered as the energy began to spill sideways, veering toward instability. He tightened his will, trying to force it back into shape, but the magic twisted harder against him, vibrating with dissonance.

"Stop," Ildan said sharply.

Caelan released the spell with a breath that left him trembling. The light dispersed without damage, but the glyph remained hot beneath his fingertips.

"What did you learn?" Ildan asked.

"That I was trying too hard," Caelan admitted, sweat clinging to his temple.

"Not quite," Ildan said, stepping forward. "You were trying without aligning intention to capacity. You offered will, but not form. You asked magic to obey you without giving it proper shape."

He took the chalk again and adjusted two of the outer glyphs with swift strokes, realigning their angles to mirror each other more precisely. Then he handed the chalk back.

"Again. This time, let the form guide the flow. Magic follows paths. You do not carry the current. You build the channel."

Caelan nodded, heart still racing, but steadier now. He redrew the pattern, slower than before, placing each line with deliberate thought. He matched the pressure of the chalk to the breath in his chest, remembering the rhythm of the Sanctum, the weaving of his trial.

When he cast again, he didn't reach outward. He allowed the energy to rise.

It came more gently this time, slower, but obedient to the path he'd drawn. The glyphs glowed in sequence—first the center, then the ring, then the outer line. The tension built, then softened, and finally settled.

The stone at the center shifted.

Its texture shimmered, grain becoming sheen. The dull gray surface took on a muted shine as the material reshaped at the molecular level. It did not become pure silver—but a sliver of the stone had altered, thin as a coin's edge.

It was enough. Ildan observed the result, then gave the faintest nod.

"You restrained yourself. And the weave responded."

Caelan let out a long breath, his arms hanging heavy at his sides. "That was harder than the trial."

"It always is," Ildan said. "Magic resists certainty. That is its nature. But when it sees discipline in place of desire, it yields more willingly."

He turned, returning the chalk and rings to a polished wooden case near the wall.

"You've made your first step into true practice," he said without turning. "Tomorrow, we begin the foundations of shielding and transference. You'll need rest."

Caelan nodded slowly, the weight of the spell still clinging to his shoulders.

He had shaped something that answered back.

And it had not rejected him.

Sleep eluded him.

Though Caelan's body ached from spellwork and discipline, his mind refused to rest. The lessons from Ildan still echoed through him, not as words, but as a strange tension—a pressure that hadn't quite left. Even within the quiet comfort of his stone-hewn quarters, he felt watched, or perhaps remembered. The walls held more than silence. They held memory.

He rose well before morning, slipping into his outer cloak and stepping barefoot into the corridor beyond his chamber. The light had changed. What had once been steady and golden now glowed pale blue, its source unclear. Faint strands of luminous glyphwork pulsed along the seams of the stone, not bright enough to cast shadows, yet enough to guide his steps.

There was no sound in the passage. No voices. No hum of magical currents. Just the rhythmic hush of his own breath and the occasional shift of air brushing through the temple's arteries.

He wandered without intent, letting instinct carry him. The halls wound in wide arcs, folding in upon themselves in a pattern too deliberate to be random. The deeper he moved into the Sanctum, the more the space felt... aware. Not oppressive, but watchful. The walls did not press in, yet he couldn't shake the sense that they remembered every step.

Eventually, his path narrowed into an archway he didn't recall seeing before. Unmarked and dim, it stood half-shrouded at the far edge of a spiraling corridor. No runes etched its surface. No glow emanated from within. Just a quiet beckoning. Familiar in its stillness. Dense with meaning.

He hesitated at the threshold. The air was different here—thicker, as though the corridor ahead had not been stirred in years. Yet something within him leaned forward, not in fear, but recognition.

He descended the spiral steps, each one smooth and perfectly shaped, worn only at the center by time. The light above faded behind him, replaced by a subtler glow rising from below.

At the bottom, the chamber opened into a circular vault. Its design was plain, almost austere, with no banners, no decoration, and no visible source of light. At the center stood a single pedestal carved from polished obsidian. Upon it rested a massive tome.

Caelan approached carefully.

The book's cover pulsed faintly, not from heat or magic, but something older. Something embedded. Symbols drifted across the surface—unfixed, ethereal. They moved like threads in water, rearranging themselves each time his gaze settled.

He reached out, and the air changed, inviting him. His fingers touched the cover.

The symbols halted their dance, collapsing inward and resolving into a single glyph. His mark. The same sigil that burned across his chest, mirrored here in radiant light. It pulsed once—warm, steady—then faded into the leather, which parted with a soft inhale as the book opened itself to him.

The pages were blank at first.

Then, from the center of the parchment, lines of glowing script began to form—slow, deliberate strokes appearing as if written by an invisible hand.

We do not seek power to change the world. We seek understanding, to know why it must.

The words struck deeper than spellwork or philosophy. They weren't a lesson. They weren't a prophecy. They felt like a memory rising from the soul of the paper itself—spoken not for him, but through him.

He lingered in the silence that followed, hand still resting on the open page. No other lines appeared. Nothing shifted. The moment was complete.

With reverence, he closed the tome. The glyphs on its cover stirred once, then settled back into motionless drift. He stepped away and left the chamber without another glance.

Whatever this place had offered, it had done so freely—and without expectation.

But something within him had changed.

The temple had shown him a truth. And now it waited to see what he would do with it.

Far beneath the chambers where Caelan walked, the Sanctum's deepest hall stood shrouded in shadow. No torches lit its walls. No glyphs pulsed in welcome. The air here was heavy with age, and even the stone seemed reluctant to echo.

Three figures stood within a carved recess of the chamber, their faces hidden beneath hoods marked by faded sigils of office. At the center of them, a tall stone basin glowed faintly with residual light—magic drawn from the upper sanctums, funneled through channels so old their origin had been lost.

Eryndor stood apart from them, his robes less ornate, but no less respected. His hands were folded within his sleeves, and his expression bore none of the serenity he showed his students.

"He passed the chaos trial," he said. "And by force. Through a steadied stillness."

The figure to his right gave a slight nod. "The mark did not resist?"

"No. It responded." Eryndor hesitated. "It harmonized."

That drew a shift in posture from the second master—a subtle stiffening. "That has not happened in generations. The last bearer..."

"We are not to speak of that," interrupted the third. Her voice was softer, but carried weight. "Not here."

Eryndor turned toward the basin. Within its glow, shapes flickered. Echoes. Residue left behind by the trials. The weave trembled faintly around one particular thread, bright and coiled in motion.

"He found the tome," Eryndor said after a moment. "The one in the silent chamber."

The others remained still.

"And it opened for him."

That, more than anything, settled the silence with unease.

The first master spoke again. "He must be guided carefully. Watched more closely than the others."

"He must be told," the second countered. "He deserves to know what the mark truly means."

Eryndor's voice remained calm, but firm. "Not yet."

The glow in the basin dimmed as the thread faded, slipping from view.

CHAPTER EIGHTEEN
JOURNALS OF OLD

The air shifted as Caelan stepped across the threshold of the archive chamber. A hush fell over him—not the silence of an empty room, but the solemn quiet that belongs to places meant to be remembered. Here, even footsteps seemed reluctant to echo. The scent of aged parchment, pressed leather, and faintly smoldering incense lingered like a memory held too tightly.

Columns of carved stone stretched to a vaulted ceiling above, their surfaces inscribed with ancient runes that shimmered faintly in the dim light. Shelves upon shelves lined the room in concentric rings, like the inner bark of a great tree. Scrolls wrapped in faded silk, books bound in unfamiliar skins, and relics sealed in glass cases filled the space. Magic hummed softly here—not the wild, crackling kind that surged during spells—but a residual thrum, quiet and eternal, as if the very walls remembered every spell ever whispered in their presence.

He took a step forward, his fingers brushing the edge of a low shelf. Dust clung to some of the older tomes, undisturbed for decades, perhaps centuries. Others, more frequently read, bore soft creases in their spines and faint thumbprints pressed into their covers.

For a moment, Caelan stood still.

This place... it wasn't just a library. It was a vault of thought. Of warning. Of legacy.

He thought of Elaria and her quiet rituals by the hearth, of long nights copying herbal lore by candlelight, of the first time she showed him how yarrow could draw blood to the surface, how symbols meant nothing until given purpose.

And now, here he was.

He crossed deeper into the chamber, drawn toward the central ring where a luminous globe floated gently above a pedestal—its surface swirling with faint magical currents. Around it were inscribed plaques, etched in dozens of languages he could barely comprehend. Some he'd seen in passing, others not at all. This was the index. The compass.

A soft whisper moved through the chamber, though no one else was present. He turned slowly, half-expecting a guardian spirit to appear between the stacks.

But there was nothing. Only the quiet hum of time pressing forward. Only the weight of a thousand voices waiting to be remembered.

Caelan stepped forward. He was ready to begin. Each morning began the same.

Before the bell tolled, before the halls filled with footsteps and murmurs of spellcraft and ritual, Caelan would slip into the archives—often with the dew of dawn still clinging to his boots. He preferred it that way. The stillness gave him space to think. To breathe. To listen to the stories waiting in the bindings of those ancient tomes.

The archives were organized with the precision of a scholar obsessed with order. Not just by school of magic, but by era, by dialect, by the inclination of thought behind each text. Aisles marked with obsidian-inlaid plaques divided sections into categories: **Elemental Invocation**, **Philosophies of Transmutation**, **Principles of Harmonics and Resonance**, **Post-Cataclysmic Theories**, and **Speculative Realms Beyond the Veil**.

He began with the elemental section—familiar ground. Texts on waterbinding, pyric lacing, and the formation of runic storm wards. Some scrolls included diagrams so precise, they felt more like architectural blueprints than magical treatises. The deeper he read, the more the foundation Elaria had given him began to make sense within a larger tapestry. Her lessons weren't isolated—they were fragments of something vast and structured, curated across generations.

He spent two days copying a passage on "Sympathetic Channeling," trying to reconcile the philosophy of emotional attunement with the harsh logic of sigil convergence. On the third day, he found an alchemical ledger from the First Cycle—its recipes blending potioncraft with lunar cycles and the magnetism of ley lines. He stared at it for hours, lost in thought.

By the end of each session, Caelan's satchel was weighed down with borrowed texts and scribbled notes. His fingers often bore smudges of charcoal ink from transcribing diagrams late into the evening. Master Ildan had given him permission to borrow what he could carry—though the older mage often remarked, half-joking, that Caelan would bankrupt the Temple's candle stores with how often he read past nightfall.

The routine grounded him. The repetition. The rhythm. Wake, study, reflect, repeat. The structure of the archives became a sanctuary of its own. Not just for knowledge—but for clarity. For purpose.

Because hidden between the lines of those ancient texts, something was changing in him.

It wasn't just about learning spells anymore.

It was about understanding why they were written at all.

It was on the forty-second week of his studies that Caelan wandered beyond the primary halls of the archives.

The corridors here were less traveled, and the glow-crystals embedded in the walls dimmed to the faintest pulse, responding only sluggishly to his presence. Dust thickened atop the ledges and bookspines. The polished stone floor gave way to older flagstones, uneven and time-worn, etched with sigils no longer in use.

He hadn't meant to stray so far.

He'd been tracing a reference cited in three different treatises—a passage discussing the metaphysical convergence of elemental fields—but each author seemed to contradict the next. One scroll led to another. A cited work referenced a different catalog. And before long, he found himself before a narrow passage flanked by two serpent-shaped sconces, their mouths open in silent warning.

He paused.

The temperature shifted here—cooler, heavier. Magic clung to the air like cobwebs. No signs marked the archway, but something pulled at him. A sense of presence. Familiar, but forgotten.

He stepped through.

Beyond lay a chamber unlike the others. Smaller. More intimate. No soaring ceilings. No gilded cataloging system. Just a half-circle of stone shelving surrounding a single pedestal at the room's center. And upon that pedestal rested a tome unlike any he had yet seen.

It was thick—wider than a shield—and bound in dragonhide that had faded to a deep maroon. The leather was traced with gold filigree that had tarnished in places, but still shimmered faintly when he approached. Across the front, runes were etched so finely they looked burned into the hide. As he reached toward it, the markings responded—not with light, but with warmth. A slow, pulsing recognition.

Caelan hesitated.

This book was watching him.

He opened it.

The pages whispered as they turned, dry but not brittle, like bark peeled from an ancient tree. The text was written in a formal, archaic dialect, but he recognized enough to begin reading. And when he did, he realized what he was holding.

The Chronicles of the Elders.

Accounts of the first generation of mages who built the Hidden Temple—not just as a refuge for magic, but as a beacon to safeguard balance itself. There were names here he had only ever heard in passing. Elanara. Vaelin the Boundless. Thorell of Ashenlight. Writings that told of their arguments, their philosophies, and their fears.

He leaned over the pedestal, engrossed. One section detailed the creation of the Temple's boundary wards—woven with raw elemental convergence and anchored by ritual sacrifice. Another described the earliest attempts at codifying magic into "disciplines," born from debates on whether power should be wielded or withheld.

But it was a passage deep in the back—faded, nearly smudged into oblivion—that caught his breath.

A reference to an artifact known as the **Orb of Harmony**. Not a weapon. Not a ward. A balance point. A vessel forged from the convergence of all four elemental forces, locked into a perfect state of stasis. It had been used to anchor wild energies in unstable regions. The text suggested that the artifact could harmonize even corrupted magic—if one could wield it properly.

Caelan read the passage three times, then sat back.

Something about it stirred him. The idea of balance—of harmony—not as a spell to be cast, but as a truth to be understood. It wasn't power. It was purpose. It was why the Elders had built the Temple. Why they had sacrificed so much.

And for the first time, Caelan wondered...

Was he meant to do the same?

Caelan didn't move for a long time.

He stood with his hands still resting on the edge of the pedestal, eyes drifting across the illuminated page. The script was dense, winding in elegant loops that shimmered faintly when viewed at the right angle—as though the ink itself had been infused with lingering intent. The words didn't simply inform; they invited reflection.

The more he read, the more the Elders ceased to feel like legends. They were flawed, stubborn, brilliant individuals who had shaped the arcane world not by force of might, but by force of thought. Their disagreements filled entire pages—debates about containment versus dispersal, the role of magic in governance, the ethical quandaries of memory alteration and elemental binding. The writing didn't hide their failures. If anything, it highlighted them.

One passage recounted a ritual gone awry during the early forging of the Temple's foundation. A stabilizing weave meant to anchor the surrounding ley lines had reacted violently with underground quartz beds. The resulting surge had killed two apprentices and scarred the western cliff face permanently. Elanara had written in the margin: *"Balance, when forced, becomes conquest. Let that be our warning."*

Caelan traced the faded ink with a finger. He could almost hear her voice. Tired. Wise. Remorseful.

He thought of the Orb of Harmony again. Not just what it could do—but what it represented. It wasn't a tool for dominance. It was a mirror. A living embodiment of magical coexistence. Fire, water, air, earth—forces that so often clashed, yet within the orb, existed in perpetual tension and unity.

Caelan closed the book gently, his hands lingering on the dragonhide cover. The runes pulsed once more beneath his touch—acknowledging him, or perhaps remembering him. He wasn't sure which.

He felt different now. As though the space between who he had been and who he was becoming had narrowed. Not vanished—but drawn closer. The boy who once feared his own power had been replaced by a young man who sought to understand it. Not for glory. Not for vengeance. But for meaning.

He stepped back from the pedestal, a slow breath easing from his chest.

This knowledge... it wasn't something to be learned and forgotten. It was something to be carried.

And that burden, he now realized, had always been his to bear.

The sky outside the archives had shifted by the time Caelan emerged—washed in deep blues and streaks of gold as the sun angled toward evening. He blinked against the change in light, the hush of the archives still lingering in his ears. The world outside seemed louder now, more insistent. Footsteps echoed distantly in the Temple corridors, muffled voices passed through archways, but none of it reached him fully.

His thoughts were still with the Elders. With Elanara. With the Orb.

That night, in the quiet of his chamber, Caelan lit a single taper candle and sat at the small desk beneath the arched window. The journals and loose parchment sheets he'd been filling for months were already stacked neatly in the corner—his earlier musings on spellcraft, small transcriptions of alchemical theories, drawings of runic forms Elaria had once taught him. But this felt different.

This wasn't transcription. It was reflection.

He dipped his quill into the inkwell and paused, the point hovering above the page. The candlelight danced along the edge of his writing hand, casting flickers of gold across his knuckles.

"The Elders did not seek dominion. They sought understanding. The difference, I think, is what allowed them to endure... and what now calls to me."

He paused. The words felt both natural and foreign—like someone else speaking through him, or perhaps him speaking with more clarity than he ever had before.

He wrote of Elanara's warning etched into the page: *"Balance, when forced, becomes conquest."* He sat with that line for a long time, repeating it silently.

He thought of Mother Elaria—of the steady way she'd taught him to feel the world before trying to shape it. He thought of her soft voice during late nights, of how she'd taught him to brew wild sage tea before ever letting him try a flame-binding spell. And of Torin, gruff and ever-watchful, who'd shown him how to center his stance, but more importantly, how to center his breathing when fear threatened to take over.

They had all been preparing him for this. Not for a battle. Not for some grand spectacle of magic. But for the choice to *listen*.

He leaned back in the chair, quill resting against the parchment. A breeze passed through the window arch, lifting the edge of the page. The candle sputtered briefly before regaining its rhythm.

In that moment, Caelan didn't feel powerful. He felt... anchored. And in that stillness, he felt something else, too. Gratitude. The journal began as an act of reflection. But it did not stay that way.

In the days that followed his discovery in the archives, Caelan wrote with purpose. Each page became a vessel—not only for what he had learned, but for how he *felt* learning it. These were not sterile transcriptions from a master's lecture. They were lived thoughts. Internal reckonings. The braided rope of wonder and doubt, of awe and responsibility, pulling tighter with each passing entry.

He titled the first page simply: *"Inheritance."*

There, he chronicled the first lesson that struck him hardest—not a spell, but a sentence: *Magic must never seek to correct the world, only to understand it.*

He wrote about the Orb of Harmony—not just its purpose, but the implications of its creation. Could something so powerful truly exist without cost? Had its harmony been a gift of nature, or a triumph of discipline and restraint? And why had it disappeared from the later records?

In other entries, he outlined spells he was beginning to understand—not just how they worked, but what they demanded of him. A wind-folding incantation that required letting go of tension in the fingers. A heat-channeling charm that backfired unless one held stillness in the breath.

He saw magic less as command, and more as conversation. You couldn't bend it without first *listening.*

Then came the philosophical notes—questions, mostly. Half-finished thoughts inked into the margins:

What does it mean to be balanced if the world itself is not?

Is restraint noble—or simply fear in disguise?

If knowledge must be earned, then what price have I paid?

Some of the most private passages spoke directly to Elanara, as if her journals had opened a quiet, invisible dialogue across time. He would quote her, then answer in his own voice, trying to grasp her reasoning, or admit when he struggled with it.

One such line read: *"True power lies not in domination, but in understanding and harmony."*

His reply: *I want to believe that. But what if I am called to act when harmony is not enough? Will understanding protect anyone when the blade is already drawn?*

Still, he kept writing.

Because some part of him knew that someday—perhaps long after his own life had ended—another would read these pages. Another student might one day sit beneath a window's light, fingers ink-stained, heart uncertain, and find comfort in his words.

He closed the journal one evening after inscribing a protection glyph on the final page—not to ward it from others, but to shield the words themselves from time. A preservation charm, imperfect but intentional.

Caelan placed the book beside his bed and whispered softly to the silence:

"If anyone ever reads this... let them remember not who I was, but what I chose."

The late afternoon sun cast long shadows through the colonnades of the Temple, pooling amber light across the stone floor. Caelan crossed the training hall with purposeful strides, clutching a weathered scroll wrapped tightly in protective cloth. His heart beat with a mixture of anticipation and resolve, each step echoing faintly as he approached the archway leading into Master Ildan's study.

He found the elder mage seated near a circular window, its lattice frame shaped like a sigil of warding. The light illuminated the streaks of silver in his dark hair and the deep lines carved by decades of discipline and thought. Master Ildan was reviewing an array of parchment diagrams spread across a low table—notations on elemental latticework and ritual harmonics.

Caelan stood in silence until Ildan glanced up.

"Caelan," he said, arching a brow. "You look as though your thoughts have finally caught fire."

"In a way, they have," Caelan replied, stepping forward and offering the wrapped scroll. "I found this in the deep archives. It's called the *Rite of Equilibrium*. I've read through it... twice now. I believe I'm meant to study this."

Ildan accepted the scroll and slowly unwrapped the cloth. The runes on the parchment shimmered faintly, even in the daylight. His eyes narrowed slightly as he scanned the first few lines. For a moment, he said nothing.

Then, a quiet exhale.

"This isn't merely a ritual," Ildan murmured. "It is a convergence rite. An attempt to harmonize internal and external magic simultaneously."

Caelan nodded. "It's unlike anything else I've seen. It's not about control—it's about balance."

Ildan looked up at him, his gaze sharp. "And balance is harder to hold than power."

He rolled the scroll slowly, fingers trailing across the edge. "This rite has not been taught in decades. Not because it is forbidden, but because most who attempt it misunderstand its nature. They treat it as a solution to chaos. It is not. It is a mirror. It reveals whether you carry imbalance within yourself. And if you do... it punishes you for it."

Caelan did not flinch. "That's why I want to learn it."

There was no arrogance in his voice. Only calm certainty.

Ildan studied him, the silence between them thick with the weight of judgment. Then the old mage gave a small nod, returning the scroll into Caelan's hands.

"Very well. You've taken your first step." He gestured to the empty chair across from him. "But understand this, Caelan—this rite will not teach you how to wield magic. It will teach you whether you deserve to."

Caelan lowered himself into the seat. "Then I'll earn it."

A faint smile ghosted across Ildan's face, as fleeting as a cloud parting the sun.

"We begin tomorrow at dawn."

The training began in silence.

Not the silence of inaction—but of discipline. Of stripping away all noise that did not serve the lesson.

At dawn, Caelan met Master Ildan in the high atrium of the Temple—an open-air space framed by stone arches and columns that sang faintly when the wind passed through them. This place was chosen for its natural balance: four cardinal pathways aligning with the elemental poles, a fountain at the center fed by a mountain spring, and trees that had grown undisturbed for generations. Harmony had to be felt before it could ever be conjured.

"Sit," Ildan had said on that first morning, gesturing to the platform beside the fountain. "Before you attempt the Rite, you must unlearn how to reach for magic—and instead, let it come to you."

For the first week, there were no incantations. No sigils. No casting. Just breathing. Stillness. Listening to the current of energy that moved through the world as naturally as blood through veins. Caelan had grown used to shaping magic through will and motion. Now, he had to feel it before touching it at all.

Ildan would walk around him slowly, tapping the earth with his staff, intoning questions more than instructions:

"Do you feel the heat in your hands when your anger rises?"

"What part of your body tightens when you doubt yourself?"

"Where does your power live—your heart, or your ego?"

Caelan didn't always know how to answer. But he listened. He *watched himself*.

By the second week, the lessons turned to practice. Not casting—but alignment. Caelan stood in a ring of sand, each quarter marked with a rune representing one of the four elements. He had to hold a different posture within each quadrant, channeling only the matching elemental energy while remaining centered in thought. Fire demanded resolve without rage. Water, flow without surrender. Earth, stillness without rigidity. Air, movement without chaos.

When one element overpowered the others, the sand would react—crackling, freezing, hardening, or vanishing into a sudden gust. More than once, Caelan collapsed in exhaustion, frustrated by how easily balance could slip away when the body tired or the mind faltered.

Ildan never scolded. Only asked:

"What did you *feel* when the balance failed?"

They meditated beneath hanging crystals tuned to resonant frequencies. They walked barefoot across temple gardens, testing focus while navigating terrain meant to provoke imbalance. They discussed ancient texts and argued over philosophical contradictions in magic's role across ages—questions Caelan once read with awe, now debated with conviction.

In the third week, Ildan placed a single copper ring into Caelan's palm.

"Close your hand around this," he instructed. "Feel the cold metal. Now... warm it."

Caelan furrowed his brow. "What does that mean?"

"You've studied enough theory," Ildan said. "Now, show me what you've learned."

It took him hours.

But when he finally centered himself—letting go of his need to *do* something—the ring began to warm. He sensed the metal's vibrations and accelerated it. A subtle glow, faint but real. He had found the current.

And from that day forward, Ildan began speaking less like a master, and more like a peer.

"The Rite of Equilibrium," he told Caelan one evening, as the two of them stood atop the Temple's southern balcony, watching the valley shift into dusk, "is not meant to fix the world. It is meant to remind it how to breathe again."

Caelan nodded.

"I understand."

"No," Ildan replied. "But you're beginning to."

The afternoon light slanted low through the arched windows of the archive's east wing, painting long, golden streaks across the marble floor. Caelan's hands were smudged with ink and dust. He had spent the better part of the day cross-referencing manuscripts related to ritual stabilization methods, but his mind had started to wander—back to Elanara's quote in the *Chronicles*, and the quiet certainty in her words.

On a whim, he returned to the alcove where the tome had been found. Not the pedestal chamber—but a narrow shelf along the outer curve of the wall, where smaller, personal volumes were kept in warded niches. Most were sealed behind locking glyphs—preserved legacies from masters long gone.

One, however, was not.

A leather-bound journal, worn and softened with age, sat slightly askew on the shelf. No clasp. No seal. Just a faint trace of silver thread-work along the edges and a name pressed into the spine:

Elanara of the Verdant Spire

His breath caught.

He reached for the book and lifted it carefully. It was lighter than he expected—delicate, as though it had never been meant for many hands. As he opened the first page, a familiar warmth pulsed across his fingertips. Something akin to memory.

The script was unmistakably hers—measured, elegant, but unafraid to waver. Her voice bled through the ink, candid and unfiltered.

I fear we are failing the world already. Not because we lack strength, but because we are tempted to believe that strength is enough.

Caelan read the first passage aloud in a whisper. It felt like she was speaking directly to him.

The journal did not read like doctrine or treatise. It read like a soul unraveling its burden in secret. She wrote of the founding of the Temple. She spoke of compromise, of friendships strained over decisions made in fear. She chronicled sleepless nights spent second-guessing her own teachings. She questioned the very idea of order in a world that was constantly shifting.

And yet, again and again, she returned to one theme:

Balance must be *chosen*, not enforced.

She admitted to failure. She grieved students lost to ambition, to fear, to martyrdom. She wrote of a ritual nearly gone wrong because she had underestimated her own bias. And in one particularly raw entry, she wrote of love—unspoken, unfulfilled—abandoned for the sake of duty.

I gave up a life that might have been whole, to hold together a world that never would be. Would I do it again? I don't know. But I would not trade the knowledge gained for peace of mind.

Caelan swallowed hard, his throat tightening. This was no flawless paragon. This was someone who had stood where he now stood. Who had questioned, faltered, and still chosen to carry forward.

He turned to the final page.

If this Temple survives me, let it not be a monument to our power. Let it be a sanctuary for those who seek wisdom with trembling hands. Let them know: it is not the certainty of our answers that defines us—but the sincerity of our questions.

He closed the journal slowly, reverently, and sat with it in his lap for a long, quiet while. That night, Caelan didn't sleep.

He sat in the quiet alcove outside the archives, the journal of Elanara resting in his hands like a tether to something larger than himself. The stars shimmered faintly through the high window above, their light barely touching the stone below. Yet here, in this hush, he felt more seen than in any hall of accolades or rites.

He opened his own journal once more—his fingers now more careful, more reverent—and began a new entry.

Elanara, I hear you.
You questioned, and I am questioning still. You doubted, and I doubt too. You sacrificed what might have been... and I don't yet know what I'm willing to give up. But your words didn't vanish into time. I found them. I needed them. Maybe others will too.

He copied entire passages from her entries, not for preservation, but for reflection. As he wrote, he annotated them in the margins with his own thoughts:

She feared power becoming doctrine. So do I.
She trusted others to challenge her. Who do I trust?
She walked the edge of despair and chose to hope anyway.

Caelan paused, staring at the last line. Then added a note beneath it.

I want to be worthy of that choice.

As dawn's light began to stir at the window's edge, he finished the entry and ran his hand over the page, as if pressing the ink into permanence.

Elanara was gone. Centuries past. Her bones long turned to dust.

And yet, through ink and thought and shared struggle, she lived again—if only in these quiet conversations between pages.

He placed her journal alongside his on the table, not as a relic beside a record, but as a conversation continuing forward.

In that moment, he no longer felt like a student tracing shadows.

He felt like an heir.

The ritual chamber sat in the oldest part of the Temple, tucked behind a staircase that spiraled downward through a shaft of stone so ancient it bore no carvings. Its entrance was unmarked, its threshold unadorned, as if to remind those who stepped inside that ceremony was not the purpose here. What lay within was not meant for spectacle or applause—it was a place of reckoning.

Caelan entered first, guided only by the glow of the ritual torches that lined the walls, their flames swaying gently despite the absence of wind. The chamber's interior was circular, enclosed with smooth stone and ringed with etched runes that shimmered faintly beneath the candlelight. In the center, a wide glyph had been drawn fresh that morning—silver chalk spread across the floor in symmetrical arcs and intersecting circles, its design both beautiful and severe. This was not the kind of ritual drawn for show or tradition. It was a pattern of convergence, carefully aligned with the forces it meant to tame.

Master Ildan walked in silence behind him, his robes trailing slightly over the floor as he moved to the outer edge of the circle. He said nothing at first, only adjusted his stance and watched as Caelan knelt at the center. No lecturing. No reminders. The time for theory had passed.

Caelan exhaled slowly and closed his eyes, letting the air settle within his lungs. He could feel the shift almost immediately—the change in atmosphere within the boundary of the circle. Magic here wasn't summoned. It simply *was*, lingering in the stone, in the runes, in the quiet breath between moments. He placed his hands flat upon the floor, palms against cool stone, and began to speak the words of invocation.

The chant flowed in even cadence, measured and low. The language of the rite was older than the Temple itself, preserved only in fragments through layered traditions. It was not spoken loudly or forcefully. There was no need to shout into the ether. The words were meant to *resonate*, to align, to invite the primordial forces into a shared space without resistance. Caelan's voice did just that, each syllable deliberate, each phrase a thread pulling the weave of the circle tighter around him.

Energy began to stir in response, rising gradually like water filling a basin. He felt the weight of it moving through him—not as raw power, but as tension. Earth pressed low in his spine, grounding his body into stillness. Fire coiled through his chest, testing his conviction. Water pooled behind his sternum, tempering impulse with memory. And air, always the most elusive, circled the crown of his skull, threading thought with instinct.

The runes at the edges of the circle came alive, glowing softly at first and then gradually brightening until they pulsed in time with his breath. The candles flickered once and then steadied again. The chamber hummed—not with sound, but with balance just beginning to form.

But that was only the first layer.

Caelan shifted into the second phase of the rite, altering the tone of his chant and drawing opposing elements into proximity. Harmony was no longer the goal—it was the test. True equilibrium could only be forged in contrast, and the rite demanded that contradiction be invited in fully.

The reaction was immediate.

Heat surged through one arm as cold gathered in the other. The floor vibrated beneath his knees. The breath in his lungs thinned, as if the air itself were being stripped from the room. Magic didn't rush him in a wave. It constricted, folding in upon itself like a spiral coiling around a still point. Pressure mounted from every direction, not to crush him, but to determine whether he could endure the convergence without collapsing beneath it.

He gritted his teeth and held firm, locking his muscles into practiced stillness, not out of resistance, but acceptance. He recalled Ildan's voice echoing through their earlier meditations: *"You are not the master of the forces. You are the space between them."*

The glow of the runes flared brighter, surging with concentrated intensity. Threads of light danced across the chalk lines, tracing the edges of the circle and looping into the inner glyph where Caelan remained motionless. Sweat formed at his brow, but he did not falter. His breath slowed. His mind cleared.

He wasn't wrestling the chaos. He was making room for it.

And slowly, almost imperceptibly at first, the tension began to settle. The forces did not recede—they aligned, orbiting one another, not as enemies, but as opposites made whole through the gravity of his will. The ritual was beginning to listen.

Caelan's eyes remained closed as the forces spun around him, threading tighter into orbit. The ritual circle was no longer just a structure on the floor—it had become a living thing, its runes pulsing in tempo with the energies he struggled to harmonize. Each breath he took echoed inside his chest like a drumbeat. His hands trembled against the stone, not from fear, but from the effort of keeping his will steady beneath the mounting pressure.

The convergence was nearing its peak.

Where once there had been tension between the elemental forces, now they pressed closer together, clawing for dominance. Earth pulled his body downward, threatening to root him where he knelt. Fire rose through his spine like a blade, sharp and demanding. Water rushed beneath his skin, cool but forceful, testing the boundaries of emotion and restraint. Air hissed around his shoulders and temples, unraveling coherent thought with whispers and uncertainty. They did not move in concert—they collided, intersected, folded into each other like opposing rivers forced into the same bed.

This was the true danger of the rite. Harmony was not granted; it was *earned*, and the price was focus without falter.

Caelan inhaled slowly, then exhaled in exact rhythm, using the breath to anchor his thoughts. He began the third phrase of the rite, not aloud, but within—allowing the cadence of the chant to play in his mind, threading it through the opposing currents. His will shaped the flow of energy, not by force, but by example. He did not command the chaos. He carried it.

Pain flared behind his eyes as the effort took hold. His limbs locked into position, resisting the urge to shift under the weight of conflicting power. The air thickened around him, hot and cold in turns, each breath harder to draw. Sweat beaded down his back and into the curve of his palms, but he refused to break the circle. Movement would fracture the ritual. Hesitation would undo it.

The chalk lines closest to his hands began to shimmer more brightly, as if responding to his resolve. Light trailed along the etched lines of the glyph like veins coming to life. In the center, where the convergence lines met beneath his chest, the stone warmed—then glowed, soft at first, and then brighter.

From beyond the ritual boundary, Master Ildan remained silent. He watched the energy swirl with surgical focus, his expression unreadable. He had seen others attempt this rite and fail—some broken by imbalance, others too arrogant to recognize it within themselves. But Caelan had not reached for power. He had offered stillness. And now the rite tested whether that offering was enough.

The final line of the chant echoed in Caelan's thoughts. This was the closing breath, the tether that would bind the opposing forces not in suppression, but in recognition. He shaped the energy inward, coaxing the wildness into motion that mirrored his own heartbeat. The light within the circle surged—brightening, swirling, then slowing in rhythm.

The chaos subsided.

The room began to steady. The air lightened.

Where once there had been disorder, now hovered a sphere of faintly glowing light—no larger than a cupped hand—suspended a few inches above the center of the glyph. It pulsed in slow, even waves. It was not blinding. It was not violent. It was simply *balanced*.

Caelan opened his eyes. His arms shook from fatigue, and his muscles burned from the stillness he had held for so long. But he remained upright, breath shallow but steady. His gaze locked on the orb, now hovering at chest height.

He had done it.

The elements had not been conquered, but they had been acknowledged.

And in turn, they had listened.

The orb hovered in perfect suspension, its glow steady and even, pulsing like the slow beat of a resting heart. It radiated no heat, no sound—only balance. Caelan watched it for a long moment, uncertain whether he was meant to move, speak, or simply breathe it in. He felt hollowed and filled all at once, as though something vast had passed through him and left only stillness in its wake.

He slowly eased back from the center of the circle, his legs aching with the strain of prolonged stillness. The runes beneath him dimmed as his connection to the convergence lessened, though a residual shimmer clung to the chalk as if reluctant to let go. Caelan reached out to the orb with a single hand, hesitant but unafraid, and as his fingers approached, the sphere began to unravel—not violently, but like mist dispersing under a morning sun. It unwound into thin threads of light that drifted upward, then vanished, absorbed back into the quiet hush of the chamber.

The ritual had ended.

Behind him, Master Ildan stepped forward, his boots making no sound against the stone. He moved to the edge of the circle but did not cross it, watching as the final traces of the orb faded from the air.

"You did not falter," Ildan said at last, his voice low and even. "That is rare."

Caelan turned toward him, his limbs stiff, expression unreadable beneath the mask of exhaustion. "I almost did."

"That's the point," Ildan replied. "The Rite of Equilibrium does not seek perfection. It reveals whether you understand the struggle well enough to endure it."

He studied Caelan for a moment longer, then motioned for him to step clear of the circle. Caelan obeyed, each step slow and deliberate, his breath still not fully recovered. As he exited the boundary, the light from the runes dulled further, fading into the stone as if the ritual had never happened.

Ildan retrieved a small cloth from a nearby pedestal and handed it to him. Caelan took it with a grateful nod, wiping the sweat from his forehead and the chalk from his palms. His hands still trembled faintly, but it wasn't from fear.

"I didn't expect it to feel like that," he said quietly. "I thought there would be some... surge. A moment where it all clicked."

Ildan gave a slight shake of his head. "Surges are for the reckless. You held the line. You remained the center, even when everything around you threatened to come undone."

Caelan glanced back at the circle, now inert. "It wasn't just about control."

"No. It never was," Ildan said. "Control is brittle. Balance bends and endures."

The older mage placed a hand on Caelan's shoulder—not as a teacher correcting a pupil, but as one who recognized the path the boy had just walked. "You understand now why this rite is rarely taught. Most believe magic is something they shape to their will. The truth is... it shapes us just as much."

Caelan nodded, feeling the truth of that settle somewhere deep in his chest. The rite had left its mark—not on his skin, but in the quiet spaces between thought and action. He hadn't conquered the ritual. He had endured it. Met it. Learned from it.

And he would carry that forward.

Together, they left the chamber in silence, the door closing behind them with a soft echo that reverberated through the stone. Whatever came next, Caelan knew this much—he had crossed a threshold that would not allow return.

Not just in magic.

In himself.

CHAPTER NINETEEN

ADJOURN IN
SHADOWS

The western quarter of Arden's Wake always held a different texture at dusk. The cobbled streets, usually crowded with merchants and townsfolk during the day, emptied by twilight. Lanterns cast flickering halos against the soot-stained walls, but they did little to chase away the shadows that grew longer with each passing minute. Lysa moved like a thread pulled through fabric—intentional, silent, and precise.

Her cloak was drawn low over her face, the city guard insignia tucked beneath the folds to avoid recognition. The scent of old iron, soot, and the sour tang of refuse clung to the alleyways here. Rats scattered ahead of her boots, and from one of the upper windows, a burst of drunken laughter echoed before vanishing back into the murk of the tenements.

She reached the alley—a narrow sliver between two storage buildings, walls marked with mildew and old chalk sigils she didn't recognize. One lantern flickered on its rusted hook at the entrance, its oil running low. The deeper she stepped into the passage, the colder it became, as though the stone itself exhaled.

He was already waiting.

A tall man cloaked in dark robes stood against the far wall, half-obscured by shadow. His posture was unhurried, arms crossed beneath the folds of his cloak. She could make out the faint glint of metal beneath the edge of his sleeve. Not a weapon—too small—but something.

"You've done well to keep your movements hidden," he said, his voice smooth, almost musical in its cadence. "But the king's spies are narrowing the net. You need to be more careful."

Lysa halted a few paces from him, her stance loose but ready. She didn't reach for her weapon, but her fingers twitched, itching for the familiar grip of steel.

"Who are you?" she asked flatly. "And why should I trust anything that comes from a voice hiding in the dark?"

The man exhaled a slow breath and tilted his chin forward. With deliberate grace, he raised a gloved hand and pushed back the edge of his hood just enough for the lantern light to catch his face.

Sharp cheekbones. Cropped black hair. A single scar trailing beneath his left eye—just enough to make his face memorable, if you were inclined to survive long enough to remember it.

"My name is Thorne," he said, eyes steady on hers. "And I have my reasons for wanting to see Aldric dethroned. Consider me an ally. For now."

His voice didn't carry the brittle urgency of a rebel or the hollow bravado of a spy. It was measured. Calm. Dangerous in its confidence.

Lysa studied him in silence. The air between them carried the weight of interest.

"I don't have time for liars or glory-hunters," she said. "If you're with the resistance, prove it."

Thorne reached into his cloak slowly, his movements practiced and deliberate. He withdrew a folded scrap of parchment and extended it toward her. Lysa stepped forward and took it, careful not to let her hand linger.

Unfolding the parchment, she found a sketched diagram of the inner chambers of Castle Dunmoh. Hallways, guard rotations, supply routes. Some of it matched the intelligence Jaxon had gathered. But other sections—new wings, deeper corridors—hadn't yet been confirmed. No one outside the inner garrison should know these details.

She refolded the paper and slid it into a hidden pocket inside her tunic.

"You could've sold this to someone far more interested in coin than rebellion," she said.

"I don't trade in coin," Thorne replied. "And I don't fight for fame. I fight because I've seen what he's done. And I have no more patience for it."

His tone didn't waver. There was something under it. A fracture maybe, buried deep beneath the stone facade. She couldn't read it. Not yet.

"If this map is real," she said, "it means you had access to the inner circle."

"I had access to many things, once."

She didn't like how he phrased that. The past tense. The vagueness. But it was a thread she might tug on later.

"This isn't a game," Lysa said. "If you're trying to use us, I will find out."

Thorne smiled faintly, but there was no warmth in it.

"I would expect nothing less."

A gust of wind funneled through the alleyway then, carrying with it the far-off sound of a patrol's boots against the main thoroughfare. Lysa adjusted her cloak.

"I'll pass this along," she said. "But if this turns out to be a trap—"

"You won't need to finish that sentence," Thorne replied. "I'm quite aware of the consequences."

Without another word, Lysa stepped back into the flickering lamplight and disappeared down the alley's edge. Behind her, Thorne remained in the shadows, unmoving. Watching.

Lysa kept her pace steady as she exited the alley and merged back into the quieter lanes near the outer ward. She didn't glance over her shoulder. Didn't adjust her stride. Her breathing remained calm, measured, even as her thoughts twisted beneath the surface like roots breaking through stone.

Thorne.

The name didn't mean anything on its own—not in her circles, not in Jaxon's network, not among the few sympathizers embedded in the city's fractured guard ranks. But the map he'd given her... that meant everything.

She slipped through a narrow passage beside a shuttered apothecary and emerged into a walled courtyard obscured from the main road. The moon hung low overhead, partially veiled in a smear of clouds. She approached a small wooden hatch embedded in the stone foundation of an old grain storage building, knelt beside it, and knocked three times in a rhythm that mimicked a raven's call.

A moment passed before the latch lifted.

"Was starting to worry," came a familiar voice. Jaxon emerged from the hidden stairwell beneath the hatch, his hair unkempt and face lined with fatigue. "You're late."

"I had a reason," Lysa replied, pulling the scrap of parchment from her tunic and handing it to him. "New contact. Name's Thorne."

Jaxon took the parchment with a frown. His eyes scanned the contents, the lines of his brow deepening with each passing second. "Where did he get this?"

"He didn't say. But he claims he wants the king gone as much as we do."

"Everybody wants the king gone these days," Jaxon muttered. "Doesn't make them allies."

"Then look at the map again," she said. "He knew about the inner supply tunnels. The vent shafts beneath the stone barracks. That's not the kind of information you just overhear in a tavern."

Jaxon folded the parchment slowly, his lips pressed into a hard line.

"And he just handed it to you?"

"He warned me. Said the king's spies are closing in on us. That I've drawn attention."

"You have," Jaxon replied flatly. "The last two raids you led came up empty. High-value targets vanished hours before we arrived. The Guard Commander's starting to ask questions."

Lysa's gaze dropped briefly to the moss-lined cobblestones beneath her boots.

"I know."

"Then why risk a meeting like this?" he asked, lowering his voice. "You've kept your cover this long because you don't make impulsive choices."

"He wasn't following me," she said. "He was waiting. He knew where I'd be, and when."

"That's what worries me."

She looked back at him then, her expression firm but wearied.

"If this man's for real... if he knows half of what he claims, then we can't afford to ignore him. We need leverage. We need a way in."

Jaxon stared at her for a long moment, weighing the truth behind her words.

Finally, he gave a short nod. "Then arrange a second meeting. But not alone this time. I want eyes nearby. Somewhere we can pull out if it goes wrong."

"I'll make contact again," Lysa said. "He'll expect it."

Jaxon glanced toward the open hatch, then back to her. "You trust him?"

"I don't," she admitted. "But I'm starting to believe he might be useful."

He folded the parchment once more and tucked it inside his jacket. "That's good. Just don't forget how dangerous useful people can be."

Lysa said nothing. She stepped away from the hatch and vanished once more into the night, her thoughts already spinning toward what Thorne might want in return—and whether she'd be willing to pay that price.

By the time Lysa reached her quarters within the guard barracks, the city was stilling. The drunken roars from the taverns had thinned into laughter that echoed off stone walls and dissolved into nothing. Rainclouds loomed over the horizon, their bellies heavy and waiting. Thunder rumbled, distant but nearing.

Her bunk was unmade, just as she had left it. The uniform draped over the nearby stool remained untouched, creased from earlier wear. She sat on the edge of the bed, removed her boots in silence, and unfastened the hidden sheath beneath her tunic. Her fingers moved on instinct, disarming the blade, checking the hilt, counting the notches she'd carved into it as mental markers.

Each one was a memory. Each a promise she hadn't yet broken.

She leaned forward, resting her forearms on her thighs, and stared at the grain of the wooden floor. Thorne's voice replayed in her head—measured, controlled, unflinching. There was no plea for trust. No fumbling justification. He hadn't asked for her to believe him. That made it harder to dismiss him as a liar.

People who wanted your trust usually begged for it.

He didn't.

That meant something. Whether it was a virtue or a red flag, she hadn't decided yet.

She stood and moved toward the corner of the room where a faded ledger sat beneath a small lantern. The pages were encoded with shorthand only she and Jaxon understood—notes on guard movements, supply shortages, names of sympathizers hidden among the ranks. She pulled a fresh scrap of parchment and inked only four words:

Tomorrow, western canal bridge.

The words looked too plain on the page, too vulnerable in their simplicity. She didn't like how that felt.

She folded the parchment and sealed it in wax, stamping it with a symbol they'd agreed upon—a closed eye with a single vertical line crossing through the lid. She'd pass it along through a runner known to Jaxon, someone quick and careful, someone who knew not to read the message. It would reach Thorne, one way or another.

She blew out the lantern and let the quiet settle again. Her bunk creaked softly as she lay back against the thin mattress, arms folded behind her head. The ceiling above her blurred as the shadows shifted with each flicker of torchlight from the hallway.

This was a line she couldn't uncross.

If Thorne was genuine, she'd be stepping closer to the very heart of the machine she hoped to dismantle. If he wasn't... then the trap was already sprung.

Her eyes drifted shut, but her mind stayed alert. Even in dreams, she wasn't safe anymore. Every choice pressed tighter against her ribs like a vice.

She would meet him again.

But she would not come unprepared.

The courtyard behind the barracks had long fallen into neglect. Ivy clawed over the outer walls, and the moss-softened stones underfoot were uneven with age. Once, it might've served as a training yard or a place for recruits to catch their breath between drills. Now, it served a different purpose—quiet, forgotten, and overlooked.

Lysa arrived just past the hourbell, her cloak drawn tight against the wind. The moon cast broken beams through the skeletal branches above, tracing latticework patterns across the old paving stones. She waited by the archway, back to the wall, her breath a shallow rhythm she kept deliberately steady.

She heard his steps before she saw him.

Sir Reginald emerged from the far corridor with his tabard unfastened and his sword conspicuously absent. His shoulders were hunched slightly against the cold, though his pace remained deliberate. He didn't speak until he crossed beneath the shadow of the arch and joined her beside the wall.

"This isn't one of our usual spots," he said, low and wary.

"No," Lysa replied. "But it's quiet. No patrols in this quadrant tonight."

Reginald gave a single nod, eyes scanning the courtyard before settling back on her. The dim light revealed deeper lines at the corners of his eyes. His usual measured calm hadn't faltered, but something behind it had sharpened.

"You said it was urgent."

"It is," she replied. "There's going to be a crackdown. Western district. Two nights from now, just before curfew. Not a routine sweep this time. They're mobilizing full squadrons. Clearing whole buildings."

Reginald's jaw tightened.

"They'll call it a loyalty check," Lysa continued, "but it's an operation. Mass arrests. Anyone without papers gets dragged in. Doesn't matter who. Doesn't matter why."

"How do you know this?" he asked.

"I have a source," she said. "Reliable. Embedded."

Reginald didn't press. He was too careful for that. But she saw the flicker in his eyes. Concern. Not disbelief—but calculation.

"There are families still hiding in the brick rows," she said. "Refugees from Snowhaven. Some of them are barely standing. Children, elders. If this sweep happens as planned, they won't make it out."

"You want me to intervene," he said quietly.

"I want you to buy them time. A distraction. Something small. A blocked route. A redirected patrol."

"You understand what you're asking me."

"I do."

Reginald exhaled through his nose. His gaze drifted toward the far wall of the courtyard, where the moonlight didn't quite reach. His silence wasn't hesitation—it was the careful balancing of risk. When he finally spoke again, his voice had softened slightly, though the steel beneath it remained.

"I've already stretched the line thin for you," he said. "I've redirected suspicion. Smoothed over missing reports. Told Varek half-truths to keep him off your scent."

"I'm not asking you to lie for me," Lysa said. "Just this once, I need cover for them. Nothing elaborate. A delay. Something that buys me twenty minutes."

He turned to look at her fully. "And what happens if that delay points back to me?"

"Then I'll take the fall," she said, without flinching. "If they press, I'll make it mine."

Reginald studied her, his expression unreadable. There was a kind of weight in the silence that followed—something too dense for words. Not suspicion. Not scorn. Just a long, tired pause as one man weighed how much more he could afford to risk.

At last, he spoke.

"There's a livestock shipment scheduled for the southern gate that night. Supply detail is always a mess when they arrive—smells foul, slows everything down. I'll have the roster reshuffled. That should tangle the inspection detail for a while."

Lysa's posture eased by a fraction. "Thank you."

"I'm not doing this for you," he said, stepping back toward the archway. "I'm doing it because there are still things in this city worth preserving. Try not to get them killed."

"I don't plan to."

He paused just before exiting the courtyard. "The guard's watching more closely now. Your name's come up in more than one briefing. Commander Varek doesn't like inconsistencies. If you keep walking this line, you'll eventually fall off it."

Lysa nodded once. "Then I'll fall knowing I did something."

Reginald didn't respond. His steps faded down the corridor, the hush of his departure leaving her alone in the dark.

She remained there for another minute, listening to the wind rustling through the ivy. Then she turned and slipped out the opposite way—no hesitation, no sound. Already moving toward the next fire she'd need to put out before morning.

The barracks had a stillness at night that didn't sit right with Lysa. Even when the halls were quiet, they were never truly at rest. The low hiss of lantern oil, the distant clank of armor being adjusted, the murmurs of off-duty guards speaking too quietly for her to make out—all of it blended into a hum that seemed to underscore the fact that nothing here ever truly slept.

She returned through the east entrance, choosing the longer route to avoid the more traveled corridors. Her boots moved soundlessly across the stone, her body coiled with the awareness of being watched even when no one stood in sight. It wasn't paranoia, not anymore. There was a rhythm to how long glances lingered when she passed through the mess hall. A weight behind certain greetings. And now, Reginald's warning had solidified the shape of it—Varek wasn't just annoyed. He was circling.

The records alcove was just ahead, tucked into the eastern wing where clerks filed patrol logs and rotation orders. Its wooden door remained slightly ajar, as it always did at this hour. She stepped inside and immediately spotted the clerk hunched over a ledger near the far wall, his face barely illuminated by the small, flickering lantern that hung from a bracket beside him. He didn't look up as she entered but gave a subtle wave toward the inbox stacked beside the shelf of recent assignments.

"More rotations in from command," he said, his voice dry and disinterested. "Varek's rattling the chains again. Wants tighter documentation. Something about operational inconsistencies."

Lysa approached the pile without comment and began flipping through the parchment. The reports were routine—double watches on the merchant square, updated curfews for the lower district, a request to requisition supplies for outpost reinforcement. Then her fingers paused on one sheet. Her name was listed mid-column, annotated with a directive written in the commander's familiar slanted hand.

Immediate debrief. Commander Varek. Sunrise.

She held the paper for a breath longer than necessary before tucking it neatly beneath her arm. The clerk, still engrossed in his transcription, offered no reaction. Lysa gave a curt nod, turned on her heel, and stepped out into the corridor.

The walk back to her quarters was slow by design. Every hallway she passed through was empty of life but not of presence. The walls, the torches, the polished floor beneath her boots—all of it had a way of amplifying silence, as if the fortress itself had become a watchful thing. She kept her shoulders loose, her eyes forward. Any show of tension might be noted. Anything out of place might be whispered about in the wrong ear.

Once inside her quarters, she secured the door behind her and crossed to the small desk set against the far wall. She sat without removing her cloak, her movements mechanical. The parchment was unfurled, the ink and quill already laid out beside her in tidy order. She wrote slowly, every word chosen for balance—truths clipped into safe shapes, enough effort to appear thorough but never enough to uncover more than she intended.

PATROL REPORT - NIGHT WATCH, WESTERN BOUNDARY Region: South of the river bend through the merchant quarter Activity: Minimal. Civilians compliant. No magic incidents observed. Informant report received regarding potential sympathizers—lead deemed unreliable, passed along for secondary vetting. Recommendation: additional guard visibility to maintain deterrent posture.

She folded the report, sealed it with wax, and left it in the tray beside the door. It would be collected by the shift runner come morning. Varek would read it, skim it at best, and search for any inconsistency that justified his growing suspicions. If he wanted to find fault, he would invent it. If he couldn't, he'd dig deeper.

She leaned back in her chair, staring up at the ceiling beams overhead as her mind ran through every move made over the past week. Every carefully coordinated exchange. Every false lead sown into her official work. The space between her two lives was narrowing, and the more useful she became to the resistance, the more visible she became to the crown.

After a moment, she stood and moved to the locked footlocker at the end of her bunk. Inside, beneath a folded tunic and a second pair of boots, she withdrew a book bound in cracked leather. Its spine was hollowed just deep enough to conceal the real item—a compact journal she used sparingly and only when the weight of her thoughts demanded space.

She flipped to a blank page and pressed the tip of her quill down.

Varek is watching. Reginald warned me, and now the summons confirms it. I'll go. I'll answer his questions. But every word I say will be a performance. I can't afford a single mis-step.

She paused, dipped the quill again, and continued.

I asked too much of Reginald tonight. I know that. But I didn't have a choice. They need the time. If this sweep goes unchallenged, it will be a slaughter.

The next line came slower.

Thorne hasn't asked for anything. That worries me more than if he had. I don't trust his silence.

She closed the journal, slid it back into the hollowed book, and returned it to its hiding place. Then she sat on the edge of her bunk, elbows on her knees, the heels of her palms pressed against her temples.

She would sleep for a few hours, just enough to survive the next day. Just enough to stand in front of Varek without blinking.

The price of caution was exhaustion.

And it was getting harder to pay.

The entrance to the old cellar sat behind a boarded stable in the forgotten quarter of the city, a district once bustling with traders and laborers before the war and the King's decree drove them away. Now it was little more than crumbling stone and hollow silence, its empty buildings rotting from the inside while the outer walls still clung to the illusion of purpose. Most guards avoided it unless directly ordered, not because of danger, but because it felt abandoned by the city itself—too quiet, too watchful.

Lysa approached through a narrow alley, her steps light, every move-ment rehearsed. She'd changed her cloak for a faded brown one, frayed at the edges and smeared with ash to dull the color. The sigil of the city guard had been tucked beneath a false hem, hidden even from an accidental glimpse. She moved past the carcass of a long-dead cart, now no more than a collapsed frame and rusting wheel, and reached the side door of the stable.

It was already cracked open.

Inside, the stench of mildew mixed with the scent of old straw and damp timber. She slipped through the narrow passage between collapsed beams and a pile of crumbled bricks, finding the trapdoor where it had been last time—beneath the dislodged feeding trough. She crouched, checked for signs of tampering, then knocked twice, waited, and knocked once more.

The door lifted with a soft groan.

Thorne waited below.

He was crouched by a makeshift table in the corner of the cellar, a low-burning lantern casting long shadows that danced behind him along the stone walls. His hood was lowered this time, hair pulled back tightly at the nape, features lean and sharp in the flickering glow. A set of rolled parchments lay spread before him, weighted by a broken iron plate and an empty glass vial.

"You're early," he said without looking up.

"I don't like surprises," Lysa replied as she stepped down the narrow wooden steps. "And I don't enjoy small talk."

"Then we're well matched."

He gestured toward the map. She crossed the space carefully, her eyes scanning the corners of the room, taking in the subtle exits, the structure of the beams overhead, the position of the lantern. No escape routes beyond the one she came in through. Not ideal. She kept that detail in mind as she stepped beside him.

The parchment was a rendering of the city's interior defensive quad-rant—the fortified portion of the capital where the garrison command, the siege stockades, and the King's inner armory were housed. But it wasn't the layout that made her pulse quicken. It was what had been sketched at the center of it.

A construct.

Massive in scale. Not simply a battering ram or fortified carriage. This was something different. Reinforced iron plating on the hull. An unusual mixture of pulleys and gears throughout. Steam vents. Cooling compartments. Internal chambers for the operators. Four men to operate it.

"What is it?" she asked, her voice low.

Thorne leaned back from the table, folding his arms across his chest.

"A siege engine," he said. "But not like any you've seen before. It's gnomish engineered machinery—unstable, but powerful. They call it the Breaker. They conscripted the gnomes of Noxhold, north of the mountains, to build it."

The name hung in the air like dust.

"It was built to move through city streets," he continued. "Not for war against foreign armies. It's for here. For Dunmoh. For us."

She looked at the sketch again, tracing the placement of the power core. It pulsed in her mind's eye like a living thing. "You're sure this is more than a design?"

"It's already almost functional," Thorne said. "They've tested it in the dead hours, just before dawn. Quiet runs. No casualties yet, but they're close to deployment. Once it rolls into a district, it doesn't need guards to arrest anyone. It simply makes fear visible. That's the point."

"Where is it now?"

"Under the Garrison Ward. Below the foundry near the east barracks. You'd never know it was there unless you've been beneath the blacksmith quarter."

She studied his expression. No trace of hesitation. No misdirection in his tone. He wasn't trying to scare her—he was trying to prepare her.

"Why tell me this?" she asked.

"Because you're the only one still inside the structure who might be able to stop it," he said plainly. "Jaxon has influence, but no reach. You, on the other hand, wear the uniform. You've been in the tunnels. You've memorized the patrols. If we're going to disable it before it rolls out, it has to be soon. And it has to be from within."

Lysa's jaw clenched. The image of the machine lingered in her mind, its monstrous silhouette towering over cobbled streets filled with frightened faces.

"How do you know all this?" she asked.

Thorne looked at her then—not with defensiveness, not even with pride. Just tired certainty.

"Because I helped build it," he said. "Not with my hands. But I was there when the designs were drawn. I stood beside the engineers. I signed the manifest that allowed the components to be moved beneath the foundry through mountain route passing through Corin's Reach."

Lysa went still.

"You were part of the Crown's design board," she said slowly.

"Once," Thorne answered. "Before I understood what Aldric intended to use it for. Before I realized what we were building."

There was a long silence between them.

Then Lysa looked down at the sketch again, her fingers tightening around the edge of the parchment. The room felt colder now, the lantern's light too fragile to ward off what she was beginning to feel press in from all sides.

"If you're lying to me, I'll end you myself."

"If I'm lying," Thorne said, "then we'll both burn when the Breaker rolls through the capital."

Lysa didn't flinch. She carefully re-rolled the map and tied the cord at its edge.

"Then we stop it," she said.

The cellar air pressed heavy with dust and the scent of rusted metal, the kind that clung to skin and settled in the back of the throat. Lysa stayed near the edge of the table, her eyes lingering on the blueprints as the silence between them stretched. The longer she stared, the more details began to emerge—rows of segmented iron plates, retractable pylons designed for vertical pressure, a central chamber large enough to carry a full detachment of guards.

The thing looked like a siege tower had been reborn for urban warfare.

"It's not just for breaking walls," she muttered. "It's for breaking people."

Thorne stood across from her with arms crossed, his face angled downward, watching her read more than speaking himself. He finally answered, voice low and deliberate.

"It's a mobile suppression platform. Designed to intimidate first, subdue second, and destroy last. Aldric's planning to bring it into the outer districts under the pretense of maintaining order. He won't need a dozen men with swords—just one of these."

Lysa's gaze remained on the schematic. "No magic. No enchantments. Just steel and fire."

"He wouldn't allow anything else," Thorne confirmed. "It's powered by a twin-boiler compression system. The core converts steam into hydraulic pressure strong enough to crush barricades, rip doors from their hinges, and tear stone free from foundations. It can clear a city block in minutes—faster if it's given free movement."

She looked up, brow furrowed. "And the noise?"

"It's deafening. Deliberately so. The heat, the pressure, the sound of it tearing through the streets—it's all part of the psychological effect. Aldric doesn't just want obedience. He wants fear in every brick."

Lysa stepped away from the table, pacing slowly, her hand brushing the cellar wall. "How did you get this close to it? These aren't public diagrams."

"I didn't steal them," he said plainly. "I drafted them."

She turned back toward him. Her tone sharpened. "You built this?"

"I engineered the frame. The early designs. I wasn't told what it was for. Not at first. They made it sound like a breakthrough in mobile logistics. Something to reinforce outposts on the borders. I didn't realize the purpose until I saw the crowd suppression notes. The riot dispersal modules. The ventilation systems meant to carry smoke and gas through narrow quarters."

He didn't raise his voice, didn't look for sympathy. His words landed like iron dropped on stone—quiet but too heavy to ignore.

"I left when I realized what it was really for," he added. "I disappeared before they could assign me to its deployment team. Burned the last of my credentials and made sure the orders traced back to another division."

Lysa crossed her arms. Her eyes narrowed slightly as she studied him. "If they knew you were gone, why haven't they come for you?"

Thorne didn't flinch. "Because I vanished the right way. And because they're arrogant. They don't believe someone like me could matter once I've walked away. Men like Varek assume the only threats are the ones who scream rebellion in the streets. They don't account for ghosts."

She said nothing for a moment, but her eyes drifted back to the schematic again. The Breaker's silhouette dominated the page. Not magical, but mechanical in the worst way—industrial, practical, unstoppable. A hammer designed not for battlefields, but for neighborhoods.

"How soon before they roll it out?"

"Four weeks," he answered. "They're staging it below the Garrison Foundry. It's hidden behind freight lifts. If you walked by, you'd think it was a lumber warehouse."

"And the crew?"

"Minimal. Five engineers, maybe six guards on site. They're keeping it quiet. There's no official documentation of its existence. No one talks about it, even among the officer ranks. Only command-level authorization has clearance."

"Which means even Reginald wouldn't know."

Thorne nodded. "Not unless someone tells him."

Lysa ran a hand through her hair, the weight of it all pressing hard against her temples. "You said it was designed to intimidate. Is there a way to stop it before it's ever seen?"

"There is," he said. "But it won't be easy."

He walked to the opposite end of the table and unrolled a second sheet—a cross-section diagram of the Breaker's undercarriage.

"The main pressure valve is here," he said, pointing near the core. "A manual override could trigger a catastrophic system failure. You wouldn't need explosives. Just heat and time. If someone could ignite the secondary feed while the boiler was active, the pressure spike would rupture the piston housing and disable the entire rig."

"Someone would have to get inside it while it's powered up."

"Yes."

"And they wouldn't survive the heat."

"No."

His answer was blunt. Cold.

Lysa stared at the diagram, then shifted her gaze back to him. "You volunteered for this?"

"I designed the failure point," he said. "I'm the only one who knows exactly how to reach it before the safety seal locks."

The silence stretched between them again, thick with implications.

"You really believe this thing can break the city?" she asked.

"No," Thorne said quietly. "I believe it's already started."

Lysa took the map, rolled it with slow precision, and tucked it under her arm.

"We'll need clearance papers, equipment, a way to get into the garrison undetected. If you're serious, we start moving now."

"I already have the uniforms. I'll get the rest."

"Then be ready," she said as she stepped toward the cellar steps. "We're not going to wait for it to move. We'll stop it before it ever sees daylight."

She climbed the stairs without another word.

The cellar door closed behind her with a soft, deliberate click. Outside, the city had not changed. Rain slicked the stones beneath her boots, and the air clung thick with smoke from the forges still burning in the distance. But inside Lysa, something had shifted. She moved faster now, cutting across the back alleys of the western quarter like a blade through cloth. Her path wasn't random. Her purpose had been crystallized.

She no longer carried questions—only the beginning of a plan.

She arrived at the tannery just before the hour bell, slipping through the side passage where the walls sweated with damp and the air smelled of hide and brine. No one would follow her here. No one ever did. The tannery's reputation for rot and chemical sting worked in her favor. Behind a storage wall, half-concealed by stacked crates, stood a narrow door with a lock that had been filed clean of any marking.

She gave three precise knocks. Pause. Two more.

The door opened just wide enough for Jaxon's eyes to meet hers. Without a word, he stepped aside.

The room inside was a repurposed drying chamber, long since stripped of its original use. The walls were lined with maps, strings, and charcoal markings that tracked city patrols, safehouse rotations, and known sympathizer routes. A narrow table held a pair of oil lamps and a water-stained ledger. Jaxon shut the door behind them and folded his arms.

"You weren't supposed to meet again until next week."

Lysa didn't sit. She walked straight to the nearest map, unrolling the new schematics she'd taken from Thorne. She pinned them at the edge and smoothed them out. The Breaker's outline stared back at them—twenty feet of riveted iron plates, reinforced hydraulics, layered treads, and heat exhausts. A weapon that wasn't made for war, but for control.

Jaxon stepped forward. The color drained from his face as he took in the scale of it. "What in the hells is this?"

"Aldric's next step," Lysa replied. "They call it the Breaker."

He said nothing for several long seconds. Then he reached out and traced the reinforcement lines near the front treads.

"This is a siege engine."

"No," she said. "This is a suppression device. They're keeping it quiet. No mention in the outer command chains. But it's finished. And it's weeks from being deployed into the districts."

She turned to him, her voice sharp. "This is why patrols have shifted. Why foot traffic's being redirected around the foundry quarter. He's not preparing to defend the kingdom. He's preparing to enforce it."

Jaxon didn't answer immediately. He reached for the side table, pulling out a logbook and flipping it open. He searched through the columns until he found a name, cross-referenced it, then snapped the book shut.

"There's a freight lift near the back of the foundry. No one's used it in over a year. I assumed it had been decommissioned—now I'm guessing it was repurposed for moving this... thing."

Lysa gave a short nod. "Thorne confirmed it. He's the one who gave me this."

At that, Jaxon's expression soured. "You're still dealing with him?"

"He's the one who worked on the Breaker."

"And now we're trusting the man who helped build the regime's new favorite weapon?"

"We don't have the luxury of picking our allies, Jaxon. He knows how to stop it. He's willing to go back inside the foundry to do it."

Jaxon moved to the other side of the table and studied the schematic again. His fingers tapped once on the corner of the map, then paused.

"Even if this works," he said, "we'll need clearance badges, uniforms, access tokens, guard schedules, and a secure exit strategy. The city garrison isn't like the outer patrols. There are officers there who don't blink before killing their own for disobedience."

"I'll handle the entry," Lysa replied. "He'll handle the sabotage. We just need a small team to maintain cover near the freight station. No contact. No interference. Just presence."

"You'll have it."

She watched as Jaxon ran both hands through his hair, his jaw clenched tight as if restraining the full weight of what this meant. Then, quietly, he asked the question she'd been dreading.

"If this fails... what's your fallback?"

Lysa didn't look away.

"There isn't one. Unless the old tunnels in that district are still passible."

Jaxon gave a short, bitter laugh and shook his head. "That's what I was afraid of."

"I'm not looking for a clean end," she said. "I'm trying to make sure this city gets the chance to fight back before it forgets how."

Jaxon looked at her then, his gaze not unkind, but heavier than usual.

"You're not invincible, Lysa."

"No," she replied. "But I'm already inside the machine. I might as well jam the gears."

She reached for the edge of the map and rolled it tightly. As she turned to leave, Jaxon's voice stopped her.

"Three weeks," he said. "If we're doing this, we move before the Breaker ever rolls through a street."

She nodded once, then slipped through the door and disappeared back into the night.

The inner offices of the barracks sat high above the courtyard, behind shuttered windows and reinforced doors that didn't creak when opened, even in the cold. Everything here was precision. Polished tile instead of stone, sconces trimmed in blackened brass, and walls too thick to hear through. Lysa's boots made no sound on the corridor's rugs, and she didn't intend to give them any. She already felt the weight of every step.

She passed two guards at the end of the hall who didn't greet her, didn't even glance. They stared forward as if she didn't exist.

That alone told her enough.

When she reached the commander's office, the door was already ajar. A voice from within—measured, sharp—called, "Enter."

Lysa stepped inside and closed the door behind her.

Commander Varek stood with his back to her, hands clasped behind him as he looked out the window overlooking the training yard below. His dark blue uniform hung immaculate, every seam aligned, every button catching just a glint of morning light. A single parchment rested on his desk, flanked by two candles that had yet to be lit.

The silence in the room was cultivated. Not uncomfortable. Not accidental.

"Your reports," Varek said, still facing the window, "have been consistent. Predictable, even. Nothing out of place. Nothing suspicious."

Lysa said nothing.

He turned slowly, eyes locking onto her with the kind of gaze that tested posture, tone, and conscience all at once. There was nothing casual in the way he moved. His stare wasn't accusatory—it was surgical.

"Which is precisely what concerns me."

She held her stance. "I wasn't aware that consistency warranted scrutiny."

"In this city," he said, walking toward the desk, "anything repeated long enough begins to sound rehearsed."

He tapped the parchment in front of him. Her patrol logs. "I had this cross-checked against two independent reports from officers in your assigned quarter. One reported minor unrest. The other reported none. You claimed both."

"I cover a wider radius than most," Lysa replied, evenly. "And I know how to get people to calm down before they attract attention."

"Do you?" he said, tilting his head slightly. "Because that sounds more like manipulation than discipline."

She let the insult settle between them, but gave it no purchase. "I was under the impression the guard valued discretion."

"We value loyalty," he said, voice dipping. "And lately, your discretion has become selective."

He moved around the desk and sat, fingers steepling beneath his chin. "Tell me, Evern. Do you know what happens to those who mistake my patience for disinterest?"

She didn't respond.

"They find themselves reassigned," he continued. "Usually somewhere remote. Someplace where the people don't ask questions—because they already know the answers."

Lysa remained still. "If you're considering a reassignment, sir, I'd prefer it be direct."

Varek allowed himself the faintest of smiles. It didn't reach his eyes.

"Oh no. No reassignment. Not yet." He leaned back in his chair. "But I've begun observing your movements more closely. A curious number of detours. Off-duty hours spent in districts with no patrol assignments. Supply requests for equipment never claimed. And of course, your association with Sir Reginald."

Lysa's pulse steadied only through practiced control. "Is there a regulation against speaking with a superior officer?"

"There is if that officer has been flagged for sympathizing with citizens marked for detainment."

So that was the angle. She saw it now—the trap was already set, and Varek was watching to see if she recognized the bait.

"What is it you're accusing me of?" she asked.

"Nothing," he said, smiling as he stood once more. "Not yet. I simply wanted to inform you that you're being watched. More closely than before. You should consider that the next time you choose to take the long route home."

He moved past her toward the window again.

"You may go."

She didn't linger. She turned on her heel and exited with the same calm expression she'd entered with. But once the door was closed behind her, she felt the pressure swell behind her ribs like a corked scream.

She walked the corridor without rushing. No change in pace. No shift in rhythm.

But inside, the message had landed.

The Breaker wasn't the only thing counting down.

The sun had already dipped past the rooftops when Lysa found Reginald at the training grounds, his silhouette framed in the muted glow of torchlight. He stood alone, blade drawn—not for combat, but for the quiet ritual of repetition. Each movement flowed into the next with the kind of elegance that only came from decades of habit. His footwork was precise, shoulders relaxed, the sword cutting the air in clean arcs as if shaping something invisible just beyond reach.

She waited until he finished the sequence before speaking.

"You always do the same forms."

Reginald didn't turn. "There's comfort in repetition. It reveals what's changed."

Lysa stepped closer, her arms folded across her chest. "You ever find something that shouldn't have?"

"More often than I'd like."

He finally turned to face her, and for a moment they simply looked at one another. The air between them was quiet, not strained, but not easy either. There was too much unspoken tension to allow for ease. Varek's words from that morning still sat sharp beneath her ribs.

"I saw the commander," she said, cutting directly to it.

Reginald's brow shifted subtly. "And?"

"He knows I've been off-route. He mentioned you. He's not coming at either of us directly, but he's watching."

Reginald wiped his blade clean with a cloth and slid it back into its sheath. "He's been circling for weeks. I've kept him distracted where I can. But he's methodical. Eventually, he lands."

"Then we don't give him time to."

She unfolded the parchment she'd carried folded at her side. Not Thorne's full schematic—just the portion showing the foundry entrance and access routes through the rear alleys. She laid it across a bench beneath one of the unlit torches.

"This is happening," she said. "The Breaker's real. The deployment schedule is set. We have less than three weeks before it moves into the districts."

Reginald didn't ask how she'd gotten it. He didn't challenge the details. He simply studied the lines on the parchment and listened.

"We've got uniforms, a forged clearance sigil, and the freight rotation logs from an old quartermaster contact of Jaxon's. We enter before first light, two weeks from now, during the crew rotation. Thorne and I go in through the supply lift. Jaxon's team maintains a perimeter block in the alley behind the foundry in case we need an exfil route."

"And if it goes wrong?" Reginald asked, his voice low.

Lysa didn't flinch. "Then I'll make sure it only costs me."

He looked at her carefully, something unreadable flickering behind his eyes. "You can't keep doing that."

"Doing what?"

"Treating yourself like the only expendable piece on the board."

She opened her mouth, but he held up a hand, quiet but firm. "You're not the only one who wants to stop this. You're not the only one who's angry. But if you keep charging into fire without trusting the people around you, you're going to burn through more than just your chances. You'll burn the whole thing down before we ever get a chance to fix it."

The words landed harder than she expected. She lowered her gaze, folding the map again, slower this time.

"I trust you," she said, softer than before.

"That's not enough," he replied. "You have to trust that we'll stand beside you when it counts. Or this all ends with you alone in the smoke."

They stood in silence for a long moment, the last light of the sky fading into the cold hush of nightfall. The torches remained unlit. The only glow came from the embers buried deep in the forge pits behind the training wall.

Finally, Lysa slid the folded map back into her cloak.

"When it happens... we won't get another chance. The King's eyes are narrowing, and once that machine rolls, every district will fall in line or fall apart."

Reginald nodded once. "Then we stop it."

She turned to leave but paused just before the steps. "Thank you. For not asking me to walk away."

"I wouldn't waste the breath," he said. "You never would have."

And with that, she disappeared back into the dark, one step closer to the line she would not come back from.

CHAPTER TWENTY
INQUISITOR INTERRUPTION

The city was quiet in the way only a fearful city could be. Arden's Wake didn't sleep—it held its breath.

Lysa's boots moved in rhythm with the cobblestones, the soft scuff and tap echoing faintly through the narrow corridor between merchant rows. Gaslamps guttered overhead, casting amber halos that distorted the shapes of shadows. Every few paces, the light from one would flare too bright or sputter low, like it was unsure whether to give warmth or warning.

Sir Reginald walked beside her in silence.

They wore their uniforms as armor, not just in protection, but in pretense. Cloaks pinned cleanly at the shoulder. Emblems polished, crests crisp. Authority wrapped over conviction like a second skin.

A cluster of tavern lights flickered dimly ahead. Lysa noted the sound of drunken laughter from within, the tail end of a shanty shouted off key. A couple of off-duty guards slumped outside against a barrel, mid-conversation, voices too low to catch. One nodded as they passed. Reginald returned it with a flat glance.

Their steps continued.

Only when the alley swallowed the last traces of sound did he finally speak. Not in command. Not in mentorship.

"They added another name to the roster for night raids."

Lysa didn't look at him. "How many this time?"

"Seven." His voice was measured, unflinching. "Mostly herbalists. One suspected of hiding a healer. The rest? Vagueness weaponized."

A breath left her lips, slow. "All sanctioned?"

He didn't answer immediately. His hand reached inside his cloak and pulled free a folded parchment. He passed it to her without breaking stride.

She took it and read while walking. Familiar ink. The King's seal. Commander Varek's signature—clear as ever. There were no details beyond names and sectors. No charges. No specifics. Just quiet death written in calligraphy.

"They're accelerating," she muttered.

Reginald nodded. "Because they're afraid. That's when they tighten the noose."

They reached the edge of the square and turned east. The moon crested over the gables, and light pooled down into a stretch of cobbled silence. Lysa paused here. Her eyes scanned the empty street, then the rooftops above.

A half-second flicker from a window on the second floor across the lane. One lantern flick. Pause. Two short flicks after. Then darkness again.

She gave no visible reaction, but her posture shifted. "We're clear. Continue."

They walked again. Reginald's voice lowered, his tone subtly shifted. "How much longer do you intend to play the dutiful enforcer?"

Lysa met his gaze briefly. "As long as I have to."

His eyes lingered on her face. Not judgment—assessment. Measuring her for cracks.

"You're not the same girl I met in training. She would have snapped by now."

Lysa allowed herself a small breath of something that wasn't quite a smile.

"She died the night I joined the guard."

Reginald nodded, accepting the answer for what it was. "And what rises in her place?"

"Something that knows how to hide the blade until the strike matters."

He slowed, and they stopped beneath the awning of an old, shuttered bakery. The scent of yeast still clung faintly to the wood, stubborn in its nostalgia. He turned toward her now, his voice no longer softened.

"If you go forward from here, there is no middle ground. You understand that?"

"I do."

"You won't be the whisper behind the curtain. You'll be the one holding the knife when this city bleeds."

"I've already accepted that."

The silence after held weight. Not discomfort—but finality.

Reginald took a slow breath and straightened his shoulders. "Then we stop walking lines. From tonight on, we operate together. Covertly. Strategically. But no more hedging."

Lysa folded the parchment again and slipped it back into his cloak. "Then let's begin."

He gave a curt nod. A flicker of something—respect, perhaps—passed between them before he turned back toward the main street. As they stepped from shadow into light once more, they moved not as mentor and subordinate.

But as co-conspirators beneath the king's banner.

They took the long loop back toward the barracks, cutting through the artisan's quarter where forge fires still glowed behind shuttered smithies. The clang of hammer against metal had long since quieted, but the scent of scorched iron and coal lingered in the air like an old ghost.

Neither of them spoke again until the tower bell tolled twice, its resonance rolling across the city like a low, sluggish heartbeat. Second bell after nightfall. By now, most of the other patrols were returning. This was their last window to speak freely.

Reginald turned down a narrow passage beside a mason's yard, slipping behind a stack of chiselled limestone slabs. Lysa followed, boots crunching on grit. Here, the walls closed in tight—no lanterns, no prying windows. Only the dim silver cast of moonlight and the weight of what needed saying.

He leaned against the stone and folded his arms.

"This is more than bending orders now," he said, keeping his voice low. "You know that. If we're caught falsifying reports, rerouting guard details, hiding suspects... this doesn't end in exile. It ends in a noose."

Lysa stepped opposite him, eyes narrowed. "You think I haven't accepted that?"

"I think you've accepted the risk to yourself." His tone was steady, unreadable. "But you haven't yet accounted for what that risk costs others."

She didn't reply right away. The distant echo of a dog barked somewhere near the western gate. The city exhaled around them, unaware of the crucible forming between two cloaked figures in a forgotten alley.

"I was raised to think justice meant protecting the innocent," she said finally. "Then I watched my mother get dragged from our home for healing sick children."

Her voice didn't tremble. It hardened.

"I've watched these streets long enough to know the truth: the law doesn't care about justice. Not anymore. It serves the throne. And the throne serves fear."

Reginald stared at her. Not dismissively. Not even with approval. Just listening. Measuring her not as a subordinate, but as someone who might just outpace him.

"You once told me," she continued, stepping closer, "that fear shapes good men into obedient ones. That was the first honest thing you ever said to me. The second was tonight."

He arched a brow. "Which was?"

"That you're done hedging."

Her hand drifted beneath her cloak. She pulled free a small folded slip of parchment, worn at the creases, sealed with no crest. She handed it to him. He unfolded it.

Inside were four names. Not the ones from the raid roster. Different ones.

Reginald scanned them, then looked up sharply. "These are officers."

"On rotation next week," she replied. "Two of them flagged a healer's home for inspection. The third has been intercepting messages. The fourth reported a child for spontaneous magic. I don't have the full proof yet, but it's building."

"You want to remove them?"

"I want to replace them." Her tone was cold, clear. "With people we trust. Or at least, people we can control."

For a long moment, Reginald held the paper like it might ignite between his fingers. Then, slowly, he folded it and tucked it into his inner pocket.

"You're playing a dangerous game."

"We're already playing it. I'm just ready to stop pretending I'm not."

Reginald stared at her another moment, then nodded once. It was not approval—it was recognition. She had stepped across the threshold. There would be no going back.

"We'll need to speak with the others," he said. "The ones who've been feeding us quiet intel. Start setting meetings—low frequency, random locations. No patterns. Nothing traceable."

Lysa nodded.

They stepped from the alley. Their pace returned to that of patrolling guards—shoulders back, eyes sharp, uniforms crisp under moonlight. But something in their cadence had changed.

Not step for step.

Step in sync.

The mentor had fallen away.

And in his place, a partner had risen.

The stairwell behind the old archives door wasn't on any current map.

Dust clung to the hinges and corners, disturbed only by the rare maintenance clerk or drunk recruit looking for a place to piss without being caught. But deeper still—beyond the second landing and behind a warped, iron-banded door—waited a chamber that hadn't seen formal use in decades.

A storeroom once. For weapons, maybe. Or prisoners, in older reigns. It didn't matter now.

Now it served another purpose.

Lysa eased the door shut behind her. The iron let out a low groan, but no one would hear it this deep. A single oil lantern hung on a hook beside a collapsed shelf, casting broad, uneven shadows across the stone floor. A table had been dragged to the center—splintered, its legs wedged with slats to keep it standing. Around it stood three figures, cloaked in the dark greys of the city watch.

Reginald stood at the head of the table. His eyes lifted as she entered. The others followed suit.

One was lean, older than he looked, with the hard-set jaw of a veteran and a crooked nose that had never healed straight. He offered no name, only a nod.

The second was wiry, pale, always fiddling with something. Tonight, it was a wax-sealed scrap she twirled between her fingers—half nervous habit, half compulsion.

The third was new. His eyes flicked too quickly, still calculating whether he belonged in this room. But he had brought intel before—reliable—and that had earned him a seat. For now.

Lysa approached the table and removed a rolled parchment from beneath her cloak.

"Schedule for outer district sweeps," she said, laying it flat. "Patrol routes, gate coverage, and the new watchtower shift handovers. It'll give us three gaps this week. Two small. One large."

The pale one—Callie, Reginald had said her name once—murmured, "The large gap... that's Market Row?"

"North Quarter entrance," Lysa corrected. "There's a three-hour lapse when the watchtower rotates and the patrols both reroute due to a livestock levy inspection. We can't use it often, or they'll notice the wear. But it's clean."

Reginald added, "Use it for message runners only. And no more than once a week. Random days. No pattern."

The older guard—the veteran—leaned forward, pressing a calloused finger to the map. "We still don't know who's feeding reports to Varek."

Callie gave a sharp exhale through her nose. "Everyone is. No one is. Half of them parrot what they're told without thinking."

Lysa met Reginald's gaze. "We'll need a test."

He frowned. "You want to bait them?"

"I want to know how deep the rot goes."

Silence settled. The kind of silence that meant consideration, not dissent.

Finally, Reginald said, "We plant a false arrest report. One too clean, too obvious. Say it comes from a black-hooded source who witnessed illicit spellwork outside the city. Then we wait to see if Varek asks about it."

"If he does," said the veteran, "we have our leak."

"And if he doesn't?" Callie asked.

Reginald's tone darkened. "Then someone else higher up has their hands on our threads."

No one spoke for a beat.

The small chamber was quiet but alive—pulsing with danger, with conviction, with the fragile thread of hope stitched between the fear. A spark, still flickering.

Lysa pulled from her satchel a small object: a blackened brass token etched with the symbol of the city guard. Around its rim, someone had scratched a pattern of intersecting lines and arcs—simple geometry, nothing a superior officer would question unless they knew exactly what they were looking for.

She set it on the table.

"This will be the marker," she said. "Pass it only to someone who's already helped. Someone who hasn't been caught looking twice."

The others nodded.

The quiet network wasn't born with fanfare. No oaths. No banners. No speeches about what would come next.

It was born in silence, with careful hands and glances, in the marrow of the city's oldest bones.

And it was growing.

The old table groaned beneath the weight of more than just plans. It bore the burden of intent—of knowing that every step forward meant stepping deeper into treason.

Reginald placed a sealed satchel at the center of the table. Its contents shifted faintly with the sound of paper against wax and glass. Lysa recognized the preparation—decoys, false orders, forged requisitions, and enough supplies to vanish if it all fell apart.

"We're not just organizing," Reginald said quietly. "We're committing."

He unrolled a second parchment. This one wasn't a map—it was a cipher key. Carefully hand-penned, it detailed a system of rotating signal phrases, courier marks, and symbols to be carved or chalked in alleys, under gate arches, or on supply crates. Each symbol would shift weekly. Each phrase was designed to pass as benign within normal conversation.

Lysa leaned over it, tracing the key with her eyes. The symbols weren't magic. They were simple. Practical. A curled leaf meant "stand down." A pair of stacked squares meant "danger confirmed." A diagonal stroke meant "new contact." There was nothing mystical—only clarity and risk.

"This is good," she said. "Simple. Scalable."

The veteran frowned. "Too simple. If they crack it—"

"They won't," Lysa cut in. "Because no one writes the key down. After tonight, this copy burns."

Callie gave a crooked grin. "I like her."

Reginald's gaze swept across them all, pausing on each pair of eyes. "We're not playing heroes. No speeches. No open defiance. Not yet. This is information, protection, subversion. We disrupt the gears until they grind."

The young guard at the table—the quiet one—shifted, discomfort flickering across his face.

"What if someone talks?" he asked. "If one of us breaks... or worse, if we're watched?"

The tension didn't rise. It cooled.

Reginald spoke without venom. "Then we've failed. But we prepare for that."

From beneath his cloak, he produced a second satchel. Inside: identical uniforms, guard insignias scraped nearly clean, forged travel orders. The kind of things a deserter might carry to impersonate a passing patrol unit. Enough to get someone out of the city—if they moved fast and didn't ask questions.

"There's one of these for each of you," he said. "We don't talk about them again. If you need it, use it. But know this—if you disappear without cause, don't expect us to cover your absence. We cannot afford the breach."

The quiet guard's jaw worked, but he said nothing more. He gave a tight nod.

Lysa stepped forward again. "And if one of us is captured?"

Callie tilted her head. "You have a plan?"

"I do." Lysa opened her palm to reveal a small strip of waxed linen. Folded inside was a sliver of iron, dulled at the edges. "If someone's taken, they burn the signal flare. Mix of oil, pine resin, and blackpowder—small enough to light in a cell without killing yourself. Big enough to be seen from any eastern-facing window."

Reginald arched a brow. "Where'd you learn that?"

Lysa met his gaze. "My mother was a healer. She taught me how to make smoke draw eyes. To bring help where screaming never reached."

He gave the faintest nod.

No one questioned her further.

At last, Reginald rolled up the cipher sheet, held it over the lantern's flame, and watched it curl to ash. They stood in silence as the parchment blackened and twisted inward on itself—silent witnesses to the death of plausible deniability.

When it was gone, he ground the ashes beneath his boot. "From now on," he said, "this room doesn't exist. These meetings didn't happen. We speak of them only in the right time, the right way."

Lysa reached for the brass token still lying at the center of the table. She turned it over once, then pressed it flat to the wood.

"We are not the revolution," she said.

"Not yet."

"But we will be the fault in the foundation."

The summons came at dawn, folded and sealed in red wax with the king's crest pressed deep into the edge. It waited on Reginald's desk like a coiled serpent—no courier, no witness, just the mark and the silence of its arrival.

He cracked the seal without ceremony.

The parchment was brief.

Orders from Commander Varek: Immediate mobilization. Suspected magical sympathizers at Slatestone Crossing, tenement row 3-B. Full compliance expected. Minimal tolerance. The king's decree is not a discussion.

There was a second slip tucked beneath it. Handwritten. No seal.

You're being watched. Choose your route carefully.

Reginald let the note fall between his fingers as he stood from the desk. His jaw worked quietly. The pretense was falling away. They weren't being tested anymore—they were being measured for the noose.

He exited his quarters with practiced calm.

The barracks stirred with morning drills. Armor clinked. The rhythm of boot to stone echoed in disciplined cadence. Recruits barked responses to instructors across the yard. But beneath it all, a murmur had started to creep into the daily routines—a low buzz of tension, of something unseen curling under the skin of the garrison.

He found Lysa already geared and waiting by the courtyard steps. Her posture was straight, but her eyes caught his before he even spoke. She already knew.

"Raid?" she asked.

"Slatestone Crossing. Section 3-B. No evidence provided. Varek's orders."

Her brow tightened slightly. "That's the old merchant block. Mostly widows, craftsmen, and traveling laborers."

"Exactly." He handed her the slip of paper. She didn't need to read it. She burned it without a word.

They walked to the armory in silence. There, a trio of guards waited—handpicked for the raid. None of them were part of the quiet network. One leaned against a post with the smirk of someone eager for violence. Another adjusted his gloves compulsively. The third, a sharp-eyed officer named Braen, nodded respectfully to Reginald.

Reginald addressed them with the ease of command. "You three are with us. We move light—no horses. Foot patrol through market row. Orders are direct. Full sweep. Contain and interrogate, but no executions unless met with force. Understood?"

They all nodded, though one of them muttered something beneath his breath that Lysa didn't quite catch. She didn't ask him to repeat it.

The squad moved through the outer gate an hour later.

Arden's Wake yawned to life around them. Bakers pulled bread carts into street stalls. A cobbler tossed water onto the cobblestones to keep the dust down. Children ran barefoot past them and fell silent as they noticed the guards approaching. Eyes lowered. Doors shut.

As they reached the edge of Slatestone Crossing, Lysa caught Reginald's glance again. It was subtle. A pause in step. She mirrored it.

Behind them, the other guards fanned out.

Lysa peeled away slightly toward the east end of the alley, where a cluster of laundry lines flapped in the breeze. She slipped her gloved hand against a crate and drew a quick, sharp mark across its side: a downward stroke intersected by a jagged curve. A signal. **Delay point active. Scatter formation.**

Thirty seconds later, two sharp knocks rang out from the corner where Callie had agreed to stage herself earlier in the week. Unseen. Unacknowledged. But heard.

The response was immediate.

A child tripped in the street, sending a basket of flour tumbling. The resulting white cloud burst into the air with a chaos that startled the guards just long enough for Lysa to disappear into a side stairwell.

Reginald stepped forward, taking advantage of the distraction. "Clear the west wall first. Lysa, secure the back stair—"

"She's already gone, sir," one guard barked, annoyed.

Reginald narrowed his eyes, tone sharpening. "Then you two split the building. I'll take the roof access. Go!"

The guards scrambled into position.

Inside the building, Lysa moved quickly, weaving through shadowed halls and up narrow staircases. She knew this block. The resistance used it often. A sympathetic weaver housed coded messages beneath floorboards. A smith on the third level provided cover for transport routes out of the city.

She didn't need to find evidence. She needed to erase it.

Upstairs, she found the signal already waiting for her—an open window with its curtain pinned at a sharp angle. The safehouse had been evacuated.

Still, she moved through each room with practiced speed, wiping clean the traces—burning parchments, scattering ash, overturning ink.

She paused only once, in the smallest room. A child's wooden horse rested beneath the bed, carved with care. Lysa hesitated, then gently pushed it deeper into the shadows.

When she emerged back onto the street, Reginald had reassembled the squad. Braen looked irritated.

"No signs of spellwork. Just some burned parchments and abandoned goods."

Reginald crossed his arms. "They knew we were coming."

Braen muttered something under his breath. "Or someone warned them."

Lysa didn't flinch.

Reginald's tone darkened. "We report the site as purged. No arrests. No findings. They'll move the next time, but the message stands."

Braen gave a curt nod but didn't look convinced.

As the squad moved out, Lysa fell back a step behind Reginald.

"That was close," she said quietly.

He didn't look back.

"It won't be the last."

The report was filed by nightfall.

Reginald stood over his desk, quill poised, as he carefully scripted the events of the day—omitting everything that mattered. The sweep was recorded as routine. No magical artifacts recovered. No evidence of harboring spellcasters. All residents accounted for, all assets seized for inspection.

He knew the phrasing well. Just enough vagueness to avoid suspicion. Just enough finality to prevent follow-up.

Across the room, Lysa leaned against the stone archway, arms folded. Her uniform was dusted from the streets, hair tied back tighter than usual. There was still soot on her gloves from the parchment she burned.

"Varek will want to know why we came up empty," she said.

"He'll assume we were sloppy," Reginald replied. "Or that the lead was bad."

"Too many clean reports and he'll start asking where we're sourcing them."

He signed the parchment with deliberate care, then poured wax and pressed the seal.

"Then we give him one that isn't clean," he said.

Lysa raised a brow. "You want to plant something?"

Reginald shook his head. "I want to leak something."

He walked to the shelf behind his desk, pulling a scroll that had already been prepared—an old report from two years ago involving a suspected hedge-witch in the north quarter. The charges had never been confirmed, the subject never arrested. But the file still existed. Dormant. Forgettable.

Reginald tapped the edge of the scroll. "We rework this. Alter the date, add a false witness statement. Mark it as urgent but misfiled."

Lysa crossed the room. "And who finds it?"

"Braen." Reginald met her gaze. "He's ambitious. And he didn't believe us today. We let him find the file himself. Let him think he's the one rooting out negligence. He'll push for a raid without us involved."

She considered this, then nodded slowly. "If it backfires—"

"He takes the blame. And if it doesn't, the real sympathizers in that block are already gone."

They worked in silence for several minutes, adjusting the scroll's contents, reshaping the margins, weathering the edges with a flick of flame and oil to make it look as though it had sat forgotten in some neglected filing chest.

When it was done, Lysa tucked it into a leather folio and placed it near Braen's assigned stack on the document table.

By morning, it would be 'discovered.'

By noon, the Varek would be briefed.

And by the next night, a ghost raid would tear through an empty tenement, chasing after shadows.

But in the space between, the resistance would move two new families out of the city.

Lysa slid her gloves off and placed them on Reginald's desk. "You're good at this."

He met her eyes, no pride in his expression. "I shouldn't have to be."

A beat of silence passed.

Then Lysa turned to go. As she reached the door, she paused. Her hand rested against the worn wood, fingers splayed in thought.

"Every time we do this... bend the law to stop it... do you ever wonder if we're becoming what we're fighting?"

Reginald didn't answer immediately. When he did, his voice was low.

"Every day. But I'd rather break the law than break a child's neck for holding a spellbook."

She didn't respond, but the door opened and shut quietly behind her.

Reginald sat in silence for a long time afterward, the fire in the hearth burning low, casting long, jagged shadows across the chamber floor.

The inquisitors arrived unannounced.

There was no fanfare, no herald, no formal scroll read aloud in the square. Just a hush that swept across the barracks like a cold front the moment the first grey-and-gold cloaked figure passed beneath the archway.

Three of them dismounted in the courtyard at dawn. Not one spoke.

Their horses were immaculate—jet black, braided reins, no dust on the saddlebags. Their armor bore no rust, their boots no scuffs. And their expressions... blank, cold, practiced.

At their head stood a tall, narrow-shouldered figure whose presence filled the space more than his voice ever would. He removed his riding gloves with slow, deliberate precision. His face was sharp, angular, like someone who'd never smiled in his life and saw no reason to start now.

Reginald knew who he was the moment he stepped forward.

Inquisitor Cale Veyron.

A name passed in whispers through the capital's lower courts. Silent judgments. Unappealable sentences. A man who didn't need to raise his voice because his silence was threat enough.

Varek greeted them in the upper courtyard, flanked by his lieutenants. Reginald and Lysa lingered back with the gathered officers, observing the exchange from a measured distance.

"Inquisitor Veyron," Varek began with a stiff nod. "We weren't informed of your arrival."

Veyron tilted his head slightly. "We weren't obligated to inform you."

Behind him, the other two inquisitors began unbuckling scroll tubes, extracting ledgers marked with royal glyphs and cordoned seals. One bore a long ribbon of orders—deployment charts, patrol rosters, arrest records, all collected and cataloged from the last four months.

"You're here to inspect our raids?" Varek asked, his tone clipped, defensive.

Veyron didn't blink. "We're here to weigh your performance."

Varek's jaw twitched. "Everything has been conducted within full alignment of the King's decree. We've detained over two hundred suspected magic users and sympathizers in the last year alone."

"And how many of those led to confirmed magical prosecution?"

A pause. Not long, but enough for every officer nearby to feel it.

Veyron didn't press further. He simply turned to the courtyard, his gaze sliding across the gathered guards like one assessing tools on a shelf. When his eyes passed over Reginald, there was a flicker. Not recognition—calculation.

The kind that cataloged threat potential.

"Commander Varek," Veyron said, "you and your captains will surrender full access to your administrative records, supply inventories, and patrol logs."

Varek nodded stiffly. "Of course."

"We will also perform independent interrogations."

That turned a few heads.

Veyron continued, unaffected. "Random selections. A cross-section of guardsmen. Command included."

The courtyard grew quiet.

Reginald and Lysa exchanged a single glance. No words. Just enough.

This wasn't a visit.

This was a hunt.

By dusk, the mood within the barracks had curdled into something heavy and suffocating. Conversations dulled into half-murmured sentences. Eyes lingered longer than usual across corridors. The usual thrum of routine—the shuffle of boots, the clatter of gear, the occasional barked laugh—had been hollowed out, replaced by the measured silence of people trying not to be noticed.

The inquisitors had split their efforts like a scalpel through soft tissue. One took residence in the command wing, cross-referencing arrest records against dispatch logs with ruthless precision. Another prowled the outer halls, never speaking, only watching—his gaze enough to scatter the gathered knots of soldiers like rats from a lit cellar. And Veyron himself drifted through the structure without pattern, his movements unpredictable, deliberate, and without warning. No questions. No accusations. Just eyes like frost and silence like rope being pulled tighter with every passing hour.

Lysa held her expression with practiced calm, but the coil in her chest had begun to wind. Her paperwork, though sometimes forged, was flawless. Her patrol routes always double-checked. But perfection drew attention just as quickly as incompetence. She began making small adjustments—leaving minor errors, smudging a date here, re-filing something under the wrong tab there—not enough to be suspicious, just enough to blend in among the merely diligent.

Still, she caught it—the half-second hesitation in a recruit's wave, the sudden silence in a barracks room when she stepped through the doorway.

And worse, twice that afternoon, footsteps shadowed hers a beat too long through the lower corridors. She paused to tie her boot, slowed her pace, doubled back through the mess hall, but whoever it was never revealed themselves. Nothing provable. Nothing actionable. Just the sensation of breath on the back of her neck, never quite there when she turned.

She found Reginald in the armory's lower antechamber just before the evening bell. The racks of weapons loomed around them, orderly and silent. He stood near the eastern wall, arms folded, face unreadable beneath the low torchlight. The moment she stepped in, his gaze flicked toward her—not sharp, not tense, but alert. Cautious.

"They pulled Maren and Tavyn for questioning," he said, not wasting time on formality.

Lysa's brows tightened. "Are they connected to us?"

"No. Just collateral. But that's not the point." He lowered his voice. "They're not hunting information. They're hunting reactions. Who flinches when someone disappears. Who asks where they've gone. Who suddenly remembers being elsewhere during a raid."

She stepped closer, reaching to remove her gloves, slow and deliberate. "How long before they look at you?"

"They already have," he muttered. "Veyron passed me in the corridor earlier. Didn't say a word. Just looked. You know that kind of look—it's not evaluation. It's the moment before judgment."

Lysa turned toward the doorway, pretending to adjust the buckle on her bracer as a passing guard clomped by overhead. When the footfalls faded, she spoke without looking at him.

"We're going to lose someone," she said quietly. "Soon."

Reginald nodded once. "The goal is to make sure it's not both of us."

She turned back to him. "We keep quiet, we keep loose. Disband the tunnel meetings for now. Message drops only. No group contact until the inquisitors leave."

"Already done," he replied. "Callie passed word down. Everyone's on half-sleep, half-paranoia."

A silence settled between them—not empty, but full of shared weight. Reginald leaned against the rack, exhaling slowly through his nose.

"When this is over," he said, "we'll have less trust, more eyes, and a smaller window to act. We'll need to move soon. Before Varek tightens the leash."

Lysa's jaw clenched, not from fear, but from the hard knowledge of truth settling into place. "Then we move on our own timeline," she said. "Not theirs."

They didn't linger. Silence was no longer a sanctuary—it was a spotlight.

Night descended with a stillness that felt neither peaceful nor natural. Arden's Wake, in the hours after curfew, became something else entirely—a city hollowed out. The cobbled streets, always worn but familiar, now looked foreign in the half-light. Homes sat shuttered and silent. Lamplight, usually warm and scattered across windows like falling stars, had dimmed. Doors stayed bolted. Curtains never moved. The people had learned not to look too long, not to speak too late, and not to notice when the shadows grew longer than the flame.

Lysa moved across the parapets of the outer wall with measured steps, her cloak pulled tightly to her frame against the wind. It wasn't her patrol night—she had traded it subtly, a favor exchanged with one of the newer recruits who hadn't yet learned when to ask questions and when to be grateful for a change in routine.

From this height, the city's sprawl unfolded below her like a map left out in the rain—edges curling, colors faded. She could make out the districts by how they breathed. Market Row still flickered with a few smuggled candles. The noble district stood dark and lifeless, all stone and silence. And near the river bend, just above the tenement roofs, a window blinked once—long, then twice in quick succession.

The signal.

A new contact. Someone else ready to listen.

She let her breath out slowly, frost curling around the edge of her scarf. The signal hadn't come from anyone they knew. That made three this week, all from different sides of the city. The network wasn't just holding. It was growing.

A part of her wanted to feel hope—but she couldn't afford the softness of it. Not now. Not while inquisitors walked their halls. Not while every shadow might be an informant and every kind smile a test of loyalty.

She stepped away from the ledge and made her way down the rampart stairs, boots silent on worn stone. Her route back to the lower levels twisted behind the old barracks, past a row of unused storage rooms and toward the auxiliary wing where the oil lamps burned lower than regulation allowed. She passed no one. That was the point.

At a narrow alcove behind the old infirmary wall, she paused. A crate of dried kindling sat just inside the covered arch. She knelt beside it and reached beneath the bottom slat, fingers brushing cold metal.

The token was there.

Not a message. Just a confirmation.

Callie had checked in.

Lysa replaced it exactly as she found it, then stepped back into the corridor. The torchlight behind her barely reached, and in the dim wash of shadows, she allowed herself a moment to close her eyes.

The break was coming.

Not yet. But soon.

She could feel the city shifting beneath its skin, like something trapped in a shell too tight, pressing against every seam. It wouldn't take much—a raid too brutal, an order too cruel, one voice raised at the wrong time—and the fracture would split clean through.

She thought of Reginald, still putting his name on reports written in the margins of lies. She thought of Callie, clever and cutting beneath her sarcasm, staying one whisper ahead of suspicion. She thought of the families they had moved out of the crossing under cover of a false raid report. And she thought of her mother—not the memory, but the absence. That hollow space where a voice should be, where answers should have lived.

Somewhere far below the city walls, she heard the long cry of a nightbird. Sharp. Singular. Then silence.

Lysa opened her eyes and turned back toward the barracks.

The signal had been lit.

And before long, fire would follow.

The barracks felt colder that night.

Lysa slipped through the halls like a wraith, her cloak brushing softly against the stone as she passed sleeping quarters, offices, and storage bays. She knew every creaking board, every loose tile, every blind corner that could hide a second set of footsteps. Her route was never the same twice. She took detours, doubled back, waited when needed. It had become second nature now. Not fear—instinct. A rhythm formed not from paranoia, but survival.

She reached her quarters without being seen.

The room was sparse by design. One bed. One desk. One trunk. A single high window offered no view, only the faint cast of moonlight reaching across the floor like a silver blade. She bolted the door and crossed to the edge of the bed where a worn satchel waited beneath the frame. Pulling it out, she laid it flat and undid the straps, unfolding its contents with care.

Inside, her secret world lay hidden—three neatly folded sets of falsified field orders, a coil of wax cord, several coded reports on troop movements and inquisitor patrols, and a small bundle wrapped in soft cloth.

She paused on the last two items.

Unwrapping it, her fingers touched the smooth surface of a carved wooden pendant. It was simple—unfinished, even—but the grooves along its edge were familiar. Her mother's hand had shaped them. It was a fragment of a larger piece once, part of a family charm that had hung above their hearth in Snowhaven. She had kept it hidden through training, tucked deep within her uniform lining, never once letting it show. The other was her mother's knife.

Now she placed them at the center of the unfolded satchel, anchoring everything else around it like the eye of a storm.

She lit a small oil lamp at the edge of her desk, adjusting the wick low so only the faintest light filled the room. It cast soft shadows over her face, washing the stone walls in flickering warmth that did little to ease the cold within her.

Her eyes moved across the documents. Each one represented something undone. Someone spared. Someone smuggled past the chokehold of the guard. For every report she altered, every false signature she copied, another act of cruelty had been delayed. Another day won.

But it was never enough.

She reached for her quill, then hesitated. Instead, she picked up the pendant and held it in her hand, thumb brushing across its edge. The wood was worn smooth in some places, sharp in others, as if time couldn't decide whether to soften or preserve it.

"Where are you?" she whispered—not aloud, but just under breath. Not for an answer, but because the silence demanded to be filled with something.

Outside, the wind stirred against the shuttered window. Faint and directionless.

She set the pendant down and tucked the satchel away once more. Everything was folded precisely. The satchel's weight was the same as before. Nothing shifted. Nothing betrayed what it held.

Lysa stood, the light still flickering across her eyes as she moved to the window. She rested her palm against the cold stone sill and looked out—not at the view, which was nothing—but at the feeling of being perched on the edge of something unseen.

This was no longer about surviving.

It was about *undoing*.

Undoing the silence. Undoing the rot. Undoing the long, slow, calculated erosion of truth.

And she would not stop.

Not until every name that had been erased from the records of this kingdom was spoken aloud again—starting with her mother's.

The flame danced behind her, the pendant catching its light for a moment longer before the room faded to stillness.

CHAPTER TWENTY-ONE

TRIAL OF ELEMENTS

The stone corridor deep beneath the temple sloped downward, the torches along the walls dimming the farther they walked. Caelan followed in Master Ildan's wake, their footsteps echoing against carved stone. He'd never ventured this far below before. The air grew heavier, charged—not stifling, but dense with something ancient.

They came to a wide archway marked by four elemental runes etched in weathered script: flame, tide, stone, and wind. The door parted on its own, groaning softly as if stirred awake. Caelan stepped through and drew a sharp breath.

The chamber beyond was enormous, its ceiling lost in shadow. At each corner of the room, the elemental forces pulsed in carefully warded pockets: tongues of fire flickered behind one barrier, swirling water danced within another, a floating disk of soil rotated slowly over stones in the third, and a funnel of air spiraled silently in the last. Intricate carvings of ancient sigils laced the walls, telling stories of harmony and discord—of forces bound, broken, and reconciled again.

Master Ildan came to a stop near the chamber's center, where faint lines were etched into the stone floor, forming a circle that bisected the space between the four elements.

"Today begins your first trials in elemental fusion," he said, his tone calm but firm. "It is one thing to command a single force. Another to balance two. Balance is not a trick of control—it is an act of understanding."

Caelan nodded, stepping into the circle. He could already feel it—the radiating heat from the fire quadrant to his left, the cool mist drifting from the water quadrant to his right. The sensations pulled at him in different ways. They weren't hostile, but they weren't tame either. They were waiting to see how he'd approach.

"Start with fire and water," Ildan instructed, taking a measured step back. "Opposing elements. Find the tension. Don't force them to merge—guide them."

Caelan lowered his stance, centering his breath. He extended his hands, palms out. With one hand, he reached for flame. With the other, the mist. Heat surged up one arm, burning against his skin without pain. Cold crept down the other, damp and fluid, resisting shape.

The two forces tugged at him, each trying to assert its nature.

Control won't hold them, he reminded himself. Listen instead.

He slowed his breathing. Let his thoughts still. In his mind's eye, he didn't see fire and water as adversaries—but as opposites in rhythm. One beat quick. One beat slow. He matched his breath to their tempo. Let them pull toward each other through him.

A shimmer appeared between his hands. First mist, then heat. Then steam.

It thickened, condensed, and slowly began to spiral—a sphere of swirling vapor, hot but stable, hovering in his grasp.

Ildan raised an eyebrow. "Good. You're beginning to feel it, not just shape it."

The sphere flickered briefly, then faded, dispersing into tendrils of rising steam.

Caelan exhaled, breath shaking. "It's harder than it looks."

Ildan's voice held a rare hint of pride. "Because it's not about what it looks like. It's about what it is. Fusion isn't a trick, Caelan. It's truth. You can't fake it."

Caelan flexed his fingers. "Then I'll learn the truth of every one of them."

The master gave a single nod. "Then let's move to the next."

Caelan stepped once more into the center of the elemental chamber, the echo of his boots swallowed quickly by the quiet hum that lingered in the stone. He rolled his shoulders, loosening the tension in his arms, and took a centering breath. The previous attempt had taught him something vital—these forces could not be commanded. They had to be respected, understood, invited.

The air between the quadrants already began to respond to his focus. To his left, the flames stirred, rising in flickering arcs of gold and orange, their heat pulsing outward in slow waves. On his right, the moisture in the air thickened. A curtain of mist crept along the floor, seeping from the water quadrant like breath on glass. Both elements seemed to recognize his intent this time and approached not as enemies, but as wary guests.

He extended his hands, palms open, facing the opposing sides. Rather than drawing the elements directly to him, he allowed them to come at their own pace. Flame licked at the invisible boundary before him, while mist coiled delicately around his fingertips.

Fire is hunger, he thought. *It thrives in passion, chaos, need.*

Water is memory—steady, yielding, and deep.

His breathing slowed. In through the nose, out through the mouth. He recalled the warmth of Elaria's hearth, the quiet of moonlit walks through the forest, the way steam curled from tea when she poured it on cold mornings. Emotion became tether. Focus, the conduit.

The heat surged forward, not in a burst this time but in a rolling push. Water followed, cold and slow, resisting the urge to collapse. As they met in the space between his hands, they collided with a violent hiss, releasing a cloud of steam that momentarily obscured his vision. The pressure shook his arms. For a heartbeat, he thought the whole chamber would rupture.

He closed his eyes and pressed inward—not with force, but with will. Not to bind them, but to allow each to express its shape.

The chaos lessened.

Steam thickened, then bent inward, forming a slowly swirling orb. At its core, fire churned like a heartbeat. Around it, the vapor tightened into a translucent veil, wrapping the heat in a shimmering cocoon. The orb hovered—unstable but holding—spinning slowly between his outstretched palms.

Caelan's arms trembled with strain. Not from raw energy, but from the delicate balance he had to maintain. One breath too deep, and it would rupture. One flicker of doubt, and it would collapse.

But he held it. Not because he forced it, but because he *trusted* it.

He watched it pulse in the quiet, this strange unity of fire and water—a thing that should not exist, but did, because he allowed it to.

Finally, he released it.

The orb unraveled gently into mist, trailing away in elegant wisps that floated upward and vanished against the ceiling lost in shadow.

Master Ildan stepped forward, his expression unreadable at first, then nodding slowly.

"You didn't try to tame them. You let them meet. That is the first real step toward elemental fusion."

Caelan exhaled, long and steady. "They didn't want to be together. Not at first."

"No. And many mages would have forced it. You didn't. That's why it worked."

There was silence between them then—not of discomfort, but of understanding. The lesson was not just about power. It was about humility, about listening, about presence.

Ildan turned toward the next quadrant. "Come. Let's see how you fare with earth and air."

Caelan followed, the warmth of steam still clinging to his fingertips.

The stillness of the chamber returned as Caelan crossed the circle, approaching the next two quadrants. Behind him, steam faded into the air like breath on winter glass. Before him, the grounded hush of earth and the gentle murmur of moving air stirred, waiting.

The elemental barrier to the left rose like a small hill of shifting stone. Rocks rotated slowly in the air, bound by invisible threads, their weight undeniable even as they drifted. From the opposite side, wind whirled in a lazy spiral, brushing leaves and dust in playful eddies across the smooth floor. It had no single source, only movement, as if born of thought and whim.

Master Ildan stood beside the stone sigil carved into the wall. "These will not clash," he said. "They'll pretend the other isn't there. Earth doesn't move unless forced. Air won't stay still long enough to notice. If fire and water were a storm, this is silence and distance."

Caelan stepped once more into the center, his boots ringing slightly against the stone. This time, he knelt—not to draw in power, but to feel where he was.

He pressed his palm to the floor, feeling the hum beneath the stone. Earth was steady. Its rhythm slow. Patient. Deep beneath the surface, it did not hunger or yearn. It endured. He closed his eyes, breathing deep until his heartbeat slowed to match that rhythm.

Then he raised his other hand, reaching toward the air.

A breeze curled around his wrist, lifting a loose strand of hair. Air was alive, curious, but easily bored. It responded quickly but moved on just as fast. To hold it, one had to offer something more than command. You had to offer direction without weight. A reason to linger.

He opened both hands.

Earth resisted, refusing to rise. It would not move unless asked with care.

Air drifted without concern, ignoring structure, seeking freedom.

How do you bridge something that stands still with something that never stops moving?

He slowed his thoughts. Instead of pulling, he waited.

Let air circle. Let earth rise.

And slowly—so slowly it almost went unnoticed—a coil of dust began to lift from the floor. A single thread at first, then a second. Tiny grains of soil caught in an upward current, swirling in tandem with the breeze. The motion was delicate. Caelan didn't force it into shape. He let it form itself around his stillness.

The dust danced.

It spun around him in looping arcs, wrapping his body like a second skin. Earthborne particles guided by the breath of the wind, suspended just above the surface. He moved one hand slightly, and the spiral shifted with him, responding not to magic, but to his intent.

He rose slowly, the coil moving with him. Dust hovered above his shoulders and wrists like a constellation drawn in sand and air.

Then, with a flick of his fingers, he extended the spiral outward. It unfurled in a wide ring before collapsing in a soft sigh, settling back onto the stone floor without a sound.

Master Ildan approached, folding his arms. "This fusion requires patience. It is not flash. It is not force. But if you ever forget the ground beneath your feet, the wind will scatter you."

Caelan nodded. His breath was steady. His heartbeat calm. "It felt... peaceful. Like listening, not speaking."

"Good," Ildan said quietly. "Because the more complex the combinations, the more vital that quiet becomes."

Caelan looked down at the dust still lingering in the air, catching the chamber light like fine ash.

"How long until I combine all four?"

"When you stop thinking of them as four," Ildan replied. "And begin to feel them as one."

Weeks passed. Then months.

The elemental chamber became as familiar to Caelan as the corridors above or the forest paths of his childhood. Every morning, he descended its spiral steps alone. Master Ildan watched only occasionally now, offering guidance when needed, but more often observing in silence from the high alcove above. This was no longer instruction—it was refinement.

Caelan's robes grew more worn. His hands became calloused from the repeated effort of channeling raw magic, fingertips perpetually tinged with soot or dust. Yet the deeper toll showed in his eyes. The weight of focus, the strain of exacting control, the persistence of failing and starting over again—all of it had carved a new shape into him.

He no longer forced the elements to obey. He met them in the spaces between their extremes.

Some days, fire and earth proved stubborn—too volatile together. On others, water and air would spiral into chaos unless held with precise timing. He learned to breathe with them, not command them. Each pairing had its own rhythm, its own tempo, and each demanded something different from him.

Control was not about domination.

It was about surrendering to the shape the elements wanted to become.

He failed often.

Fire lashed out unexpectedly, burning lines into the chamber walls. Wind once knocked him from his stance with a sharp backdraft. He spent hours sweeping shattered stone from the training circle after a misaligned combination of earth and flame collapsed into an explosion of molten dust. But every failure taught him where the boundaries were—and how to bend them, carefully, without snapping.

He kept a journal beside his bed. Each night, he documented the feel of the magic, how each element resisted or yielded. Diagrams filled the margins—spirals for air, slanted lines for fire, half-moons for water, and nested squares for earth. Over time, his notes became less about formula and more about feeling. The writing changed. Less analytical, more instinctive.

The discipline reshaped him.

His body grew leaner. Stronger. The constant pull and motion honed not just his magical intuition but his physical precision. Movements that once relied on concentration became reflex. The elements no longer waited for his focus—they met his momentum, responding to thought as swiftly as muscle.

One morning, while meditating in the center of the chamber, he opened his eyes to find the air already circling him. Dust lifted with his breath. A faint pulse of warmth stirred in his chest. Without words or effort, the elements gathered—not in conflict, but in anticipation.

He was no longer guiding them one at a time.

He was beginning to understand how they wove together.

That day, Master Ildan finally spoke from the gallery above. His voice echoed with quiet pride.

"You're ready for the Trial."

Caelan didn't smile. He simply stood, brushing ash from his sleeves, and nodded.

He was tired. But he was ready.

The central chamber lay at the heart of the temple, far below the mountain roots. Few ever reached it. Fewer still were allowed to stand within its center.

Master Ildan led the way in silence, his footfalls measured, ceremonial. Caelan followed, each step echoing louder than the last as the hall narrowed and then opened into a vast chamber. The ceiling stretched high above them, lost in darkness. The walls were carved with reliefs of ancient mages whose names had long been forgotten, their forms caught in moments of elemental mastery—summoning flame, riding wind, calling stone to rise beneath their feet.

This was no place for beginners. It was a crucible.

At the center of the floor was a great circle, larger than the elemental chamber, bordered by concentric rings of runes that shimmered faintly in the torchlight. Four pillars stood equidistant around it, each marked with a different symbol: a flame cast in iron, a stream in blue glass, a twisting wind carved into silver, and a stone column veined with crystal.

As Caelan crossed the threshold, the energy in the room changed. The air grew thicker. Not oppressive—more like expectation. The chamber recognized him. It felt like the moment before a storm breaks, not in chaos, but in charged stillness. The elements were here, waiting. Watching.

He stepped into the circle.

Master Ildan remained at the edge, arms folded, his expression unreadable.

"This is where theory ends," he said. "Where lessons fade, and truth begins. The Trial does not measure skill alone. It measures balance—within you, and between the elements. Do not try to tame them. Do not try to dazzle me. Simply do what you have learned. Trust in that."

Caelan nodded. "What happens if I fail?"

Ildan's gaze held steady. "Then the chamber will let you go. But you'll know the difference. That's punishment enough."

The rune beneath Caelan's feet flickered to life. A pulse of light expanded outward, circling the room. The four pillars responded in kind—flame flickered higher, water churned in its vessel, wind coiled in anticipation, and stone groaned beneath unseen pressure.

The trial had begun.

Caelan took a slow breath. He closed his eyes and let the world fall away—not to ignore it, but to feel it more fully. He reached inward, toward the stillness he had earned through months of discipline. From that quiet, he extended himself outward.

Each element answered.

Heat coiled beneath his fingertips. Cool moisture gathered at the edges of his awareness. The weight of stone pressed behind his heels, while air lifted around his shoulders like the breath of unseen wings.

They did not arrive in harmony.

They came as they always did—independent, insistent, unwilling to wait.

He stood still as they surged toward him, not in rage, but in challenge. They demanded not submission, but presence. Not commands, but communion.

And so, he began.

The elements stirred in full as Caelan extended his awareness outward. Heat swelled from the fire pillar in rippling waves, distorting the air around it. Moisture from the water quadrant thickened with a pulse, gathering along the stone like coiling fog. Wind slipped across the chamber in quick, probing currents, testing the seams of stillness. From below, the earth answered with a slow, resonant groan—a grounded presence that settled like a weight in Caelan's bones.

He didn't move at first. Movement wasn't yet needed.

Instead, he focused on his breath, aligning his center. Each inhale became a point of invitation. Each exhale, a gesture of balance. He didn't summon the elements. He acknowledged them. And in turn, they came.

Fire responded first, spiraling outward in a slow arc, forming a flickering band around his right hand. Its warmth was not harsh, but insistent—a presence eager to act. From the opposite side, water rose in tandem, lifting in a silver ribbon that traced the line of his left arm, cool and deliberate, winding upward in soft motion.

Neither touched. Neither yielded. But neither resisted his presence.

The air stirred next, slipping in from the edges of the circle like a breath held too long and finally released. It coiled gently around his shoulders and swirled along the floor, wrapping his stance in motion without mass. Last came the earth. It did not climb quickly or erupt with force. Instead, the stone beneath him shifted with quiet intent, raising a platform just beneath his feet—a subtle lift, steady and sure.

All four elements were now present, circling him in their own patterns. He stood in the center of their rhythm, not commanding, not containing—only guiding.

He began to move.

His steps were measured, not for show, but for purpose. As he rotated his shoulders and shifted his weight, the elements adjusted with him. Fire curved along the movement of his wrist. Water dipped and coiled in response to his open palm. Air fed the dance between them, while the floor beneath rose or stilled in time with each transition.

It wasn't choreography. It was conversation.

Flame met wind and flared briefly, spinning into a braided coil of heat and motion. Caelan pivoted, drawing water through the center and tempering the fire, producing a sudden burst of steam that hissed and curled but did not lash outward. The mist hung in the air for a moment, soft and shimmering, before dispersing into the air, leaving behind a ring of condensed droplets suspended in weightless orbit.

Earth rose next, lifting small fragments of stone around him. He timed his breath, shifted his footing, and used air to scatter the debris into a slow spiral. He wrapped fire through the stones, igniting them with molten traces, and guided water around the perimeter to cool and contain the heat.

The room shifted with him, element by element, reaction by reaction. Where before they had fought to remain separate, now they yielded space to one another. Their resistance had not vanished—it had been acknowledged and balanced.

His body ached. Shoulders burned. Jaw tightened in concentration. Every movement required precision, not because the magic demanded control, but because imbalance meant collapse. He didn't dare let his focus slip—not even for a moment.

Yet he wasn't afraid.

As the elements rose and fell, spiraled and broke apart, Caelan moved through their rhythm with calm resolve. This was no longer about technique. This was presence. Discipline. Truth.

He stepped back and slowly extended his arms, lifting each element one final time. The wind encircled the fire. Water flowed through the stone. Sparks danced across his palms as a final current of heat traced the spiral of his breath.

Then he released them.

Not with a flourish, but with silence.

The fire dimmed. The water settled. Air fell still. Earth anchored again beneath his feet.

The chamber was quiet once more.

His breath echoed faintly against the dome overhead. Across the runed circle, the elements returned to their pillars. Not repelled. Not expelled. Simply... done.

Master Ildan stood at the edge of the chamber, arms crossed, expression solemn. He did not clap. He did not offer praise. But he bowed his head once, a gesture deeper than any applause.

Caelan lowered his hands and let the breath leave his chest completely. The ache in his limbs was profound, but behind it, a calm had taken root—quiet, stable, and absolute.

The weave had held.

And more than that—he had held himself through it.

The last of the elemental light faded, leaving the chamber cloaked in its natural quiet—a silence vast enough to feel sacred. Only the soft hiss of settling dust remained, the residual magic gently exhaling back into stillness.

Caelan stood at the center of the circle, arms loose at his sides, breath finally beginning to slow. The tension in his shoulders had not fully left him, nor had the fine tremor in his legs. But neither came from uncertainty. They were the marks of labor, of a body pushed to its edge and held steady by choice, not desperation.

He didn't need to speak.

Neither did Master Ildan.

The old mage descended the shallow steps at the edge of the chamber with slow, deliberate strides. He approached the outer ring of the elemental circle but did not step within it. His eyes traced the runes now glowing faintly across the stone. Residual patterns, still humming with what had just taken place.

When he finally met Caelan's gaze, there was no smile, no dramatic proclamation—just the weight of measured approval.

"You listened," he said. "You didn't just remember your training. You let it become part of you."

Caelan nodded, still catching his breath. "It didn't feel like passing a test."

"It wasn't." Ildan's voice was quiet, though it carried easily in the echoing space. "This trial was never about proving your strength. It was about showing you whether you understood what you've become. And whether you're ready for what comes next."

Caelan looked to the elemental pillars, each now dormant again. "I thought it would be more... dramatic. Something final."

"There is no final," Ildan replied. "Not for magic. Not for balance. There's only movement. Reflection. Then the next path."

Caelan was silent for a long moment.

The trial hadn't left him triumphant. It had left him centered. Worn to the core, but steady in a way he hadn't felt before. The elements had responded not because he forced them to—but because he had offered them something real.

"I can feel the difference," he said at last. "It's not just energy anymore. It's part of how I move. How I breathe."

"That's the beginning of mastery," Ildan said. "And the end of needing instruction."

He took another step forward and reached into the folds of his robes, drawing out a small metal token etched with an intricate sigil. It was neither ornate nor decorative—just a circle containing the four elemental glyphs, balanced in perfect symmetry.

Ildan placed it in Caelan's hand.

"This marks the completion of your formal training. From this point on, you walk the path of your own design. I will guide you when needed, but your lessons are no longer measured by my standards. Only by your own."

Caelan turned the token over slowly in his fingers. The metal was warm, the etching precise. It felt heavier than it looked.

He gave a faint nod. "I'm ready."

Ildan studied him for a long moment, then gestured toward the stairwell that led back to the temple above.

"Then go. Rest. Reflect. Tomorrow, we begin again—but not as teacher and student. From here forward, we are brothers of the same path."

Caelan bowed—not out of ceremony, but respect—and crossed the threshold of the chamber.

As he climbed the stone steps, he didn't feel taller. Or stronger. Or more powerful.

He felt still.

For the first time, truly still.

Chapter Twenty-Two

The Noose Tightens

Dawn had come, but the city made no celebration of it. Dunmoh stirred only in small, hesitant movements—shutters opening a sliver before closing again, doors cracking wide enough for a single glance, then shutting with quiet finality. The usual sounds of morning were absent. No calls from the baker's lane, no hammering from the forges, no gossip spilling from the cloth markets. The streets felt starved of sound, drained of routine, as if the people themselves had vanished and left behind a husk of a city pretending to function.

Lysa walked her patrol route without slowing, her boots falling in steady rhythm across stone that should have echoed. Instead, the sound was swallowed by the stillness around her. Her cloak barely stirred in the morning breeze, and her armor, though recently polished, seemed dull against the gray cast of the sky. The uniform she wore had not changed from the night before, but the weight of it now pressed heavier against her shoulders, as though stitched with the burden of knowing what had been done.

Each intersection she passed revealed another absence. The corners where children once played were now deserted, their chalk drawings washed away by the city's cleansing crews. The windows of the apothecary—normally fogged with condensation from brewing tinctures—stood empty and dry. Even the street cats had disappeared, their usual scavenging paths silent and still.

Her route took her along the spine of the southern merchant quarter, where signs once hung with pride from painted beams. Today, most had been stripped down. Only a few remained, their painted letters faded, their edges scorched or scratched. One bore a smear of dried pitch across the carved crest above the door. Another had been removed entirely, the anchor bolts still protruding from the wood like broken teeth.

She passed a fountain at the corner of Myre and Holloway, its basin dry, the marble stained with soot and ash. Someone had thrown a handful of wilted flowers into the bowl—a quiet act of defiance, or perhaps mourning. Lysa allowed herself no pause. Her expression did not change. Her movements remained crisp and disciplined, every step placed with deliberate control. No one could afford to be seen hesitating this morning, least of all her.

Across the way, two guards stood at attention near a posting board. Their armor was too clean. Their faces were unfamiliar. She recognized them as replacements—brought in from outlying provinces, assigned here for one purpose. They were not trained to protect. They had been stationed to remind.

Lysa kept her distance, crossing to the far side of the road before resuming her route. She did not look at the notice board. She already knew what it said.

The farther she walked, the more familiar the damage became. The quarter ahead had once been one of the livelier neighborhoods—less formal than the central ward, but full of working families and independent trades. Children ran barefoot through its alleyways during the warmer months, and during the colder ones, the scent of spiced broth often drifted from the cookhouse chimneys. The people here had little, but they clung to each other. Now, their doors bore the signs of intrusion. The wood had been split and re-nailed. Hinges hung slightly off-center. A few of the homes had boards across the windows, nailed from the outside.

At the corner of a narrow alley, Lysa paused to adjust the strap of her cloak. It was a simple motion, enough to justify the brief stop if anyone questioned her. From where she stood, she could see the remains of a cobbler's stall—the one with the painted blue shutters and the brass bell that never quite stopped ringing when the wind caught it. The shutters now lay shattered near the steps, and the bell, twisted from its hook, had been stomped into the dirt. A few pieces of broken leather and cobbling tools had been swept into a pile near the threshold, waiting for someone who would never return to reclaim them.

A boy used to work there—barely old enough to grow stubble, always covered in flecks of polish and dye. He had repaired her boots once after a winter patrol and refused payment. She hadn't seen him since the raid began.

She continued walking.

At the far end of the street, a line of ash curled from the gutter. It trailed across the stones like a scar, evidence of something burned in haste. The smell still lingered—charred cloth, oil, something thicker that clung to the back of the throat when she inhaled through her nose. A building had gone up here. Maybe more than one. No one was clearing the debris. No one was standing nearby to mourn. The silence of the neighborhood was absolute, broken only by the sound of distant boots on stone and the faint creak of wood settling beneath pressure.

Someone had scrubbed graffiti from the back wall of a nearby warehouse. The wash left streaks of pale residue across the bricks, but enough pigment remained to hint at what had once been written. The loop of a crescent still clung to the corner. Three slashes cut through it diagonally—old symbols of the resistance, familiar only to those who knew what to look for. The effort to erase it had been thorough, but careless.

Lysa stepped through a narrow pass between two buildings and emerged into an open courtyard where laundry lines once ran from window to window. Most of them had been taken down. A few still remained, the cloth torn or sagging, forgotten in haste. A wicker basket had been kicked aside near the stone steps, its contents scattered and stained with soot. She recognized the layout of the homes surrounding the square. She had visited this block during a food drop two months ago. A woman had let her in through the kitchen door and given her tea while they waited for the signal to come through. The tea had been bitter, but warm.

Now the windows were dark. The door was gone.

A voice called out from the far end of the street. It was sharp, clipped, and authoritative. A name followed, one she did not recognize. Then came the sound of a door slamming, a scuffle of feet, and the rhythmic clatter of armor. Lysa did not react. She turned down a different path, sticking to her assigned route, never quickening her pace.

These weren't her streets anymore. They belonged to fear now.

And fear did not welcome strangers.

She approached the central square as the bell from the old chapel rang once, marking the half-hour past sunrise. The sound barely carried across the plaza, muffled by the stone buildings and the absence of life between them. The square should have been busy by now, filled with vendors arranging their carts and townsfolk bargaining over bread and fresh greens. Instead, a few lone figures moved along the outer edges with cautious glances, their heads bowed as they slipped between shadows. No one lingered. Even the fountain at the center of the plaza had gone dry, the basin cracked from neglect, its tiles dulled to a sallow gray.

At the edge of the square, just beneath the northern wall, a new posting board had been erected overnight. It stood taller than the one it replaced, its frame reinforced with iron and painted in the king's colors. The parchment nailed to its face gleamed with fresh ink, the script sharp and deliberate. Guards had posted it before dawn. She could still see where their bootprints had scuffed the dust in wide circles around the base. The earth had been churned near the foot of the board as if someone had fallen or been dragged across it.

Lysa drew closer, scanning the area before allowing her gaze to settle on the document. She stood as any loyal officer would—upright, composed, her hands folded behind her back. The official seal of Dunmoh had been pressed into the top of the parchment, its wax still clean and unblemished. Below that, the text began.

Royal Edict 72-B: Declaration of Complicity and Custodial Seizure *By command of His Majesty King Aldric Ravenmark, the following individuals have been identified in coordination with subversive elements acting in violation of royal decree. Property and assets will be seized under the au-*

thority of Commander Varek. Further adjudication is pending.

A list followed.

Eleven names.

She read each of them without blinking, though her eyes hesitated on a few. Some had gone by aliases. Others had no connection to the resistance at all. They were shopkeepers. Artisans. A scribe from the upper quarter who had once lent her a forged ledger. Two others she had helped relocate before the crackdown began. The remaining names were strangers, but their placement here marked them just the same.

At the bottom of the list, a second column had been added by hand. The ink was darker, pressed harder into the page.

Status: Confessed. Awaiting Sentencing.

The implication was unmistakable. No trial. No review.

Just the procession.

She let her gaze rest there for a long moment, then shifted it toward the scaffolding being constructed in the center of the square. It stood low for now, still in the early stages of assembly, but its purpose was already evident. The beams were raw, the ropes freshly coiled. No effort had been made to disguise what it would be used for.

A guard nearby straightened at her presence. He was young, unfamiliar, likely brought in from the provincial garrisons. His stance was rigid, and his eyes flicked to the posting before settling on her. He said nothing. Neither did she.

After a moment, she offered a curt nod, turned from the board, and continued on.

Her route diverted through the stonework alley that split off from the square and wound past the east wall of the armory. The passage was narrow, just wide enough for two men shoulder to shoulder, with moss clinging to the lower edges of the wall and runoff channels carved into the center of the path. The space between buildings here felt colder than the rest of the city, always in shadow, and rarely traveled by anyone but runners, off-duty guards, or those who knew exactly what they were doing.

Lysa's pace slowed slightly as she moved beneath the overhang of an arched walkway. Her eyes scanned without turning her head. The usual layers of weathered stone and soot-covered brick revealed little at first glance, but near the base of a low corner column, half-hidden by grime and runoff, was a faint mark.

It had been drawn in chalk—light gray, nearly the same color as the stone behind it. A crescent shape arced across the mortar line, the bottom edge fractured by three diagonal slashes carved through the curve. The strokes had been done quickly, without flourish, but with purpose. She recognized the symbol immediately. It wasn't just a call sign—it was a message. That particular variation of the crescent wasn't a summons. It was a warning.

Someone had tried to reach her. Someone had passed through this alley within the last few hours and left behind a silent signal: the network still watched, but movement had become dangerous. The resistance hadn't scattered entirely, but their routes had changed. Their safehouses might no longer be safe.

Lysa kept her posture neutral. She crouched near the base of the wall under the pretense of adjusting her boot. Her fingers brushed against the stone briefly, just long enough to confirm the texture of the chalk and the direction of the strokes. The mark was fresh. Still sharp around the edges. Likely placed during the night while the sweep teams focused on more public areas.

She rubbed her thumb across the symbol once and left it obscured, a smudge blending into the soot. If she passed through the same alley tomorrow and the mark had returned, she'd know it had been meant specifically for her. If it remained erased, the message had reached the intended eyes.

Standing again, she didn't glance back.

The alley remained empty as she stepped out onto the next road. The weight of the message traveled with her, quiet and unshakable. Even with chains rattling in the public square, and names posted like warnings, there were still those who carried information through the cracks in the wall. They hadn't stopped. They had only grown quieter.

And in the quiet, she had always known how to listen.

By the time Lysa returned to the main thoroughfare near the outer garrison ring, the clouds above Dunmoh had begun to thicken. The sun remained hidden behind them, casting no warmth, only a dull sheen across the rooftops. Her route curved past the supply yard and the west gatehouse, where a new guard rotation stood at attention beneath the stone arch. No one spoke. They didn't need to. Orders had already made their rounds.

The silence wasn't born from discipline. It came from something deeper, more rigid. The sort of stillness that took hold when too many had seen something they couldn't forget and knew better than to speak of it.

She crossed the length of the barracks courtyard, her eyes flicking briefly to the row of training dummies along the eastern wall. One of them had been split at the shoulder, its cloth padding torn and left unrepaired. Another lay on its side in the mud, half buried from neglect. Normally, that would've earned a rebuke from the sergeant. This morning, no one seemed to care. The training field was empty. The practice blades stacked in the rack remained untouched.

As she passed beneath the arch leading to the administrative wing, the signal horn sounded. Its tone was short and sharp—precisely pitched to carry through stone corridors and reach every soldier within earshot. The call was not unfamiliar. Its cadence meant report immediately. No delay. No excuses.

She didn't change her pace, but she adjusted her cloak as she walked, drawing it across the front of her uniform with calculated neatness. Her gloves were already fitted. Her posture had never slackened.

Others were already converging on the command hall by the time she reached the inner corridor. Pairs of guards arrived from different patrol sectors, some marked by road dust, others still carrying the sweat of the garrison interior. She recognized a few faces but didn't acknowledge them. None of them met her eye. A few nodded toward the outer walls. One muttered something under his breath to a companion, his voice falling quiet the moment her boots approached the edge of the stone platform.

The heavy door at the center of the corridor stood open. Light spilled from within—cool and bright, filtered through the stained glass high above the command hall. The shadows inside moved with purpose. Lysa could see the back of Commander Varek's uniform as he leaned over the war table, the flame sigil of the Ravenmark crest stitched between his shoulders like a brand.

She took a steadying breath.

Then she stepped through the doorway and into the room.

The command hall retained none of the warmth its design suggested. Light filtered through stained glass in muted colors, casting long patterns across the floor in amber and violet, but the effect did little to soften the austerity of the room. Stone walls stretched high overhead, lined with banners bearing the royal crest, and flanked by iron sconces that flickered with cold torchlight. The chamber was made to feel imposing, not inspiring.

At the far end stood the war table—a massive slab of carved oak set with inlaid silver and notches worn from years of heavy use. It was surrounded by a small assembly of officers, each wearing the polished dark armor of the inner command. Their expressions held the detached sharpness of soldiers long past sentiment. A few shifted as Lysa entered, though no one spoke. Commander Varek stood at the head of the table, his back straight, his posture rigid enough to seem carved from the same stone that lined the hall.

He turned only after a long pause, letting the sound of her approach fill the silence between them. His eyes swept over her with precise calculation. There was no recognition in his stare, no familiarity. Only the measured coldness of a man who had spent years molding fear into compliance. His hair had grayed since she'd last seen him up close, but his eyes remained unchanged—sharp, unreadable, devoid of softness.

"Officer Evern," he said at last, his voice low and deliberate. "Report."

The other officers stepped back slightly, clearing space around the table without being told. Their movements were fluid, practiced, as if the room itself bent to the authority of Varek's presence.

Lysa kept her expression composed. She met his eyes, gave the customary incline of her head, and stepped forward.

"Sector patrol complete. No disturbances reported along the southern and merchant corridors. Civilian presence limited. No sign of further subversive activity."

Varek remained still. His arms crossed behind his back, his gaze steady. The silence following her statement stretched long enough to become its own challenge.

"Your route passed through Myre's Hollow," he said eventually. "The cobbler's row. I'm told it was quiet there."

"It was," she answered, keeping her voice level. "Shops shuttered. No open resistance. No contact with civilians."

He nodded slightly, as if filing the detail away.

"You knew the man who owned the stall there, didn't you?" he asked. "Sevrin. He patched boots for half the garrison. Worked late. Liked to talk too much."

The air in the hall shifted. It wasn't in the words, but in the way the others watched him speak—as if they were waiting for something. Lysa didn't flinch.

"I knew of him," she replied. "I interacted with him as needed for field repairs."

Varek studied her face for a long moment. His silence was more pressing than his questions. He stepped around the side of the table, slow and deliberate, his boots falling in perfect rhythm against the stone floor.

"He confessed during the sweep," Varek said flatly. "Claimed to have passed messages. Said they came through an officer contact. Never gave a name."

Lysa remained still. Her hands were clasped behind her back, fingers relaxed, shoulders squared. Every inch of her posture had been trained for this moment, prepared for the day when the inquiry became personal.

"I wasn't aware he was under suspicion," she said. "He never indicated anything unusual during our interactions."

Varek stopped just short of her left shoulder. He didn't speak for several seconds. When he did, his tone was quieter, but not gentler.

"Of course not," he said. "No one ever does."

He turned again and walked back to the table.

Commander Varek returned to the head of the table, his hands resting lightly on its carved edge. He did not sit. He rarely did during interrogations that were not called by name. The command hall itself served as his platform, and silence remained his preferred weapon.

Lysa didn't shift her stance. The placement of her feet, the position of her shoulders, the measured distance between her and the edge of the table—all of it remained exactly as it should be. Not too stiff to draw suspicion. Not too casual to give insult. Discipline masked tension, and she wore it well.

"You've served under my command for three years," Varek said, eyes fixed on the surface of the table, as though reading from a memory instead of a report. "I recall you first came to us from the northern circuit. Small garrison near Drellwyn, wasn't it?"

"That's correct," she answered. "Assigned to perimeter patrol and supply inspection detail before transfer."

He nodded slowly, tracing a line along the inlaid silver filigree with the side of his thumb. "No disciplinary marks. No requests for reassignment. No special commendations. You've kept your head down, performed your duties, and followed orders." He looked up again, this time meeting her gaze directly. "Would you say that's a fair assessment?"

"I would," she replied.

"And yet," he said, letting the words settle, "you were one of only three officers within the city center when the raids began. Your patrol took you through two areas later identified as compromised. And your report this morning offers very little insight into the attitudes of the civilians you encountered."

She held his gaze. "There were few civilians present. Most remained indoors. Those I passed did not speak. There were no gatherings. No open signs of unrest."

"No unrest," Varek repeated. "Despite the arrests. Despite the disappearances."

She didn't respond immediately. Her silence wasn't hesitation—it was the exact length of a thoughtful pause.

"Fear keeps people quiet," she said. "Not peace."

One of the officers near the table stirred slightly at her response, but Varek raised a hand, silencing the room without needing to speak.

"I find it interesting," he said, "how well you understand the difference."

Lysa did not blink. "It's a distinction that matters when enforcing order."

Varek turned again, this time walking toward the far wall where a slate board had been mounted beside the tactical display. A list of sectors was marked in chalk, each annotated with timing notations and guard rotations. He studied it for a moment before speaking again.

"There's an ongoing review of officer records," he said. "In light of recent events, every patrol assignment is being reevaluated. Every movement, every report, every name passed through chain of command. The king demands clarity."

She nodded once. "Then I trust the review will show my record as consistent."

Varek didn't answer right away. When he turned back to her, his expression had shifted only slightly, but the change was noticeable. The coldness remained, but beneath it was something less direct—calculation, perhaps, or curiosity.

"Tell me," he said, "do you ever wonder why you were never promoted?"

The question landed like a stone dropped into a still pond. It wasn't hostile. It didn't need to be. It was the kind of question that carried weight only because of who was asking, and when.

Lysa's reply came without the faintest tremor. "I assumed I hadn't earned distinction."

He watched her closely. "You're competent. Efficient. Respected by your peers. But you've never been... ambitious. You don't reach. You hold position. You watch. You wait. That isn't a flaw, Officer Evern. But it is something I notice."

She said nothing.

Varek stepped forward once more, crossing the space between them until the distance had narrowed again.

"Be careful," he said quietly. "Sometimes it's the ones who wait too long that fall hardest when the wind shifts."

Then, just as quickly, he turned his attention to the officers behind him.

"You're dismissed, Officer Evern," he said. "We'll speak again soon."

Lysa offered the appropriate salute, then turned without hesitation and walked from the hall with the same deliberate calm she had entered with.

The moment the door closed behind her, the sound of it echoed longer than it should have. The corridor outside the command hall stood empty, the vaulted ceiling rising overhead in mute indifference to whatever might pass beneath it. Torches along the walls burned low, their flames still and thin, giving off just enough light to make the hall feel like a passage between thresholds rather than a place of purpose. Lysa kept walking, her stride unwavering, though her heartbeat had yet to settle.

She could feel the imprint of Varek's voice in the space between her shoulders, the way his words still trailed after her, measuring each step she took. He hadn't accused her of anything outright, but the dance around suspicion had been far from casual. Every question had been selected with care. Every statement had served more than one purpose.

The mention of Sevrin hadn't been a test of loyalty—it had been a probe into memory. Varek already knew the cobbler had passed messages. What he wanted to know was whether Lysa would flinch when reminded of it. And she hadn't. Not even once.

Still, the weight remained.

Her boots struck the stone floor in even rhythm, but beneath the surface of her composure, a thousand calculations reeled. He hadn't called her in for punishment. He hadn't exposed her. But he had looked at her the way an executioner might regard a blade—wondering if it had dulled, or if it had simply not yet been used to its full potential.

At the corridor's end, a narrow stairwell led to the barracks wing. She took it without pause, descending into a space where the flicker of lantern light danced across walls lined with bunks and footlockers. A few guards lingered near the common table, speaking in low voices, their words blunted by exhaustion. No one stopped her as she passed. No one asked what had been said behind the door.

Inside her quarters, the silence deepened.

The room was small, spare, and kept deliberately impersonal. A cot, a basin, a narrow chest. Her uniform hung from a wall hook, and a stack of folded cloth sat untouched atop the chest beside her pack. Everything was in order. Everything was as it should be.

She closed the door, unfastened her cloak, and folded it with careful precision. The act gave her hands something to do. Something small. Something quiet.

Then she sat on the edge of the cot and stared at the far wall.

Varek's voice still echoed. Not his words—but the pause between them. The restraint.

He suspected something.

And if he hadn't, he would soon.

The knock at her door came softly—three measured taps spaced just wide enough to avoid suspicion. It wasn't the sort of knock a superior would use, nor the kind that suggested urgency or threat. It was familiar. Intentionally restrained. She didn't rise right away. She listened first, waiting to hear the creak of boots shifting outside or the sound of another body waiting just out of sight. Nothing followed.

When she opened the door, Reginald stood alone in the hallway, hands behind his back, posture easy in the way of a man who had mastered the art of appearing unremarkable. His uniform bore no visible rank insignia today, just the standard grey tunic and dark sash of the outer guard. He had shed his usual scarf. The absence made his features appear more hollow, more tired around the eyes. He glanced over her shoulder once before speaking.

"You're not on rotation again until dusk," he said in a voice just above a whisper. "Walk with me."

She didn't answer immediately, but she stepped aside just enough to grab her cloak. If anyone was watching, it would look like a casual meeting between off-duty officers. A shared route. A private conversation had no place in these halls anymore.

They moved together without speaking until they had exited the barracks wing. Reginald led her through a lesser-used corridor beneath the outer rampart, where the air smelled faintly of old lye and weathered limestone. The lanterns here burned lower than the rest. Most who passed through only did so by necessity. It was the kind of place where secrets had room to breathe.

When he finally spoke, he kept his eyes forward. "One of the names came off the list," he said. "Before it went to the wall."

Her footsteps didn't falter, but her focus sharpened.

"How?"

"I made it happen," he answered, his voice low but firm. "Couldn't pull more than one without drawing attention. Had to pick someone without ties that would raise flags. The ledger boy from the old scribe post. Barely sixteen. Quiet. Forgot how to lie without shaking. Wouldn't have lasted the day."

"You took a risk," she said.

He offered the barest of nods. "I know. But I couldn't watch it happen again."

They walked in silence for several paces. The corridor narrowed ahead, and he waited until they had turned a blind corner before continuing.

"You were named."

The words were simple. Quiet. Undramatic. But they hit like a dropped blade.

"Sevrin gave no names during the first sweep," Reginald continued, "but during holding, he cracked. Spoke in circles. Mentioned a contact, female, within the garrison. Described someone careful, someone who asked questions but never too many. Varek's been piecing it together. He hasn't said it outright, but he knows the shape of the shadow. He's looking to match it to a face."

Lysa absorbed the words without changing pace. "And you?"

"I rerouted the intake chain," he said. "Scrubbed the cross-reference between patrol logs and supply requisitions. It'll buy you time, but not much."

She kept her voice even. "Why are you telling me this?"

Reginald stopped walking. She halted beside him.

"Because I used to think I could help from the edges. Stay clean. Keep you covered without stepping past the line." He turned to look at her fully for the first time. "But that line's gone now. After what I saw last night—what they did—I'm in this. Whatever it costs."

The corridor remained empty. No voices reached them from the stairwell beyond. Just the low crackle of a nearby torch and the sound of both their breathing.

"I've done what I can from inside," he said. "But you'll need to move soon. Before he stops playing games."

She gave a faint nod.

"I'll be ready."

They resumed walking without speaking, their footfalls soft against the worn stone floor. The corridor led them to a side exit near the west archery platform, one that opened to the lower courtyard rarely used during rotation hours. The morning haze still clung to the air, thinning now, but not yet burned off by the sun. Everything in the light looked slightly washed, as though the city itself hadn't decided whether it wanted to be seen.

Reginald stepped to the edge of a low stone planter and sat on its lip with little ceremony. Lysa remained standing, her arms folded across her chest, cloak wrapped tighter than the temperature demanded. The walls here didn't echo. The wind moved slowly between the towers, bending the nearby flags just enough to keep them from falling still. It was the kind of place meant for brief reprieve, not reflection.

"You never wanted this," he said after a time, eyes still fixed on the far side of the yard.

She didn't answer right away. When she did, her voice remained low. "Want has nothing to do with it."

He tilted his head, watching her carefully. "You could've just survived. Played the part. Stayed invisible."

"I tried."

Reginald looked away again. His jaw tensed briefly, then released.

"I think about that sometimes," he said. "What it would look like to walk away from all of this. Let the city devour itself and find somewhere quiet, far from walls and orders. Start over."

"You wouldn't stay gone," she said. "Even if you could."

"No," he admitted. "I wouldn't."

They lapsed into silence again. Around them, the city stirred faintly, though only in half-hearted movements. A few early messengers crossed the high ramparts above. A cart rolled along the edge of the inner lane. Somewhere near the kitchen wing, the sound of water being drawn echoed once before fading.

"I've got eyes in the next quarter," Reginald said, shifting back toward business. "They'll leave a signal by dusk if it's safe to move. We'll have to act soon. Varek doesn't wait long when he's circling something."

Lysa nodded once, her expression unreadable. "Understood."

He stood again, adjusting the set of his belt and checking the clasp of his cloak.

"I'll find you when it's time."

She didn't stop him as he turned to leave. His steps faded into the archway without urgency, without pretense. Just the quiet retreat of someone who had already decided where he stood—and knew it wouldn't be enough for much longer.

Lysa remained in place after he disappeared from view. The courtyard still offered its illusion of peace, but her thoughts moved far faster than the wind above them. The mask she wore for Varek hadn't cracked. Her posture hadn't faltered. But the walls were closing in, and she could feel the shape of her next choice beginning to form—sharp-edged, inevitable, and final.

She took one slow breath before turning back toward the barracks.

The moment of quiet was over.

Chapter Twenty-Three
Letters Home

The candle burned low on the writing desk, casting soft light across the parchment as Caelan dipped his quill in ink. He sat in his quarters, the stone walls still faintly warm from the afternoon sun. The air was quiet, save for the occasional rustle of wind outside and the faint hum of energy that lingered in every chamber of the temple. His shoulders were sore from training, but his mind was restless—not from fatigue, but reflection.

He let the ink settle into the nib and began to write.

Dear Mom,

I hope this letter reaches you safely and that the forest is treating you kindly. The air here smells like stone and dust most days, but I imagine Elderwood still carries the scent of sage and pine after the rain.

I finally completed the Trial of Elements. Master Ildan says I've passed into what he calls 'true instruction'—which is a nice way of saying I get to fail more often without him watching over my shoulder. I think he's proud of me, though he still only shows it with nods and long silences.

Remember when I nearly lit the cottage curtains on fire trying to impress you with that candle trick? Well, now I can guide fire and water in the same motion. Steam everywhere. There was one moment last week I may have accidentally filled half the chamber with mist. Ildan didn't say a word. Just handed me a towel and raised one eyebrow. Progress, right?

He paused, letting a small grin cross his lips. The quill hovered for a moment before returning to the page.

I've started keeping a journal—not for spells, exactly, but for how the elements feel. It's strange how much of magic isn't in the words or gestures, but in the way you listen to things that aren't speaking. Fire isn't angry. It's just honest. Earth doesn't resist—it waits. I'm learning to move with them now, not just through them.

I know you always said power without understanding is just noise. I think I finally get that. It's not about doing more. It's about being more—quietly.

I still miss your cooking, though. The bread here tastes like limestone, and don't even get me started on the stew. If I had a gold coin for every time I dreamed about your herb-roasted rabbit, I could retire and build a second temple just for meals. How's Thistle? Still headbutting the door every morning for a carrot? And are the chickens still plotting your downfall?

I think about home often. Not because I want to run back to it, but because it's part of who I carry forward. Your voice is still louder than the voices in my head when I hesitate. Your lessons still echo between my choices.

I'll write again soon. There's more to learn, more to face, and more of me still waiting to be uncovered. But for now, I wanted you to know—I'm still your son. Just with better posture, slightly singed sleeves, and a deeper understanding of why you taught me the way you did.

With love,
Caelan

He signed his name with care, then folded the parchment, sealing it with the temple's wax sigil. Rising from his desk, he stepped into the corridor and made his way toward the messenger rookery, where arcane couriers would carry the letter back across mountains and woodlands to a cottage nestled far from the reach of kings.

The path ahead was still long, but in that quiet moment, under candlelight and ink, he remembered why he walked it.

The sun had just begun to dip beneath the treetops when Elaria settled into the chair beside the hearth, Caelan's letter still folded in her lap. Outside, the wind whispered through the tall grass, and the hens made their last lazy circuit around the garden before retiring to their coop. A pot of tea cooled on the table, untouched.

She had read the letter three times already.

Not because she didn't understand it, but because it said so much between the lines.

With a slow smile, she took up her own parchment and dipped her quill.

My dear Caelan,

Your letter arrived today with a courier who smelled faintly of burnt parchment and wild berries. I suspect your "steam incident" left more than just the walls damp. Whatever method they're using to ferry messages now must be quite the adventure—though I dare say it's more reliable than the crows.

I'm proud of you. Not for passing the trial, though I expected you would. I'm proud of the way you describe it. You've begun to see what lies beneath the surface of things—not just the beauty of fire or the quiet of stone, but the will behind them. That kind of perception can't be taught. It can only be lived.

She paused, fingers briefly resting against the edge of the page, then continued.

> *You were always one to feel first and question later. As a boy, you chased butterflies into thorns, tried to hug foxes, and once tried to climb a tree just to apologize to a bird for startling its nest. You were reckless, but not careless. Now I see that same heart tempered with discipline. It's the best kind of strength.*
>
> *As for the cooking—your complaints are noted, though I refuse to believe the bread is as bad as you claim. If it crumbles like chalk and tastes like old boots, you may want to check if you're accidentally eating temple bricks. Try adding rosemary to your stew. Or just whisper kind words to it. That worked on you well enough when you were stubborn.*

She allowed herself a quiet chuckle before turning serious again.

> *Thistle still hooves at the door. The chickens are indeed plotting something. And the herb garden is thriving—though I swear the thyme has grown legs. I spend most days in the glade now, meditating beneath the trees. The forest hasn't changed much, but I have. Maybe you have too.*
>
> *You speak of becoming more. I see it. And I believe in it. But don't forget—becoming isn't something you must prove. It's something you carry quietly. Like a seed waiting for the right season.*
>
> *Keep your balance. Let the elements guide your strength, but never let them drown your voice. That part of you—the part that questions, that laughs, that writes home when your sleeves catch fire—that's the part I never want to see burn away.*

She signed her name with a firm, looping stroke.

All my love,
Elaria

Folding the letter, she sealed it with her own mark—a pressed sprig of sage, still faintly fragrant—and handed it to the returning courier with a brief nod. As she watched the magical shimmer carry it into the forest's embrace, she whispered a quiet prayer to the roots and wind alike.

"Guide him gently. He is ready, but still becoming."

The sanctum was silent, save for the steady drip of condensation falling from the high arches above. Caelan sat cross-legged in the center of the floor, palms resting on his knees, eyes closed. The outer world had faded—no rustle of robes, no flicker of torchlight, only the rhythm of breath and the ever-present thrum of ambient magic pressing gently against his skin.

His thoughts drifted beyond the temple. Beyond stone walls and elemental flow. He had come seeking clarity, but what rose in the depths of his focus felt... ancient.

It began as a whisper—not sound, not voice, but sensation. Like pressure against a door not yet opened. A pull from somewhere far beyond the boundaries of the chamber. It was neither light nor dark. Neither comfort nor threat. But it was watching.

Caelan's breath hitched.

He tried to ground himself, shifting his awareness to the elements he knew—air around his shoulders, earth beneath his seat, the steady pulse of his blood in rhythm with the fire, the soft moisture of his lungs drawing breath. But the vision came anyway.

It did not ask permission.

The floor beneath him melted away—not physically, but perceptually. In its place, a vast expanse unfolded. A battlefield stretched across a horizonless plain. The sky above was bruised and swollen, heavy with clouds that did not move. Silence blanketed everything, yet the air felt thick with anticipation.

Caelan stood, though he hadn't moved. Figures emerged from the fog—faceless at first, then clearer.

One wore armor etched with lines of fire and light, his movements graceful and sharp. Another cloaked in shadow, their steps soundless, blade trailing darkness like a wound. A third hovered at a distance, robed in symbols Caelan could not read, their eyes gleamed.

Then came the fourth.

A presence more than a form. A maleficent silhouette that didn't hold. It flickered between shapes—a tall figure in flowing robes, a body of shadow, a mask with no features. Every time Caelan tried to focus on it, the image blurred, yet the dread it carried remained fixed.

It said nothing. It didn't need to. Just being seen by it made his chest tighten, his breath shallow.

He wasn't in danger, but he wasn't untouched. This was no illusion. This was not conjured by his mind. It was something reaching *through* his awareness, testing the boundaries of who he was becoming.

In the vision, he lifted a blade—not his own, but one wrought of silver flame and crackling runes. Around him, others stood—figures he recognized but could not name. Their faces half-lit, their stances tense. Friends? Allies? Reflections?

He stepped forward in the vision... and the ground cracked. A voice rose from beneath.

You do not belong here yet.

The battlefield snapped away like paper torn from a journal.

Caelan's eyes flew open, breath sharp in his throat. Sweat clung to his brow. The sanctum was still quiet, still real. But the feeling lingered—like soot after a fire.

He rose slowly, grounding himself in the real stone beneath his feet, the real torches flickering along the walls.

But somewhere, in the silence between his thoughts, the echo of that vision remained.

Waiting.

The evening bell had not yet sounded, but the temple halls had already fallen into the stillness of early twilight. Caelan moved with purpose through the inner corridors. He hadn't meant to seek anyone out—not at first. The vision had rattled him, yes, but more than that, it had stirred something. A weight beneath the surface, like sediment unsettled by a passing current.

He found Master Ildan where he often did at this hour—in the candlelit alcove of the scriptorium, seated at a low desk surrounded by aged scrolls and open tomes. The air smelled of wax and dried ink. Quiet permeated the space, yet Caelan's presence drew Ildan's eyes before he had spoken a word.

The old mage closed the book before him and gestured for Caelan to sit.

"You saw something."

It wasn't a question.

Caelan lowered himself onto the stone bench across from him, his posture still rigid with tension. "During meditation in the sanctum. It wasn't like anything I've seen before."

Ildan folded his hands loosely before him, waiting.

Caelan exhaled slowly. "There was a battlefield. Empty at first, then filled with figures—some I couldn't name, others I could barely hold in my vision. One of them... it wasn't a person. It was something else. Shifting. Watching. It felt like it knew me. Not just who I am, but who I might become."

Ildan's gaze didn't waver. "Did it speak?"

"Not exactly. But something pushed back. It told me I didn't belong there yet." Caelan paused. "It wasn't threatening. It just... dismissed me."

For a long moment, Ildan said nothing. He leaned back slightly, fingers tracing a slow arc across the grain of the table.

"There are places the mind can touch before the body is ready to follow. You've opened pathways that few reach so soon. The elements have taught you presence. But presence alone doesn't shield you from what lies beyond the veil."

"You've seen something like this before?"

"I've guided others who have," Ildan said. "And I've glimpsed echoes, here and there. Usually not so clearly. Not so young."

Caelan searched his face. "Then what was it?"

Ildan's answer came slow, careful. "Possibility. Memory. Warning. The temple does not dictate which visions arise. Magic has no allegiance to comfort or certainty. It reveals what you carry inside—and sometimes, what waits far ahead."

He reached for a worn scroll and slid it toward Caelan. Its edges were frayed, and its surface bore the faded sigils of an older tradition. "There's a reason we train not just to shape magic, but to survive its reflection. Study this. It speaks of layered realms—of how thought, intent, and truth blur when magic deepens."

Caelan took the scroll and nodded, though his grip on it was tight. "It felt like it saw more than I'm ready for."

"Then you'll need to become someone who is ready," Ildan replied.

A silence settled between them, heavier than before.

Finally, Caelan stood. "Thank you."

Ildan's gaze softened, just slightly. "Rest tonight. Let the vision fade naturally. If it returns, you'll be better prepared. And Caelan... not every shadow that watches is an enemy. Some are echoes of what you must eventually face. Some are parts of yourself, yet unclaimed."

Caelan left the scriptorium with the scroll tucked beneath his arm, the echo of those last words trailing behind him like a second shadow.

The practice yard was empty beneath the rising sun, dew still clinging to the grass like fine threads of glass. Caelan stood alone near the far edge, sword in hand, bare arms chilled in the morning air. His cloak and outer robe had been folded neatly on the stone wall behind him. He preferred the quiet of dawn. It felt honest. Less cluttered by expectation.

Before him, four training dummies stood in staggered formation, their wooden limbs worn smooth by years of strikes. He didn't see them as targets, not today. They were tempo. Measure. Placeholders for what his movements might one day mean.

He lowered the blade to his side and closed his eyes.

There was no spell in his hands. No incantation on his tongue. Just breath.

On the inhale, he drew in the elements—not physically, but through intention. He felt the heat of the sun on his cheek. The trace of morning mist against his skin. The firm weight of the ground beneath his feet. The whisper of wind curling through the trees at the courtyard edge.

On the exhale, he moved.

The first strike was slow—deliberate.

A horizontal slash paired with a pulse of wind, not enough to cut deeper, but enough to add pressure behind the blade. The dummy rocked gently from the force, just as Caelan turned on his heel into a follow-through step. His left hand extended in a reverse guard, and from his palm, a faint flicker of flame curled, no larger than a candle's tongue. It danced briefly before he let it fade.

He wasn't casting spells.

He was listening—to motion.

Again.

This time, his blade traced a vertical arc, and as it reached its apex, he released a short burst of water magic from his opposite hand. The mist followed the arc of the swing, trailing like a tail of vapor behind the steel. As it landed, he twisted his foot, drawing strength from the ground, and finished the motion in a low stance reinforced by a subtle tremor in the stone—earth bracing his balance.

The elements responded not as weapons, but as partners.

Their presence did not announce itself in thunder or flame. It moved in the gaps between strikes—in the timing of his step, the angle of his wrist, the centering of his core.

He repeated the form, faster this time.

Slash, pivot, breath.

Air lent speed. Fire marked direction. Water cooled the transition. Earth steadied the shift.

Over and over, he drilled the sequence until his muscles hummed with effort and the morning sun had climbed halfway to its peak.

By the time he stopped, the dummies were untouched. But the space between them felt changed—charged, as if magic had passed through and remembered its shape.

Caelan stood, the blade lowered again to his side, breath steady.

From the high stone balcony overlooking the temple's training yard, Master Ildan stood with both hands resting lightly against the carved railing, his eyes following Caelan's every movement below. The boy—no, the young man—moved with rhythm, blade in hand, no longer chasing mastery as he once had but shaping it in the space between muscle and intention. Each motion traced clean arcs through the air, not with flourish, but with form; not to display power, but to balance it.

Elemental energy responded not in dramatic flares but in subtle partnership. Gusts of wind gathered just enough to redirect a strike. Heat flickered along the edge of his steel before fading back. His footing shifted with the support of unseen stone, a breath before it might have faltered. Water was not summoned, but suggested—sliding like vapor across the arc of a reversed guard, vanishing the instant it served its purpose.

Ildan remained silent as he watched, though the breath he released was touched with something rare: approval. Caelan had reached a point that no mentor could chart forward from. He was not mimicking forms or executing remembered steps. He was interpreting. Integrating instinct, theory, and rhythm into something lived. It was a threshold only few ever approached, and even fewer crossed with such quiet discipline.

A memory stirred in the stillness. Another student, years ago, had stood on that same stone yard. Her magic had been sharp, all frost and pride, her ambition greater than her patience. She'd advanced too quickly, ignoring the spaces between breath and motion, chasing control before learning to listen. The elements had punished her for it—not out of cruelty, but necessity. They could not be owned. Only understood.

Caelan, at last, was beginning to understand.

His sword work no longer asked permission from the elements. It moved in harmony with them, not as a master, but as a companion. Even now, as he shifted into a low stance, channeling a gust to twist behind the dummy's flank while his blade flowed through the empty air, there was a subtle gravity to him—a weight to his presence that had not been there in the boy who had first arrived.

Footsteps approached behind Ildan, quiet but intentional. One of the instructors from the inner hall stepped up beside him, pausing just long enough to observe the final sweep of Caelan's blade.

"He's taken to the fusion work faster than I expected," the younger mage said, voice pitched low out of respect for the moment.

Ildan didn't turn, his eyes still on the courtyard. "He's not rushing. He's listening."

The instructor hesitated, watching as Caelan concluded the form and sheathed his sword in one fluid motion. "He's changed."

"He's begun to understand the difference between control and clarity," Ildan replied. "He no longer asks the elements to obey him. He joins them."

They both watched as Caelan retrieved his folded robe from the wall and slung it over one shoulder. His stride was calm, unhurried, but not idle. There was purpose in the way he moved now. Not to complete something. To continue it.

Ildan allowed himself a faint nod. "He's nearly ready for the next phase. But readiness is a fragile thing."

The instructor cast a sidelong glance. "Do you think he knows what that means?"

Ildan's reply came after a pause. "No. But he will."

Every morning the upper terrace of the temple stood bathed in golden light as the morning sun rose above the surrounding cliffs, casting long, dappled shadows across polished stone. It was a place untouched by daily lessons or ceremonial rites—a space reserved for quiet practice, reflection, and the shaping of discipline into something personal. Caelan had claimed it as his own. It had become the one place where he could move without scrutiny, speak through motion rather than words, and test the boundaries of everything he had learned.

He stood at the terrace's center, sword drawn, breath steady, body loose but alert. The wind stirred the edges of his tunic, brushing against bare forearms as if waiting. This was not a session guided by instruction or bound to routine. There would be no drills. No pattern to memorize. Only movement.

He stepped forward, blade low, and let the first current of magic rise with the shift of his body. Air gathered behind his shoulders, drawn by the tilt of his stance and the intention behind his form, lending speed to his strike before slipping away like breath. As he turned into the next motion, heat pulsed faintly along the inner line of his forearm, a trace of fire that warmed the swing and extended its force without needing to ignite.

There was no pause between sword and spell. No boundary between gesture and will.

He flowed from one stance to the next. A rising cut became a downward arc, then a spinning redirection across his centerline. Water lifted briefly from the terrace surface, coalescing from morning dew and faint humidity, trailing his movement like a silver ribbon before he dispersed it with a flick of his fingers. He shifted his weight into a grounded stance, drawing from the earth beneath his boots—not to raise stone or cause tremors, but to feel the way it stabilized him, held his frame as he pivoted low and rose again into a ready posture.

What once had been elements called in sequence had become something more—an unspoken alignment of breath, blade, and arcane rhythm. He was not layering magic atop swordplay. He was weaving them together from the start. The blade no longer led and the magic did not follow. They moved as one.

Each step, each strike, each adjustment of his hips or shoulders shaped the flow of magic in real time. A sharp forward thrust carried a burst of air with it, subtle but tangible, enough to carry weight behind the point. A rising guard curved flame around his forearm in a defensive shimmer before fading into the ambient light. As he reversed direction, the heat softened into steam, and moisture pooled in the air for only a moment before falling away.

The more he moved, the more natural it became. There was no need to remember which spell to use or which form to follow. His instincts, sharpened by repetition and molded through vision, carried him forward. Where there had once been hesitation, there was now fluidity. Where magic had once been a separate craft, it now answered the arc of his motion as readily as it answered his will.

When the sequence finally slowed, his blade came to rest at his side, and the air around him grew still again. No lingering heat, no echo of frost, no residue of conjured force remained—but the space felt different, as if something unseen had passed through and taken notice.

He sheathed the sword with care and stepped back from the terrace center, muscles warm, breath even. There had been no audience. No praise.

But he didn't need it. He knew what this was. Mastery in motion

CHAPTER TWENTY-FOUR
ON THE MOVE

Night fell early.

Not because the sun had vanished any sooner, but because the city had learned to darken itself before the horizon finished the task. Windows shuttered before twilight. Doorways emptied. Voices sank low and rarely rose again. The lanterns lining Arden Wake's inner streets were fewer now, spaced at uneven intervals. Some remained unlit, their oil never replaced. Others flickered dimly behind stained glass, casting narrow slivers of amber that barely touched the cobblestones beneath them.

Lysa moved through those slivers like a shadow unwilling to be fully seen. Her uniform had been stripped of its outer markings, leaving only the plain, charcoal fabric of the underlayer. A cloak draped over her shoulders, dark enough to vanish into corners and alley edges. She carried no visible weapon, though the knife at her belt was easy to reach, and her boots had been wrapped to mute their tread.

This was not an assigned patrol. She had passed off her rotation to a willing recruit with no questions asked. The exchange had required a favor owed, but it had been worth the cost. Tonight's route was not sanctioned. It followed no charted sector and passed through no known checkpoints. The way had been chosen for what it avoided—torchlight, familiar faces, curious eyes.

She kept to the western quarter first, weaving between narrow lanes and ducking through gaps in half-fallen fences. The further she moved from the barracks, the more the city returned to its wounded quiet. The scars of the raids still lingered. Burn marks on doors. Broken hinges. Soot-smudged brick. Every street whispered reminders of what had been taken, or who had vanished. Every corner offered the possibility that someone might be watching.

She reached the edge of the river canal before slowing. A low bridge arched across the water, its stonework weathered and uneven. At the base of its eastern pillar, half-hidden in moss, a faint crescent had been drawn in chalk—familiar, subtle, and fresh. The slashes through its arc confirmed what Reginald had promised.

It was safe to proceed.

Lysa stepped carefully across the bridge, keeping to the darkest side. Her breath was steady, but her thoughts ran taut beneath the surface of her calm. Varek's eyes still lingered in her memory—sharp and patient, like a knife waiting for its moment. The reprieve she'd earned would not last. This night might be her only opportunity.

And if she failed to reach them now, the resistance would fade before the next posting arrived. Executions would begin by the end of the week. The scaffolds would rise. And her silence would make her complicit.

The wind off the river was sharp as she crossed, but she welcomed the cold. It cleared the last of her hesitation.

She didn't look back.

The path on the far side of the bridge narrowed quickly, hemmed in by crumbling stone walls and overgrown ivy. Few patrols came this far, and fewer civilians. The district had been marked years ago for future reconstruction, but the plans had never materialized. The city had always chosen to build outward rather than heal what already stood.

Lysa turned down a side lane tucked behind a collapsed grain store. The air here smelled faintly of wet stone and mold. A single lantern flickered at the far end, its glass half-shattered, casting broken shapes across the ground. She passed beneath its reach and continued another dozen steps before pausing near a crooked archway that had once belonged to a stonemason's storefront. Only the frame remained, the door long since taken for firewood. She stepped inside without hesitation.

The space beyond was hollowed out but still held the bones of what it had once been. Shelves lined the walls, though most were empty or broken.

A worktable rested beneath a window covered with a ragged curtain. The floor bore faint outlines of where larger stones had once been stacked. At the center, a single stool waited beside a covered lantern. No light shone through the cloth, but its outline was familiar.

Lysa knelt beside it and gave three taps against the base. Then two. Then one.

Silence stretched. Then came a soft shuffle of fabric from the back of the room.

From behind a draped partition, a figure emerged. Hooded. Cautious. Taller than she expected.

He stopped just short of the lantern and lifted the edge of his hood. Jaxon.

His eyes caught the dim ambient light and held it with a quiet steadiness. The sharpness she remembered from their earlier meetings remained, but there was something new threaded beneath it—tension, frayed by too many close calls. His jaw was darker now, lined with unshaven stubble. A fresh scar trailed near his temple, mostly hidden by his hood.

"You made it," he said, keeping his voice low.

She nodded. "So did you."

"Barely."

He reached for the lantern and pulled the cloth free. The light inside had been shuttered, but now he opened the side slightly. A narrow beam spilled across the floor, just enough to illuminate the edges of the room without reaching the window.

"There's not much time," he said. "Half our runners are gone. The safehouse in Alder Hollow was breached yesterday. We're assuming compromised code."

She stepped in closer, keeping her back to the wall.

"How many left?"

"In the city? Fewer than ten we can reach without risk. Fewer than that who still have a way to move unnoticed."

"And outside?"

"Maybe two contacts past the ridge. Maybe."

He didn't offer false comfort. There wasn't any.

Lysa drew in a slow breath and looked to the map Jaxon now unrolled across the table. Several streets were marked in red chalk. One circle in black.

She pointed to it. "What's here?"

His expression tightened. "The transport manifest. Final copy. If we can get it, we'll know where the prisoners are being held, and where they're being sent. If it's a transfer, we have one chance."

She leaned over the table, studying the lines. "Then we take it."

Jaxon's eyes met hers again. "We do. But if we're caught—"

"We won't be."

She said it without bravado. Only certainty.

Jaxon gave a slight nod. "Then we move before first light."

They remained inside the ruined stonemason's shop long after the final strategy had been drawn. The lantern had been dimmed again, its light reduced to a faint pulse against the fabric covering its sides. Outside, the wind had picked up, carrying with it the scent of smoke from a distant hearth and the faint trace of wet stone. Somewhere deeper in the city, a bell rang—not from the palace, but from the riverwatch quarter. Off-schedule. Deliberate.

Jaxon moved to the corner of the room where a fire bowl had been set beneath a grate of iron. It wasn't meant for warmth. The embers inside had been coaxed from a piece of coal and burned low and smokeless, just enough to light a page or reduce it to ash. He crouched beside it and unrolled a strip of parchment with steady hands. The wax seal was already broken.

"This came in before you arrived," he said. "Courier dropped it in one of the wall vents east of the canal. Markings match the outpost in Falden Hollow. No other confirmation yet."

He held it toward the flame and read the words once—silently, eyes narrowing slightly as they scanned. Then, without pause, he passed it to her.

Lysa took it carefully. The parchment was thin, folded three times, and scrawled in a hurried but practiced hand. The language was coded—tradespeak layered with phrases that only the resistance would recognize.

The message was brief:

Movement confirmed. Detainments not local. Transfer planned. Break lines or break silence. Signal by dawn. The rest will follow.

No names. No dates. But the meaning was clear.

"If they're moving the prisoners," she said, folding the parchment again, "they're doing it before anyone can speak on their behalf."

"They already have," Jaxon replied, tossing a handful of dried husk into the coals. The fire flared orange, then settled. "Just not loud enough for it to matter."

He held out his hand. She passed him the parchment, and he placed it into the fire. It curled, blackened, and dissolved without a sound.

The two of them sat in silence for a long stretch. The kind of silence that didn't demand filling. Only the soft hiss of the coals remained.

When he finally spoke again, his voice was quieter.

"You don't have to be part of this."

Lysa looked at him fully, her posture unmoved.

"I already am."

Jaxon didn't argue.

He simply nodded once, stood, and began preparing the packs for the night's work.

The maps were cleared without a word. Chalk marks were scrubbed clean with the edge of a cloth, parchment rolled and bound with twine that would be burned before they left. Jaxon moved with precision, his gestures stripped of flourish. Every motion was practiced, shaped by repetition born of necessity. He packed only what was essential—rations, flint, rope, two glass vials of oil sealed in wax-stopped pouches. No documents. No sigils. Nothing that could be traced.

Lysa checked the dagger at her belt, then reached beneath her cloak to adjust the strap that held a second blade beneath her tunic. It pressed against her ribs uncomfortably, but its presence calmed her. In a place where words were dangerous and names were currency, steel remained the only truth she could rely on.

Jaxon handed her a folded satchel. Inside it were gloves dyed with ash soot, a thin veil that could be drawn beneath her cowl, and a pair of waxed cloth wraps for the soles of her boots—meant to soften footsteps across stone and break the pattern of prints in dust.

"They've pulled the sentries from the west wall checkpoint," he said. "Likely redeployed to the guard tower north of the square. The ledger house sits between the two. We'll need to cross the alley blind."

"How many windows face the path?"

"Four," he answered. "But only two are lit. The others are boarded. Watch for silhouettes."

She nodded once, slipping the gloves into place and drawing her hood over her hair. The feeling of fabric against her jaw was grounding.

Outside, the wind had picked up again. A shutter banged against the far wall. Neither of them flinched.

Jaxon stood and shouldered his pack. "We move in ten. No signals once we cross the bridge. If something goes wrong—"

"I'll improvise."

His eyes lingered on her for a moment longer than necessary.

"You always do."

He offered the ghost of a smile, then turned and vanished through the back curtain, where a passage led to the hidden entrance beneath the broken cistern. She followed a moment later, her cloak settling across her shoulders.

The gate hadn't even closed behind them when Jaxon returned.

He didn't speak at first. Didn't have to. The blood soaked into the side of his cloak told its own story, but it wasn't his. The courier who'd brought the message was somewhere behind him now, slumped in an alley drain with half his face missing.

Jaxon held the parchment like it burned his fingers. His eyes locked on Lysa, jaw set. His voice was dry stone scraping dry stone.

"You need to read this."

Lysa took the note. The paper had bled through in places, water-warped and soft at the edges, but the ink still clung to the middle in harsh, ragged strokes. The words were scrawled—no spacing, no thought, just the last gasp of someone running out of time.

> Manifest wrong. No prisoners aboard. Final component.
> Breaker nearly armed.

She read it again.

Then again.

The corners of her vision pulsed.

"I—" Thorne stopped halfway through tightening his pack. "That's a mistake, right?"

Jaxon didn't blink. "They confirmed it before the runner was hit. Cargo never touched the cells. It was transferred through the forge lines. Straight into the foundry quarter."

Reginald swore low under his breath. He turned away, hand braced against the wall like he suddenly needed help standing. Thorne just stared at the ground, as if he could will the truth back into the shadows.

Lysa didn't move.

She let the silence press against her chest until her lungs started to burn. They'd spent weeks chasing rumors, risking lives for information, clinging to the hope that what they were fighting for had a face—a name—a soul that could be pulled out of the dark and brought home.

But there were no names. No prisoners.

Just gears and steel and death wrapped in the bones of a machine they had no blueprint for.

"How long until it's active?" she asked.

"Less than a day," Jaxon said. "Maybe hours."

Lysa folded the paper in half, slow and deliberate. Her voice didn't shake.

"Then we don't stop a transport. We stop the Breaker."

Reginald looked up at her, and for the first time in days, there was no trace of doubt in his expression. Just quiet fury.

Thorne gave a soft, bitter laugh and unslung his pack. "Well. That changes the night, doesn't it?"

No one argued. There was no time.

"Looks like we'll have to take the tunnels. No time to prepare otherwise," Lysa stated with a sigh.

Chapter Twenty-Five

THE BREAKER

They passed through the last cistern arch in silence, the lantern shuttered, the steps steep. The undercity opened its throat beneath their feet—stone soaked in damp and rust, foundations built on rot and forgotten things.

The tunnel beyond the gate sealed them in like a throat closing. Lysa adjusted the strap across her chest as she followed Reginald's lead, one hand skimming the wall to steady her steps. The stone was slick with moisture, the air heavier now—no longer cold, but warm with the kind of industrial heat that spoke of furnaces and pressure, not fire. Thorne moved behind her, quiet save for the occasional rasp of fabric against stone. None of them spoke. There was nothing left to discuss.

The path narrowed to a single file chute, forcing them into a crouch beneath low-hanging conduit and sagging pipework. Rust had eaten into the fittings overhead, and more than once the floor dipped without warning, threatening to twist an ankle or snap a knee. Reginald kept the lantern low and shuttered, its faint light barely enough to paint the next few feet in orange-gray shadow.

A creak passed through the pipe system above them. It wasn't loud, but it had weight behind it. Lysa paused mid-step, instinct tightening the muscles at the back of her neck. The sound faded slowly, echo swallowed by the tunnel's curve, but she didn't like the feel of it. Something had shifted.

She reached up and pressed her glove to the nearest pipe. It was warm—not from residual heat, but from pressure moving through it. The same kind she'd felt in a forge channel right before a vent opened. Steady. Purposeful. Fed.

"Line's active," she said quietly.

Reginald was already crouching beside a cracked vent grille up ahead. He leaned in, bracing a hand against the floor as he pressed his ear to the metal. After a moment, he pulled back and stood.

"Airflow's high. System's pulling draw," he said. "The engine's live. It's not waiting anymore."

Thorne frowned. "Wait. I thought we had more time."

"So did I," Reginald replied.

Lysa stepped up beside them. "How long?"

"No way to know for sure," Reginald said. "Gnomes keep their mechanisms secret, it might still need time to stabilize. Could be half an hour. Could be ten minutes. Depends how far along they were before the component got here."

She swallowed the curse building in her throat. There was no comfort in the uncertainty—only pressure. They'd already lost time on a false mission. Now the cost of delay was measured in moments, not hours.

"How far to the core housing?" she asked.

"Ten minutes if we're careful. Seven if we're not."

Lysa adjusted the blade at her hip. "We don't have ten."

Reginald gave a single nod and turned back toward the corridor.

They moved again, deeper into the warm dark. The sound of the city was long gone now. All that remained was the breath of old machinery, pulsing slow and steady through the pipework overhead like a sleeping beast drawing breath. The walls felt closer with every step. The light behind them faded as the heat grew.

The corridor widened just enough to let them move shoulder to shoulder again, though the space still carried the choking heat of an active line. Condensation slicked the walls in patches. The air tasted of copper and iron filings, undercut by the sour tang of grease. Pipes ran the length of the ceiling now—some narrow, others thick enough to walk across if someone dared. Each one pulsed with steady warmth, a heartbeat of machinery building toward something terrible.

They passed a fork in the tunnel. Reginald slowed, tilting the lantern toward the wall. Scratched into the stone near the corner was a mark—two intersecting triangles with a line through the center.

"That's the old guild code," Thorne whispered. "Used to mark pressure lanes. Still accurate?"

Reginald glanced at Lysa. "Only one way to find out."

She motioned forward.

They followed the left-hand path. The incline dipped slightly, enough that Lysa felt it in her thighs. This tunnel was descending, curving beneath the outer rim of the foundry. As they moved, the steady hum above them grew louder. It wasn't chaotic like a forge—no hammering, no sudden bursts of flame or steel striking anvil. This was colder. Calibrated. Mechanical.

She didn't like the way it felt in her ribs.

They reached a section where the wall had partially collapsed. A steel support beam jutted out at an angle, forcing them to duck beneath it one by one. Loose gravel crackled underfoot. Lysa crouched and kept her weight centered, careful not to scrape her gear across the debris.

Reginald was waiting just ahead, crouched low near another vent opening. A soft glow filtered through the grate—faint orange and flickering like firelight behind heavy glass.

"Eyes," he said.

Lysa dropped beside him and peered through the slats.

Beyond the vent stretched the undercarriage of something massive. Steel columns supported thick scaffolding that rose into darkness, vanishing past the limits of their view. Dozens of conduit lines snaked from the ceiling into a central hub—thick, black, and humming faintly with power. Shadows moved through the glow: engineers, guards, someone hauling a chain loop over a massive gear-tooth wheel.

It wasn't the full Breaker. It was its gut. The core was just beyond this wall.

"How many?" she asked.

"Too many for a straight fight," Reginald answered. "But they're not guarding the lower perimeter. Focus is on top-side."

Lysa pulled back and wiped the grit from her gloves. "Then we go under. Fast and quiet. Disable the relay and collapse the intake shaft if we can."

Thorne gave a low whistle and nodded. "Finally, something with teeth."

"Stay sharp," Reginald said. "This isn't a forge. It's a war engine."

They moved back from the vent, already adjusting packs, checking weight, freeing tools. The pressure hadn't peaked yet, but Lysa felt it building.

The corridor narrowed before opening into a shallow, half-flooded antechamber. The water was barely ankle deep, but it stank of iron and machine grease. Somewhere up ahead, deeper in the structure, the Breaker groaned to life in slow rhythmic pulses. It wasn't a roar. Not yet. But the sound carried weight—like pressure building behind a closed valve.

A segmented gate stood between them and the final stretch. Thick bars crossed its surface, bolted together with reinforced bracing. Steel mesh had been welded behind the frame, crude but solid. Not built for style—built to hold something in. Or keep something out.

Thorne stepped forward, crouching beside the left bracket without a word. His fingers ghosted along the lower edge until he found it—nearly invisible, submerged just beneath the murky waterline.

"Tripwire," he muttered.

Lysa leaned in beside him. A faint shimmer stretched across the base of the gate—tight and hair-thin, anchored just below the central support plate. It looked like a trickle of filament clinging to rust. She wouldn't have noticed it on her own.

Thorne clicked his tongue. "You love to see it."

Reginald's voice stayed low. "Can you bypass it?"

Thorne was already unrolling his tool wrap. "Not if you keep asking questions."

He drew a slender hook and narrow clamp, running his thumb down the shaft before sliding the tools beneath the gate's base. His posture changed. Joking gone. Joints loose. Shoulders relaxed. Whatever twitch lived behind his usual sarcasm vanished as his attention narrowed to a single point.

Lysa kept watch over his shoulder, blade drawn but lowered. She counted heartbeats. Above them, something in the pipework gave a low shudder. Steam hissed, drawn through the system like breath behind a clenched jaw.

"We don't have long," she said.

"I know," Thorne replied. His voice was steady now, calm in a way that only came from repetition. "Rig's basic. Trip it and you send a pull chain to the tower block above. Probably lights up the floor. Maybe worse."

"Disable it," Reginald said. "No alarms. No delay."

Thorne didn't look up. "I wasn't planning on leaving a thank-you note."

A soft click echoed under the gate. The wire slackened, then settled.

"Trip's dead," he said. "Gimme another minute for the locking pins."

The gate's upper plate creaked slightly as he moved his tools higher. Lysa felt the hairs on her arms rise. Every second felt wrong—too still, too close. They were brushing the edge of something that hadn't woken yet, but would. Soon.

Reginald checked the tunnel behind them. Still clear. But the pulse in the floor was growing louder now. That mechanical rhythm was no longer just powering up.

It was counting down.

The lock gave way with a muffled click, barely audible over the soft hiss of steam behind the walls. Thorne exhaled through his nose, the tension in his shoulders easing just slightly as he removed the last pin and slipped his tools back into the wrap. He tapped the gate's hinge once with the butt of his knife.

"It's loose," he whispered. "But heavy. Won't open quiet."

Lysa exchanged a glance with Reginald. They didn't have the luxury of waiting for quiet.

"Open it slow as you can," she said. "We'll adjust on the fly."

Thorne braced his foot and eased into the motion. The gate shuddered as it shifted, metal grinding against stone. Not loud, but not silent either. Lysa clenched her jaw. Any sharp ear in the chamber beyond would hear it, if they were listening. But the hum of the engine masked most of the groan.

Three inches. Six.

Enough space for one person to slip through.

Reginald went first, crouched low and blade drawn. Lysa followed, keeping her steps tight and close to the wall. The passage on the other side of the gate opened into a curved maintenance corridor, unfinished and clinging to the back wall of the Breaker's primary staging platform. Pipes ran across the ceiling in clustered tangles, feeding in and out of thick conduits that snaked through reinforced support beams. The deeper thrum of the machine echoed through the floor now, pulsing beneath their boots like a second heartbeat.

Thorne came last, letting the gate ease shut behind them. He didn't latch it—just let it rest in place. The moment it clicked, they were in hostile ground.

Ahead, a grated overlook stretched outward. Through it, they could see the heart of the Breaker's understructure: massive coiled belts of steel, chained counterweights, arc housing tubes threaded like arteries through the walls. The platform above was cast in copper glow, figures moving between suspended walkways and control spires. Lysa could make out two guards posted near the core hatch and another pacing beneath the cooling tower.

No alarms. No signs of detection. Yet.

She crouched beside the overlook and scanned the lower perimeter. There—beneath a column of hanging chain spindles—was the relay box. A housing unit wired directly into the control lattice. If they cut it, the Breaker would seize. Maybe not permanently. But long enough.

She pointed to it, tapping Reginald's arm. He nodded.

Thorne edged in beside them and whispered, "You're sure that's the relay? Looks like a lever box from an inn's cellar."

"It's not the box," Lysa said. "It's the lines running through it."

Thorne traced the cabling with his eyes. "Damn. That's tight rigging."

"Can you disable it clean?" Reginald asked.

"Not from here," Thorne said. "Too exposed. We'll have to drop to the support trench below. Get behind it."

"How many eyes?" Lysa asked.

Reginald looked again, watching the pacing guard. "Three. Maybe four if they've got a floater."

Lysa narrowed her focus. The platform above was still active, engineers moving in rhythm with the core's cycle. No one was looking down. No one had noticed the shadow growing beneath them.

But they would. Soon. She drew her knife.

"Split and strike. Quiet and fast," she said. "We don't get another chance."

They moved like water through the dark.

Lysa led the descent, sliding between the beams beneath the overlook platform. She dropped into the trench below without a sound, landing in a crouch among the dusted debris of long-forgotten maintenance scraps. Reginald followed with military precision, his weight controlled, blade already drawn and angled downward. Thorne came last, easing his pack against his chest to soften the impact as he landed behind them.

The trench offered little room for error. Reinforced with rusted steel supports and split along the center by a drainage channel, the narrow passage left just enough space to crouch and crawl along the underbelly of the Breaker's core platform. They kept low, pressed into shadow. Overhead, the rhythmic drone of the arc engine pulsed louder now, accompanied by a soft, unsettling tremor that vibrated through the steel supports.

It wasn't the sound of something starting. It was the sound of something preparing to unleash.

Reginald raised two fingers and pointed toward a side wall lined with cabling. The arc relay housing was bolted against a curved support strut, its lines feeding directly into the platform's central engine casing. A thick black conduit extended from its base and ran along the floor into a containment stack surrounded by heat baffles. Heat shimmered faintly in the air around it, distorting the edges of the metal.

Thorne leaned in, close enough to whisper without breath escaping.

"That's it."

Lysa nodded. "What do you need?"

"Thirty seconds," he said. "And nobody breathing down my neck."

Reginald glanced upward. The pacing guard was still moving, back turned. No alert. No deviation.

"I'll intercept the roamer," he said.

Lysa hesitated. "Keep it silent."

He didn't reply. He was already moving, angling toward the slope that led up to the side platform where the guard would loop next. His steps were deliberate, not rushed. Controlled. He disappeared into shadow, blade held low.

Thorne was already on one knee beside the relay box. His fingers moved like they were wired into the metal—steady, unshaking, each motion deliberate. He stripped a wire, spliced a bypass, adjusted the grounding rod, then started counting under his breath.

Lysa held position at the rear of the trench, eyes tracking both directions of the narrow corridor. The tremor in the walls increased—faint, but pulsing, as if the engine was flexing against its restraints. She gripped the hilt of her dagger harder.

A muffled sound echoed above. Not a shout. Not a clash. Just a shift. Reginald's doing.

A moment later, Thorne exhaled. "Cut."

Lysa turned.

He stepped back from the relay. The engine's drone dropped in pitch for the briefest of seconds, like something vital had skipped a beat. No alarms. No surge. Just that dip—small, subtle, but unmistakable.

Then—

The Breaker growled. A new pulse rippled through the core. Thicker. Angrier. Like it felt the interference.

Lysa grabbed Thorne by the arm. "Move."

Reginald reappeared at the top of the trench. His cloak was streaked with dust, but his expression was steady. "One down. No alarm."

She nodded once. "We've got minutes now, not more."

From the depth of the chamber, a grinding shift began to build—metal straining, something massive winding into alignment.

The Breaker wasn't just reacting. It was waking up. The chamber trembled.

It began low—just a groan through the floor supports—but within seconds it grew. The walls flexed with the weight of moving machinery, the pressure inside the arc housing pushing against its constraints. Pipes above them hissed and vibrated. One cracked along a seam and spat a fine spray of steam that rolled across the upper walkway in silver coils.

Lysa didn't wait for confirmation. She pulled Reginald back into the trench and motioned for Thorne to move. They ran low and fast, feet silent across the steel mesh floor. The relay sabotage had worked—partially. Whatever delay it caused, the Breaker was still accelerating toward ignition.

Reginald was the first to speak. "If we can't shut it down—"

"Then we bury it," Lysa said. "Collapse the whole chamber if we have to."

Thorne shook his head. "Not enough detcord for a full collapse. Maybe a partial. We'd have to bring the ceiling down at the right point."

"Is the containment stack linked to the cooling shaft?" she asked.

"It's mounted against the rear load wall, opposite that relay," he said. "If we push enough heat through the casing and drop that wall—"

"The chamber goes with it," Reginald finished.

"And we go with it," Thorne added, not joking.

Lysa turned back toward the trench opening. From here, she could see the cooling baffles beginning to pulse with light. The pressure gauges on the control platform spun as the engine ramped up. They had minutes, maybe less. The whole place would ignite from within if the containment reached threshold.

She didn't hesitate.

"We sabotage the cooling line," she said. "Force a feedback loop. Reginald, you clear the platform. Take out what guards you can quietly. We don't need them pulling that safety override."

Reginald nodded once and moved. Thorne didn't move.

He looked at her for a beat, face tight. "You sure about this?"

"No," she admitted. "But it's the only shot we've got."

He drew a knife and followed, leaving only her in the trench. Above, the first alert klaxon began to flicker red.

Lysa scaled the ladder inset into the support column, climbing with swift, practiced motion. Her boots struck the rungs in silence. The overhead klaxon began to pulse faster now, but still without sound—just that angry red glow spinning across the chamber like a searchlight. A visual warning only. Audible alarms were still offline.

Thank the relay for that.

She reached the upper walkway just as Reginald struck. The first guard went down without a cry, his throat cut before he knew someone was behind him. Reginald caught the body mid-fall and eased it against the railing, turning fluidly toward the next. Thorne moved behind him in the shadow of the engine column, eyes scanning, blade drawn but not yet bloodied.

Lysa crossed toward the rear wall.

The containment stack loomed in the center of a multi-tiered array—baffled with heat vents and wrapped in safety conduit. Pressure valves hissed from the top of the chamber like an animal venting rage. It wasn't designed to rupture. But it could be tricked.

She reached the far panel and dropped to one knee beside the emergency coolant valve. Thorne slid in beside her.

"Bypassing this will spike the internal temp in under sixty seconds," he said. "After that, there's no stopping it."

"Understood."

He hesitated. "You're sure we're not trying to run?"

Lysa met his eyes.

"We run after it explodes."

Thorne blew out a breath and began pulling back the paneling. Wires spilled out in a tangle, and he sliced through the grounding loop first, then the temp regulator. Sparks jumped across the edge of his blade, and a red light inside the stack housing began to flash.

The core's hum changed. Lower now. Deeper. The machine didn't whine—it growled.

Reginald appeared from the far stairwell, blood trailing down one gauntlet, his movements were steady, but slowing. He was trying to hide the severity of the gash on his arm.

"Clear," he said. "No one left who can stop this."

Thorne pulled back the final switch and jammed a fuse fork into the control socket. A hiss built behind the wall like a thousand kettles boiling at once.

"There," he said. "Coolant's locked. It's going to overheat in thirty seconds."

"Time to leave," Reginald said, blood starting to spittle as his spoke.

Lysa turned toward the east ladder. "Extraction route?"

Thorne slung his pack back on. "Through the south vent chute. We saw it earlier."

The chamber around them began to shudder. The engine's core gave off a low, resonant whine, now climbing in pitch. Red warning lights spun faster. A vibration rolled up through the steel—faint at first, then stronger, shaking bolts loose from the railings.

They ran.

Down the staircase, through the trench, back toward the vent gate they'd come through. Behind them, the Breaker moaned like something ancient and wounded.

And then—the first explosion hit.

A flash of white light spilled down the corridor behind them as the containment stack cracked open. Steam and pressure ripped through the chamber, shearing bolts and lighting the walls in arcs of fire. The blast wasn't focused—but it didn't have to be.

Lysa hit the floor as the air behind them turned to flame.

The explosion tore through the chamber like a living thing.

The containment stack ruptured in full, and the blast wave caught the far walkway mid-frame. Steel peeled like bark under flame, girders snapping, the upper catwalk shearing from its mounts in a shriek of metal. A wall of pressure chased them through the access tunnel—fire and steam slamming into the stone just seconds behind their heels.

Lysa hit the floor hard, shoulder-first, and rolled through a slurry of hot ash and soaked debris. The heat bit through her gloves. Something sizzled near her neck, but she ignored it. She pushed herself up and kept moving.

Ahead, Thorne was already at the vent chute, wrenching open the bolted hatch they'd spotted earlier—a pressure dump line used for exhaust. It wasn't meant for human passage. But it was the only thing that wasn't collapsing behind them.

Reginald appeared through the haze of smoke, coughing through his sleeve, half-limping with one hand pressed to his side.

"You hit?" she shouted.

"It's nothing," he replied, voice hoarse as he coughed. "Move!"

Thorne kicked the hatch fully open. A rush of hot air blasted outward, nearly knocking him back. Inside, the shaft was angled steeply down, its walls slick with residue and heat. Barely wide enough to crawl through—but it would lead away from the core.

Lysa went first. She didn't think. She dropped into the chute and slid.

Metal screamed behind her as the Breaker gave way. She could feel the ceiling folding in, the tunnel above choking on debris and fury. Light blinked and vanished behind her as stone and steel caved in across the trench.

The chute twisted, then dropped sharper, and suddenly she was airborne—falling into a reservoir chamber half-filled with black water and runoff.

She crashed through the surface hard.

Cold met her like a fist, shocking against the heat that had followed them down. She surfaced gasping, coughing, eyes burning from the fumes. Reginald hit the water a second later, followed by Thorne with a grunt of pain as he landed hard beside a floating piece of duct panel.

Above them, the shaft sealed itself with thunder. Dust and sparks bled through the seams, but no more fire.

Just silence. Just breath. They floated for a moment in the dark.

Then Lysa turned toward the sloped ledge at the edge of the chamber and began to swim.

They crawled out of the reservoir one by one, dragging themselves onto the slick stone ledge that ringed the lower basin. The chamber was quiet now, save for the slow drip of runoff and the hiss of cooling metal somewhere deeper in the system. No alarms. No footfalls. Just the heavy stillness that follows destruction.

Lysa pushed to her feet, water pouring from her cloak and hair, boots slipping slightly on the angled ledge. Her limbs ached from the fall, the crash, the cold. Every breath felt tight in her ribs. But she was alive. They all were.

Thorne sat slumped against the wall, blinking through a smear of blood that trailed from his brow. His coat was scorched along one sleeve, a piece of shattered gear still strapped uselessly to his pack.

"That," he muttered, voice ragged, "was the worst exit plan I've ever committed to."

Reginald lowered himself beside a broken pipe jutting from the wall. He peeled back the fabric at his side, inspecting the wound. It was deep, and nasty—shrapnel or something sharp during the drop. His vision was blurring. Blood was already drenched through his tunic, thicker than the water they just crawled out of, pooling below him.

"You're lucky we made it out at all," he said with a cough, spitting up some blood. "The ceiling was seconds from collapse."

"I wasn't lucky," Thorne said. "I was brilliant. Just... damp and underappreciated."

Lysa ignored them both for a moment. She walked to the far edge of the chamber, where a grated service duct rose into the wall. A rusted ladder led upward into darkness. Possibly into another maintenance corridor. Maybe a vent line. She couldn't tell, but it went up and would take another hour to reach the surface.

She looked back over her shoulder.

"We're not out yet," she said. "We still need a way to surfa—"

Reginald nodded slowly, then fell over where he sat.

"Reginald!" Lysa screamed as she rushed over to his side, grabbing his hand.

He was barely conscious as he looked up at Lysa, light fading from his eyes as with a final squeeze "Go..." slipping from his lips.

Lysa lingered there for a moment, before Thorne startled her.

Thorne groaned from his own bruises but rose, pulling the strap on his satchel tighter. There was a tunnel of to the right. They didn't know where it went, but it was the only option from here.

"We wont be able to carry him with us." Thorne stated. "I'm too wounded. You're not strong enough, and that passage way is too narrow."

She took a final look back at Reginald, "Goodbye old friend. and Thank you." Then turned back to Thorne. "Let's go."

It coiled through several turns and twists. After about half an hour, they happened upon a small opening with a ladder heading up.

"Up the ladder, then?" Thorne remarked.

Lysa stepped forward and placed her hands on the rungs. The metal was cold, slick with condensation, but it held her weight.

"Yes," she said. "Up. And out."

She climbed.

Behind her, one man followed, wounded, soaked, and bruised, but alive. The shaft above them swallowed their light, and as they rose, the noise of the reservoir faded, replaced by the distant murmur of the city above.

The Breaker was gone. But its shadow would linger.

The access ladder ended at a rusted panel, the bolts half-eaten by time and steam. Lysa tested it with one hand. It didn't give easily, but it wasn't welded shut. A hard shove rattled the hinges loose. She braced her shoulder and pushed again, and the panel finally creaked open with a groan that echoed through the shaft like a distant warning bell.

Cool night air spilled in.

She climbed through first, emerging into a narrow alley behind a row of storage sheds lined with soot-dark brick. The street was empty, save for the muffled churn of patrol wagons farther west. No alarm bells rang. No soldiers sprinted toward them.

Not yet.

The blast hadn't reached the surface—not fully. But something down there had changed. She could feel it in the air. Pressure. Residue. The faint smell of burned ozone that had no business being in the open air.

Thorne climbed out behind her, hands scraping across the wet stones.

"You know, for a moment there, I thought we were going to die."

"We still might," she said.

"True, but we'll smell better doing it."

He caught his breath, then looked toward the sky. Smoke curled faintly from the direction of the foundry. Not a towering inferno, but a wound opened in the belly of the city. It hadn't collapsed completely—but it was damaged. Set back. Sabotaged.

"It'll take them weeks to rebuild that," he said.

Lysa didn't answer. She was looking elsewhere.

Her eyes were fixed on the corner of the alley, where a posted flier flapped in the breeze—half-burned, but still legible. A wanted notice. Her face. The sketch was poorly rendered but close enough. Someone had written TRAITOR in red paint across the top.

Thorne saw it too. He reached forward and ripped it down with a grim smile.

"Suppose we'll need new faces."

"No," Lysa said quietly. "They need to remember ours."

The city around them was stirring. Somewhere in the distance, a bell began to ring. Not an alarm, but a shift call. Midnight or just after. The world above had no idea what had just been prevented beneath their feet.

But they would.

Soon.

Chapter Twenty-Six

TRAITOR

The floor of the safehouse was cold, but not clean. Damp stone, layered with old soot and the faint scent of rusted iron, pressed against Lysa's back as she stared at the cracked ceiling above. Her lungs still burned from the smoke, and her hands—though scrubbed raw at the basin—carried the scent of scorched leather and broken steel. Every part of her ached. Muscles gone tight. Skin stinging from half-healed scrapes and bruises.

They had survived.

Barely. Reginald was gone. They had to leave him there in the tunnel.

Thorne was seated near the wall, one leg stretched, one bent, with his pack half-open beside him and a torn sleeve knotted tightly at his bicep. Blood still streaked his temple from a shallow gash above his brow, and his hair was crusted at the edges where ash had clung to sweat. He was quieter than usual—no jokes, no smug smirks. Just the hollow gaze of a man running calculations on what could've gone wrong, and what still might.

No one had spoken since they'd reached the safehouse.

The entry door was stone-set and reinforced with three locking braces. It hadn't been opened since Jaxon had locked it from the inside. One of the younger runners had passed through earlier with word from the eastern quarter—quietly, nervously—but hadn't lingered. Everyone knew better. The air was too heavy for conversation. Even victory tasted like iron.

Lysa stood near the far basin, where a rusted pipe dripped yellowed water into a shallow stone bowl. She had washed her hands four times already, but the grime beneath her fingernails clung like guilt. She turned the valve again and let the water spill across her gloves one last time.

Something caught her eye.

A parchment square, nailed unevenly into the support beam beside the wash. It had curled at the corners, warped slightly from steam or damp. Not the one Thorne had torn down earlier. Another. This one fresher.

She reached for it slowly, knowing full well what it would be.

The ink had run in places, but not enough to blur the face. A crude sketch—red hair, narrow eyes, sharp cheekbones. Her likeness, or close enough that anyone passing it on the street would know who to whisper about. Across the top, in thick strokes of red paint, the word TRAITOR had been slashed so deeply into the paper it tore the surface in three places.

She stared at it in silence.

"Guess they printed more," Thorne murmured from behind her. His voice was hoarse. Unmocking. "Didn't take long."

She didn't answer. She folded the paper once, then again, and slipped it into the inner pouch of her coat.

"Should burn those," he added after a moment.

"I will."

"You won't."

She didn't argue. Thorne let the silence hang and returned to tightening the knot in his makeshift sling.

Behind her, "The eastern forgehall's sealed," Jaxon said. "They've pulled new patrols from the garrison—posted them at the outer wall and near the lower causeway. Blocked the entire intake descent."

Thorne grunted. "So they think we're still underground."

Jaxon nodded. "For now. They're choking off every access vent and flooding the lower tunnels with torch teams."

Thorne snorted. "Good luck to them. Most of those vents haven't held a proper scaffold in years."

"They're not worried about structural integrity," Jaxon said. "They're worried we're still breathing."

Lysa turned back toward them. Her gaze swept the room—scorched coats, split knuckles, the stink of blood and ash still clinging to them all. They looked like survivors. But barely.

She walked to the far wall and knelt beside her pack. The side pocket was scorched. The straps half-torn from the slide down the chute. She'd have to rebuild it from scrap again.

But that could wait. They had minutes, maybe an hour, before the next ripple of consequence hit the city. And this time, it had her name on it.

The room had thinned out by the time Lysa stepped away from the far wall. Thorne had curled into his coat and was half-snoring in the corner, his breath shallow but steady. Jaxon was gone, off to relay orders and scout a second route out of the lower quarter. The young runner hadn't come back. No one expected him to.

Lysa crossed the chamber without a word and sank down on the edge of the stone bench.

The silence stretched. She didn't fill it.

Callie spoke up from the corner, "Jaxon says they posted fliers in five districts. Not just the upper quarter. Not just the guild halls." She paused. "Slums, too. Border villages. Even the quarry camps."

Lysa let her hands rest in her lap. She could still feel the folded parchment in her coat. "Then they're serious."

"They were always serious," she replied. "Now they're afraid."

A flicker of light caught the edge of Lysa's cheek, where dried blood crusted the corner of a long-healed scar. She hadn't cleaned up. There hadn't been time. Or the need.

"You knew it would happen eventually," Callie said.

"I did," Lysa admitted. "Just not like this."

Callie turned her head slightly to look at her. "Like what?"

"Like I stepped into it." Her jaw clenched. "Like I chose to wear a name I didn't ask for. I wanted to fight. Not... brand myself."

She studied her face. "You didn't."

"No?" She looked away. "That poster says otherwise."

"That poster is a weapon," she said. "Nothing more."

Lysa let out a slow breath. "It's my face, Callie. My name. People saw me. In the tunnels. On the scaffolds. That wasn't just a mission. It was a message." She looked back at her, eyes sharp with the weight of it. "And now the message has a target."

She looked down at her gloves, still wet from the basin. Her fingers curled slightly.

Callie watched her. "You're not just a name now. You're a symbol. And that's what terrifies them."

She shook her head. "I didn't want to be a symbol."

"No one ever does." She glanced toward the door. "But that's what we're left with. People don't remember sabotage reports. They remember faces."

Lysa's voice was barely a whisper. "And if they catch that face?"

Callie was quiet a moment.

"Then they parade it," she said flatly. "Hang it from the high wall. Burn it in the square. Make children watch." She turned back to her. "But only if we let them."

The lantern overhead flickered once. The wick hissed in the oil, then settled. Outside, the city exhaled.

Lysa looked past the door. Past the stone and steel and blood still clinging to her boots. Somewhere above, the foundry still burned. The people hadn't seen the fire yet, but they would.

And they would remember her name. Even if they never said it aloud.

She reached into her coat and pulled the flier from her inner pocket. The folds were damp. The edges curled. She looked at her own eyes drawn in ink and shadows.

Then she tore it in half and tossed it into the lantern flame. Neither of them spoke as it burned.

The fire in the war chamber burned high but gave off no heat. It snapped and hissed within the hearth, yet the room remained cold. Not the cold of wind or stone, but something else—something pressed into the air like an unseen weight, a stillness that made the shadows seem thicker than they should have been. No one said it aloud, but the walls felt closer than before. The ceiling heavier. The tapestries along the back wall swayed ever so slightly though no draft passed through.

King Aldric stood over the table with both hands braced on its edge. He had stripped off the outer layer of his royal regalia. The heavy crimson cloak remained, but his crown had been left behind in the antechamber. His jaw was clenched. The only movement was the twitch of his gloved thumb against the wood. A single parchment lay in front of him, pinned flat beneath a ceremonial dagger that had split it through the middle. The sketch on the poster was unmistakable. Red hair. Narrow eyes. A mouth drawn in tight defiance. Lysa Evern's likeness stared back at him in silence, her image bisected by the blade. Across the top, the word "TRAITOR" had been printed in heavy red dye—official, sanctioned, and now publicly displayed in every quarter.

"She stood atop the forge," Aldric said, his voice low but even. "She set fire to my judgment. And the people applauded."

None of the gathered men dared respond immediately. Commander Varek stood just beyond the table's edge, his posture sharp and measured. His armor had been cleaned but not polished, blackened steel still showing the scratches of recent engagements. Two senior advisors flanked him, both more cautious in their demeanor. Their eyes rarely left the floor for long.

"We have begun securing the lower sectors," Varek said after a beat. "The break lines near the eastern causeways have been sealed. We're posting patrols at all five inner walls. So far, no movement suggests she's escaped the city."

Aldric didn't move. His eyes remained fixed on the table, though his stare had grown distant.

"She hasn't escaped," he said. "Not yet."

One of the advisors took a hesitant step forward. His voice was careful, deferential. "We've begun authorizing dusk raids, as per your standing orders. The fliers bearing her image are posted in every major square. Minor collaborators will be dealt with by the local magistrates—those harboring her directly will be handed over to the Black Hall. Quietly."

Aldric's gaze lifted at that. He looked toward the man, but something in his expression made the advisor falter. The king's eyes had always been sharp, but now they looked strained in a way that felt unnatural—too wide, too focused. As though looking through the man, not at him.

The shadows around Aldric squirmed and writhed with malicious intent.

Raze the city! Flush her out with fear and fire!

"No," Aldric said. "There is no quiet."

The words sat heavy in the air. Somewhere behind the tapestries, a faint sound stirred—so faint it could have been nothing at all, a shift in the timber of the walls or the creak of ancient stone. But none of them spoke. None of them breathed too loudly. The king's voice was calm, but the temperature in the room felt colder now. The fire cracked again, but the shadows did not retreat from the corners.

"She has given them something to believe in," Aldric continued. "A story. A face. That's the danger." He lifted the dagger from the parchment and turned it slowly between his fingers. "People don't riot for nothing. They riot for ideas, for memory. For the illusion that something once was better. And that it can be again."

He let the dagger fall. It struck the stone floor point-first and rattled once before toppling over.

"I want her face everywhere," he said. "Not just on parchment. Paint it on walls. Carve it into wood. Make it unmistakable. Let the people choke on it."

Commander Varek gave a small nod. "And when we find her?"

"When we find her," Aldric said, "we parade her through every district she dared to ignite. We let the people see the price of defiance before we put her to the fire."

Varek hesitated, but only briefly. "And if she's not found soon?"

The king turned fully toward him then, the firelight catching the sharp lines of his face. His skin looked drawn tighter than usual, paler, like a man who hadn't slept properly in weeks, years even. The glow behind him cast long shadows along the floor, but they didn't seem to align with the flames. They stretched too far. Moved too slowly. One of the advisors shifted his weight, glancing once toward the rear of the chamber, and then away again.

"She will be found," Aldric said. "She wants to be seen. Let her. The more she burns in their minds, the easier it will be to crush her spirit when the city turns cold."

He stepped away from the table and crossed to the hearth, his boots scraping softly across the stone. The fire blazed high, but the warmth never reached him. He stared into the flame without blinking.

One hand dipped into the inside pocket of his cloak. From it, he drew a small locket—the same one he always kept near, but never opened in public. He turned it over in his fingers. The advisors did not move. Varek didn't speak. None of them asked.

Aldric's tone dropped to a murmur, his voice barely audible above the fire. "Those like her took her from me."

The room remained silent.

But from somewhere just beyond the hearthlight—where the glow did not touch the far wall—the shadows seemed to shift. Not drift or flicker, but swell, as though some unseen shape leaned forward from behind the stone, watching through eyes that didn't exist. Content with Aldric being it's puppet.

Aldric didn't flinch. His hand tightened around the locket. The firelight didn't warm the room, and none of the men dared speak again.

The orders had been given.

The retaliation had begun.

The city did not sleep. It never had, not truly, but something had changed in its rhythm since the fire beneath the forgehall. People moved differently now. Streets emptied sooner than usual. Taverns grew quiet before the moon reached its peak. The air smelled of ash and cold steel, even in districts far removed from the blast. And everywhere, from the merchant rows to the tenement gutters, the name Lysa Evern passed between lips not as gossip—but as weight.

In the market square, a butcher's boy swept the stone stoop with slow, cautious strokes. He paused when he saw the pair of soldiers nailing another parchment to the post outside the grainhouse. He didn't speak. Just stared. The soldiers didn't acknowledge him. When they moved on, he stepped forward and tilted his head at the sketch. His father had called her a reckless fool. His mother hadn't said anything at all. But the boy had seen her—two nights ago, silhouetted against firelight atop the shattered tower. She hadn't run.

He took a piece of charcoal from the edge of the ledger post and, with a glance over his shoulder, scrawled a thin red line beneath her name. Then he picked up his broom and kept sweeping.

At the edge of the inner district, an old man lit the lanterns outside his bookstall with a shaking hand. He could still hear the soldiers from earlier—boots on cobblestone, barked orders, the tearing of old volumes used to light the torches. When they left, he found a torn fragment of one of the wanted fliers stuffed between the shelves. He didn't hang it back up. Instead, he folded it and placed it beneath the loose board in the floor with the rest. There were seven now. All of them different. Some said "traitor." Some didn't say anything at all. But the faces were always the same.

On the third tier near the collapsed aqueduct, a mother sat in silence while her son reenacted the explosion using carved sticks and bits of glass. He had given one of the figures red hair, drawn with wax pencil. It rode the back of a hawk, knocking over the soldiers' pieces with a twig for a sword. She didn't scold him. But when he wasn't looking, she gathered the toys and placed them in a cloth satchel, folding it twice before hiding it beneath the floorboards. She didn't tell her husband.

Elsewhere, in an alley behind the tannery, three young men passed around a wineskin and stared at the freshly painted symbols left behind by resistance runners. A rising sun etched in charcoal. A broken crown split down the center. Beneath one, someone had written a name. Not Lysa's real name, but one the streets had given her.

Fireblood.

One of the men crossed it out. Not out of fear. Out of disagreement. Then he etched something new below it.

Queen of Ash.

The others didn't speak, but none of them erased it.

In the upper districts, where soldiers walked in pairs and the gates closed early, a tailor kept her head down and stitched in silence while her neighbor's home was searched. No resistance fliers were found, but the family was dragged into the street anyway. The father begged. The mother held her child so tightly she nearly dropped him when they pulled her arm away. The tailor didn't move. She kept sewing until they were gone. But that night, she took down her warding sigil from above the door and replaced it with a black strip of cloth. No words. No symbols. Just black.

The city did not erupt overnight. It did not riot or crumble. But something beneath the stone had shifted. People watched their windows more carefully. They whispered in lower tones. They passed news not in full sentences, but in gestures and glances and the smallest exchanges of silver. And always, always, her name hovered behind it.

Not all believed in her. Not all wanted her to win.

But every one of them now knew who she was.

The safehouse beneath the blacksmith's quarter was colder than the last. The forge overhead hadn't been lit in weeks, and the stone walls carried every echo of bootsteps and shifting breath. Lamplight cast long shadows across the table at the center of the chamber, where a half-unrolled city map lay pinned with rusted nails. Scraps of parchment, coded slips, and marked routes scattered its surface, weighted down with knives, bolts, and the butt of a hammer.

Lysa stood at the edge of the table, her arms crossed over her chest, eyes fixed on the newest markings scrawled in red. Three of the routes had been blocked since the night of the Breaker's fall. Patrols doubled. Interrogations reported at every known gate. Even some of their safehouses, ones never used by her directly, had gone silent.

Jaxon stood to her right, flipping through the latest field reports brought in by the runners. His jaw worked silently as he read, but the tension in his brow made the outcome clear.

"We lost the Yarrow bridge route," he said, voice tight. "They pulled a patrol off the merchant road and stationed a full watch at the north bend. And there's word the Iron Crescent has been turned into a holding pen."

Lysa exhaled through her nose. "How many taken?"

"Two dozen. Maybe more. Some had ties to us. Some didn't."

Across the room, Thorne cursed under his breath and paced a tight line behind the benches. His shoulder had been bound better this time, but he still moved with a hitch in his step. The quiet had never suited him. Now it was starting to fray the edge of his voice.

"We should've kept the pressure up," he muttered. "They're scrambling. We had them chasing ghosts. We should've hit again while they were still off balance."

"We weren't in position to strike twice," Jaxon replied, not looking up. "Half the cell leads haven't reported back. We're still patching comms between the third and sixth circles. And the runners are stretched too thin."

"Then we replace them," Thorne snapped. "There's no shortage of hands willing to throw a torch."

"Throwing a torch is easy," Jaxon said. "Lighting a fire that doesn't burn out of control—that takes more than anger."

Thorne scowled, but didn't argue. He just paced again, slower this time.

The silence returned, thick and waiting. Lysa didn't move. She felt every eye settle back on her, even when none of them said her name. It was in the room now, every time they gathered. Every decision carried her weight. Every risk balanced on what she would allow.

She looked back to the map. A dozen red slashes. Too many unknowns. Too few options.

"We go quiet," she said.

Thorne stopped pacing.

Jaxon glanced up. "You're certain?"

She nodded once. "For now. No new strikes. No large gatherings. We split the operatives into pairs and fade into the districts. I want observation only—supply lines, patrol patterns, internal cracks in their formations. They're pressing too hard. If we hit again now, we give them an excuse to turn the city into a prison."

A voice from the edge of the room spoke—young, sharp, uncertain. One of the newer recruits. Lysa didn't know his name. He stood near the rear door with arms crossed, trying too hard not to look afraid.

"So we do nothing?"

The room stilled.

Lysa turned to face him, her expression unreadable. "We survive."

He didn't speak again. But he didn't look away, either.

Jaxon stepped forward, placing one hand on the table. "There's no shame in restraint," he said. "You only get to play martyr once."

Lysa didn't answer him. Not aloud. She just stared at the map and the thin black line running from the foundry ruins through the heart of the city and up toward the palace hill.

A line drawn in soot and memory. They weren't just fighting soldiers anymore. They were fighting silence. Fear. The kind that didn't need swords to kill.

She had made herself visible, and now the city was watching. The others dispersed without ceremony.

Thorne took his leave with a half-hearted shrug and muttered something about checking the watch signals along the southern wall. The new recruits trailed after, whispering low between themselves, casting brief glances in Lysa's direction as they left. None of them lingered long enough to meet her eyes.

Only Jaxon remained.

He stood at the edge of the room, arms folded, his back to the door that hadn't yet shut behind the others. His posture was relaxed, but his eyes tracked her carefully. Not with suspicion. With concern that he was trying not to show.

"You should've let us hit them again," he said after the silence had stretched too long. "Just once. Not to win. Just to remind them we could."

Lysa stayed where she was. Her fingers rested on the corner of the table, knuckles white against the stone.

"That's not what they need right now," she said.

Jaxon pushed off the wall and stepped forward. His boots scuffed the floor lightly, but he stopped short of crossing the table's edge.

"They need to believe the fight is still theirs," he said. "You're starting to look like the whole movement. That's not a compliment."

She looked up at him. "You think I asked for that?"

"No. I think you've handled it better than most would. But it's a fire that's already burning out of your control."

"I didn't start it."

"No," he said, softer now. "But you poured the oil."

Lysa's jaw tightened. She turned away from the table and began gathering the scattered slips, folding them into a leather pouch. Her movements were precise. Mechanical.

Jaxon didn't move. "You're visible now, Lysa. That means something."

"I know."

"No, you think you do. But it's worse than you imagine." He took another step forward. "You can't walk a street without being recognized. You're not a rumor anymore. You're not a whisper. You're a symbol. And symbols are targets."

She paused, slipping the last piece of parchment into the pouch. "So what would you have me do? Run? Hide while they tear down the walls looking for a ghost?"

"I'd have you leave the city—just for a while. Let the face fade. Let them forget the shape of your shadow."

She looked at him then, really looked, and for a moment the mask of command faltered. Just for a breath.

"If I vanish now, that flier becomes prophecy."

Jaxon didn't answer.

The fire in the corner brazier crackled softly, but the silence between them held heavier than heat.

He finally broke it, his voice quieter this time. "Then make sure they remember something worth believing in."

Lysa nodded once, but it wasn't agreement. It was acknowledgment. A recognition of the line she had already crossed.

She turned back to the table and unrolled the map again. Not to change orders. Not to redraw the plan. Just to see it. To remind herself what they were fighting through, and what lay on the other side.

Jaxon didn't speak again. He simply stepped back and slipped out the door, leaving her with the flickering maplight and the weight of a city now watching too closely.

The air in the stairwell was colder than the chamber below. Not from altitude, but from absence. These were the forgotten veins of the city—service corridors never completed, rooms half-carved and left to rot beneath the merchant tier. Lysa stepped carefully through the narrow passage, her boots barely making a sound across the dust-coated stone. She had memorized this path during the early days. Back when their meetings fit in single rooms. Back when her name hadn't been whispered on every street.

She passed a rusted doorframe and ducked through a collapsed entryway into what had once been a courier hall. Crates lined the far wall. Most were empty. One still held a scattering of blank parchment and dried inkpots. In the corner, a low table had been dragged near a stack of chairs. A tattered satchel lay on top, half-open, with a stencil plate peeking from the flap.

She crossed the room without pausing.

A single lantern burned low on the wall bracket. Its flame barely reached the floor. That suited her fine.

She opened the satchel and pulled out the stencil. The edges were nicked from repeated use, but the shape still held: a rising sun split by a line down the middle. Hope and fracture. Their message. Their mark.

But it wasn't enough anymore.

She set it aside and withdrew a blank plate. The steel was cold beneath her fingers as she worked. No ornate calligraphy. No flourishes. Just deliberate, steady cuts with the carving blade she kept in her belt. It took time. Her hands moved slower than they used to. Not from doubt, but from exhaustion.

When it was done, she held the new plate to the light.

Not a name. Not a phrase.

Just a face. Her face—rendered in sharp, simple lines. No grandeur. No crown. Just a woman staring straight ahead.

She set the stencil down and pulled a fresh piece of parchment from the stack. A block of charcoal. A brush of ink. The ink would smear if rushed, so she didn't. She worked silently, efficiently, the way she had when copying orders and courier codes. She didn't stop until she had ten.

Then she began pinning them to the message slips meant for the runners.

They would go out by nightfall. Carried in pouches and pockets, tucked into doorframes, slid beneath crates, pasted to the backs of water troughs.

No slogans. No rallying words.

Just a face in charcoal.

Let them look.

Let them wonder whether the stories were true.

Let them see her—not as a traitor drawn in red ink, but as something they hadn't yet decided how to name.

She folded the last slip, pressed her palm flat against it, and exhaled.

If she was to be seen, it would be on her terms.

The rooftop above the tannery offered little shelter from the wind, but it gave them the space they needed. Smoke still hung over the southern ridge of the city, faint and distant now, but the scent of scorched timber carried farther at night. Lysa crouched near the chimney stack, holding the lantern steady against a loose stone outcrop while Thorne finished tying the last of the fastenings. His hands moved quickly, despite the bruises along his knuckles and the half-healed gash above his temple.

They had worked in silence since arriving. No need to speak. The message was already written.

A crude rack of split timber had been mounted to the stone lip, reinforced with iron nails scavenged from the cart depot. Folded fliers had been stacked between thin wooden braces, their edges already curling from the rising heat of the lantern. The stencil plate had done its work. Dozens of sheets bore the same image now—her face, drawn in clean lines, neither smiling nor defiant. Just present. Watchful. Intentional.

Thorne stepped back and checked the kindling at the base of the rack. He glanced at her once before opening the latch on the firepot.

"You're certain about this?" he asked, keeping his voice low.

Lysa didn't look away from the rack. "Yes."

"It's going to draw attention. Patrols, wardens, maybe worse."

She nodded. "That's the point."

He gave a small exhale and lit the flame.

It caught with a dry hiss and a rush of heat. The kindling went first, then the paper edges, curling upward as the fire spread through the rack. The fliers began to lift, carried on the wind in soft, uneven spirals. Some flared too quickly and crumbled before clearing the rooftop. Others held their shape longer, drifting into the night with edges blackening as they spun.

From a distance, they would look like nothing more than ash and scrap.

But up close, each one carried her image. No words. No slogans. Just the face they had tried to paint in red.

The wind shifted. A handful of the burning slips were swept over the eastern wall, scattering toward the outer rings. Lysa could already picture them catching on windowsills, doorframes, and awnings. The guards would tear them down. They always did. But not before someone saw them. Not before someone recognized what they were meant to remember.

Thorne watched in silence for a long moment. Then he stepped beside her, his tone even.

"You understand what this does. There's no stepping back after this."

Lysa kept her gaze forward. "They already branded me. This doesn't change that."

"It changes how they remember you."

She didn't answer immediately. Her hands were steady, her breath even, but her mind lingered on the names she had seen scratched into alley walls. Fireblood. Queen of Ash. None of them had been hers, not really. But this... this was different. This wasn't a story they told in her absence. This was something they would have to see with their own eyes.

"They won't forget me now," she said, not with defiance, but with resolve.

The last of the slips pulled free from the rack and rose into the dark above the city. The fire had burned through the frame, leaving only embers and a scorched patch of stone. Lysa stepped back and retrieved the lantern, shielding the flame as the wind picked up again.

She didn't look at Thorne as they turned toward the stairwell, but she knew he would follow. They didn't speak as they descended. The fire was done. The message had been sent.

Chapter Twenty-Seven

POWER IN A NAME

The candlelight in the study chamber flickered with each turn of the page as Caelan traced his fingers along the margin of a weathered tome. The text was dense, packed with archaic theories and diagrams that blended martial stances with sigils—long-discredited concepts that once attempted to unify combat forms with arcane expression. The scribes who authored them had spoken in metaphors more than methods, their intent buried under layers of poetic language and frustration.

Most had failed to make it work, but Caelan saw the patterns differently now. What they described wasn't just academic folly. It was familiar.

He recognized the shift in momentum described in a margin note on elemental absorption. He had felt the described backlash of an overloaded weave during his early fusion attempts. Where the book described consequence in abstract, Caelan could name the exact bruises and muscle tears. He knew what it felt like to misjudge the weight of a spell when pivoting mid-strike, to cast too late and unbalance a stance, to let fire linger a heartbeat too long and feel it catch the edge of his sleeve.

He wasn't reading theory. He was reading memory.

The door opened with a gentle creak. Master Ildan stepped inside, his eyes moving first to the tome, then to Caelan.

"You found it."

Caelan looked up, brow raised. "You knew this was here."

"It's not forbidden," Ildan said, crossing the chamber and setting down a second scroll. "Just... neglected. Most who read it dismiss it as romantic nonsense. No one's applied it with clarity in generations."

Caelan closed the book slowly, resting his hand on the cover. "They were reaching for something real. They just didn't have the rhythm."

Ildan nodded, his gaze thoughtful. "And you think you do?"

"I'm not trying to recreate their failure," Caelan said. "I'm building from what they couldn't finish. Not because I know better, but because I've felt it."

The silence that followed was not one of doubt, but of consideration.

"You've given shape to something that hasn't had a name in a long time," Ildan said, after a moment. "Not a battlemage. or a duelist with a spellbook. Something else."

Caelan looked down at the lines of notation and the rough sketches of sword arcs intertwined with glyphs. "I don't care what it's called."

"You should," Ildan replied. "Names matter. There's power in a name... for lineage. For those who come after."

Caelan thought of the terrace, the practice yard, the elemental chamber. He thought of fire moving through his blade, of wind guiding the angle of a cut, of earth steadying his heel, of water softening his recovery. He thought of the vision in the sanctum. The battlefield. The presence in the fog.

"I don't want to be the only one," he said quietly. "If I survive what's coming, others should know this path exists."

Ildan stepped beside him and rested one hand on the tome.

"There is a name buried in older records," he said. "Used sparingly. Not often understood. They called it the Eldritch Path. Or sometimes, the Eldritch Order. It implied not a school of magic, but a fusion—fluid, evolving, formed at the edge where arcane and physical discipline intersect. A blend of chaos and order, radiance and shadow."

Caelan's eyes narrowed slightly. The word resonated in a way titles rarely did. Not because it sounded powerful. Because it felt true.

He reached for a fresh scrap of parchment and began to write.

Ildan watched, then stepped back toward the door.

"I won't tell you what to call yourself," he said. "But whatever shape you walk, make sure it carries your own truth."

As the door clicked shut behind him, Caelan continued to write, the lines of the form unfolding with each motion of the quill.

He didn't need a title to move forward, but somewhere deep within, something steady had taken root. A name not of vanity, but of foundation.

Eldritch Knight.

Time passed quietly within the temple walls, marked not by urgency or decree, but by the steady rhythm of disciplined routine. The sun rose and set in familiar arcs across the stone terraces, casting long shadows through the meditation halls and warming the practice grounds with the soft heat of late afternoon. Meals were taken in the same quiet spaces, scrolls returned to their shelves only to be studied again, and the sound of footsteps along polished stone echoed with the soft constancy of a place designed to endure.

Yet beneath that surface calm, change had begun to take root.

Caelan no longer trained beneath watchful eyes or sought approval from the instructors who had once measured his progress in lessons and corrections. His days were now his own, shaped by an internal rhythm forged through experience and quiet resolve. At dawn, he walked alone to the upper terrace, where he blended swordwork with the elemental disciplines he had come to master—not as separate arts, but as one. His movements carried intention rather than spectacle, each stance refined through countless repetitions, each gesture guided by the flow of magic drawn not from command but from understanding.

Afternoons were spent in study. Not in pursuit of rote knowledge, but in discovery—cross-referencing forgotten manuscripts, tracing the arcane theories of long-dead philosophers, and annotating the flaws and insights of those who had once attempted to do what he now did instinctively. He did not seek answers so much as he shaped the questions more clearly. On quieter evenings, he wandered the inner sanctum corridors, not to be seen, but to think. There was clarity in the solitude, in the subtle hum of magic that lived in the foundation stones and open arches, in the echoes of his own footsteps when no one else walked beside him.

The instructors gave him space, and though they said little, their silence was no longer dismissive. They had begun to understand that his path was diverging from theirs—not in rebellion, but in purpose. Master Ildan remained watchful, but his presence had softened. Where once he offered correction, he now offered context, speaking less often but with more weight when he did. There was no ceremony marking Caelan's shift. No new robe. No formal title. Yet all who observed him now did so with a quiet respect.

In the elemental chamber, the pillars no longer resisted him. The runes etched into the floor flared with a gentler light at his approach, as though they had come to recognize the rhythm of his presence. The elements waited not to be summoned, but to be heard. And Caelan, in turn, moved with the confidence of someone who no longer saw his power as something to wield, but something to integrate. He no longer sought mastery over the arcane or the blade. He was learning to live between them.

Though he focused on the present, his thoughts often returned to Elaria's words. Her letter remained folded inside one of his journals, but the words themselves stayed with him. He recalled the scent of sage from the hearthside in the cottage, the way she once leaned against the doorframe after a long day in the garden, and the softness of her voice when she warned him not to confuse strength with noise. These memories anchored him more than any incantation, more than any scroll, and though he did not speak of them aloud, they lived within every step he took forward.

The temple, too, had begun to shift. Runners arrived more frequently from distant provinces, carrying messages wrapped in urgency and sealed in wax not often used. Discussions among the senior mages lingered longer after dusk, and though no alarm was sounded, there was a change in the air—an awareness that the world beyond their walls was stirring. Whispers of unrest reached the inner sanctum, and preparations began beneath the surface, quiet but deliberate.

Caelan listened without pressing, watched without drawing attention to himself, and continued to refine the path he was walking. He was not naïve enough to believe peace would hold. The signs were too clear. Something was coming. Something that would pull him from the calm of the temple and test all that he had built in silence.

He did not know the shape of it yet. Only that it approached, and with it, a new turning point.

Somewhere far beyond the mountain range, someone else had begun their journey as well. She was not yet within the temple's reach, but her steps were drawing closer with each passing day.

Though they did not know one another, they were bound to meet.

And when they did, nothing would remain as it was.

EPILOGUE

The city slept uneasy that night. Even hours after the flames had guttered on the tannery roof, smoke still clung to the alleys, faint enough to mistake for mist until the wind shifted and the sting of ash reminded otherwise.

Lysa sat alone on the narrow balcony outside the loft they had claimed, her arms resting against the iron rail. From here, she could see the eastern quarter: rooftops sagging beneath the weight of old stone, the faint glow of watchfires near the gatehouse, and farther still the dark beyond the walls. The night was quiet in ways she had not expected. No patrol horns. No shouting in the streets. Just the creak of old beams as the wind pressed at the eaves, and the low hum of a city holding its breath.

She had not lit a lamp. The only light came from the waning moon, painting the rail in pale silver. It was enough. Her thoughts did not need more company than the shadows already gave her.

A faint sound broke the stillness—a shuffle of claws against wood, too deliberate to be the wind. Lysa turned just as a small shape slipped up onto the rail.

A black cat balanced there, its fur sleek enough to catch the moonlight, eyes a sharp, unblinking green. It gave a short, low meow, as if to announce itself, and then sat, tail curling neatly around its paws.

Lysa studied it for a moment. Strays were not rare in Arden's Wake, yet this one did not hold itself like the others she had seen slinking near the markets. It met her gaze directly, calm, expectant even, as though the balcony belonged as much to it as to her.

"You're bold," she murmured, her voice soft enough not to carry.

The cat tilted its head, one ear flicking back at the wind, but did not move.

For a moment, she considered reaching out. Her hand rose, hesitated in the air, then lowered again. She did not know why. Perhaps it was the steadiness in its eyes, or the quiet sense that this was no ordinary visit. Whatever the reason, she remained as she was, watching.

The cat gave another sound, almost a purr, and then turned away. With an easy leap, it vanished back into the dark.

Lysa exhaled slowly. The city stretched before her again, unchanged, yet the silence felt different now—less empty, more like a pause before something yet to come.

She stayed there until the moon dipped lower and the chill of morning crept into her bones. When at last she rose, she glanced once more toward the rail, half-expecting to see green eyes waiting for her in the dark.

But the space was empty.